PRAISE FOR C. L. WILSON'S EPIC DEBUT!

"An absolutely wonderful new voice for romance with all the bells and whistles for pure escapism! It exceeded all my expectations."

—Kay Meriam, RWA Steffie Walker
Bookseller of the Year 2003

"I LOVE this book! A thrilling, captivating story that stays with you after you put it down. The best book I've read in years."

—*New York Times* bestselling author
Christine Feehan

"Lush and evocative. A powerful epic fantasy to savor."
—*New York Times* bestselling author
Gena Showalter

"Brilliant and breathtaking! *Lord of the Fading Lands* debuts a fascinatingly unique world populated with characters I fell in love with—and can't wait to read about again."

—Alyssa Day, *USA Today* bestselling
author of *Atlantis Rising*

"This debut will draw you into a magical weave of spirit and air that won't release you until the last word is read."

—Jessica Stachowski, Bookseller,
The World's Biggest Bookstore

CLAIMED BY HER TRUEMATE

She felt him bow his head to rest his jaw on her hair, the touch feather light. Tears beaded in her lashes at the simple beauty of it.

"Ver reisa ku'chae. Kem surah, shei'tani." He whispered the words against her hair.

"You said that before," she murmured. "What does it mean?"

His gaze moved slowly over her face as if he were committing her likeness to memory for all time. "I don't even know your name."

She blinked in surprise. Since the moment she had put her hand in his and he had pulled her into his arms, she felt as if he knew everything there was to know about her. It was surprising and disconcerting to realize that, in fact, they knew each other not at all. "Ellie," she told him solemnly. "My name is Ellysetta Baristani."

"Ellie." Liquid Fey accents savored the syllables of her simple name, making it something beautiful and exotic. "Ellysetta with hair like tairen flame and eyes the green color of spring. I've seen the mist of your reflection in The Eye of Truth." His gaze returned to hers, filled with wonder and regret. "*Ver reisa ku'chae. Kem surah, shei'tani.* Your soul calls out. Mine answers, beloved."

C. L. WILSON

LORD OF THE FADING LANDS

TAIREN SOUL

LEISURE BOOKS NEW YORK CITY

*For my Dad, Ray Richter. Every person should
have a hero. You've always been mine.*

*And for my Mom, Lynda Richter. I couldn't have
done this without you.*

*Thank you both, for everything. I'm so lucky
you're my parents.*

A LEISURE BOOK®

October 2007

Published by

Dorchester Publishing Co., Inc.
200 Madison Avenue
New York, NY 10016

ISBN-10: 0-8439-5977-0
ISBN-13: 978-0-8439-5977-2

Visit us on the web at www.dorchesterpub.com.

ACKNOWLEDGEMENTS

I am blessed to have the most wonderful friends, family and supporters. A special thanks to Michelle Grajkowski, my agent, for taking a chance on a 1,000 page fantasy romance from an unpublished author, and to my editor, Alicia Condon, for the same reason. You both made my dream come true. Thanks to all the critique partners who've helped me in so many priceless ways: Christine Feehan, Diana Peterfreund, Mom, Betina Krahn, Sharon Stone, Kathie Firzlaff, Carla Hughes, my sister Lisette, Tanya Michaels, Sheila Clover English and Alesia Holliday. Thanks to my dear friends Kim Klein, Keith Stringer, and April Rice who have cheered me on, and to my husband Kevin and our children Ileah, Rhiannon, and Aidan for being so understanding of all the long hours I've spent sequestered in my office.

A special thanks to bookseller Kay Meriam Vamvakias: you have no idea how much your support and encouragement meant to me. You are a true friend of the Fey.

Thanks to the richly talented artist, Judy York, who so perfectly captured my vision of Rain, Ellysetta, and the tairen on my absolutely gorgeous covers—and for letting me use them on my Web site!

And, last but not least, thanks to the wonderful men and women of Tampa Area Romance Authors (TARA) who've been my writing family for the last five years. TARA Rocks!

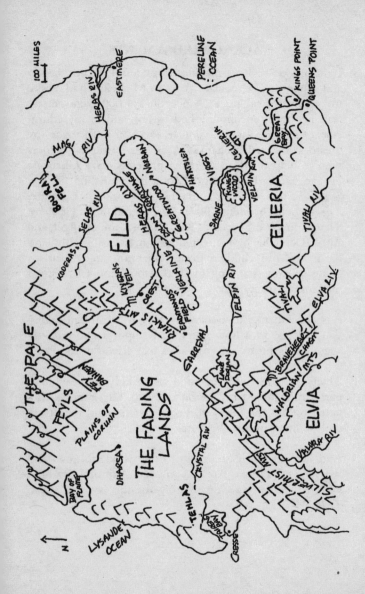

LORD *Of The* FADING LANDS

PROLOGUE

Loudly, proudly, tairen sing,
As they soar on mighty wings.
Softly, sadly, mothers cry
To sing a tairen's lullabye.
                    The Tairen's Lament, Fey Nursery Rhyme

The tairen were dying.

Rain Tairen Soul, King of the Fey, could no longer deny the truth. Nor, despite all his vast power and centuries of trying, could he figure a way to save either the creatures that were his soul-kin or the people who depended upon him to lead and defend them.

The tairen—those magnificent, magical, winged cats of the Fading Lands—had only one fertile female left in their pride, and she grew weaker by the day as she fed her strength to her six unhatched kitlings. With those tiny, unborn lives rested the last hope of a future for the tairen, and the last hope of a future for Rain's people, the Fey. But today, the painful truth had become clear. The mysterious, deadly wasting disease that had decimated the tairen over the last millennium had sunk its evil, invisible claws into yet another clutch of unhatched kits.

When the tairen died, so too would the Fey. The fates of the two species were forever intertwined, and had been since the misty time before memory.

Rain looked around the wide, empty expanse of the Hall

of Tairen. Indeed, he thought grimly, the death of the immortal Fey had begun centuries ago.

Once, in a time he could still remember, the Hall had rung with the sound of hundreds of Fey Lords, warriors, *shei'dalins* and Tairen Souls arguing politics and debating treaties. Those days had long passed. The Hall was silent now, as silent as the long-abandoned cities of the Fey, as silent as Fey nurseries, as silent as the graves of all those Fey who had died in the Mage Wars a thousand years ago.

Now the last hope for both the tairen and the Fey was dying, and Rain sensed a growing darkness in the east, in the land of his ancient enemies, the Mages of Eld. He couldn't help believing the two events were somehow connected.

He turned to face the huge, priceless globe of magical Tairen's Eye crystal called the Eye of Truth, which occupied the center of the room. Displayed on the wings of a man-high stand fashioned from three golden tairen, the Eye was an oracle in which a trained seer could search for answers in the past, the present, and the infinite possibilities of the future. The globe was ominously dark and murky now, the future a dim, forbidding shadow. If there was a way to halt the relentless extermination of his peoples, the answer lay there, within the Eye.

The Eye of Truth had been guarding its secrets, showing shadows but no clear visions. It had resisted the probes of even the most talented of the Fey's still-living seers, played coy with even their most beguiling magic weaves. The Eye was, after all, tairen-made. By its very nature, it combined pride with cunning; matched passion with often-wicked playfulness. Seers approached it with respect, humbly asked it for a viewing, courted its favor with their minds and their magic but never their touch.

The Eye of Truth was never to be touched.

It was a golden rule of childhood, drummed into the head of every Fey from infant to ancient.

The Eye held the concentrated magic of ages, power so pure and undiluted that laying hands upon it would be like laying hands upon the Great Sun.

But the Eye was keeping secrets, and Rain Tairen Soul was a desperate king with no time to waste and no patience for protocol. The Eye of Truth *would* be touched. He was the king, and he would have his answers. He would wrest them from the oracle by force, if necessary.

His hands rose. He summoned power effortlessly and wove it with consummate skill. Silvery white Air formed magical webs that he laid upon the doors, walls, floor, and ceiling. A spidery network of lavender Spirit joined the Air, then green Earth to seal all entrances to the Hall. None would enter to disturb him. No scream, no whisper, no mental cry could pass those shields. Come good or ill, he would wrest his answers from the Eye without interruption—and if it demanded a life for his impertinence, it would be unable to claim any but his.

He closed his eyes and cleared his mind of every thought not centered on his current purpose. His breathing became deep and even, going in and out of his lungs in a slow rhythm that kept time with the beat of his heart. His entire being contracted into a single shining blade of determination.

His eyes flashed open. Rain Tairen Soul reached out both hands to grasp the Eye of Truth.

"Aaahh!" Power—immeasurable, immutable—arced through him. His head flew back beneath its onslaught, his teeth bared, his throat straining with a scream of agony. Pain drilled his body like a thousand *sel'dor* blades, and despite twelve hundred years of learning to absorb pain, to embrace it and mute it, Rain writhed in torment.

This pain was unlike any he had ever known.

This pain refused to be contained.

Fire seared his veins and scorched his skin. He felt his soul splinter and his bones melt. The Eye was angry at his daring affront. He had assaulted it with his bare hands and bare power, and such was not to be borne. Its fury screeched along his bones, vibrating down his spine, slashing at every nerve center in his body until tears spilled from his eyes and blood dripped from his mouth where he bit his lip to stop screaming.

"*Nei*," he gasped. "I am the Tairen Soul, and I will have my answer."

If the Eye wished to cement the extinction of both tairen and Fey, it would claim Rain's life. He was not afraid of death; rather he longed for it.

He surrendered himself to the Eye and forced his tortured body to relax. Power and pain flowed into him, through him, claiming him without resistance. And when the violent rush of power had invaded his every cell, when the pain filled his entire being, a strange calm settled over him. The agony was there, extreme and nearly overwhelming, but without resistance he was able to distance his mind from his body's torture, to disassociate the agony of the physical from the determination of the mental. He forced his lips to move, his voice a hoarse, cracked whisper of sound that spoke ancient words of power to capture the Eye's immense magic in flows of Air, Water, Fire, Earth, and Spirit.

His eyes opened, glowing bright as twin moons in the dark reflection of the Eye, burning like coals in a face bone white with pain.

With voice and mind combined, Rain Tairen Soul asked his question: "How can I save the tairen and the Fey?"

Relentlessly, absorbing the agony of direct contact with the Eye, he searched its raging depths for answers. Millions of possibilities flashed before his eyes, countless variations on possible futures, countless retellings of past events. Millennia passed in an instant, visions so rapid his physical sight could never have hoped to discern them, yet his mind, steadily commanding the threads of magic, absorbed the images and processed them with brutal clarity. He stood witness to the deaths of millions, the rise and fall of entire civilizations. Angry, unfettered magic grew wild in the world and Mages worked their evil deeds. Tairen shrieked in pain, immolating the world in their agony. Fey women wept oceans of tears, and Fey warriors fell helpless to their knees, as weak as infants. Rain's mind screamed to reject the visions, yet still his hands gripped the Eye of Truth, and still he voiced his question, demanding an answer.

"How can I save the tairen and the Fey?"

He saw himself in tairen form, raining death indiscriminately upon unarmed masses, his own tairen claws impaling Fey warriors.

"How can I save the tairen and the Fey?"

Sariel, his beloved mate, lay bloody and broken at his feet, pierced by hundreds of knives, half her face scorched black by Mage fire. She reached out to him, her burned and bloodied mouth forming his name. He watched in helpless paralysis as the flashing arc of an Elden Mage's black *sel'dor* blade sliced down across her neck. Bright red blood fountained—

The unutterable pain of Sariel's death—tempered by centuries of life without her—surged back to life with soul-shredding rawness. Rage and bloodlust exploded within him, mindless, visceral, unstoppable. It was the Fey Wilding Rage, fueled by a tairen's primal fury, unfettered emotions backed by lethal fangs, incinerating fire, and access to unimaginable power.

They would die! They had slain his mate, and they would all die for their crime! His shrieking soul grasped eagerly for the madness, the power to kill without remorse, to scorch the earth and leave nothing but smoldering ruins and death.

"Nei!" Rain yanked his hands from the Eye and flung up his arms to cover his face. His breath came in harsh pants as he battled to control his fury. Once before, in a moment of madness and unendurable pain, he had unleashed the beast in his soul and rained death upon the world. He had slain thousands in mere moments, laid waste to half a continent within a few days. It had taken the combined will of every still-living tairen and Fey to cage his madness.

"Nei! Please," he begged, clawing for self-possession. He released the weaves connecting him to the Eye in the frantic hope that shearing the tie would stop the rage fighting to claim him.

Instead, it was as if he had called Fire in an oil vault.

The world was suddenly bathed in blood as his vision turned red. The tairen in him shrieked for release. To his horror, he felt his body begin to dissolve, saw the black fur form, the lethal curve of tairen claws spear the air.

For the first time in twelve hundred years of life, Rainier vel'En Daris knew absolute terror.

The magic he'd woven throughout the Hall would never hold a Tairen Soul caught up in a Fey Wilding Rage. All would die. The world would die.

The Tairen-Change moved over him in horrible slow motion, creeping up his limbs, taunting him with his inability to stop it. The small sane part of his mind watched like a stunned, helpless spectator, seeing his own death hurtling towards him and realizing with detached horror that he was going to die and there was nothing he could do to prevent it.

He had overestimated his own power and utterly underestimated that of the Eye of Truth.

"Stop," he shouted. "I beg you. Stop! Don't do this." Without pride or shame, he fell to his knees before the ancient oracle.

The rage left him as suddenly as it had come.

In a flash of light, his tairen-form disappeared. Flesh, sinew, and bone re-formed into the lean, muscular lines of his Fey body. He collapsed face down on the floor, gasping for breath, the sweat of terror streaming from his pores, his muscles shaking uncontrollably.

Faint laughter whispered across the stone floor and danced on the intricately carved columns that lined either side of the Hall of Tairen.

The Eye mocked him for his arrogance.

"Aiyah," he whispered, his eyes closed. "I deserve it. But I am desperate. Our people—mine and yours both—face extinction. And now dark magic is rising again in Eld. Would you not also have dared any wrath to save our people?"

The laughter faded, and silence fell over the Hall, broken only by the wordless noises coming from Rain himself, the sobbing gasp of his breath, the quiet groans of pain he didn't have the strength to hold back. In the silence, power gathered. The fine hairs on his arms and the back of his neck stood on end. He became aware of light, a kaleidoscope of color bathing the Hall, flickering through the thin veil of his eyelids.

His eyes opened—then went wide with wonder.

There, from its perch atop the wings of three golden tairen, the Eye of Truth shone with resplendent clarity, a crystalline globe blazing with light. Prisms of radiant color beamed out in undulating waves.

Stunned, he struggled to his knees and reached out instinctively towards the Eye. It wasn't until his fingers were close enough to draw tiny stinging arcs of power from the stone that he came to his senses and snatched his hands back without touching the oracle's polished surface.

There had been something in the Eye's radiant depths—an image of what looked like a woman's face—but all he could make out were fading sparkles of lush green surrounded by orange flame. A fine mist formed in the center of the Eye, then slowly cleared as another vision formed. This image he saw clearly as it came into focus, and he recognized it instantly. It was a city he knew well, a city he despised. The second image faded and the Eye dimmed, but it was enough. Rain Tairen Soul had his answer. He knew his path.

With a groan, he rose slowly to his feet. His knees trembled, and he staggered back against the throne to collapse on the cushioned seat.

Rain gazed at the Eye of Truth with newfound respect. He was the Tairen Soul, the most powerful Fey alive, and yet the Eye had reduced him to a weeping infant in mere moments. If it had not decided to release him, it could have used him to destroy the world. Instead, after beating the arrogance out of him, it had given up at least one of the secrets it was hiding.

He reached out to the Eye with a lightly woven stream of Air, Fire, and Water and whisked away the faint smudges left behind by the fingers he had dared to place upon it.

«*Sieks'ta. Thank you.*» He filled his mental tone with gen-

uine respect and was rewarded by the instant muting of his
body's pain. With a bow to the Eye of Truth, he strode
towards the massive carved wooden doors at the end of the
Hall of Tairen and tore down his weaves.

«*Marissya.*» He sent the mental call to the Fey's strongest
living *shei'dalin* even as he reached out with Air to swing
open the Hall's heavy doors before him. The Fey warriors
guarding the door to the Hall of Tairen nodded in response
to the orders he issued with swift, flashing motions of his
hands as he strode by, and the flurry of movement behind
him assured him his orders were being carried out.

«*Rain?*» Marissya's mental voice was as soothing as her
physical one, her curiosity mild and patient.

«*A change of plans. I'm for Celieria in the morning and I'm dou-
bling your guard. Let your kindred know the Feyreisen is coming
with you.*»

Even across the city, he could feel her shocked surprise, and
it almost made him smile.

Half a continent away, in the mortal city of Celieria, Ellysetta
Baristani huddled in the corner of her tiny bedroom, tears running freely down her face, her body trembling uncontrollably.

The nightmare had been so real, the agony so intense.
Dozens of angry, stinging welts scored her skin . . . self-
inflicted claw marks that might have been worse had her fingernails been longer. But worse than the pain of the
nightmare had been the helpless rage and the soul-shredding
sense of loss, the raw animal fury of a mortally wounded
heart. Her own soul had cried out in empathetic sorrow, feeling the tortured emotions as if they had been her own.

And then she'd sensed something else. Something dark and
eager and evil. A crouching malevolent presence that had
ripped her out of sleep, bringing her bolt upright in her bed,
a smothered cry of familiar terror on her lips.

She covered her eyes with shaking hands. *Please, gods, not
again*.

CHAPTER ONE

"Ellie, don't be such a soggy *dorn*." Nine-year-old Lorelle Baristani pouted at her older sister.

It was, in Ellysetta's opinion, an adorable pout. Lorelle's outthrust lower lip was plump and pink, her round cheeks soft as satin, and her big brown eyes heart-tuggingly soulful. The whole enchanting picture was complemented by masses of mink-brown ringlets, and more than one seasoned adult had been known to abandon common sense in the face of such considerable infant artillery. Unfortunately for Lorelle, Ellie was made of sterner stuff.

Ellie smiled and bent to kiss her sister's cheek. "A soggy *dorn*, am I? Just because I don't want to spend the whole day caught up in what's sure to be the worst crush in the past year? And for what? To catch a brief glimpse of a Fey warrior as he walks past?" Ellie shook her head and punched down the bread dough she was making for tonight's dinner rolls.

Tomorrow was the much-anticipated annual visit of the *shei'dalin* Marissya v'En Solande. Her arrival was always a spectacle as she and her guard of one hundred fierce leather-

and-steel-bedecked Fey warriors entered the city and marched down the main thoroughfare to the palace.

A week ago, Ellysetta would have gone, no matter how long the wait, just for the chance of glimpsing the glint off a Fey blade. But that was before that disturbing nightmare and before the dark dreams that had continued to haunt her ever since. When she woke each morning, her skin felt tight, her muscles inexplicably sore and weary, as if each night she fought a battle in her sleep. As if she were fighting to keep something out . . . or worse, to keep something in.

Memories flashed—of horrifying convulsions racking her body, Mama's fear, the Church of Light exorcists with their fervent, shining eyes and merciless determination to drive the demons from her soul.

She shuddered from the awful memories and quickly sketched the sign of the Lord of Light. No, all things considered, now was a bad time for her to go anywhere near the Fey and their powerful magic.

"Besides, I'm busy tomorrow," she told Lorelle, grateful for the genuine excuse. "Lady Zillina ordered an entire new suite for her receiving room, and Mama wants me to get started on the embroidery for the pillows."

"But, Ellie, the Feyreisen is coming!"

Ellie's breath caught in her throat. The Feyreisen? Despite her well-founded fear of magic, she'd dreamed all her life of seeing Rain Tairen Soul in the flesh.

Then common sense returned, and Ellie cast a stern sidelong glance at her sister. "Who told you that bit of silliness? Everyone knows the Feyreisen hasn't set foot outside the Fading Lands in a thousand years." Not since the end of the horrendous magical holocaust known as the Mage Wars.

"It's not silliness!" Lorelle protested indignantly. "I heard it straight from Tomy Sorris." Tomy Sorris, son of the printer, was the local town crier and usually well on top of the latest news and gossip.

Ellie was unimpressed. "Then Tomy's been smelling too

much printer's ink." She transferred the dough back into its rising bowl and covered it with a damp cloth.

"He has not!" A stamp of one small foot expressed the child's outrage.

"Well, perhaps he's just misinformed then," Ellie replied. If Rain Tairen Soul were coming, they'd have heard about it long before now. The Fey who'd once nearly destroyed the world in a rage of tairen flame wouldn't simply end his thousand-year exile without someone knowing about it in advance.

With a few quick swipes of a clean cloth, she swept the light dusting of flour off the tabletop into her palm and disposed of it in the waste bin beneath the kitchen sink. She cranked the sink pump twice and rinsed her floury fingers beneath the resulting cold spurt of water, then cast a glance back over her shoulder at Lorelle.

"Besides, why would the Feyreisen come here? He never had much use for mortals even before the Wars."

She recalled a story in yesterday's paper about a small caravan of travelers attacked near the Borders by *dahl'reisen*, the frightening mercenaries who'd once been Fey warriors before being banished from the Fading Lands for the darkness in their souls. Would Rain Tairen Soul come to Celieria because of that?

She dismissed the idea instantly. All her life she'd heard tales of *dahl'reisen* raids—such tales were so common they were used to frighten small children into behaving—but none of those stories had ever lured the King of the Fey beyond the Faering Mists that circled the Fading Lands. No, Lorelle must be wrong.

Ellie untied her apron and hung it on a wooden peg in the corner of the modest, cozy Baristani family kitchen and smoothed slender hands over her serviceable tan muslin skirts. Her shirtsleeves were bunched up around her elbows, and she tugged the plain cuffs back down to her wrists, unable to stifle a wistful sigh as she imagined a fall of ivory lace draped over her hands. It was, of course, a foolish daydream. Lace would only get dirty and torn as she went about her chores.

She smiled at Lorelle, whose pout had now become an outright scowl. "Come now, kitling, don't be cross. I'll take you to the park instead. It won't take up the whole day, it's bound to be less crowded, and we can still have a fine time."

Lorelle crossed her arms over her chest. "I don't want to go to the park. I want to see the Feyreisen."

Before Ellie could reply, Lorelle's twin, Lillis, came skipping into the kitchen, all atwitter. A mirror image of her sister, Lillis would have been indistinguishable from Lorelle except for the radiant excitement stamped on her face, which contrasted vividly with Lorelle's dark scowl. "Ellie! Ellie! Guess what!"

Ellie made a show of widening her eyes with exaggerated interest. "What?"

"The Feyreisen is coming, and Mama says you can take us to see him enter the city tomorrow!"

"Ha!" Lorelle exclaimed. "I told you so!"

This time the breath that caught in Ellie's throat stayed there. Tomy Sorris might have sniffed too much printer's ink, but Mama was never wrong. Seeking confirmation, Ellie glanced towards the door.

"Mama? Is it true? Is the Feyreisen really coming to Celieria?"

Lauriana Baristani nodded, her fingers deftly untying the bow of her large-brimmed sun hat as she crossed the threshold and entered the kitchen. There was a light of excitement in her eyes that Ellie had never seen before. "It's true," she confirmed.

Ellie watched in astonishment as her mother tossed her hat and woven shawl over the back of a nearby chair rather than hanging them neatly on the wooden pegs provided for that purpose. Her mother was a firm believer in a place for everything and everything in its place. Something was going on,

something that had nothing to do with the unexpected am-
bassadorial visit from a twelve-hundred-year-old Fey who
could turn himself into a tairen.

"Mama?" She picked up the hat and shawl and hung them
in their place. "What is it?" She gave her mother a searching
look. Lauriana was a handsome woman in her mid fifties,
with a solid build and strong arms that could help her husband move heavy pieces of handcrafted furniture or hug her
children close. She had the same rich brown hair as the twins,
though her soft ringlets were threaded liberally with silver,
and her eyes were a pleasant hazel. Her brown dress was
neatly made of sturdy, sensible cloth, and her shoes were
sturdy, sensible brown leather to match. But at the moment,
she did not look sensible at all. She looked . . . *giddy*.

"Oh, Ellie, you won't believe it!" Lauriana reached out to
grasp Ellie's hands. "Queen Annoura," she said, squeezing Ellie's fingers tight, "sent Lady Zillina to commission your father to produce a special carving in the Feyreisen's honor.
He's to have it finished and ready to present to the Feyreisen
at the Prince's betrothal ball!" When Ellie gasped again and
the twins squealed, Lauriana beamed and nodded. "Commissioned by the queen. At last!"

"Oh, Mama," Ellie breathed. "Papa must be singing with
pride!" After ten years as a master woodcarver, Sol Baristani
had finally received a coveted royal commission. When word
got out, nobles and rich merchants would be banging down
his door to commission his work. Money, always rather scarce
in the Baristani household, was sure to flow into the family
coffers.

Lauriana flashed her eldest daughter a devilish grin. "And
won't that just put Madam Rich and Snooty Minset's knick-
ers in a twist?"

"Mama!" Ellie gasped, giving her mother a shocked look.

Her mother—definitely not her staid and sensible self—
laughed out loud, then clapped a hand over her mouth. "Oh,
that was evil. Just evil."

Ellie couldn't help laughing herself. It was so unlike her calm, unflappable mother to say something nasty, even about the social-climbing Madam Minset, the banker's wife. Though if ever a woman deserved to have something nasty said about her, Madam Minset did—and that went double for her daughter Kelissande.

"But, Mama, why is the Feyreisen coming to Celieria?"

Lauriana shrugged. "No one knows, but it's sure to be a spectacle. And I promised Lillis you would take her and Lorelle to see the Feyreisen." Ellie stared in surprise, and her mother blushed a little. "I know what you're thinking, and this doesn't mean I approve of Fey sorcerers. I don't. Not in the least. But the Bright Lord did select Rain Tairen Soul as the vehicle through which He has delivered this latest blessing upon our family. I wouldn't want Him to think us ungrateful. You will take the girls, won't you?"

Ellie glanced at Lorelle, who was now sporting a grin as large as a dairy cow, and had to laugh. "Of course I will," she agreed. The twins shrieked with happiness and danced about the kitchen.

No matter how dreadful her nightmares, Ellie would never have missed this once-in-a-lifetime opportunity to see the one and only Rain Tairen Soul. He was living history, the Fey who'd once in a fit of grief-induced madness almost destroyed the world.

How many ballads had been written about that terrible day? How many plays? Celieria's Museum of Arts held no less than twenty enormous oil paintings that commemorated the entire series of events, masterpieces painted by Celieria's greatest artists over the past thousand years. Ellie couldn't count the number of times she'd stood in front of Fabrizio Chelan's immortal *Death of the Beloved* and wept at the unspeakable anguish the great master had depicted on the face of Rain Tairen Soul as he held Lady Sariel in her death swoon and cried out to the heavens.

To see Rain Tairen Soul in the flesh. It was more than she'd ever dreamed possible.

She wagged a finger at the twins. "You two had best plan to go to bed early. We leave at the break of dawn, so we can be sure to find a place with a good view."

Her mother shook her head. "You and your love of the Fey." But for once, she didn't add her usual lecture about the evils of magic and the danger of temptations that wore a pretty face.

Though Ellie shared her mother's fear of magic, all things Fey had fascinated her since she was a small child. "That doesn't mean I'm any less excited about your news, Mama." She reached out to grasp her mother's hands. "Indeed, I want you to tell me everything. What, exactly, did Lady Zillina say? Don't leave out a single detail."

Lauriana pulled up a stool and related the whole story, including the ultimate pleasure of having Stella Morin, the neighborhood's biggest gossip, witness the entire event. She'd come into the shop to tell Lauriana that Donatella Brodson, the butcher's youngest daughter, was officially contracted to wed the third son of a wealthy silk merchant.

"Oh—" Lauriana snapped her fingers. "That reminds me. Den is coming for dinner tonight."

"Den?" Ellie repeated with dismay. Den Brodson, the butcher's son, was a stuffed pork roast of a young man. And ever since his first wife had died in childbirth six months ago, he'd been following Ellie around like a starving hound on the trail of a juicy steak. He'd made a habit of catching her in dark corners, standing so close she could smell the reek of onions and bacon on him, and looking too intently down the neckline of her dresses as if he could see straight through the fabric to the soft curves beneath. His thick fingers were ever clutching at her arm, as if he had some right to her. She shuddered with revulsion. She'd never liked him much, even as a child. Now he made her skin crawl.

Beside her the twins rolled their eyes and clutched at their throats, making gagging noises. They didn't like Den either.

"Mmm." Lauriana paid no notice to the rolling eyes and gagging faces, but she did shoo the twins out of the kitchen.

"Go play in your room, girls." Then, to Ellie, "Wear your green dress, kit. It makes you look rather pretty."

"Why would I want to look pretty for Den?"

A stern hazel gaze pinned her in place. The laughing, flighty Mama was gone. Practical, no-nonsense Mama was back. "You're twenty-four, Ellysetta. That's long past time to be making a good match and starting your own family. Look at your friends. All of them married for years, with at least one child walking and another on the way."

"Kelissande's not wed," Ellie reminded her mother.

"Yes, but Kelissande's not lacking for offers." The stern look in Lauriana's eyes remained the same, but her voice softened. "She's got beauty, girl, and wealth. You don't."

Ellie ducked her head to hide the glimmer of tears that sprang to her eyes. She knew she was no beauty. She'd seen her reflection often enough to understand that. And Kelissande Minset had always been happy to point out her shortcomings in case she missed them.

"Even though you've got a fine, kind heart," Lauriana continued, "and a strong back to make any man a treasured helpmate, young lads and their parents don't look for those blessings first. The lads want beauty. The parents want wealth. The queen's commission will probably be enough to bring Den's family up to scratch, but you don't have the time to wait for Papa to make a fortune so you can take your pick of men." Unspoken was the common knowledge that if a girl was not wed by twenty-five, she was obviously defective in some way. Spinsters were to be pitied—and watched carefully lest the hand of evil that had blackened their futures laid its shadow over those around them.

Ellie couldn't believe what she was hearing. It was obvious her mother had already decided whom Ellie would marry. "But I don't love Den, Mama." To her horror, her voice wobbled.

"Ellysetta." There was a rustle of skirts and then the unexpected warmth of her mother's arms wrapping around her thin shoulders and drawing her close. "Ah, girl. This is my fault." Lauriana sighed. "I should have done my duty by you long ago. But you were such an . . . awkward . . . creature, and we were poor. I thought you'd never be wed, so where was the harm in letting you keep your dreams?"

Awkward. Such a mild euphemism for the fearful truth Mama never voiced. Ellie knew her parents loved her, as did Lillis and Lorelle. But that had not stopped her from hearing the talk of others—or seeing the fear that Mama could never quite hide whenever . . . things . . . happened around Ellie.

"But you've changed, Ellie, and so have our circumstances. You've grown rather pretty in your own way, and this royal commission puts a few coins in our coffers, with the promise of more to come. Look at me, child." Obedient to the command and the accompanying hand raising her chin, Ellie met her mother's solemn gaze. "Life is never certain, Ellie. This is your chance to wed, and you must take it."

"But, Mama—"

Lauriana held up a silencing finger. "Despite everything that happened when you were young, I've never curbed your love of Feytales or your dreams of truemates and happy endings, but that's for Fey, not mortal folk like us. We don't have centuries to wait for true love."

"I know that, Mama."

"Love will come in time, Ellie."

"But not with Den, Mama!" How could it, when the very thought of his touch revolted her?

"Hush! You've not even given him a chance, Ellysetta. Den's not a bad sort, and he's certainly shown interest in you these last few months. His family's well enough, both in manner and position, and your children would never lack for food. Believe me when I tell you there's nothing worse for parents than hearing a child cry for food they cannot provide. Even if that child is not of their own blood."

Ellie dropped her gaze as the reminder that she was not the

Baristanis' natural child knifed through her. Almost twenty-four years ago, on a journey from Kreppes to Hartslea in the north, Sol and Lauriana had found an abandoned baby in the woods near Norban. A girl baby with a shock of orange hair and startling green eyes.

Despite the fact that they were grindingly poor—Sol's hands stiff and nearly crippled by an accident that had left him unable to work as a journeyman woodcarver—they had taken in the baby rather than leaving it to die. And they had kept her, even while Sol barely eked out a living on a few coppers a week as an apprentice carpenter, his broken hands managing to hold hammer, nail, rasp, and lathe, though they could no longer do the intricate detail work he loved.

They kept her even when mysterious, violent seizures afflicted her and the priests declared her demon-cursed. They'd even left their home in Hartslea rather than cast her out or give her into the Church's keeping as the exorcists and the parish priest advised them to do.

After that, thankfully, the family fortunes changed. Sol's hands had miraculously healed, and he'd been able to return to his first love, woodcarving. Ellie's ghastly seizures had dwindled, then stopped almost completely—a fact that Mama attributed to Ellie swearing her soul into service of the Light at her first Concordia in the Church of Light.

Still, Ellie had never forgotten all they'd sacrificed on her behalf. Now there was a chance for her to wed, if not well, at least well enough. It would ensure that Lillis and Lorelle would have the opportunity to make a truly fine match.

"You must trust your parents to do what's best, Ellysetta. For you and the family."

"Yes, Mama," she whispered. She owed them that much and more.

"I know he's not the man you've dreamed of, but give Den a chance. And if another young man of good family asks to court you, we will consider his suit as well."

"Yes, Mama."

"And wear your green dress tonight."

Ellie's shoulders drooped. "Yes, Mama."

That evening, Ellie donned her green dress and tried not to feel like a lamb being led to slaughter. At her mother's insistence, she wore Lauriana's bridal chemise beneath the green gown, and aged ivory lace fell over the backs of her hands, looking beautiful and feminine and delicate. Ellie wished she were wearing her own plain cuffs instead.

She stared hard at her reflection in the mirror. Startling green eyes stared back at her, looking too big in a too wan face, accentuated by prominent cheekbones and a slender nose. In the last year or so, her eyebrows and eyelashes had darkened to a deep auburn. The slashing wings of her brows were now exotic rather than pale and washed out, and once her eyelashes had darkened, their thickness and length had become apparent. She had been grateful for that, though at this moment she could have cheerfully wished them back to the transparent pale orange of her childhood. Her mouth was too wide, she acknowledged critically, her lips too full and too red. Her teeth, however, were white and straight, one of her best features.

She decided not to smile tonight—at least not so she showed any teeth.

She had ruthlessly subdued her wild tangle of hair into a knot on the top of her head, and for once was glad of its bright, unfashionable color and the rather severe style. She stepped back from the mirror. Unfortunately, Mama had been right about the dress making her look nice. The green color was flattering, and the bodice, laced tight to push up her breasts, made her look slender rather than skinny. She was still too tall to be considered feminine by Celierian standards. Flat-footed, she could look Den straight in the eye. Ellie thrust her feet into her highest-heeled shoes and immediately grew three inches.

Satisfied that she'd done exactly as her mother asked, and

as much as possible to mitigate any hint of prettiness, Ellie made her way downstairs to the family parlor.

Den was already there, sitting across from her father on one of Sol Baristani's finely carved settees and chewing a chocolate caramel with relish. His stocky body was clothed in what appeared to be a new dark blue plaid suit, cut just the tiniest bit too tight, with a yellow neckcloth tied in folds about his thick neck. A gold pin, shaped like a rather ungainly bear, glinted from the folds of the neckcloth. His brown hair, greased with a strongly scented pomade, was slicked back from his face, with a puff of curls carefully formed at the top of his broad forehead. His skin was ruddy, his nose partly flattened from a series of childhood scuffles, and his eyes were pale blue rimmed with stubby black lashes.

He was attractive enough, in a rough, butcher's son sort of way. That wasn't what bothered Ellie.

He looked up, caught sight of her, and jumped to his feet, crossing the room to stand uncomfortably close to her. His gaze swept over her, then homed in on the swell of bosom thrust up against the delicate fabric of her mother's best chemise. A bosom that was three inches closer to his face thanks to her decision—poorly considered, she now realized—to wear high heels. His tongue came out to lick his full lips.

That was what bothered Ellie.

Fighting the urge to cross her arms over her chest, she forced a stiff little smile—no teeth—and said, "Good evening, Den. How nice that you could join us tonight."

"You look very pretty, Ellysetta." That came from Papa, of course. Den was still salivating over her bosom.

"Thank you, Papa." She was grateful for the warm love shining from Sol Baristani's eyes. And for his presence in the parlor. The gods only knew what Den would have tried had they been alone. Judging from the look on his face, she wouldn't have liked it much.

"Mmm. Yes," Den agreed, licking his lips again. "Very pretty." His pale blue gaze traveled up her neck and paused at her mouth. When finally he met her gaze head on, there were spots of color in his cheeks.

For a moment she imagined she felt a disturbing hunger. *His* hunger, she realized, and it wasn't for food. Sudden panic roiled inside her, tying her stomach in knots and making her break out in a clammy sweat. If he touched her, she knew she would be sick.

"Ah, Ellysetta. Good." Mama's voice snapped through the strange emotions that had captured Ellie, and she dragged in a gasp of air. No wonder she felt ill. She'd held her breath until she was dizzy!

"—to ask you to help me," Lauriana was saying, "but I've changed my mind. You look far too pretty to risk soiling your gown in the kitchen. Don't you agree, Den?" It was an embarrassing maternal attempt to draw a compliment from Den, but the young man didn't hesitate to oblige her.

"Indeed, Madam Baristani." Den bowed at the waist as if he were a lord's son rather than a butcher's. "Ellysetta looks lovelier than I have ever seen her." The smug smile was back.

"Sol, perhaps you would give me a hand instead?" Lauriana suggested with a pointed look.

Ellie's eyes went wide with panic. "I don't mind helping you, Mama!" She heard the shrill desperation in her voice. "Really, I don't."

"Nonsense. You stay here and entertain your young man. Your father is happy to help me." As they exited the room, her mother flashed an indulgent smile at Den and said in a coy, entirely un-Mama-like voice, "We won't be but a few chimes, children."

There was no mistaking her humiliatingly obvious scheme, and Den was quick to take up the unspoken invitation. As soon as Lauriana's skirts disappeared down the hall, he stepped closer to Ellie, his square hands reaching for her. She stumbled backwards to escape his pursuit, only to find herself stuck in a corner, trapped between his arms, staring in horrified revulsion as his thick, wet lips tried to attach themselves to hers.

Ellie escaped the kiss with a quick twist of her body, and tried to duck under his arm. She wasn't quite fast enough, and her slender muscles were no match for his solid bulk. After a brief, undignified tussle, she found herself back in the corner, pulled tight against his body.

"Come on, Ellie." His breath was starting to come a little faster. "We both know why your parents left us alone. There's no need to play the coy maiden. I don't want anything more than a kiss or two." He grinned, showing two rows of sharp and slightly crooked teeth. "For now."

"Den, we hardly know each other."

He laughed. "We've known each other since childhood, Ellie."

"But not like this . . . we've just been . . . er . . . friends." They'd never been friends. He'd been a taunting bully who liked to make her cry.

"I want to be more than friends now." His hands roved over her waist, and his lips descended, glancing off her cheek as she jerked her head away. Den drew back slightly and chuckled. "I've been watching you for some time now, Ellie," he murmured, his voice thick and possessive. "Granted, you weren't much to look at as a kid, all orange hair, freckles, and knobby knees. But lately, you've started to show a little promise." That smug, secret smile flashed again, and one thick-fingered hand came up to cup her chin. "I've decided to make you my wife, Ellie Baristani."

He didn't ask. He just said it, as if she had no choice in the matter. She stared at him, aghast, wondering how in the names of all the gods she was going to get out of this with any measure of grace. "Den, you . . . er . . . honor me, but—"

"Shh." The hand on her chin moved to cover her mouth. "There's no need to say anything." Her eyes widened in outrage and sudden fear as the hand on her mouth clamped down harder and Den lowered his head to her neck.

Her stomach lurched as something warm and wet touched her skin. Was that his *tongue*? A stinging pain at the base of her throat made her yelp against his silencing hand. The little bloat toad had *bitten* her! He sucked at the spot he'd just bitten, and once more that warm, wet tongue licked her. Oh, gods, she was going to be sick!

Outraged and repulsed, she grabbed two handfuls of his hair and yanked. Hard. She kicked his shins, too. He just grunted and shoved her against the wall, pinning her with the heavy, unmovable weight of his stocky body. Before she could draw breath enough to scream, his mouth was on hers. His lips were wet and slippery, and that horrid tongue was on the loose again, this time trying to get inside her mouth.

Without warning, one hand closed around her breast. Instinctively, she opened her mouth to scream. It was exactly the wrong reaction, and one he'd obviously been counting on. His hand shot up to hold her jaw open, and his tongue thrust deep into her mouth. Her screams, muffled by his mouth, came out as frantic little squeals that seemed only to excite him further.

Never in her life had Ellie been assaulted this way. Where were her parents? How could they have abandoned her to this . . . this . . . mauling?

Beneath the revulsion and feeling of helplessness, a darker emotion burst into smoldering life. A wild, fierce anger. Her skin flashed hot and tingling, drawing tight as if something inside her flesh were struggling to get out.

Terror grabbed her by the throat as the room began to tremble.

Two hundred miles away, beside a campfire burning in the chilly night, Rain Tairen Soul felt a woman's emotions stab into him. Fear. Outrage. Desperation. He leapt to his feet, his nostrils flaring as if he could scent the emotions on the wind. His mind raced to find their path, to identify their source.

Another wave of feelings arrowed into him. Revulsion. Rage. Then stark terror. A wordless cry screamed in his mind. She was calling out to him. She was afraid, and he was not there to protect her.

He flung himself from the ground into the sky, flashing instantly into tairen-form. Flames scorched the night sky and his roar of fury rent the air as he followed the path of the mind that called out to him in fear.

But then, as suddenly as the call had come, it fell silent. Confused by the abrupt termination of the connection, Rain faltered in mid flight. His fury was still there. Licks of flame still curled from his muzzle and venom pooled in the reservoirs in his fangs, but his rage had lost its focus. The woman's fear and desperation were gone, no longer fueling his wrath. Banking right, he circled the sky and reached out with his mind, trying to find the one who had called. He found nothing but silence and the worried calls of the Fey warriors he'd left behind. Then the even more worried call of Marissya.

The warriors he might have ignored, but not Marissya. All Fey men were bound to protect the females of their race, even from worry.

«*Rain?*» Marissya didn't try to hide the concern in her mental voice. She was a mere century older than Rain, had known him all his life. She was his friend. «*What happened?*»

«*She called out to me. She was afraid.*»

«*Who?*»

He hesitated. «*I don't know.*» Keen tairen eyes pierced the night. Far away in the distance, he saw the glow of Celieria. «*But I'm going to find out.*» He dipped one wing and banked again, heading towards the city in the distance.

Ellie sat at the dinner table and couldn't stomach the thought of putting food in her mouth. The terrifying anger and the disturbing sensation in her skin had passed almost as quickly as they'd come, with none but Ellie the wiser. Though she could have sworn the parlor had actually trembled, no one else appeared to have sensed it. Was she going mad? Had the demons that had haunted her youth found a different, more subtle way to work their evil on her?

Ellie knew not to let herself get upset. All her life, she'd worked to keep her emotions in check lest she accidentally trigger another seizure. She forced herself to take deep, even breaths, and filled her mind with calming thoughts.

Still, as she glanced at her mother from beneath her lashes, she couldn't quell a spurt of anger and resentment as Lauriana made pleasant small talk—small talk!—with Den Brodson. How could Mama even contemplate wedding Ellie to that odious *rultshart*?

Did Mama know what Den had been doing in the parlor? She must have known. She'd made a series of intentionally loud noises before coming back in. What had that been all about except to let Den know he should stop his assault on Ellie? He had, thank the gods. With a final wet kiss and a last painful squeeze of her breast, Den had released her and said, "You'll do, Ellie." As if she were a haunch of beef he was approving from the slaughterhouse.

Ellie's relief at being freed had rapidly turned into a sense of betrayal. How could Mama know what Den had been doing and not be outraged? Surely Mama didn't know about that awful pink slug of a tongue.

Outrage and resentment clashed inside her. She was not going to marry Den Brodson. Not now. Not ever. Anger flared, quick and hot.

Suddenly there was a feeling in her mind. A probing touch, as if someone or something was trying to reach inside her head. She had a distant sense of scarcely banked fury and a stronger sense of something powerful rushing towards her with grim purpose.

Ellie's spoon clattered to the table. Everyone looked at her in surprise.

"Ellie?" Papa's brown eyes radiated concern. "Are you all right, kit?"

She put a shaking hand to her head. "I—I think so, Papa." The feeling was gone. Had it been her imagination? Another sign of impending madness? She forced a wan smile and tugged at the neck of her chemise. "I mean, yes. I'm fine. Just a little tired."

"What's that on your neck?" Lorelle was staring at the spot where Den had bitten Ellie's neck, the spot that Ellie had unwittingly just revealed.

In an instant, everyone was staring at Ellie's neck. Embarrassed, she clapped a hand over the spot. She hadn't looked in a mirror. Had Den left a mark on her?

Apparently so, because her father was now staring hard at Den. That shameless *klat* just smiled his smug smile and met her papa's gaze straight on. Mama's eyes darted from her husband to her daughter's suitor. There was a look in Mama's eyes that made Ellie's heart stutter. Embarrassment faded—even fear of what was happening to her faded—as worry slithered up Ellie's spine.

"Girls," Papa said. Ellie had never heard his voice sound so emotionless, so hard. "Go to your rooms." The twins jumped to their feet and scurried out. "You, too, Ellysetta." He didn't look at her, didn't take his unblinking gaze from Den's.

Ellie did not immediately obey. Did her parents not know what Den had done to her, after all? Was it possible that they hadn't left her alone with him in the parlor for that very reason?

"Papa?"

"Go!" he barked, and Ellie all but fell over herself rushing from the room. She raced for the stairs and took them two at a time, not slowing down until she was ensconced in the safety of her small bedroom.

Needing to know exactly what sort of mark Den had left on her, she went to the small dressing table tucked in the corner of her room. Her fingers shook as she struck a match and lit the oil lamp on the table. Soft golden light filled the room. Ellie leaned close to the mirror, tugging the neck of her chemise to one side to reveal a small, dark, oval mark at the base of her throat. In the golden glow of lamplight, the mark looked like a smudge of soot. She rubbed at it, but it didn't come off. She felt invaded somehow, violated, and suddenly very afraid of what was going on downstairs.

She sat on the edge of her bed, and waited. She didn't know how long she sat there. It seemed like bells before she heard the creak of the stairs and the slow clomp, clomp of her father's boots. She rushed to her bedroom door and pulled it open.

"Papa?"

There was disappointment and sadness in his eyes when he looked at her. "Go to bed, Ellysetta. It's getting late." He looked tired and worn. Old.

"But, Papa . . . about Den." What could she say? She couldn't very well tell her father about the embarrassing things he'd done to her. "I . . . I know Mama thinks he's a good match, but, Papa . . . I don't like him. Please, I don't want to marry him."

Her father stared at her for a moment, then shook his head and turned away. "Go to bed. We'll talk tomorrow."

"But, Papa—"

He just continued walking down the hall and into his room, closing his bedroom door behind him.

Ellie returned to her own room and undressed in shadowy darkness, hanging the green gown and her mother's chemise in the small wardrobe resting against the wall. She didn't want to wear either of them again as long as she lived.

After donning a cotton nightdress, she sat down beside the window and unpinned her hair. It spilled down her back in long, springy coils. Brushing it with steady strokes, she stared out at the night sky. Both the large moon called the Mother and the small moon called the Daughter were three-quarters full. It was a bright night.

Please, she prayed silently, fervently, hoping the Celierian gods would hear her. *Please send me someone else. Anyone else but Den.* She laid the brush in its place on her dressing table and crawled into bed, pulling the covers up to her chin and closing her eyes.

She didn't see the shadow fall across her room as the light

from the Mother was blotted out by a large black tairen winging through the night. She didn't see the lavender eyes, glowing like beacons, turn their light upon the rooftops of Celieria. Searching. Seeking.

CHAPTER TWO

Beautifully and fearfully wrought, by dread magic
* splendored,*
With passion's fire his soul does burn, in sorrow his
* name be whispered.*

                —from the epic poem *Rainier's Song*
                        by Avian of Celieria

Celieria's main thoroughfare was already lined four deep when Ellie and the twins arrived at seven the next morning. News that the Tairen Soul himself would be coming had raced like wildfire through the city, and Ellie was convinced that before ten bells every man, woman, and child in the city would be lining the streets to ogle the legendary Feyreisen, Rain Tairen Soul, the man-beast who had once almost destroyed the world.

She began searching for a place from which to watch the forthcoming spectacle. About halfway between the city gates and the royal palace, she found a grassy knoll bordering one of the city's many small parks. From atop the knoll, the children would have an unimpeded view of the Fey procession.

Sending the twins off to play while they waited for the procession to begin, Ellie spread her brown skirts and sat down without a care for grass stains or the morning dew that dampened her dress. Her mind was still chasing itself in circles, worrying over what had passed between Den and her parents last night. She still didn't know. Papa had been gone when she came downstairs for breakfast, and Mama had told her they would talk after she returned from the Fey procession. Ellie couldn't shake the feeling that something very bad was about to happen.

Her sleep had been tormented by more dreams. Not the familiar, violent dreams of blood and death or the dark, malevolent nightmares that had haunted her most of her life, but new, frightening dreams of fiery anger and pale purple eyes, of a soundless voice that called to her, demanding that she reply. She remembered tossing and turning, remembered trying to block out those eyes and that insistent voice. Not until close to dawn had she finally found peace.

Now, staring up at the bright blue morning sky, with the Great Sun glowing like a huge golden ball, she could almost pretend that the dreams were nothing more than her imagination running wild . . . that worry about the situation with Den was to blame . . . that everything would be all right and life would return to its pleasant, comfortable routine.

She didn't believe it for a moment.

Twenty miles outside the city, two hundred Fey warriors and one Fey Lord traveled at a fast lope down the broad road that cut a swath through the Celierian landscape of lush fields dotted by small villages. Farmers and villagers bordered the road in small groups, having come with their families as they always did to see the immortal Fey run past. This year, however, their attention was directed not at the road, but overhead, where Marissya v'En Solande rode the wind on the back of a massive black tairen—the infamous Rain Tairen Soul himself.

The Fey warriors had broken camp three bells before dawn and resumed their trek to Celieria at a fast clip. Marissya had run with them until Rain returned just as the Great Sun began to light the sky; then she continued the journey on tairen-back, allowing the warriors to resume their normal, easily sustainable run. They had traversed the next seventy miles in just under three bells.

Everyone knew that something had disturbed Rain the night before and that he had gone in search of the source of the disturbance. But he had not spoken of it since his return, and not even Marissya could get him to talk.

When they neared the city, Rain landed, lowered Marissya to the ground, and shifted back into Fey form. He paced restlessly as Marissya and the Fey prepared themselves for their ceremonial entrance into the city.

Marissya shed her brown traveling leathers for a red gown that covered her from chin to toe and a stiff-brimmed hat draped with a thick red veil that covered her face. Her waist-length dark hair was braided and tucked out of sight. The garb would have been hot and stifling had her truemate, Dax, not woven a cool web of Air around her. Marissya was a *shei'dalin*, a powerful Fey healer and Truthspeaker, and none who were not Fey or kin were permitted to look upon her outside of council.

All around Marissya, two hundred Fey warriors donned gleaming black leathers and spent at least half a bell polishing and re-sheathing the scores of blades each warrior wore when he left the Fading Lands. Her mate, Dax, clad in the dark red leathers of a truemated Fey Lord, tended his own weapons with similar care. Though he was no longer of the warrior class—no Fey Lord was permitted to put his mate at risk by continuing to dance with knives—his blades would always stand between her and danger.

Marissya finished her physical preparations long before the men, and she went to join Rain. It had been many years since she'd seen him in such a state. He was restless, edgy, pacing back and forth with short, rapid steps. There was so much power in him, so scarcely contained that a shining aura surrounded him, flashing continuously with tiny sparks. His eyes glowed fever-bright. His nostrils quivered as if he were an animal scenting something in the air that set him on edge. If he'd been in tairen form, he would have been spouting flame. He was still in control of himself—she and all the Fey would have known if he were not—but he was in a high state of agitation, and that did not bode well for the long day ahead.

She knew better than to touch him—one didn't touch raw power without receiving a shock. Instead, she reached out to him on their private mental path, the one they had forged centuries ago in friendship. *«Rain, be calm.»* She sent a soothing wave of reassurance along with the words, not surprised when he shrugged it off and continued pacing.

«She is there. For a moment last night I was in her mind; then I lost her again.» Frustration boiled through the link.

«Who, Rain? Who is there?»

He snapped around, eyes flashing. His long, elegant hands clenched and unclenched. His chest heaved. He was angry and frustrated, yes, but now Marissya realized it was more than that.

«She is.*»* he snapped. *«She! The one!»* And then, the one word she was sure to understand. The one word that explained everything. He shouted it out loud: *"Shei'tani!"*

There was a sudden clattering whoosh of sound followed by absolute silence as two hundred Fey warriors jerked around to stare at their king in stunned disbelief.

Marissya's breath left her in an astonished gasp. *«But that cannot be.»*

«It can be nothing else.»

The tumult of Rain's emotions blasted over their mental link, and Marissya stumbled back in shock, recognizing those feelings for exactly what they were. Her mind reached instinctively for Dax, her own truemate, sharing the shocking truth of Rain's emotions with him.

Their gazes met across the distance, and as one they turned to look at their king.

He was pacing restlessly once more. Every few moments his head turned towards Celieria and the power in him burned a little brighter. They both knew the instincts driving him, knew that because he was the Tairen Soul those instincts would be far more intense and far harder to control, fueled by Fey and tairen passions combined. If they weren't very careful, the coming days could end in disaster.

As she caught sight of the Feyreisen riding the wind in tairen form, Ellie acknowledged that just a glimpse of him was well worth the interminable wait and jostling crowds. Long before the Fey warriors drew near, Ellie and the twins saw Rain Tairen Soul soaring through the sky. He was all that legend claimed, and more—a gigantic, ferocious black feline with glowing purple eyes, frightening and beautiful at the same time. He winged like a raptor over the city, circling again and again, emitting warning bursts of fire when the thronging crowd moved too close to the approaching warriors. Even from a distance, she could see the glistening danger of his sharp, venom-filled fangs. His ears were laid back on his head, his claws extended.

When the Fey warriors came into view, the sight of them was almost as awe-inspiring as that of the Tairen Soul. There were at least twice as many warriors as had ever come before. Row after impeccably formed row marched into view, and for the first time in Ellie's memory, magic surrounded them in a glowing aura of light.

A murmur of wonderment rose up from the crowd.

The Fey warriors presented a stunning display, clad in black leather from neck to toe and bristling with silvery swords and knives that gleamed in the sunlight. Every warrior clutched two long, curving blades called *meicha*, and what seemed like hundreds of razor-sharp throwing knives called Fey'cha were tucked into leather belts that crisscrossed their chests. As if that weren't enough, each warrior wore two massive *seyani* long swords strapped to his back.

It was said that one Fey warrior was as lethal as ten champions. Looking at their fierceness, their precision, and the tangible glow of magic enveloping them, Ellie believed it.

In the center of the formation, surrounded by an even brighter glow, walked an unarmed figure draped in voluminous folds of blood red. It was the *shei'dalin*, the Truthspeaker, Marissya v'En Solande, and the handsome, dangerous-looking man in red leather by her side was her truemate, the Fey Lord Daxian v'En Solande.

As the procession moved closer, the crowd surged forward, everyone straining for a better look. Rain Tairen Soul roared and spouted a warning flare of fire. With many screams and uplifted heads, the crowd wisely jumped back.

In the sudden shifting of massed bodies, Lillis lost her footing and fell to the ground. She howled in pain when Lorelle, trying to avoid being knocked over herself, trod on her hand.

Ellie was there in an instant, hauling Lillis to her feet and inspecting the injury. The child's little fingers were red, the skin slightly torn over one knuckle. "Oh, kitling. I'm so sorry. Would you like me to kiss it better?"

Lillis sniffled and nodded. "Yes, Ellie. You kiss the pain away better than anyone."

Giving her a fond smile, Ellie raised the girl's injured finger to her mouth. "Gods bless and keep you, kitling," she murmured and kissed the little finger. A tiny electric current leapt from Ellie to her sister, making them both jump. Ellie laughed a little. "Sorry, Lilli-pet. I didn't mean to shock you."

Rain Tairen Soul whooshed overhead, roaring, the sound like a clap of thunder in the air.

Ellie straightened in time to see the Fey warriors come to an abrupt halt, their curved *meicha* blades raised. The ones closest to the Truthspeaker drew their long swords with a hiss of metal leaving scabbard.

The *shei'dalin* turned her head from side to side as if scanning the crowd. Beside her, her mate had razor-edged swords in hand and was ablaze with power.

The crowd went silent. From her vantage point on the knoll, Ellie watched with bated breath and clutched the twins to her side. She didn't have any idea what was happening, but it was something unusual. Something important and frightening. The crowd around Ellie began shoving, everyone trying to get a better glimpse of what was going on.

"Lillis! Lorelle! Stay close to me!" She grabbed the twins

and hugged them tight, afraid they were about to be pushed off the knoll into the trampling feet below.

Rain Tairen Soul roared again, clawing the air, now obviously agitated about something. Flame seared the air, followed by another roar of tairen fury. From the street, the *shei'dalin* raised her arms and shouted, "Rain! *Nei!*"

The crowd began to panic, and so did Ellie. Someone stumbled heavily into her back. She staggered and tried to keep her balance, but her leather shoes slipped on the grass. With a cry of alarm, Ellie toppled off the knoll. She fell forward, pushing the children to safety with one hand and reaching out with the other to break her fall. She landed hard and screamed in pain as a man's boot heel stamped on her fingers, crushing the slender bones with a snap.

Pain and terror swamped her senses. People rushed madly around her, and another boot ground into her broken hand. She shrieked again. Barely able to think, certain she was about to die, she curled her body into a tight ball and brought her broken hand up over her head.

She was dimly aware that people were screaming around her. She didn't see Rain Tairen Soul fold his wings and drop like a hurtling black meteor towards the ground. But something touched her senses, something made her realize that suddenly the sun was gone, and so were the people hurting her.

She glanced up and let loose another shrill cry of horror as the huge, terrifying, black-winged tairen swooped down upon her, metamorphosing at the last chime into Rainier vel'En Daris Feyreisen, the infamous Rain Tairen Soul, who lightly stepped from sky to ground, one black-booted foot at a time.

He towered over her huddled form. Death-black hair hung in long, straight strands that blew about his face in the windy remnants of the tairen's downdraft. His skin was pale and faintly luminescent, his face terrible in the perfection of its stunning masculine beauty, and his lavender eyes glowed with a brilliant, icy fire. With a wave of one hand, he threw up a towering cone of Air and Fire magic that surrounded the two of them in a whirling haze of white and red.

Ellie cowered in fear, and instinctively held up her broken hand to ward him away. With a sobbing gasp, she rolled to her feet and staggered back.

"Stay away!" she ordered hoarsely. Her heart was racing, her breath coming in fast, shallow gasps, but she couldn't seem to get any air. Had he used his magic to steal the breath from her lungs? She knew the Fey could do that sort of thing.

"Ver reisa ku'chae. Kem surah, shei'tani." He spoke to her in a lyrical foreign tongue—Feyan, she realized, though she didn't understand the words—and stepped towards her.

"No!" she cried out. For all she knew, he'd just told her to prepare for her impending death. "Stay back! Don't come any closer!"

He paused for a moment, frowning. *"Ve ta dor. Ve ku'jian vallar."* Then Rain Tairen Soul came towards her again, his steps slow and resolute. He reached for her, ignoring the way she sobbed and flinched away from him. His fingers, strong and surprisingly warm, curled around her forearms and trapped her with effortless strength. She had the overwhelming sensation of immense power, deep sorrow, and a terrible longing. But underlying all of those was another emotion—a violent swirl of rage. She cried out and struggled to free herself, succeeding only in grinding the bones of her hand together. Agony knifed up her arm.

A scream ripped from her throat. She fell to her knees. Unexpectedly, she found herself free. She blinked and risked a glance up at the Feyreisen.

His eyes were squeezed shut, his hands clenched in white-knuckled fists at his sides. He was shaking as if he were in pain. His eyes flashed open again. The ice was still in them, and confusion, and more than a hint of madness.

She watched him fearfully, her body poised to flee if he came towards her again.

With a flick of his finger, he fashioned a door in the whirling cone of magic. His voice, deep, ancient, commanding, called out in Feyan.

A moment later, the Truthspeaker stepped through the doorway, followed closely by her mate. The Fey Lord Dax had sheathed his swords, and as he stepped inside the cone of magic the Feyreisen had erected, his own glow of power winked out. He followed a few feet behind his mate as she approached Ellie.

Though the *shei'dalin's* face was hidden behind folds of red, she radiated waves of compassion and reassurance. Despite everything—including her own mind whispering that this was a Fey trick—Ellie felt her terror begin to abate. She needed to trust this woman. The Truthspeaker would never cause her harm. There was no need to be afraid. She could be calm. All would be well.

The soothing compassion, the compulsion to release her fear, was impossible to resist. Dazed, lulled by the powerful hypnotic spell of a Fey *shei'dalin*, Ellie didn't protest when Marissya reached for her broken hand.

The Fey woman's long, pale fingers, slender and elegant, passed over Ellie's. Warmth sank through Ellie's skin and into the flesh and bone below. Her pain evaporated. A strange ticklish tingling spread across her hand, and she watched in astonishment as her bones straightened and knit. Within moments, her hand was whole and unhurt.

She flexed her fingers experimentally. There wasn't the faintest twinge of pain.

Ellie swallowed the lump in her throat and raised awestruck eyes to the Fey woman. "How did you do that?"

"Eva Telah, cor la v'ali, Feyreisa." The voice behind the veils sounded so peaceful, so soothing, so compassionate. Ellie wanted to sink into the comfort of that voice and absorb its tranquillity. She fought off the lethargy with a brisk shake of her head.

"I don't understand you."

The Truthspeaker's head jerked up. Though Ellie couldn't

see her eyes, she had a feeling the *shei'dalin* was staring at her in surprise. "You don't speak the Fey tongue?"

"Only a word or two." Ellie couldn't understand why that would be so unusual. Had she offended them somehow? "I'm sorry," she apologized. "I read it fairly well, but very few Celierians still actually speak your language."

"You are Celierian?"

Ellie blinked. "Of course."

The Truthspeaker cast a glance over her shoulder. The Feyreisen was still staring at Ellie, and he was frowning. She began to inch away. Immediately, the *shei'dalin* turned back to her, lifting her heavy veil as she did so. Huge blue eyes, so full of compassion Ellie could drown in them, were smiling at her from a face so beautiful it would put a Lightmaiden to shame.

"Be at peace, little sister," the *shei'dalin* murmured, and her hand came out to rest on Ellie's. "Of all people, you need never fear Rainier." As the Fey woman spoke, Ellie felt a faint pressure in her head, so slight she might not have noticed it had she not already been on edge. Her eyes widened as she realized the Truthspeaker was probing her mind. It was said that a *shei'dalin* could strip a soul naked, leave even the strongest of men sobbing like infants. Truthspeakers could bend anyone to their will.

"No!" Ellie yanked her hand out of the Fey's grip and imagined a gate of brick and steel slamming shut around her mind, thrusting out the invading consciousness.

The *shei'dalin* gave a muffled cry and staggered back. The Tairen Soul's eyes flared bright, and a bubble of lavender light burst into glowing life around Ellie. A feral snarl rumbled from the Tairen Soul's chest, and he bared his teeth like a wild animal on the verge of attack. In a blur, he leapt between Ellie and the *shei'dalin*. In the same instant, the *shei'dalin's* mate also leapt forward.

«Get back!» The voice was in Ellie's head, sharp, commanding. Somehow she knew it had come from the Feyreisen.

Scared out of her wits, Ellie pushed against the purple light enveloping her, trying to escape before the two Fey Lords decided to slaughter her where she stood.

Instead, to her utter amazement, the Tairen Soul whirled on the *shei'dalin* and her mate. His hands rose, power arcing from his fingers in blinding flashes just as the other Fey Lord's power snapped into blazing light and he sent a bright bubble of energy surging forth to wrap around his mate. Like Rain's, Daxian v'En Solande's teeth were bared in naked menace, but that menace was directed solely at the Feyreisen.

The two men faced each other, faces drawn in fury, power bursting around them, scorching the air with the scent of ozone.

"Nei, Rain!" the Truthspeaker protested. Her voice wasn't calm now. It was afraid. *"Nei, shei'tan!"* Then in Celierian, "I didn't mean to frighten you. Please, forgive me! Calm yourself. Guard your feelings."

It took a startled moment for Ellie to realize the Truthspeaker was addressing her. *"Me?"*

"Yes! Can you not see he is protecting you?" Even as she spoke to the girl, Marissya sent a silent plea to Rain. «*I'm sorry, Rain. I didn't mean to frighten her. Please. She is unhurt. See for yourself. Be calm. You must be calm. It is you who frighten her now.*» And to her truemate, whose thoughts and feelings she sensed as her own, «*Dax, shei'tan, I am not hurt. She only surprised me. It is my fault. I should not have probed her. She felt it and was frightened. Rain responds to her fear, to protect her, as you protect me. Please, let go before someone gets hurt.*»

Neither Rain nor Dax relaxed his grip on his power or his rage. It wasn't surprising. A Fey Lord reacted violently to even the smallest perceived threat to his mate.

«*Please, Rain. She needs you strong for her, in control of yourself. You must control the tairen in you. She was hurt, and you came. You protected her. She is safe.*»

«*She fears you.*» Blazing, half-mad lavender eyes pinned her. «*I will not permit it.*»

«*I'm sorry. I—*» The weave of Fire and Air appeared without warning. With incredible speed and dexterity, Rain had rewoven the protective cone of magic, shutting Marissya and Dax out, closing himself and the Celierian girl within.

It took Rain several chimes to beat back the tairen's fury, to shove it into a small corner of his mind and keep it there. Only then did he turn to face the woman whose emotions ripped at his sanity. Her fear—of him, he knew, despite his wanting to blame Marissya—tore at him in ways he'd never known. The web of Spirit he'd woven around her winked out as he released his power back to the elements. Still, she cowered from him. Rain would have torn out the heart of any other man who dared to frighten her this badly, yet he would not—could not—leave her.

"Come." His tone was imperious, yet the hand he held out trembled. "I could never harm you, *shei'tani*." His Celierian was rusty, deeply accented with Fey tones, and his attempt to appear nonthreatening was equally out of practice. The tairen in him still clawed at the edges of his control, all fiery passion, possessiveness, and primitive instinct. "I am called Rainier."

"I know." Her eyes were huge in the too-thin oval of her face. Twin pools of verdant green, they stared at him as if he were a monster. "You scorched the world once. It's in all the history books."

"That was a very long time ago." He tried to summon a smile, but the muscles in his face couldn't seem to remember how to form one. "I promise you are safe with me." His fingers beckoned her. "Come. Give me your hand."

The exotic flares of her brows drew together in a suspicious frown. "Why? So you can try to invade my thoughts like the Truthspeaker?" Rain could see she was still afraid, very afraid, yet she was working hard to master her fear.

"I . . . apologize for Marissya. She had no right."

"Then why did she do it?"

"She was . . . curious about you." She had done it to find answers, of course. Answers to the questions of how a Celierian child-woman could wield the power he had felt, and more importantly, how she could possibly be Rain's *shei'tani*.

"Did she never think to just *ask*?" The asperity in her voice was unmistakable. The delicate, frightened *shei'tani* had steel in her spine after all.

"She will now. Believe me." The tairen in him was slowly subsiding. It had ceased pounding the door of its cage and was now pacing restlessly within, edgy but contained. For the moment. But it, like him, had a great need to touch this woman. Once more he held out his hand. "Come. Give me your hand. Please." The last was more a genuine plea than an afterthought. "I would give my life before allowing harm to come to you."

Ellie stared at the outstretched hand in stunned silence. Was Rainier vel'En Daris, King of the Fey, truly standing before her, vowing to sacrifice his immortal life to protect her? Her, Ellie Baristani, the woodcarver's odd, unattractive, and embarrassingly unwed adoptive daughter? Surely she was dreaming.

But this all seemed so real. And he was so beautiful. *Beautifully and fearfully wrought*. Her dazed mind supplied the quote from Avian's classic epic poem, "Rainier's Song." Avian, she now knew, had barely got the half of it. She had dreamed of Rain Tairen Soul all her life, and here he was. She felt herself moving towards him, her hand reaching out. He had asked, and she had to touch him. If only to be sure he was real.

Her fingers trembled as they slid into his. She trembled as his hand closed about hers. Warmth, like the spring heat of the Great Sun, spread through her body, and a sense of peace unlike anything she'd ever felt came over her. She heard him inhale deeply, watched his eyes flutter closed. A nameless expression, an unsettling mix of joy and pain, crossed his face.

He drew her closer, and she went without protest, dazed

with wonder as his arms, so lean and strong, wrapped her in a close embrace. Her ear pressed against his chest. She felt the unyielding bristle of the countless sheathed knives strapped over his chest, heard the beat of his heart, and was oddly reassured. There was safety here as no other place on earth.

She felt him bow his head to rest his jaw on her hair, the touch feather light. Tears beaded in her lashes at the simple beauty of it.

"Ver reisa ku'chae. Kem surah, shei'tani." He whispered the words against her hair.

"You said that before," she murmured. "What does it mean?" It sounded familiar, like something she had heard or read somewhere. She felt the stillness in him, the hesitation, and she pulled back to look up into his eyes.

His gaze moved slowly over her face as if he were committing her likeness to memory for all time. "I don't even know your name."

She blinked in surprise. Since the moment she had put her hand in his and he had pulled her into his arms, she felt as if he knew everything there was to know about her. It was surprising and disconcerting to realize that, in fact, they knew each other not at all. "Ellie," she told him solemnly. "My name is Ellysetta Baristani."

"Ellie." Liquid Fey accents savored the syllables of her simple name, making it something beautiful and exotic. "Ellysetta." His pale, supple hand brushed the mass of her hair. His gaze followed the path of his fingers as they delved deep into the untamable coils. "Ellysetta with hair like tairen flame and eyes the green color of spring. I've seen the mist of your reflection in The Eye of Truth." His gaze returned to hers, filled with wonder and regret. *"Ver reisa ku'chae. Kem surah, shei'tani.* Your soul calls out. Mine answers, beloved."

At last Ellie remembered why the Fey words seemed so familiar. She'd read them before in a slim volume of translated Fey poetry. It was the greeting a Fey man spoke to a woman when recognizing and claiming her as his truemate.

The strange buzzing in her ears was all the warning Ellie received before her knees buckled.

Rain caught the girl as her legs gave way and held her tight to his chest, even as his own legs trembled beneath him. She was not the only one stunned by his claim.

Never in recorded history had a Tairen Soul claimed a truemate.

That was the price of the Tairen Soul, one he had accepted eleven hundred and eighty-seven years ago when his adolescent Soul Quest had shown him flame and fang. And on the day of his First Change, when all the tairen and Tairen Souls of the Fading Lands gathered in Fey'Bahren to guide him through his first transformation, he had trembled with fear and exaltation—but no regret—as his Fey form dissolved and re-formed as a massive, black-furred tairen who rode the winds on mighty wings. He had known then that he was destined for loneliness. Never to find a truemate, the one who was his other half. Never to bear a daughter of his loins. Never to know relief from the souls that darkened his own.

Sariel had joined her life with his, even knowing their souls would never follow where their hearts had led. Then she had died, and he had survived her death. Ah, gods, how he had railed against that. If Sariel had been his truemate, the mate of his soul rather than simply the mate of his heart, nothing could have chained him to life after her death. But he was a Tairen Soul, and Tairen Souls did not have truemates.

Until now.

Rain shook his head in disbelief. This girl in his arms was the first truemate to be claimed in a thousand years. The first truemate ever to be claimed by a Tairen Soul. Among the many wonders of the *shei'tanitsa* bonding, not the least of its benefits was the guarantee of fertility and the continuation of the strongest magics of the Fey.

There was no doubt in his mind that she was the reason the Eye had sent him to Celieria.

Somehow, for some reason beyond his understanding, the gods had granted this slender Celierian girl—scarcely more than a child—the power to save the tairen and the Fey.

Somehow, though he did not want it, they had granted her the power to save him.

CHAPTER THREE

Ellie woke wrapped in warm strength, the music of a steady heartbeat sounding in her ear. His strength. His heartbeat. Rainier vel'En Daris Feyreisen. Rain Tairen Soul. The man who had claimed her as his truemate, the missing half of his soul.

"I'm all right," she murmured, pulling away to stare up into the watchful lavender gaze of the stranger who named her his beloved. "I just got a little dizzy for a moment." Something warm and hungry unfurled within her as their eyes met. She backed away from him, hoping he had not noticed. "Why did you . . . say what you did?"

"That you are my *shei'tani*?" he growled. "Because it is the truth. Because I must." A muscle flexed in his jaw. She was suddenly aware of a sense of driving need, of a hunger not warm like hers but hot and demanding; then the feelings faded as Rainier vel'En Daris turned his back to her and took several deep breaths. "We must go," he said abruptly. "Your countrymen grow restless and too bold by half. The girl children who were with you are worried."

Her hands clapped over her cheeks. "Lillis! Lorelle!" How

could she have forgotten about them? She spun around, only to find her wrist clasped in his hand.

"Stay close to me, Ellysetta Baristani. I can allow no harm to befall you." He gestured. The cone of magic surrounding them disappeared, revealing them both to the swarming crowds jamming the streets. The throngs were so thick, with more bodies pushing into the area by the second, that Celierians dared to crowd within five feet of the small, lethal army of Fey warriors. There was a dull roar of sound— thousands of bodies shifting restlessly, voices murmuring— but all fell silent when Ellysetta and Rainier appeared.

"Wait here a moment, *shei'tani.*" A bubble of multicolored magic enveloped her as Rain Tairen Soul walked several paces away to speak with the *shei'dalin* and her truemate.

"Ellie!" The high-pitched shrieks heralded the twins' arrival as they raced towards her. Their faces were splotched with tears, their dresses torn, their lovely curls disheveled. Two Fey warriors, looking much worse for wear than the girls, hurried close on their heels.

"*Nei,* little Fey'cha." One of the Fey, a tall young man with silvery blond hair, a swollen eye, and a set of four bleeding scratches down the side of his face, snatched up Lorelle just as she would have flung herself into Ellie's arms. Lorelle immediately convulsed into a howling, screaming fit, her little fingers curved into claws, which explained the battle wounds on the man's face. He subdued her, admonishing in a gentle, genuinely concerned voice, "*Nei, nei.* Do not touch the Feyreisa when the bright light surrounds her. It would do you much harm."

Lillis stopped a few feet away, her lower lip trembling, tears pouring from her eyes. She looked so pitiful, so woefully in need of a hug that Ellie instinctively stepped towards her. When the warrior behind Lillis grabbed her up, Ellie froze in her tracks.

A lump rose in her throat. She turned towards the Feyreisen. "Please," she called out. She pushed at the light surrounding her, but it merely flowed around her hands. "Release me from this thing."

The look he turned upon her was once again the cold, frightening Tairen Soul's gaze. With no expression on his face, he scanned the crowd for several long moments, then dissipated her shield without a word.

As soon as it was gone, she lurched forward to snatch Lillis and Lorelle into her arms, hugging them close as they wrapped their little bodies around her and cried into her neck. "Shh, kitlings. Shh. It's all right. I'm safe." She showered kisses upon their curly heads. "I'm so sorry you were frightened. Hush, now. Please don't cry."

"What's going on, Ellie?" Lorelle asked once she had calmed down enough to speak. "Why did the tairen-man attack you, then put you in the fire cage?"

"It's all very confusing," Ellie told them. "And it must have looked very frightening." It certainly had scared the wits out of her. "But the Feyreisen didn't attack me. He knew I was hurt and came to my rescue."

"Why wouldn't the Fey let us come to you?" Lillis asked. "We cried and cried, but they wouldn't let you out of the cage and they wouldn't let us in!" Lillis wasn't used to her tears being so ineffective. She glared at the brown-haired, blue-eyed Fey who had kept her from going to Ellie. He only grinned back at her and bowed.

"I know," Ellie soothed. "I'm sorry. But I'm here now and we're together again and safe."

"I want to go home." Lorelle's brows drew together in a scowl.

"Me too, kitling." Ellie murmured. "Me too."

A few feet away, Rain watched the reunion. Her love for the children was obvious, as was theirs for her. He had known love once, but it had died along with all his gentler feelings at the Battle of Eadmond's Field, where Sariel had breathed her last. That day had changed him forever, stripping him of kindness and compassion, leaving him with sorrow, anger, duty, and the stain of millions of lives darkening his soul. Had he not been the last Feyreisen, he would have been cast out by the Fey for the blood on his hands and the taint on his soul.

Yet now, in a fit of wicked humor, the gods had thrust Ellysetta Baristani in his path and decreed he must mate, binding the darkness of his ancient soul to the shining innocence of hers. He didn't want it. The responsibility for her safety and happiness was yet another burden, the reawakening of violent tairen-passions a potential danger to them all. But he was the Feyreisen, the last Tairen Soul, repository of all the ancient Fey magics and the only remaining Fey capable of entering the tairen's lair, Fey'Bahren. He had lost the freedom of choice with the death of all the other Tairen Souls. What remained was his duty to protect the Fey. To live when he would rather die. To mate when he would rather remain alone.

The tairen in him roared again. The Fey in him roared back. The tairen hungered for his mate, was furious at the delay, while Rain, the beloved of Sariel, didn't want to let another in his heart, as he must in order to fulfill the matebond.

«*Rain, be calm,*» Marissya warned.

«*I am calm,*» he snapped back, but he grabbed the unraveling threads of his emotions and pulled them tight. "Celieria unsettles me." There were too many memories here, of Sariel and happier days, of death and war. "My *shei'tani* is not safe here. She must return with me to the Fading Lands. The courtship will take place there."

"You cannot just abduct her, no matter how much you worry about her safety. She has parents, a family. Do you think she will accept you if you take her from everything she knows?"

"I will permit her family to enter the Fading Lands. They can remain until the matebond is complete." That was fair. More than fair. No one but Fey had been allowed to enter the Fading Lands since the Mage Wars. "She will accept me."

"Don't be so sure you know a *shei'tani's* heart," Marissya warned him. "She may be young, but she would never be your truemate if she weren't very strong."

"Marissya is right, Rain," Dax agreed. "She doesn't trust any of us. If you take her from her home, you may never win her. And where will that leave the Fey? We can't afford to risk losing you any more than you can afford to lose her."

Rain knew they were right. If Ellysetta Baristani didn't accept him, he would die. No gift from the gods ever came without a price, and that was the price Fey warriors paid for the truemate bond. He had recognized her as his mate. His soul, for good or ill, was already bound to hers. She, on the other hand, had yet to accept him, and he was ancient enough, powerful enough, that the debilitating effects of an unfulfilled matebond would begin to take their toll on him quickly. Madness first, then death, either at his own hands or the hands of his people.

"My Lord Feyreisen."

Ellysetta stood beside him, holding tight to the children with the lovely hair. He could feel her fear, and her determination not to be cowed by it. She didn't trust him, even though she felt the pull of his soul—or perhaps because of that—and she definitely didn't trust Marissya or Dax. The tairen within pushed against its cage, sensing its mate, seeking release.

"My Lord Feyreisen," she repeated. "My sisters and I must return home."

Logic evaporated. Cold fury took its place. She thought to leave him? "*Nei.*"

Ellysetta's jaw went slack.

"What Rain means is that you are welcome to walk with us," Marissya hurried to explain. «*Rain! Do you want to drive her away?*» She held out a hand. "I would be honored if you would join me."

"No!" Ellysetta all but leapt back to avoid Marissya's outstretched hand. "I mean, no, thank you. We've had enough excitement for one day. I'm sure you understand." Her eyes turned back to Rain and she said slowly, as if he were thick in the head, "My parents will be worried if we don't come home."

"Your sisters may go," Rain told her. "You stay with me."

"I can't send them home alone!" she exclaimed. "They're just children!"

Her defiance angered him. The tairen's cage rattled. "The Fey will take them. You stay."

Her hands fisted. Her body trembled. "I won't!"

The tairen screamed in rage. *She is our mate. She will not leave us! She will submit. We will make her submit!* Power flamed in his eyes. "You will."

She cried out and shrank back in fear. Suddenly there was a glow of power around her, and it wasn't his. Baring his teeth in a snarl, he whirled around. Who dared? His eyes narrowed on Dax, who wore the telltale shining aura about him.

"Rain, stop it." With seeming fearlessness, Marissya stepped between her king and her mate. *«This anger is the bond-madness talking. The girl must return to her home. She is not leaving you. She has not rejected the bond. Think, Rain! Stop feeling, and think!»* She didn't touch him, but he felt the insistent presence of her power in his mind, urging calm upon him.

He shook his head. He couldn't think. That was the problem. Since the Mage Wars, caging the tairen required constant vigilance and concentration. His centuries-old vise hold on it had been weakened by the Eye only days ago, and the tairen had reawakened with a vengeance, hungry for freedom. Here in Celieria, memories and the thoughts of millions pounded at him, sapping his concentration. Added to that, the visceral power of the matebond had him in its teeth. Just touching his *shei'tani's* hand caused a rush of feelings the likes of which he'd never felt—not even for Sariel. Was it any wonder he was going mad?

"I must leave this place. I need to find peace . . . and strength . . . to do what must be done."

Marissa nodded. "*Aiyah*, but you cannot take the girl with you. We will watch over her until you return."

He looked at his *shei'tani*. Her lips were almost bloodless with fear, and the sight stabbed at his Fey heart. He was a monster. And this poor child had just been offered up as a sacrifice. "She may return to her home for now," he informed Marissya abruptly, adding on a private weave, *«She must be well guarded. Half of the warriors will accompany her to her home, stay there to guard her. The other half will remain with you. Bel»*—he looked at the tall, dark warrior who had been his friend since before the Mage Wars—*«Guard her. Use Kieran, Adrial, Rowan, and Kiel for her quintet.»* At Bel's nod, Rain released his power and glared at Dax until he did the same. Only when his *shei'tani* was no longer enveloped in another's light did Rain begin to relax.

He crossed the short distance to Ellysetta Baristani, ignoring the tairen's hissing command to dominate her when she backed away from him. "I know I have given you cause to fear me, and I am sorry for that. I am . . . not myself." He held out his hands, shamelessly used a push of Earth to make the ground beneath her feet shift so that she stumbled forward into his arms. His eyelids lowered as the intense pleasure flowed up from his hands where his bare skin touched hers. He breathed in her scent, knowing he would never forget it. "Of course you may return to your home, but you must allow me to send warriors to accompany you."

"I—" She looked at the grim-faced army of Fey and gulped. "I really don't need—"

"It is for your protection," he interrupted. "They will guard you until I return."

She looked up at him, green eyes wide. "You are leaving?" Her relief was so obvious that he didn't need to read her emotions to know it. His young *shei'tani* thought to be rid of him!

"Only for a short while." There was tairen-wicked satisfaction in dashing her ridiculous hopes. "I will come for you tomorrow." Releasing her hands, he made a sharp gesture and half the contingent of Fey warriors circled her.

She gathered the twins closer and eyed the warriors with naked fear. "This isn't necessary. Really. One or two to serve as an escort would be fine."

"Be at peace, little sister," Marissya said. "They will not harm you." There was understanding and sadness in her voice. "Indeed, they would each die to protect you from the slightest harm."

«Go.» Rain saw Ellysetta jerk when his voice sounded in her head. «*They will protect you while I am gone. No harm must come to you.*» He could not compel her with a thought—she was his *shei'tani*, so free access to her mind was denied him until she accepted their bond—but he knew she feared him enough to obey. Fear was his specialty. He stood there, alone, remote, imperious, until she bowed her head to his will and began walking.

One hundred Fey accompanied her, with five of the Fey's greatest warriors ringed protectively around her. Belliard vel Jelani, the oldest unmated warrior of the Fey and Rain's most trusted friend, walked at Ellysetta's side. Bel and the other four warriors Rain had designated to be part of his *shei'tani's* personal guard would kill hundreds and die themselves before allowing harm to come to her. Magic glowed bright around the procession as it departed from the main thoroughfare, heading into the narrow, winding side streets of Celieria.

Rain waited until Ellysetta was out of sight before he broke into a run, then leapt into the air, transforming in an instant into a massive black tairen. Powerful wings beat the air, lifting him above Celieria into the freedom and silence of the skies. He rocketed high up into the icy coldness of the ether, released a scream of tairen fury, and disappeared over the horizon.

As the Tairen Soul took to the sky and half of the Fey warriors escorted the Celierian girl away, dark eyes watched with interest. Black eyes that glowed with red lights. Elden Mage eyes, steeped in Azrahn, though the magic was tightly leashed to avoid Fey detection.

The Tairen Soul had a truemate. A truemate with tairen-flame hair and green eyes like those of the child that had been stolen from the High Mage of Eld more than two decades earlier. Kolis Manza, apprentice to the High Mage, knew his master must be informed. The decision of how to proceed belonged to the High Mage alone. In the meantime, the girl must be watched.

Kolis made a quick gesture, little more than a flick of one wrist, accompanied by a brief command sent on a filament-thin weave of red-tinged black carefully hidden within a subtle Spirit weave to avoid Fey notice. Two young lads beside him, unfortunate children of the street who'd given Kolis access to their souls in return for full bellies and warmth in the winter, darted after the Celierian girl's entourage.

Marissya sent calming thoughts over the curious crowds as she, Dax, and the remaining contingent of Fey warriors continued on their way to the royal palace. Despite the long delay, the King and Queen of Celieria and a host of Celierian dignitaries were still waiting on the steps of the palace to greet the Fey with even more ceremonial pomp than usual.

It seemed as though the entire court had turned out for their arrival. They were hoping to get a glimpse of the Feyreisen, Marissya knew, and disappointment hung like heavy smoke in the air. She had never seen so much bosom on display, many ladies bordering on indecency with the amount of skin they revealed. They were so obvious, these women, with their foolish hopes of attracting the Feyreisen's attention.

Unlike the women of their court, King Dorian X and his queen had clothed themselves with both extravagance and decorum, and if they were disappointed that Rain was absent, they did not show it. They stood side by side in royal splendor, King Dorian outfitted in robes rich with gold thread, queen Annoura shining in silver. The queen's pale hair had been piled high and decorated with shimmering silver birds and jeweled butterflies. The pair of them remained cool and composed while the rest of their court had melted in the summer heat. Marissya suspected King Dorian had wrapped himself and his wife in the same cooling Air magic that Dax had woven around her. Dorian had inherited at least a minor command of magic from her sister's bloodline.

Standing before the royal couple, Marissya raised the heavy outer veil from her face and uttered the traditional blessing of the *shei'dalin*. "Peace, health, and fertility upon the house of Marikah of the Fey. Greetings from the Fey, your kin."

"Greetings, Lady," returned King Dorian. "Truth and light upon you. We welcome the *shei'dalin* into our walls and vow to protect her from harm. Enter in peace."

Marissya lightly embraced the king and queen, sending them a wave of healing and peace as she did so. Her brows drew together in the tiniest frown as her fingers touched Annoura.

«Marissya?»

«It is nothing, shei'tan. A whisper of darkness that I don't remember.» She felt Dax's concern and smoothed the frown from her face. *«She is mortal. It is to be expected.»* But it was more than that, too. During the procession, she'd been aware of an unusual level of hostility in the crowd. She'd thought it was in response to Rain's presence—he was responsible for more Celierian deaths than any other individual in history—but now she wondered if that was the case. She touched Prince Dorian and his chosen bride, Lady Nadela, and was pleased to find little trace of darkness in either of them.

As they moved towards the doors of the palace, the Fey warriors fanned out around them. Several broke off from the main group to stand guard outside the palace. Inside, Dax and five Fey remained with Marissya while the rest of her guard took up pre-assigned protective positions throughout the palace. Dax walked beside his mate, and Marissya rested her fingers on the back of his wrist in the Fey way, leaving his fingers free to call magic or unsheathe weapons should the need arise.

"Your journey was pleasant, I hope, Lady Marissya, Lord Dax," Queen Annoura said as they made their way through a labyrinth of halls and winding corridors. Liveried servants and richly garbed courtiers bowed as the entourage passed.

"*Aiyah,*" Dax replied. "Celieria is beautiful as always."

"All seemed peaceful," Marissya added.

"Yes, well . . . Ah, here we are. A nice quiet spot for a private discussion." King Dorian led the way into a small, comfortably appointed antechamber. As soon as the door closed, Dax wove shields of Air and Spirit to seal the room and ensure privacy.

Marissya took a seat on one of the cream velvet sofas and removed her heavy veils and hat. She captured Dorian's gaze and opened up her empathic senses. "Your concern weighs heavy on your mind, bond-nephew. All is not as peaceful as it appeared on our journey, then. Tell us."

"A minor disturbance in the north, but the Border Lords have matters in hand."

"Disturbance?"

"*Dahl'reisen,*" Dorian admitted. "They've been raiding a few of the small villages along the northern borders. They killed about half a dozen men last month."

Marissya sat back. *Dahl'reisen* were banished Fey who had turned their backs on honor and chosen to walk the Shadowed Path. "You are certain it was *dahl'reisen*?"

"As certain as one can be." Dorian reached into his robes and pulled out a cloth-wrapped object. "Usually they leave no weapons and no witnesses, but this was recovered from one of the raid sites."

Dax took the small parcel and pulled back the folds of cloth to reveal a small, shining dagger with a red-silk-wrapped handle. He examined the blade and checked the marking on the pommel. "I do not recognize the namemark, but it *is* a true Fey'cha. Fey rarely lose their blades. If you found this, it was most likely left deliberately—either to implicate the *dahl'reisen* or to issue a challenge."

"Are there witnesses?" Marissya asked.

"Not from the attack where that Fey'cha was found, but there is an old woman who swears she saw her son murdered in his bed by the Dark Lord himself." Dorian said the last bluntly, but his sympathy skated across Marissya's senses.

She stifled a flinch. The Dark Lord was a phrase originally coined to refer to the God of Shadows, but since the Mage Wars, it had been used almost exclusively to refer to Gaelen vel Serranis, Marissya's brother, the infamous *dahl'reisen* whose bloody vengeance for his twin sister's murder had ignited the Mage Wars. She wanted to cry out that it was not true, that her brother would not have murdered a helpless mortal in his sleep, but she could not. For the last thousand years Gaelen had lived beyond the honor of the Fey. She no longer knew what he was and was not capable of. "Is it possible to bring this woman to me that I might question her?"

"She has refused out of fear, and her Lord is bitter enough over the recent attacks that he supports her refusal."

"Has news of these raids reached Celieria City?"

"The pamphleteers were spreading tales more than a week ago, and the newspapers began printing the story two days after that—including the bits about an eyewitness and evidence proving that *dahl'reisen* were behind the attacks."

That would explain the hostility Marissya had sensed during the procession. Most Celierians considered *dahl'reisen* and Fey to be one and the same. If *dahl'reisen* were killing Celierians, the blame would fall on the Fey.

"Enough of all this doom and gloom," Dorian announced briskly. "There will be time enough for weighty discussion in the next few days. For now, tell us what happened between the Feyreisen and the Celierian girl. Is it true that he dropped out of the sky and locked himself with her in a cage of magic, then sent her home with an escort of one hundred Fey warriors?"

"It's true," Marissya confirmed. "But those tales are only part of the whole story. Rain has found his truemate."

The king's eyes widened. "But this is excellent news."

Marissya exchanged a look with Dax. "That remains to be seen," Dax replied. "There has never been a truemated Tairen Soul before. The bonding period is difficult at best, for any Fey man. But Rain fights the tairen in him as well. It will push him to the brink of madness. Our best hope is that the girl accepts him, and quickly."

The marching Fey warriors caused an uproar along Celieria's quiet side streets as Ellysetta, the twins, and their enormous escort made their way to the merchant class district that housed the Baristani residence. Luckily, the streets were mostly deserted, or Ellie's entourage would have caused all manner of problems. As it was, a crowd double the size of her escort followed them from the main thoroughfare, and more folk joined them as they went. Ellie's face was flaming with embarrassment long before they reached her street.

Unlike Ellie, once the twins had recovered from their initial fear, they found the attention quite entertaining. They darted to and fro, giggling when they managed to catch a warrior's eye. The Fey did not smile at their antics. They just watched them, stone-faced and gimlet-eyed, except for the brown-haired, blue-eyed warrior, who would give Lillis a tiny grin each time she stuck her little snub nose in the air to show that she still had not forgiven him for not falling prey to her earlier tears.

The warrior beside Ellie was named Belliard vel Jelani. She gathered he was quite, quite old, though his face was as unlined as that of a Celierian just leaving his twenties. It was his eyes, dark and fathomless, that showed his age. Looking into those eyes, she felt an oppressive weight and terrible sorrow, as if he had lived countless centuries without joy. He did not, she noted, look directly at her for more than a moment at a time, and his stern, studious avoidance of her gaze invited little in the way of conversation.

As they neared the Baristani home, Ellie's step faltered and her stomach clenched in nervous knots. Her mother stood in the doorway of their house. Someone had obviously run ahead to announce her coming, and Mama did not look happy. As the first of the Fey neared the Baristani residence, the procession smoothly parted in two separate columns that circled around the sides of the house like a black river flowing around an obstruction in the effluvial plain. Within moments the house was surrounded and Ellie found herself deposited on the doorstep, looking up at her mother's grim face.

The twins ran to her, chattering excitedly about the Tairen Soul and fire cages and having been very afraid though now they weren't. Lauriana listened with half an ear, then shooed them into the house.

"What's this about the Tairen Soul and fire cages, Ellysetta?" she demanded as Ellie drew close. Her voice was sharp, filled with a brittle combination of fear and anger. She held no affection for the Fey. In her opinion, magic was the scourge of the earth. "And why is this . . . this *army* of Fey bringing you home?"

Ellie cast a glance at the surrounding avid faces of the neighbors. "Can we talk about this inside, please, Mama?" There was a note of desperation in her voice.

Fortunately, Lauriana firmly believed that respectable folk did not air laundry on the front steps. "Very well. Get yourself inside." Her eyebrows shot up into her hairline as Belliard vel Jelani and four other Fey—including the two who'd seen to Lillis and Lorelle—followed Ellie up the steps. "Sers, thank you for escorting my daughter, but you need not follow her into our home." Her teeth made an audible click as she gave the men a grimly pleasant smile. "Especially as you have not been invited."

Belliard gave her a deep bow. "Eternal apologies, honored one, but we must enter. We protect the Feyreisa. We go where she goes."

"The Fey-who?" Lauriana turned to Ellie. "What is he talking about?"

"Please, Mama. Let them in, if that's what they want. Let's go inside." Ellie glanced again at the crowd and tried to direct her mother towards the privacy of their home.

"And what are *they* doing?" Outraged, Lauriana turned to glare at a group of warriors weaving an intricate, nearly invisible mass of shining magic over the front of the house. "You there! Stop that this instant!" Four of the Fey behind her took advantage of her distraction to slip into the house. Belliard remained, his gaze intent and watchful as he waited for Ellie.

"Mama, I'll explain inside. *Please!*" Ellie tugged her mother across the threshold as yet another group of Fey took up guard beside the front steps. The rest seemed to melt away into the shadows of alleyways and rooftops. Ellie knew they were still there, unseen. She could feel them, like a ripple of wind on the back of her neck.

Inside the house, the five Fey guards positioned themselves by the doors and windows of the large main room. They stood silently, arms crossed over their chests, fingers a mere breath away from the countless knives they wore. After one look at their stern faces and resolute stance, Lauriana did not even attempt to oust them. Instead, she turned a dark look on Ellie.

"Well, young lady, what is the meaning of this?"

"It's a long story, Mama."

Lauriana crossed her arms over her chest. "I have time, Ellysetta."

Ellie bit her lip. When Mama called her Ellysetta and had that darkling look in her eye, she meant business. "Well . . . I took the twins to see the Feyreisen like you asked me to . . ." She related the series of incredible events, leaving out the more alarming parts like the bit about Rainier vel'En Daris claiming her as his *shei'tani*. ". . . and he sent the Fey to escort me home . . . and, well, here we are." Conscious of the five pairs of Fey eyes watching her steadily and her mother's patent disbelief, Ellie flushed and stared at her feet. Her story was a fabrication of partial truths laid over gaping chasms of omitted pertinent facts.

Before Lauriana could take Ellie to task, a commotion outside the front door drew her attention. "Now what?" Scowling, she marched to the door and threw it open.

The enormous crowd outside had grown even larger. It

now included the strangers who had followed the Fey, nosy neighbors in search of gossip, and, to Ellie's dismay, Den Brodson. He had bullied his way to the front of the pack and was now loudly demanding to know what was going on. Den's mother, a plump woman with ruddy cheeks and frizzy brown hair, stood beside him, clutching his elbow and adding her shrill voice to his.

When she caught sight of Lauriana, Talla Brodson waved a frantic hand and yelled, "Lauriana Baristani, what in the name of the gods is going on? Tell these Fey to let us pass!"

At Lauriana's insistence—and a subtle nod from Belliard—the Fey allowed the butcher's wife and her son to enter the house. As they passed the Fey guards, Talla sniffed and stuck her nose in the air, while Den puffed out his chest and eyed the warriors haughtily.

Once inside the house, Den's haughty look changed to a scowl, and he marched across the room towards Ellie. "What's the meaning of this, Ellysetta Baristani?" he demanded in a bullying tone. "You have quite a bit of explaining to do, my girl." He reached out to grab her arm in what was sure to be a bruising grip, but before he could lay a finger on her, the sound of unsheathing swords cut the air. Den, his mother, Ellie, and Lauriana froze. Each of the five guards held naked steel in his hands. Though Belliard vel Jelani was still easily the most frightening of the Fey, now even the youthful smiling one looked like death waiting to be set free. Belliard tested his thumb on the edge of his blade, eyed Den's hand, and shook his head ever so gently.

Den withdrew his hand.

The Fey clucked in approval and began sharpening his blade.

Ellie was grateful for the intervention. The feel of Den's fingers squeezing her flesh always made her ill. Lauriana, however, wasn't impressed. She planted her hands on her hips and glared. "Now, you see here, sers. This is Ellie's fiancé. Her father signed the agreement just this morning. You've no business entering my home and coming between a lad and his betrothed."

"Betrothed?" Ellie gasped.

The Fey shared looks and a patter of quick Feyan words. The young brown-haired warrior pointed at Den and laughed in disbelief. Then he grinned and shook his head.

"*Nei, nei,* little sausage," he told Den. "The Feyreisa is not for you."

Obviously feeling a bit braver after seeing Lauriana stand up to the warriors, Den thrust out his jaw. "Ellysetta is my betrothed, and you demon-souled sorcerers have nothing to say about it. She bears my mark, her family has signed the agreement. We wed in a month's time."

"Your mark?" Ellie cried. Her hand flew to her throat. "Is that why you bit my neck, you horrid little toad?"

"Ellysetta Baristani," her mother snapped, "mind your tongue!"

Den's face turned purple at the insult. Without warning, his meaty hand slashed out towards Ellie's face. Never having been struck before in her life, Ellie was too stunned even to think of defending herself.

She didn't need to. Den's arm froze in mid swing, and the intended blow never landed.

Den's eyes went wide with surprise that changed quickly into fear, then terror. He clawed at his chest, mouth opening in a soundless gasp. It was as though all the air had been sucked from his lungs. He fell to his knees.

Ellie looked at Belliard. A faint white glow emanated from him.

"You may not touch the Feyreisa," he told Den. His voice was glacial, his eyes flat and lifeless. This was a man who would kill without a qualm. "I will not take a life in the Feyreisa's home unless I must, and so I let you live."

The room echoed with the raw sound of air rushing back into Den's starved lungs. He coughed and his shoulders heaved. His mother rushed to his side, trying to hover over him, only to be batted away.

Ellie swallowed. Her innate compassion roused a twinge of sympathy, but her outrage at the way he had tried to trap her into marriage kept her standing where she was.

Talla whirled on Lauriana. "How can you stand there and allow my son to be treated this way? No young man with any pride would have allowed his betrothed to speak so rudely without punishment. Most would have taken a stick to her rather than a hand, and you know it!"

Lauriana dragged her dazed stare away from the butcher's gasping son and faced his outraged mother. "Talla, please—"

"It's obvious your daughter is a creature of loose morals. Who else has put his mark on her that you don't know about? This Fey Lord perhaps? Is that why he sends his sorcerers into your house? To watch over her until he is done with her?"

"Now, just a blessed minute!" Lauriana's cheeks flushed at the insult. To accuse a girl of loose morals was to accuse her family of the same.

"I've a good mind to break the agreement and demand the bride bond, which I scorching well know you can't afford to pay!" By Celierian custom, all families bonded their betrothed daughters with a price three times the girls' dower. It gave the families of the suitor insurance against unacceptable brides and provided strong incentive for the families of the bride to guard the girl's virtue and ensure she behaved with modest circumspection until her marriage.

"Talla Brodson, that is outside of enough! Are you threatening me in my own home?"

"My son has no need of a wife who is unattractive, poor, and loose with her favors to boot!"

"Shut up, Mother." Den had recovered his breath and gotten to his feet. He glared at his mother, glared at the Fey, then settled a narrow-eyed look of promised retribution on Ellie. "The betrothal stands. She's mine. I want her. I will have her. And Rain Tairen Soul can go flame himself. The laws of Celieria are on my side." He straightened his clothes with a few sharp tugs and stomped towards the door. "Come on, Mother. We're leaving." At the door, he stopped to pin Ellie with a final hot look. "Prepare yourself for our wedding, Ellysetta Baristani. And our wedding night."

The door slammed behind them with a resounding bang.

In the ensuing silence, Ellie began to tremble as shock set in. She clasped her shaking hands together and hid them in her skirts, then turned to face her mother. "Mama, I can't marry him. Surely you must see that."

Lauriana sighed. "Ellie, your father signed the papers. You must marry him."

"But, Mama—"

"But nothing. You let him put his mark on you. In this very house. That's the same as agreeing to wed him."

"I didn't *let* him do anything, Mama! Besides, the mark's just on my neck! I thought it had to be someplace more"—she glanced at the onlooking Fey and blushed bright red—"intimate."

Ellie knew very little about claiming marks. Both she and her best friend, Selianne Sebarre, had overhead Kelissande and her friends giggling about the marks a time or two; but Selianne's mother wasn't from Celieria and didn't know the ancient custom, and the one time Ellie had asked Mama about it, Mama's nebulous reference to "passion roses" and stern caution to "stay away from boys and dark corners" had shed little light on the subject. The suspicion and close maternal supervision Ellie had received for weeks thereafter ensured that she never dared ask again.

It was only five years ago, after Selianne wed Gerwyn Pyerson, that Ellie and Selianne finally learned what a claiming mark was. Ellie still remembered Selianne's fiery cheeks as she'd unbuttoned her chemise to reveal the dark smudge on the top of her left breast and the giggling that ensued when she explained how the mark was made. It never occurred to Ellie that a mark could be made against a girl's will—or put on a place as *non*-scandalous as her neck.

Lauriana set her straight on both counts. "The location of the mark doesn't matter, Ellie. It doesn't even matter if you were willing. Den Brodson put his mouth on your body and left proof that he did. You're now a marked woman, a claimed one."

"But—" Panic was setting in. Ellie took a deep breath and clung to the shreds of her composure. "Nobody needs to know about the mark. I'll stay in the house until it fades."

"Ellysetta, if your father hadn't agreed to sign the betrothal, Den vowed to destroy your reputation. With that mark on your throat, there's no one who would doubt him."

"Then let him! People can say and think what they like."

"Ellie, there's more at stake here than just you. There's your father's business—and the queen's commission. There's Lillis and Lorelle and their future. A stain on you is a stain on us all."

"Mama, I hate him! I can't marry him—no! I won't!" For the first time in her entire life, Ellysetta defied her mother. She didn't know who was more shocked—herself or her mother.

Lauriana's face lost all expression. "If you refuse, you'll see this family destroyed."

Ellie's fingers curled into fists. Her chest heaved. In a billow of skirts, she whirled and fled upstairs to her bedroom, locking herself within as her tears began to fall.

Rain raced through the skies, flying as fast as his tairen form was able until the worst of his wild emotions passed. He wasn't aware of the passage of time or distance until he recognized the frozen heights of the Tivali Mountains near Elvia's border and realized the Great Sun was beginning to set.

Exhausted, he set down on a mountain peak, draping his massive black tairen form across a rocky outcropping. Snow drifted around him, but he did not feel the cold. He rested his tairen muzzle on his forepaws and looked out over the snowy peaks and the fertile Celierian lowlands to the north. His mind was calmer now, more rational.

A truemate. It was not what he had ever expected, never what he had wanted after Sariel's death. He knew the agony of loss, knew it in rich, memorable, fresh detail, thanks to the Eye of Truth. Which, upon reflection, seemed a bit too tairen-devious to be coincidental. In the process of punishing him for laying hands upon it, the Eye had resuscitated centuries-dead feelings, then sent him straight into the path of the only living being capable of making him feel those feelings again. The only living being for whom he would risk an emotional attachment capable of rousing the Fey Wilding Rage.

Once recognized, the truemate bond was irrevocable. He could no more deny it now than he could deny his own body breath. Not even *sheisan'dahlein*, the Fey honor death, was an option for him. He was the last Tairen Soul, the only living Fey capable of entering the tairen's lair, Fey'Bahren. He could not seek death until another Tairen Soul was born.

«Rain.» The familiar sound of Bel's Spirit voice sounded in Rain's mind. *«You must return. There is an . . . inconvenience . . . here.»*

Bel quickly relayed the details of the recent confrontation with the man who stupidly thought to claim a Tairen Soul's *shei'tani*. Rain's exhaustion fled in an instant, along with all thoughts of Sariel, loss and death. Rising up on all fours, his tairen form crouched on the outcropping, bristling with tension, claws digging deep into solid rock. His wings unfurled and spread wide, the long, curving mid-joint claws stabbing at the air. His tail whipped against the mountain, sending showers of rock plummeting down the sheer cliff face. Venom pooled in the reservoirs in his fangs.

«I will return soon. Guard my shei'tani well, old friend.»

«Aiyah, Rain. With my life.»

Rain Tairen Soul launched himself into the air. His massive form plummeted, then soared high as his wings snapped taut on an updraft. The truemate bond tugged at him, urging him to fly faster back to Celieria City and the warmth of Ellysetta Baristani's beckoning soul.

After his angry departure from the Baristani house, Den Brodson escorted his mother back home and marched five miles across town to the imposing colonnaded white stone edifice of Celieria's Office of the King's Law. There, he headed down a twisting maze of corridors to the small, cramped office shared by four apprentice Clerks of the King's Law, including Garlie Tavitts, an old chum from Den's early school days. With Garlie's help, Den spent the rest of the day completing, filing, and validating all the legal paperwork necessary to confirm his betrothal claim to Ellysetta Baristani and obtain a Special License for an immediate wedding.

After painstakingly copying the last of a series of legal documents, Garlie pushed one final parchment across his crowded and deeply scarred desktop. "Just make your mark here, Den, so I can submit the Petition for Special License to Master Wiley. Though I still don't understand what all the fuss is about. I remember Ellie Baristani, and believe me, Den, there's an entire ocean of finer fish out there just waiting to be caught. Fish with a little more . . . meat on their bones, if you catch my drift." The young man cupped his hands in front of his chest and jiggled them suggestively.

"There's more to love than big tits, Garlie." Den dipped a ratty old quill into Garlie's tarnished inkwell and labored to scratch his name on the parchment.

"Yeah, like money, but she's got none of that either, Den. And don't even think I'm dimskull enough to fall for that 'love' line. You never liked her. 'Flat-chested, freckle-faced, wood-scratcher's git' was the nicest thing you ever called her. And stop your glaring. You know it's true."

Den gave the scrawny, big-nosed paper-pusher a last, hard look. "Careful there, Tavitts. That's the future Madam Brodson you're insulting." He sprinkled sand over his signature and helped himself to Garlie's blotter to remove the excess ink from the parchment. "There." He blew on the document for good measure before handing it back to the apprentice clerk. "She might not have tits, coin, or much to recommend her in the looks department—though that does seem to be slowly improving—but Ellie Baristani has something else that outweighs all the rest. Something that's going to make me a rich man."

"And what's that, Den?"

Den smiled, his eyes twin coins of cold blue greed gleaming in a broad, brutishly handsome face. "Magic."

CHAPTER FOUR

Water pure, the path to cleanse
Blood to bindings call
Tairen's Eye to forge the bridge
Azrahn these souls enthrall.

—Magecraft Seeking Spell

The coast was clear at last.

Night had fallen. Ellie's parents and the twins had turned in for the night, and the Fey who'd been swarming around the Baristani house seemed to have finally left. Ellie could no longer even sense the tingling awareness of their presence.

She secured a brown shawl over her distinctive hair and slipped out her bedroom window, careful not to let the leather boots hanging about her neck bang against the glass or windowsill. While the Fey warriors outside the house might be gone, the five who'd followed her into the house and declared themselves her "quintet" were still very much in attendance. They'd stayed despite Mama's outrage, despite even Papa's coming home and ordering them to leave his house.

Faced with the direct order from Papa, the Fey called Belliard had merely bowed and politely refused, just as he had with Mama. He'd offered to make himself and the other four Fey invisible, so as to minimize the family's discomfort with their presence, but the idea of invisible magical beings roaming through her house had nearly sent Mama into palpitations.

"Thank you, but no," Papa had answered. "We would

rather see you so that we may know where you are." And then, to Ellie's surprise, he'd demanded that the Fey swear an oath of honor not to use magic to hide their presence in his home, and not to read nor influence the minds of any of his family members.

The demand had obviously surprised Belliard vel Jelani, but he'd sworn the oath, first in lyrical Feyan, then in the formal eloquence of ancient Celierian court-tongue. Ellie knew enough about Fey honor to know that no Fey would go back on his sworn word.

Papa had also tried to get Belliard to swear not to call magic for any reason inside the house, but the Fey refused to do that. "*Nei*, honored one, we may need to use magic to protect the Feyreisa and her family. I will make no vow that puts her at risk." And that had been the end of it.

Ellie's bare feet made no noise on the wooden shingles as she crept across the back-porch roof and climbed down the ivy trellis to the small, bricked courtyard at the back of the house. She kept to the shadows, avoiding the brightening moonlight in the hope that no one would notice her furtive departure.

Just before supper, one of the neighbor children had smuggled a note to Ellie through Lillis and Lorelle. From Selianne, Ellie's best friend, the note had been scrawled in a shaking hand and read: *Meet me. You know where. Twenty-two bells. URGENT!!!!*

Selianne's fear all but leapt off the parchment as Ellie held the note. Her terror was understandable. A few years back, as Selianne had prepared for the birth of her first child, her mother, Tuelis, had confessed that she wasn't Sorrelian as everyone assumed, but that she'd actually been born and raised in Eld and sold in marriage to her sea-captain husband at age fourteen. Selianne had kept her mother's secret. She'd only told Ellie in a moment of fear, when she'd been plagued by nightmares of Eld Mages stalking her son Bannon to steal his soul.

Now, with Rain Tairen Soul in the city and suddenly becoming a fixture in Ellie's life, Selianne was probably terrified that he would find out the truth about Selianne and her mother and come to kill them. Despite the risk of discovery, there was no way Ellie could ignore Selianne's summons.

On the ground, she ducked into the deeper shadows of a small alcove near the courtyard gate and bent to don her boots. When she rose, she let out a strangled cry.

Belliard vel Jelani stood before her, his Fey skin shining faintly, his dark eyes watchful. "You wish to go somewhere, Ellysetta Baristani?"

"I . . ." Her cheeks burned with embarrassment. Behind Belliard stood the other four Fey of her quintet, each wearing a similar blank but watchful expression. "I wanted to go for a walk to get some fresh air."

Belliard glanced at the ivy trellis behind her and followed the path she'd taken out her bedroom window, then returned his flat gaze to hers. "You are the Feyreisa," he said. "You need only to ask, and we will accompany you to your chosen destination."

She paused a moment to regain her composure, then lifted her chin. "I'm going to meet a friend, and your presence will only alarm her."

"We will accompany you, all the same. You are Rain Tairen Soul's truemate, and all the city knows it. There are those who might think to harm the Fey through you."

For a moment, Ellie considered heading straight back to her room, but she couldn't just leave Selianne waiting at the museum. Remembering the way her father had bargained with the Fey warriors earlier, Ellie gathered her courage and said, "If you insist on coming, Ser vel Jelani, you must swear an oath of honor that you'll give my friend and me privacy. No eavesdropping or mind reading."

Belliard's expression never wavered. "*Aiyah*, Ellysetta Baristani. I do so vow." When her gaze flickered to the four Fey behind him, he added, "I speak for all of your *cha'kor*, your quintet. We are here not to spy, but to protect."

She took a deep breath. "Well, let's go, then. I don't want my friend to worry."

Surrounded by her escort of five leather-and-steel-clad immortals, Ellie hurried down the alleyway, then turned east on the lane that ran through the West End's quiet merchant district. Fire-lit lamps cast a golden glow over the cobblestones and storefronts.

"Do you climb out of your bedroom window often, *kem'-falla*?" Belliard asked as they walked.

Ellie felt her cheeks heat up. "No." Her parents were sound enough sleepers that she usually went out the kitchen door.

"But this is not the first time you have done so."

"Not the first time, no."

"I had not thought Celieria's daughters were so . . . adventurous."

"Most aren't." If her parents had known she slipped out of the house at night, they would have put an immediate stop to it. But the nightmares that plagued her all her life made sleep difficult, and alone in the silence of the small bells, Ellysetta had often found peace by walking in the night air. At first she'd kept to the private courtyard behind the house, but as she grew older the courtyard began to feel too confining and she started to roam farther. Most nights, she ended up at the same place she was going now—Celieria's National Museum of Art.

"You are either very brave or very foolish, Ellysetta Baristani. Night streets are no place for young women alone."

Ellie shrugged. In all the years she'd walked alone at night, she'd never had a problem. Indeed, no one had ever even seemed to notice her presence before. "Celieria is well patrolled, the streets are well lit, and this is an honest part of the city."

"Evil has an affinity for the night. Even in well-lit, well-patrolled, honest quarters."

"I'll keep that in mind." She glanced at the other four Fey, then back to Belliard. "Since you seem determined to guard me, perhaps you should tell me your names."

The five Fey bowed and introduced themselves one by one. The smiling, brown-haired Fey was Kieran vel Solande, son of the *shei'dalin* Marissya and her truemate Dax. The blond warrior whose face Lorelle had scratched was Kiel vel Tomar. The other two, both black-haired and brown-eyed, were brothers, Rowan and Adrial vel Arquinas.

"There are another five Fey in your secondary quintet who will guard you for the few bells in the night when we must sleep," Belliard added.

"Mama will just love that," Ellie muttered.

"Your mother does not like magic or magical races?"

"She's from the north. The magic from the Mage Wars left behind many evil things. Dangerous, mutated creatures; dark places no one dares enter." Even children with frightening afflictions. "Magic and Celierians don't mix well."

"And yet, here in Celieria City, the people accept magic and its benefits without question." Belliard pointed to the Fire-lit lamps.

"Well, the Mages never sacked Celieria City, did they? The worst of the Wars never reached south of Vrest. People here would feel different if mutated predators like lyrant roamed their woods, or if their children were born with ghastly deformities and deadly powers."

"Do you share your mother's fear of magic?"

Ellie hesitated before answering. "Magic . . . makes me uncomfortable." For the past year or so, if anyone wielded strong magic around her, she would get terrible headaches and her sleep would be tormented by particularly horrible nightmares. She didn't even want to think what her dreams held in store for her tonight.

They reached Celieria's main thoroughfare and turned north. Though most of the hardworking families of the West End were asleep, that was not true of all of Celieria's population. Carriages rolled down the cobbled street, carrying nobles in colorful silks and satins to their night's entertainment. Men and women, some well dressed, some more commonly so, strolled down the wide bricked sidewalks on either side of the road. Boisterous laughter and music poured through the doors of numerous pubs.

Normally, Ellie didn't come out until much later at night, when fewer people roamed the city. She was very aware of her Fey escort's distinctive garb. "You're going to draw attention."

Belliard vel Jelani shared a glance with his fellow Fey, then gestured. Lavender light glowed around them, and when it faded, all five warriors were dressed in simple Celierian clothing and their Fey skin had lost its luminescence. They were still too handsome to be pure mortal, but their disguises would allow them to walk without drawing too much attention to themselves.

Ellie rubbed at the goose bumps that rose on her skin in response to Belliard's magic. "Nice trick."

They turned the corner and slipped into the streams of people walking the sidewalks. A number of women gave the Fey long, hungry looks, but no one stopped them or acted as though their presence were anything out of the ordinary. Ellie led the way up the remaining half mile to the arched bridge that spanned the Velpin River.

Celieria's National Museum of Art lay on the other side of the river. The domed building was the crowning feature of a sprawling, manicured park that bordered the Velpin's magic-purified waters. Circled by Fire-lamps, the building gleamed like a jewel in the night.

Ellie hurried up the wide brick walkway to the museum's entrance and pushed open the leaded-glass doors. Though the museum staff departed promptly at seventeen bells each day, the museum doors were never locked. Something far more powerful than bolted doors protected the building's many priceless treasures. Any thief could wander in and look to his heart's content, but let him touch a single precious piece of art and he'd be paralyzed until the curator arrived in the morning.

"Don't touch any of the exhibits," Ellie warned. Her voice echoed in the marbled vestibule. She led them through the domed rotunda, where marble columns ringed a twenty-foot statue of King Dorian I holding his sword upraised in one hand, his Fey wife beside him with healing hands splayed over the upturned face of a child. At the base of the statue, deeply carved letters painted with pure gold proclaimed the majestic promise of Celieria's creed: *Might and mercy shall vanquish all foes.*

She headed down the second arching corridor on the left. Sculpted tairen heads with glowing ruby eyes flanked the entrance to the Fey wing.

Ellie's friend Selianne Pyerson was sitting on a cushioned bench beside the alcove that housed an eight-foot bronze of a tairen rampant perched on a boulder of white marble veined with gold. Selianne's normally tidy blond hair was disheveled, as if she'd been running her hands through it, and her pretty face was drawn tight in lines of worry and agitation. She jumped to her feet when she caught sight of Ellie, then froze when she realized her friend was not alone.

"Who are they?" Selianne gestured to the five men standing behind Ellie.

"They are . . . um . . . my guards." Faint lavender light shimmered, and the Fey assumed their true appearance.

Selianne stumbled back a step. "It's true, then. The Tairen Soul really did claim you as his mate."

"Apparently so." Ellie introduced the five warriors to her friend. "Selianne and I have been friends since my family first came to Celieria City." They'd been childhood outcasts together, Selianne for being the foreign-born daughter of a Sorrelian sea captain and his wife, and Ellie for her odd appearance and strange ways.

Selianne dragged Ellie back a few steps and hissed into her ear, "I can't believe you brought Fey with you. What if they . . . you know . . . read my mind or something?"

"They won't," Ellie assured her. "I made them give an honor oath not to eavesdrop or mind read before I let them come with me." She glanced at Belliard behind her. "Would you mind giving us that privacy now?"

He bowed. "I will build a privacy shield around you both. You may walk and speak freely to one another without worry that others will hear." He raised his hands, and threads of faintly glowing white and lavender magic spun out from his fingertips. Ellie felt a soft, cool wind swirl around her. It smelled of springtime, full of sweet rain and crisp morning air. As it closed about her, she felt a strangely light and tranquil silence enter her mind, as if a pressure she'd never realized existed had been lifted.

Selianne stared at Ellie. "You can feel their magic, can't you?"

Ellie raised her brows. "Can't you?"

"No. I know he's weaving magic, because he said so and his hands are glowing a little more, but even knowing it's there, I can't sense it." She lifted shaking hands to her mouth and turned away. "Dear gods. I can't believe you brought them with you, Fey oath or not."

"I'm sorry, Sel. It was either that or not come at all, and your note sounded so frightened. I did the best I could."

"I know. I'm sorry that I sounded ungrateful. I do appreciate your coming, and at least you didn't bring . . . *him* . . . with you." She jerked her chin towards one of the paintings of Rain Tairen Soul. "It's bad enough that he's here in the city—but to have him claim you. What happens when he finds out about my mother?"

Ellie clasped Selianne's hands. "He's not going to find out," she vowed, staring earnestly into her friend's terrified blue eyes. "I won't let him. I'll lock the memory away so deep inside me, he won't be able to find it, and we'll just stay away from each other until he's gone. Do you hear me? Everything's going to be all right." She filled her voice with conviction, and kept her hands clasped tight around Selianne's cold fingers until her friend's terror began to abate.

After several moments, the reassurance seemed to sink in. Selianne nodded and drew a deep breath. "All right. Good plan. We'll avoid each other until he's gone." Releasing Ellie's hands, she let out a shaky laugh. "How soon will that be? And is there anything you can do to hurry it up?"

Ellie laughed too. "You sound like Mama."

"I knew there was a reason I loved her so much." Selianne flashed a brief grin, then shook her head again. "I just can't believe it, Ellysetta. There must be Fey blood in you from somewhere." Her blond brows rose. "Maybe you're the child of a *dahl'reisen*."

"Maybe I'm the child of Celierians and I'm just sensitive to magic because I come from the north," Ellie answered repressively. She took Selianne's arm and began to walk with her away from the Fey. "What excuse did you give Gerwyn to leave the house so late at night?"

"He thinks I'm with the Ladies of Light, planning the Sun Festival."

"What will he do when he finds out you're not?"

"He won't. I actually was with the Ladies tonight. I just stopped here on my way home." Selianne waved a dismissive hand. "Enough about that. Tell me everything."

Ellie tried to recap the day's tumultuous events quickly, but Selianne insisted on details. Soon the whole emotion-filled tale came pouring out: Den's attack the previous night, the fire cage and Rain Tairen Soul's claiming of her, the shattering news of Ellie's betrothal this evening.

"Oh, that sneaking, conniving, rotten little maggot," Selianne breathed when Ellie told her about Den's assault and showed her the mark on her neck. "But I thought the mark had to be someplace . . ." She broke off, blushing.

"I know, so did I, but apparently it's the mark, not the location, that's important."

"Surely your parents wouldn't really make you marry him?"

"They've already signed the betrothal papers, and they won't break the contract for fear of how it would hurt the family and Papa's business. And now that Rain Tairen Soul did what he did, I think Mama is even more determined to see me wed to Den. She's afraid of the Fey and their magic. She hasn't said as much, but I think she'd rather marry me off to old Master Weazman than see me wed to a Fey." The ancient, toothless old Gilding Master was known as much for his lechery as for his exquisite work with precious metals.

"Well, put that way, I admit I understand her concern. The Fey are a frightening, secretive lot. And we all know what they're capable of."

Ellie stiffened. "The same can be said of several other races I could name, Selianne."

Selianne gave her a reproachful look. "There's no need to get personal, Ellysetta."

"Sorry." Ellie blew out a breath. "I'm a bit on edge." She rubbed her arms and the back of her neck to massage away the faint tension gathering there.

"Be honest, Ell. Do you really think Den or your parents stand a chance of defying the Tairen Soul? What's to stop him from just breathing a little tairen flame on Den? Problem solved. Betrothal broken."

The same thought had occurred to Ellysetta earlier, when Papa had told her that he would not break the betrothal. She'd instantly dismissed it, though the possibility still nagged at her. "He wouldn't do that. That's not honorable."

"And flaming millions of people was?"

It always came back to that whenever Selianne and Ellie discussed Rain Tairen Soul or the Fey. It was the one constant bone of contention in an otherwise flawless friendship.

"That was war, and the Mages had just killed his mate. He went mad for a while from a documented Fey phenomenon called the Wilding Rage. Gaelen vel Serranis experienced the same thing when his sister was murdered. We've had this discussion a hundred times."

"It was murder, Ellie. In both cases. No matter how you try to pretty it up."

"It was vengeance. The Eld murdered Gaelen's sister—that was true murder. She'd done nothing to provoke them. The Eld murdered Sariel—an unarmed woman healing the wounded on a battlefield—hoping to destroy Rain Tairen Soul. Well, in both cases, the Eld got more than they bargained for, didn't they?" She rubbed at the tension in her neck and arms again.

"You've never liked hearing anyone speak ill of the Fey, especially not Rain Tairen Soul." Selianne eyed her intently. "Aren't you even the least bit afraid of him?"

"Of course I am. Who wouldn't be? He's the man who

scorched the world. But, Selianne, when he held me in his arms this morning and said those things to me . . . I could have died right then and been happy. I've never felt so . . . at peace, so loved."

"It was probably Fey magic—a glamour of some kind."

"I know that. But, Sel, if you'd felt it . . . part of me thinks I would do just about anything to feel that way again. Even if it was a lie."

"I don't like the sound of that, Ellie. You've never wanted a pleasant lie over a hard truth. Never." Selianne gripped Ellie's hands, squeezing tight. "Don't let them control your mind."

Ellie smiled and shook her head. "I can assure you no one's controlling my mind. Part of me may want Fey-perfect love, even if it's an illusion, but most of me is still firmly grounded in common sense. In fact, I keep waiting for Rain Tairen Soul to come back and tell me he made a mistake in claiming me, and would I please just forget the whole thing." She laughed.

Selianne didn't laugh with her. "I'm worried for you, Ellie. Maybe your mother's right. Maybe you're better off marrying Den—or even old Master Weazman." She cast a glance over her shoulder at the five Fey standing near the wing's entrance. "Handsome as they are, I'd never want anything to do with them."

Ellie didn't answer. The sensation she'd mistaken for tension was now a tingling in her skin, an odd awareness that grew stronger by the second. She lifted her head. "He's coming."

"He? He who?"

"Rain Tairen Soul."

"He's coming?" Selianne squeaked. "Here? Now?"

"Yes." She *felt* him, felt the hunger and longing rise up within her in response to his nearness. The sensations were frightening and compelling all at once. "He's here."

Fresh panic flooded Selianne's eyes. "Ellie, the Tairen Soul hasn't sworn any vow against mind reading, has he?" Ellie shook her head. "Bright Lord save me; that's what I thought. If he picks my brain and discovers the truth, he might decide to flame me instead of just Den." She snatched up her shawl from the bench and hugged Ellie in a quick, fierce embrace. "I've got to go. Take care, dear friend." She hurried away, heading for the rear exit of the Fey wing to avoid the approaching Fey King.

Ellie saw her cast one last, frantic look over her shoulder and freeze in her tracks, but even without that, Ellie would have known that Rain Tairen Soul had walked into the room. The shields Belliard had built dissolved. Ellie could hear the clap of Rain's boots against the marble floor as he walked towards her, but it was the way her skin felt flushed and the blood raced through her veins that told her he was near.

She turned to face him. Everything about him called to every one of her senses, leaving her as giddy as an adolescent girl mooning over a handsome boy. His luminescent Fey skin shone against the blackness of his leathers. His eyes glowed with power, and Ellie saw his gaze flick from her to Selianne.

Worried that he would do just as Selianne feared—probe her mind and discover her heritage—Ellie stepped directly into his line of vision, drawing his attention away from her friend. "You're here. How did you know where to find us?" She heard the sound of racing footsteps as Selianne took advantage of the Tairen Soul's distraction and ran away.

The Feyreisen's fierce gaze pinned Ellie in place. "Bel told me. But even if he had not, I would always be able to find you, *shei'tani*." Anger rolled over her in waves. "You should not have attempted to leave the house without guard. You will not do so again."

Though his anger frightened her, the barked command made her spine go poker straight. "I'm not your prisoner. You have no right to order me to do anything. I've gone for walks in the night many times in the past and never come to harm."

"You weren't the Feyreisa before now. While the Mages

may have overlooked Ellysetta Baristani, the woodcarver's daughter, believe me they will not overlook Ellysetta Baristani, the Tairen Soul's mate."

Ellie swallowed. He sounded so certain, so ominous. "Maybe what you say would be true if there were Mages in Celieria, but there are none. There haven't been since the Mage Wars. They were banned a thousand years ago."

His lips pulled back in a small snarl. "And do you really think they've stayed away all this time? They are cunning adversaries, patient and powerful." He advanced on her, and she backed up nervously. "You can be certain they know about you by now, and they're already plotting to capture or kill you."

Ellie's heart pounded in her chest, beating with sudden fear. She told herself that since he'd claimed her as his true-mate, he couldn't possibly harm her, but that didn't seem to matter much. The way he looked right now, it wasn't hard to imagine *him* killing her.

"*Aiyah*, you should be afraid. Perhaps fear will stop you from acting foolishly."

She turned to run, but only managed half a dozen steps before he caught her wrist.

"*Nei*, Ellysetta. You will not run from me. You will . . ." His voice broke off, his attention captured by something just beyond her shoulder. Sorrow washed over her, deep and heartrending. The emotions were his, but she felt them as clearly as if they were her own.

She turned to follow his gaze, and her breath stalled. She had unwittingly run straight for the one room in the museum where she spent most of her time—the exhibit dedicated to the scorching of the world.

More than twenty oil paintings circled the room, vivid canvases painted by Celieria's greatest masters, all depicting the tragic story of Rain and Sariel and the fiery aftermath of her death. Dominating the room was Fabrizio Chelan's masterpiece, *Death of the Beloved*.

The look on Rain's face as he regarded the great master's most famous work would have made her heart ache even without the stunned, breathless pain radiating from him. Tears filled her eyes. For the first time, she didn't find the famous painting tragically romantic or tragically beautiful. For the first time, she found it only tragic.

He released her hand, and the terrible rawness of his grief faded. "Her death was nothing like that," he murmured. His gaze remained fixed on the central figures captured forever through Chelan's unsurpassed mastery of composition, color, and perspective.

"How do you mean?"

"I never got to hold her like that for the last time. They drew me away from her as part of their ambush, then attacked her to destroy me. She was badly burned. The Elden Mages cut off her head so she could not be healed. I was in the air when I felt her die, and the Rage took me then. I don't remember much after that, but they tell me I incinerated the entire battlefield in mere chimes. There was nothing left of her to hold when I finally came back to sanity." He reached up a hand as if to touch the painted image of his dead mate, then pulled back when sparks flashed from the protective weave. He stood there, staring at the image of Sariel in a dramatic, beautiful death swoon, her cheeks still rosy, unscorched, and glimmering with Fey luminescence, clutched in the arms of the mate who should have been at her side protecting her but had not. "She died alone, at the hands of an Elden Mage."

The pain of Rain's loss squeezed Ellie's heart. Her throat went tight and tears burned at the backs of her eyes. "I'm so sorry. I know you loved her."

"It was a long time ago." He frowned at Sariel's image. "That isn't even a very good likeness of her."

Ellie gave a choked sound that was half laugh, half sob. This painting was one of the most famous masterpieces in all of Celierian history, and yet Rain Tairen Soul declared the image to be not only wholly false but a poor likeness as well.

"In a way, it is good to see this painting and remember," he continued.

"That you loved her?"

"*Nei*. That I failed her. My first duty was to protect my mate, and I did not. It will not happen again." His expression hardened and he turned to face her. "Which is why you will never again attempt to leave your home unescorted."

"But—"

"*Nei!* You are my truemate. Harm to you is harm to me. The Eld know this, and that puts you in great danger, Ellysetta. The world is no longer a safe place for you."

His eyes were starting to glow again, and she could feel his anger beating at her. She should just meekly agree and go home. That was the smart thing to do. He was a powerful Fey who'd already lost control of his wild magic once before. Only a fool would actually *argue* with him.

And yet . . . something would not let her just meekly murmur her obedience and allow the Fey to lead her home like a prize dog on a leash. "I realize your concern is genuine, my lord Feyreisen, but even if Eld Mages really are hiding in the city, plotting evil, they have no reason to harm me. I am betrothed to another man."

"Bel told me of the butcher's offspring. His desires neither hold sway over our bond nor protect you from the Eld. Your soul called out, Ellysetta Baristani, and mine answered. That one moment made you a prize the Eld would kill to claim. Nothing can change that. And that means you must never again attempt to wander the streets alone."

"But—"

"No buts." His hands seized hers in a tight grip. "If you will not consider your own safety, consider the safety of others. Sariel was my mate. I should not have survived her death. But I did, and you know the results." He gestured to the fiery, violent paintings surrounding them. "Whether you want it or not, you are my truemate. Even though our bond is not yet complete, if the Eld managed to kill you, I should not survive it." Sudden intensity burned in his eyes, and his voice dropped to a low whisper. *"But what if I did?"*

Ellie's mouth went dry. Her skin burned where Rain's hands gripped hers as images and emotions flooded into her. The blinding grief of Sariel's death. The hot, wild rush of rage, driving him to rain fire and death upon the world. The haunting screams and terror of those who died in the face of his madness.

She yanked free of his grip, and the onslaught ceased.

She pressed one shaking hand to her mouth and the other to her belly. "What was that?"

"A tiny fraction of what I live with, Ellysetta, every day since I scorched the world."

"I'm going to be sick." She spun on her heel and raced for the nearest waste bin, barely making it before the contents of her stomach heaved out of her.

When she was done, he was there beside her, a glass of cold water in his hand. She could have cried with humiliation. Instead, she took the glass, rinsed her mouth, and spat. Not meeting his eyes, she handed the glass back to him. It melted into nothing. All signs of her brief, violent sickness vanished as well.

She stared at the empty space and couldn't even summon surprise. Of course the Fey could make vomit vanish. All that power had to have its practical uses. She forced a laugh. "Where were you when Lillis and Lorelle had the stomach ague last year?"

He didn't laugh or even smile at her weak joke. "*Sieks'ta.* I should not have shared that with you. I have shamed myself. Not even fear for your safety excuses me." He gestured, and Bel stepped closer. "Your quintet will take you home. As I've just demonstrated, my control is not yet what it should be." He bowed, his face a frozen mask.

If he'd meant to impress upon her the gravity of her situation, he'd succeeded. His tactics might have been brutal, but they were effective. She couldn't even summon any anger. How could she blame him for wanting to avoid reliving the horror he'd just shared with her?

She started to reach out to him, but caution made her draw

back before touching him. One taste of his torment was enough. "I won't leave the house without escort again," she promised.

As Bel led her away, she paused at the entrance of the Fey wing and glanced back. Rain stood looking up at Chelan's painting of Sariel's death, his face pale and drawn.

The young boy darted silently through the shadows of the West End's quiet merchant district. A block ahead, the pretty blond girl he'd followed from the museum turned down a narrow cobbled lane that led to a modest residential district. The boy smiled. He could practically feel the gold sovereign warm between his fingers.

Follow her, Master Manza had ordered when he'd realized the blonde was Ellysetta Baristani's friend. *Find out where she lives. She may prove useful.*

Rain remained in the museum for almost a full bell after Ellysetta's departure, sitting on the bench in the middle of the room, staring up at the countless images and remembering.

He'd loved Sariel. With all the unfettered, consuming passion of youth, he'd loved her. He'd been a young Tairen Soul, full of the power of his gift and the promise of endless skies, and she'd been a beautiful Fey healer, not as powerful as Marissya, and no match to his own strength, but so gentle and compassionate there were none who did not love her.

She'd been first in his heart since boyhood. He'd never wanted another.

And now he did.

It felt like betrayal. As if his own body, his own soul, had betrayed his heart.

Spirit swirled around his fingertips. Swaths of mystic magic poured out in a sparkling cloud that slowly began to spin. He watched it, guided it, as the magic condensed and took shape. Long, straight strands of silky black hair blew back from a luminous oval face of stunning beauty. Full, red lips smiled at him with exquisite tenderness, while eyes like blue forget-me-nots watched him with endless patience and love.

"Sariel," Rain whispered sadly. He'd woven the memories many times. He was a master of Spirit. To any other on-looker, Sariel would have seemed whole and alive and real, but Rain held the weave, and he knew—he always knew—she was an illusion. He'd managed to pretend otherwise, but no longer. The slender arms that rose to embrace him seemed hollow and faded, and when he reached out to her, his hand passed through the weave.

He would have wept if he still had tears within him. "I don't want to lose you, *e'tani*."

Sariel smiled and shook her head. She bent to kiss him, but when he tilted back his head to meet her lips, the Spirit weave dissolved. Sariel faded into mist. Rain groaned and buried his face in his hands. Not even with a kiss to a phantom love could he betray his *shei'tani*.

"Your magic knows you belong to another, even if your heart still rebels."

Rain lifted his head. Marissya stood at the entrance to the chamber. Dax was at her side, while her quintet stood guard a bit further away. Marissya was watching Rain with a strange mix of compassion and irritation. The truemate in her dis-liked that he'd even attempted to betray his bond with a kiss to his lost love, while the empath in her understood why he did.

"We all loved Sariel, Rain," Marissya continued, "but you must let her go. Your *shei'tani* will never accept you so long as you cling to the memory of another."

"I know that without your scolding." Her reprimand stung, even more because it was deserved. He rose to his feet.

"I am glad to hear it. I wasn't certain you were thinking clearly. Kieran told me you shared your torment with your *shei'tani*."

Kieran had a flapping tongue. "She tried to leave her home unescorted. Truemated to the Tairen Soul, and she tried to wander Celierian streets alone—at night! She even refused to believe her life might be in danger. Did Kieran tell you that, too?"

One cool brown brow rose. "He merely suggested you might need my help weaving control over your emotions. It appears he was right."

Rain's lips compressed. To argue would only prove her point.

Marissya sighed, and her expression softened. "The gods weave as the gods will, Rain. And even though it may not be apparent at first, they do weave purpose into all things. Even terrible things. Sariel's death was a devastating loss, but all this time I believed it was the price the gods demanded for the end of the Wars. That was the only pattern I saw in the weave . . . until today, when a Celierian girl called a tairen from the sky."

"What are you suggesting?"

"The tairen and the Fey are dying. You are the last bridge between our two species. You told me the Eye of Truth sent you here, to Celieria, to find our salvation. We both know it can be no coincidence that Ellysetta is your truemate. Some-how, she is the key to saving us all. Though we've yet to see her power, it must be vast. She could never have called your soul if she were not your equal in every way. We also both know she could never have called you if you were still bound to another—even if that bond was only *e'tanitsa*, as it was be-tween you and Sariel." Her hands closed over his, and cool, calming threads of empathy and healing stroked across his battered emotions. "You've seen the pattern, too, Rain. No matter how badly you want to deny it. Sariel had to die so Ellysetta could be born to save us."

Rain pulled free of her grasp and turned away.

"You must not blame Ellysetta," Marissya continued. "She is an innocent. She is the soul the gods shaped to save the tairen and the Fey." She circled round him, relentless. "And you, Rain, are the soul the gods shaped to protect her and bring her safely back to us so she can fulfill her purpose. You cannot shirk your duty, not to the tairen, not to the Fey, and definitely not to your truemate. Set aside your longings for what used to be. Embrace Ellysetta in your heart as well as your soul so you can win her trust and her bond and help her discover her strength. Because, Rain, one other thing seems certain to me." The *shei'dalin's* eyes grew dark with portent. "Whatever task the gods have set before Ellysetta Baristani, it is fearfully dangerous. Else she'd not need a tairen to protect her soul."

Far away to the northeast in the heart of the Elden wilderness, the subterranean palace of Boura Fell, seat of the High Mage Vadim Maur, lay buried deep in the earth, masterfully shielded from Fey senses and Fey magic by rock, soil, and wards worked from the darkest Elden wizardry. The massive complex stretched for miles beneath the surface, one of many similar fortresses hidden throughout Eld. For nearly a thousand years, the network of underground palaces had survived, thrived even, undetected and steadily growing in strength and number, like a cancer quietly spreading its deadly tentacles beneath the skin of a seemingly healthy man.

High Mage Vadim Maur, leader of the High Council of Mages and uncrowned ruler of Eld, sat at his massive desk and pondered the news from his apprentice in Celieria. Around him, sconces flickered with Fire, lighting the dark, windowless cavern of his study with a pale yellow glow, illuminating the numerous bookcases that held priceless ancient texts and centuries' worth of notes on his experiments.

Rain Tairen Soul had a truemate. A truemate with red hair and green eyes, so suspiciously like the child stolen years ago.

Vadim sat back in his chair and steepled his hands beneath his chin. Suspicion was not certainty, and not enough to make him tip his hand. Not yet, at least. There were two hundred Fey in Celieria City . . . too many to confront lightly even without the substantial added might of the Tairen Soul. Vadim had not won and held his grip on the

High Council of Mages through the blundering application of brute force. He was a man who believed in choosing his battles . . . and in preparing his battlefield.

He'd already dispatched a handful of spies to northern Celieria in case his search party had missed something so many years ago. Meanwhile, his apprentice Kolis Manza would continue his work in Celieria and learn what he could about the girl without rousing suspicions.

Vadim rose from his desk. His rich, gold-embroidered, purple velvet robes whispered around him as he crossed the room to approach a carefully warded black metal door. He dissolved the wards, placed his hand in the hollow etched deep into the door's center panel, and uttered, "*Gaz vegoth.*"

The ancient Feraz witchwords sent magic swirling. Metal groaned as the unseen bolts securing the door slid free from their anchors in the stone. The door opened inward to reveal the small round antechamber that served as Vadim Maur's private spell room.

Fire flared to life in three golden sconces as the High Mage stepped through the door, and in the flickering light, figures seemed to move and sway across the intricate patterns of the mosaic tiles that covered every fingerspan of wall, ceiling, and floor in the room. A carved black stone altar occupied the center of the room; a bowl and goblet of hammered gold rested atop it. Opposite the door, pure, cool water poured from the carved mouth of a snarling dragon's head into a rune-etched catch-basin below.

Vadim moved around the room, murmuring a cleansing spell. When he was finished and satisfied that the room held no residue of previous spells, he grasped the small golden ewer that rested on the wide lip of the catch-basin, and filled it. "Water pure, the path to cleanse," he murmured as he poured the water into the altar bowl.

From a deep left-hand pocket of his Mage robe, he withdrew a tiny vial filled with still-warm blood he had recently taken from a particular guest of his lowermost dungeon and uncorked it. "Blood to bindings call." He dribbled a thin stream of the dark red liquid into the bowl. As it broke the water's surface, the blood diluted rapidly, tiny red streamers shooting through the clear water until the bowl was filled with cloudy pinkness. With a razor-sharp black dagger, he slit the palm of his hand and added his own blood to the mix. His Mage senses grew sharp and he felt the dark, binding threads of magic that tied him to the blooded captive.

He tugged on the thin gold chain about his neck and withdrew the sparkling, dark, rainbow-hued Tairen's Eye crystal that had been resting against his chest. The stone was not warm from contact with his skin as any other pendant would be but instead remained defiantly cool to his touch, rejecting him as its owner had done for centuries.

"Tairen's Eye to forge the bridge." He lowered the crystal into the water until it was completely submerged. The pink, bloodied water grew clear again as the Tairen's Eye crystal at the bottom of the bowl began to glow and pulse like a heartbeat. Vadim dipped the small golden goblet into the altar bowl and drank. The pulsing beat of the crystal grew loud in his ears as his heart matched the rhythm.

"Azrahn these souls enthrall." The High Mage of Eld closed his eyes. He stretched his open palms over the golden bowl. Azrahn gathered at his fingertips and spiraled upwards, a spider-silk-thin filament of darkness that pulsed with red lights keeping time with the beating crystal. Threads of Spirit joined it, wrapping the Azrahn in a protective shield, hiding it from Fey senses. The weave traveled up the tiny pipe that rose from the antechamber's ceiling, through hundreds of layers of rock, into the fresh night air of Eld, then raced south towards Celieria with dizzying speed. His senses raced with it, shooting over forests, rivers, and towns until he reached the glowing brightness of Celieria's capital city.

And there, as his body stood vacant and chilling half a continent away in Eld, High Mage Vadim Maur began softly to croon, "Are you she, girl? Are you the one? Show yourself."

* * *

Well into the night, Ellie drifted in a fretful sleep, tossing and turning as she dreamed of flames and magic and horrible battles where blood flowed in rivers. The scenes changed. Shadows dimmed her vision, and a cold, frightening fog covered the world. Within the fog, something stalked her, calling to her, beckoning with familiar malevolence.

Fear gripped her, the certainty that whatever she did, she must never reveal herself to that crooning evil. *Hide deep and well. Do not let him find you.*

A strong breeze from her open bedroom window blew across her face. In a half-waking state, she imagined a shadow falling across her. She tensed with sudden fear, then sighed her relief as a tender hand brushed hair from her eyes. Her eyelids fluttering with the effort to open, but a kiss feathered across her brow and a soft-spoken caress of words soothed her. Deep, restful sleep finally overtook her and she sank into it willingly.

Crouched on the floor beside her bed, surrounded by a weave of Spirit to make himself invisible, Rain Tairen Soul watched over his truemate as she slept.

CHAPTER FIVE

Ellie woke to yet another pounding headache and the feel of something soft yet bristly brushing against her cheek. Her eyes opened, and she rose up on one elbow to find a vibrant blue feather on her pillow. It was easily as long as her forearm, with a tuft of navy down at its base and iridescent pink glimmers along its edges. The feather had come from a kolitou, a very rare species of bird that lived in the most inaccessible reaches of the Tivali Mountains bordering Elvia to the south. Hundreds of years ago, before craftsmen had perfected the delicate metal pen nib for writing instruments, the kolitou feather had been the quill of choice for kings due to its rare beauty and the danger involved in acquiring it.

Ellie had no idea why the feather was on her pillow, though she had a fairly good idea who had put it there. Climbing high enough to locate a kolitou aerie was risky for men, but it wouldn't be difficult for a Tairen Soul.

There was an old Celierian proverb: Mind what you pray for, the gods may grant it. She had prayed for someone else, anyone else but Den. She'd been hoping for a nice, quiet man like Papa. Instead, the gods had sent her the man who'd scorched the world.

The Feyreisen terrified her. He wore the promise of death like a cloak, and dread magic all but crackled around him. Yet even as her heart quailed, he drew her as no man ever had. Already, after only two brief meetings, he was like an addictive potion in her blood. She hungered for the sight of his face, the sound of his voice, the tingle in her skin when he was near. She didn't believe it was mind control, as Selianne feared. After all, what could Ellysetta Baristani possibly have that the King of the Fey would want?

She wasn't fool enough to think Rain Tairen Soul loved her just because he claimed she was his truemate. The man whose consuming, tragic love for the Lady Sariel was still celebrated throughout Celieria would not lightly cast aside the memories of his dead wife and set in her stead a young, unremarkable mortal stranger.

But Ellie also knew enough about the legends of the truemate bond to know it only formed where deep, abiding love could blossom. The temptation of knowing a love so deep, so complete, so unconditional, was a powerful lure that appealed straight to her deepest, most secret desire. Plain, awkward, simple Ellie dreamed of love. Not the gentle, friendly love that could eventually grow between two people joined in an arranged marriage, but the boundless, passionate love that only happened in Feytales.

She brushed the pink-shimmered kolitou feather across her face, remembering the feel of Rain's hands doing the same. Impulsively she kissed the feather, then tucked it with care into the top drawer of her dressing table and hurried to get dressed.

Outside, Fey minds murmured to one another in approval. It was a fine first gift, and the Feyreisa had accepted it. The courtship had begun.

At half past seven bells, as the Baristani family broke their fast in their tiny kitchen, a knock sounded at the front door.

"I'll get it," Sol said. He swiped at his lips with his napkin before tossing it on the table.

Curious as to who would call so early in the morning, Ellie followed him to the front door. She and her father both froze in surprise at the sight of a royal messenger standing on the doorstep, impeccably garbed in expensive gold-embroidered livery.

The man gave a brief bow. "You are Sol Baristani, master woodcarver?" he asked.

Her father swallowed and cleared his throat. "Yes."

"Father of Ellysetta Baristani?" The messenger's gaze flickered to Ellie before snapping back to her father's face.

Papa's gaze did the same. "Yes," he said, a little more slowly this time.

The messenger clicked his mirror-polished black heels and bowed again, a half bow rather than the previous quarter. "Then it is my honor, privilege, and duty, Master Baristani, to present you with this summons to the royal palace." He held out a rolled parchment tied with a blue satin ribbon and sealed with a large glob of gold wax bearing the crest of the royal family of Celieria. "You and your family are to make your appearance by ten bells today."

Papa cracked the royal seal and unrolled the parchment. His eyes scanned the contents rapidly. "There is no reason noted for the summons." He looked up at the messenger. "Why is our presence requested?"

"It is not my place to know, Master Baristani. I have been instructed to wait for you to prepare yourselves, and then to convey you to the palace. A coach has been provided." He waved at the covered coach waiting in the street. It was a massive vehicle, painted a rich Celierian blue buffed to a high gloss. A team of six matched grays stood patiently in their harnesses. The royal coat of arms was emblazoned in gold on the sides of the coach.

"I see. Then shall I assume this request is more in the way of a royal command?"

The messenger bowed again.

"Well." Papa rubbed his chin the way he always did when gathering his thoughts. "Give us a bell or so to ready ourselves. You are welcome to wait in the house."

The messenger eyed the Fey warriors standing like dark shadows behind Ellie's father and declined. "Thank you, Master Baristani, but I shall await your convenience outside."

Papa closed the door and turned to Ellie. "First the Fey, now a royal summons. I can't help believing they are related, Ellie girl."

She said nothing. What was there to say?

"Lauriana! Come quickly, my dear." Sol strode into the kitchen in search of his wife. The sudden commotion of chairs scraping back from the table marked the moment when he announced the surprising news. Her parents and sisters rushed out of the kitchen.

"Why are you just standing there, Ellie?" Mama demanded, herding the twins up the stairs. "We've barely time enough to get decent, let alone fit for an audience with the king."

"I'll be right up, Mama." Ellie waited until her family had hustled upstairs before she met Belliard's impassive gaze. "This is the Feyreisen's doing, isn't it?" she asked. His head inclined slightly. "Well, I wish he'd given us a little more notice. I have nothing suitable to wear for a visit to the royal palace." Was that almost a smile that twitched at the corner of the stone-faced Fey's mouth?

"The Fey can provide you a gown worthy of a queen." He gestured, and Ellie's plain homespun dress became a dazzling court ball gown of shining ivory fabric, cascading with blond lace fine as a spider's web, and sparkling with thousands of tiny jewels.

Stunned, Ellie touched the jewel-encrusted bodice and the billowing skirts. It was incredible. It was dazzling. It was . . . she frowned . . . an illusion? Though she could feel the cool, slippery satin beneath her fingers, the hard pebbles of each tiny jewel, even the crush of a corset pulling her waist in tight, something told her the dress wasn't real.

"It's beautiful," she told Belliard. "But it's not real, is it?"

His eyebrows actually inched higher. She had managed to surprise him. "No, it is made of Spirit, but you should not be able to detect the difference between my weave and a real gown."

"Spirit?"

"The magic I used for the weave. It is a mystic, not an elemental, magic. It works on the mind, not the physical. My command of Spirit is exceptional." There was a stiff tone to his voice, something that sounded very much like bruised masculine pride.

"I'm sorry." She tried to make amends. "It's a wonderful job, really. All my senses are telling me it's real." Without thinking, she reached out to pat his hand, and the Fey's board-stiff back went even stiffer.

Behind Belliard, blond Kiel coughed loudly into his hand while the brothers Adrial and Rowan studiously inspected the ceiling. Brown-haired Kieran's tiny smile was now wide and gleaming with white teeth, and his blue eyes danced with open amusement.

The gorgeous gown winked out of existence.

"I do not command Earth," Belliard told her in stilted tones. One might have thought he was confessing to some terrible, humiliating affliction, like having the uncontrollable urge to dress in women's clothing and dance beneath the light of the Mother on All Spirits' Eve. "Kieran"—he gestured to the brown-haired Fey—"controls Earth admirably. A gown made of Earth is real. He can make for you what I cannot."

Ellie could never bring herself to hurt this proud, solitary Fey's feelings by rejecting his offer and accepting that of another. She'd already unwittingly hurt him quite enough. She shook her head. "Thank you for the offer, but no. I'm not Ashleanne the hearthminder, wearing her Fey gift-father's gown to the ball. I'm just plain Ellie Baristani, woodcarver's daughter. I would feel silly and uncomfortable trying to be someone I'm not." She turned to climb the stairs.

"Ellysetta Baristani." Belliard's voice caused her to stop and turn back around. "Even should you clothe yourself in rags and dirt, you would bring honor to the Fey."

Tears sprang to her eyes. Those were quite possibly the nicest words anyone had ever said to her. "Thank you."

He was so proud, so sad in his aloneness and the dark sorrow that drowned all light in his eyes. She had thought him frightening and incapable of gentle feelings, and he had just proved her utterly wrong. Sorry for her part in hurting him, wishing she could take the shadows from his eyes, she reached out to touch his face, her fingertips gentle against his cheek and jaw. "I pray the gods grant you the peace and happiness you deserve," she whispered, meaning it with every fiber of her being. Her flesh tingled, and he flinched beneath her hand, his eyes widening.

To her amazement, Belliard vel Jelani dropped to one knee, bowed his head, and in a shaking voice declared, "Of my own free will, Ellysetta Baristani, I pledge my life and my soul to your protection. None shall harm you while in life or death I have power to prevent it." He drew one of the small, black-handled knives from the straps across his chest and slit his palm. Fisting his sliced hand, he held it over the blade and allowed six drops of blood to fall on the shining steel. "This I do swear with my own life's blood, in Fire and Air and Earth and Water, in Spirit and in Azrahn, the magic never to be called. I do ask that this pledge be witnessed."

"Witnessed," Kieran agreed, his smile gone.

"Witnessed," the other three Fey echoed with like solemnity.

The blade in Belliard's hand flared bright for an instant. He rose to his feet and offered Ellie the knife, hilt first. "Your *shei'tan* will always be your first protector," he told her, "but know that I will always be your second. So I have sworn. So it is witnessed. Take this Fey'cha as proof of my oath and keep it with you always. If you ever have need of me, simply let a drop of your blood touch the blade. No matter where I am or what I am doing, I will know you need me, and I will come."

She took the knife with hands that shook. "I don't pretend to know all your oath entails, but I know you have done me a great honor. I will strive to be worthy." She turned to hurry upstairs.

When she was gone, Belliard turned to his brother warriors. Tiny, nearly imperceptible tremors were shaking his body. He touched his cheek, still feeling the warmth, the very subtle yet incredibly strong power that had moved from her fingertips to him.

He had so much death on his soul that all but the strongest women among the Fey had avoided touching him centuries ago, unable to bear the pain of his sorrow, the ruthlessly self-enforced emotionlessness, and the dark burden of the lives he'd taken to protect the Fey. Even the *shei'dalins* only touched him when they needed to heal wounds he gained in battle. Yet this child, this incredible child whose soul called a tairen's, had reached out to touch him and sent a flood of healing warmth and love so strong that it burned straight through the block of black ice that encased what remained of his gentle Fey emotions.

He looked at Kieran, Kiel, Rowan, and Adrial. They could not feel what he felt, but they could hear his thoughts, and as Fey warriors they would understand. *«My heart weeps again,»* he told them, nodding when their faces mirrored his astonishment. *«She is more powerful than any of us suspected.»*

Aloud he added, "She's no Celierian. On this I would stake every blade I own."

Queen Annoura strolled down the stone walkways that wound through the palace's vast, manicured gardens. She'd woken early to greet the Tairen Soul and attend to the most pressing of her day's correspondence while breaking her fast. Duty would call her to service again soon, but she refused to forgo the pleasure of her regular morning walk.

The members of her Queen's Court followed a few paces behind, noble young Sers and Seras chosen as much for their

beauty as for their family connections. Annoura was no inse-
cure queen forced to fill her court with Drabs in order to
look beautiful by comparison. She was herself a Brilliant, and
she insisted on surrounding herself with nothing less than
Dazzles to set off her own beauty to its best advantage.

Of course, she also had her inner circle of Favorites, the
small knot of courtiers selected as her confidants for their
wit, shrewdness, political connections, and loyalty. Chief
among her current circle was the delicious, sultry-eyed Ser
Vale, a breathtakingly handsome nobleman whose palpable
aura of sensuality made Annoura envy ladies for whom infi-
delity was not an act of treason. He'd joined her court as a
Dazzle late last fall, but his entertaining wit and keen intelli-
gence had raised him swiftly to her inner circle.

He walked beside her now, elegant as always, his hair powdered the same pale blue as his form-fitting silk breeches and
matching gold-and-silk-embroidered velvet doublet. He
wore an alluring scent today, something deep and mysterious,
teasing Annoura with hints of wicked, forbidden pleasure.

He was not at all impressed with the news of the Tairen
Soul's truemate. "A woodcarver's daughter, My Queen? A
commoner?"

"The Fey do not share our appreciation for the purity of
noble bloodlines, Ser Vale, you know that. The Tairen Soul
claims she is his truemate, and he will not give her up." She
kept her voice low, her words private between them. "The
girl is betrothed to another and bound by a claiming mark,
yet he insists we set aside her lawful marriage contract."

"It is an outrage against Celierian sovereignty. The king
will, of course, refuse." There was earnest surety in his voice
and in his thickly lashed blue-green eyes.

"No," she said. "I doubt that he will."

"You cannot mean it!" Vale stopped in his tracks, drawing
the attention of the surrounding courtiers. "Surely His
Majesty would not truly allow this . . . this Fey sorcerer to
install a peasant—one of your own subjects, no less—as his
queen? To raise up a common woodcarver's daughter as the

equal of you, Queen Annoura of Celieria, in whose veins flows the world's most noble royal blood?"

"You go too far, lordling," Annoura snapped. "It seems I erred in raising you from Dazzle to Favorite so quickly if you think she could ever be my equal." Her skirts snapped as she resumed her walk at a brisk pace.

"My Queen!" Vale hurried to catch up with her. "Your Majesty, forgive me."

She glared at him. "He may call her his queen and seat her on the Tairen Throne, but there is much more to being *my* equal than the mere possession of a crown and a title."

"Of course, Your Majesty. I did not mean to suggest that I would ever believe otherwise. You are the Moon of Celieria, a Brilliant who outshines the Mother herself. And I hear this Celierian girl isn't even a Gem. Little more than a Drab."

Annoura arched a haughty brow. "Now you imply I am threatened by her looks?"

"Never, My Queen. You know my devotion belongs to you alone."

His hand brushed hers. An onlooker might believe it was an accidental touch, but Annoura knew otherwise. Her eyes narrowed.

"I am pleased to hear that at least." She brought the hand he had touched to her waist, out of further reach. "I am not benevolent to Favorites who betray my trust in them, nor am I a queen who shares the devotions due her."

"Your Majesty, it is not I who would claim her to be your equal. I but think how others outside of Celieria might view these unprecedented events."

Annoura kept her expression blank, but she was troubled by the suggestion that anyone might consider this upstart soon-to-be queen of the Fey equal in power and stature to Annoura of Celieria. She had spent the last two and a half decades building renown for the elegance of her court and the power of her husband's kingdom. She would not lightly share or lessen her position in the world. Especially not for some Drab of a woodcarver's daughter.

"The girl's fate is out of my hands. The king will not deny Rain Tairen Soul his truemate." There was more. The girl's betrothed had petitioned the King's clerk for a special license to wed her immediately. The Feyreisen had been in a rage when he'd found out. He'd actually threatened war if Dorian did not revoke the license and dissolve the betrothal. The arrogance of Rain Tairen Soul's demands still infuriated Annoura. Celieria was a sovereign nation, its laws inviolable. But Dorian—ever the coward when dealing with his magical kin—would not stand firm.

Another time, Annoura might have confessed some of the details to Vale, but he had irritated her with his insinuations, so she said merely, "The House of Torreval has long supported the traditions of both Celierians and Fey." She turned back to the palace. "I believe I have walked long enough this morning. I shall return to the palace." When he made to follow her, she stopped and leveled a hard, cold glance upon his handsome face. "Your attendance is not required today, Ser Vale." She lifted a hand and gestured to one of her newest young Dazzles, an exquisite blond lordling who'd been vying for her attention these last few months. "Ser Nilas. You may escort me back to the palace."

"My Queen!" The young Ser bowed so low, his golden forelock brushed the ground.

Vale bowed as well, but his eyes, vibrant and burning, held her gaze with a boldness that belied his calm acceptance of her dismissal.

At a quarter before ten bells, the Baristani family, clad in their best clothes, arrived at the royal palace. At least eighty Fey surrounded the carriage that conveyed them, with Ellie's quintet running alongside the conveyance as it rolled through the palace gates and up to the wide steps of the palace's grand entrance.

Though she had vowed never to do so, Ellie had once again donned her green dress and her mother's bridal chemise, hoping that it would bring more luck this time than it had the last. Her mother had helped her put up her hair in a soft, flattering style of curls and intricate plaits, held down by a set of long-toothed ivory combs. She wore no jewelry. She had none. But Kieran of the Fey had presented her with a girdle of delicate gold links and a sheath for Belliard's knife, decorated with six small, lovely jewels that shone red, blue, green, white, black, and lavender. The knife fit the sheath perfectly and now rested snugly on her right hip, pressed against the folds of her green gown. Belliard had said nothing when he saw it, but his eyes had flickered for a moment and she knew he was pleased.

An important-looking little man in elegant clothes met them at the top of the palace stairs. He greeted them with a gracious bow and introduced himself as the Right Honorable Ser Taneth Marcet, Undersecretary to the Minister of State. "If you and your family will follow me, please, Master Baristani."

He led them into the palace, down several marble-floored hallways, and into a luxurious antechamber. Ellie had never seen such wealth. Massive portraits of royal Celierian ancestors adorned the walls, their painted eyes looking down with imperious detachment. Gorgeous ivory brocade chairs overflowed with tasseled ice-blue and deep rose pillows. A rich, exquisitely carved sideboard of solid burlwood rested against one wall, its lustrous top covered with silver trays bearing all manner of fruits, comfits, tiny finger sandwiches, and delicate pastries. On a nearby cart rested a three-legged silver urn with eggshell-thin porcelain cups, tiny silver spoons, and a selection of sugars and creams elegantly presented around it.

After a brief investigation of the antechamber, the Fey settled themselves into the four corners of the room, and Belliard stood beside Ellie.

The Undersecretary gestured to the food and drink. "The refreshments are yours to enjoy," he told them, and he backed out of the room.

"Ser! Wait! Can you please tell us—" Sol's voice died off as the doors closed.

Lillis and Lorelle made a beeline for the comfits and had

already jammed three or four of the delicate candies in their mouths before Lauriana noticed and rapped out a sharp order to desist.

"But, Mama," Lorelle objected around the mass of sweets in her mouth, "the man said we could help ourselves."

"And have powdered sugar and chocolate stains all over you as a result? I think not. And don't talk with your mouth full, Lorelle."

The twins pouted, but as soon as their mother turned her attention back to Sol and Ellie, they each snatched another handful of comfits and hurried to plop themselves down on one of the large chairs facing away from their parents, where they proceeded to furtively nibble their purloined treats. Ellie shook her head and noticed that the Fey named Kieran was smiling again.

"Well," said Lauriana. "It looks as though they intend to keep us in suspense. As it's obvious we're being treated as guests rather than prisoners, you would think someone would tell us what's going on."

"I imagine we'll know soon enough," Sol replied in a distracted voice. Ellie cast him a surprised glance, only to smile fondly as she recognized the cause of his distraction. His attention was riveted by the carving on the burlwood sideboard, and he crouched down beside the piece to inspect it.

"Exquisite," he breathed, running a hand over the intricate designs that had obviously been worked by a master. "Laurie, my dearest, come look at this workmanship. I've never seen finer. I wonder who did this. One of the old masters, no doubt. Probably Centarro. It looks old enough, and the amount of detail—amazing!—is right for the period. Maybe Purcel . . . but no, he was never one to work with burlwood . . ." Completely absorbed, Sol pulled a small magnifying glass from his suit pocket and began looking for the tiny master's seal that was sure to be hidden somewhere on the carving.

Ellie, having skipped breakfast in the morning's rush, reached over him to help herself to a buttery fruit-and-nut-filled pastry, then moved to the cart to pour a cup of dark, steaming keflee into one of the delicate cups provided for that purpose. Holding the warm cup to her nose, she breathed deep of the spice-scented aroma and sighed happily. She poured a healthy dollop of honeyed cream into the bitter-sweet drink and took a sip, closing her eyes in bliss. Nothing should taste so lovely as this. Rich, creamy, sweet, spicy, with just enough bitterness to make it full-bodied. She rolled the flavors around on her tongue and nearly moaned in pleasure.

"The gods' blessings on whoever discovered keflee," she murmured, opening her eyes to find all the Fey watching her in fascination. Her chin came up in defiance of the blush warming her cheeks. "Well, surely some of the Fey must like it too?" she challenged.

"*Aiyah.*" That came from the blond-haired warrior named Kiel. "Many do. But few who . . . enjoy it . . . so well."

Before Ellie could respond, the doors at the far end of the room opened wide and the doorman announced in ringing tones, "Her Majesty, Queen Annoura of Celieria."

Lauriana gasped and fell into a deep, awkward curtsey while beside her Sol bent nearly double in a bow. The twins froze in the process of stuffing the last of the comfits in their mouths, then, in a flash of petticoats and pantalets, they tumbled off the chair and hid behind it, only their quivering bows visible over the stuffed arms of the chair. Ellie looked at the cup of keflee in her one hand and the pastry in the other, and spent a frantic moment searching for a suitable place to set them. Belliard came to her rescue, taking the cup and pastry so she could sink into her own curtsey.

"Please rise." If the queen found their blatant nervousness amusing, she didn't let on. Her voice was pleasant and warmly modulated. "Master Baristani, a pleasure to meet you at last."

As her father replied, Ellie rose to her feet, clasped her hands tightly together, and stared in wide-eyed fascination at the woman who was queen of all Celieria. She was a tiny woman, with delicate features and large blue eyes in a lovely heart-shaped face. Pale hair, so fine it looked like spun sugar, was piled high in an elaborate cascade of curls threaded liberally with ropes of pearls and gold. About her throat she wore a gold necklace dripping with sapphires and diamonds that must have cost the yearly wages of the entire West End. She was a walking testimony to the privilege of the upper class, and Ellie was suddenly very conscious of her own humble dress and even humbler beginnings.

"And you must be Ellysetta." The queen was standing before her, smiling, her delicate, milky white hands outstretched. "My dear, I have heard quite a bit about you."

Ellie stared at those perfect, satin-skinned hands and reluctantly placed her own much rougher ones in them. "Your Majesty," she blurted, hoping to draw attention away from her chapped skin and ragged fingernails, "I am honored to meet you. Though I am still not certain why we were summoned."

The queen patted her hand. "Patience is a virtue, my dear. All will reveal itself in good time." She flashed a small, conspiratorial smile. "In truth, I'm not supposed to be here myself, but I simply couldn't stand the curiosity any longer."

"Curiosity, ma'am?"

"About you, dear. About you." The lovely blue eyes narrowed a bit. "I would have thought the Fey would have seen to your dress before bringing you to the palace. Well, pay no mind to the gossiping tongues." She walked around Ellie, inspecting her from all sides. "You are quite a bit younger than I would have imagined. And not much to look at, though you show definite promise. Skinny. And very, very tall. Dear me, a veritable giant. Please tell me you've stopped growing."

Taken aback by the unexpected attack delivered in such sweet tones, Ellie stepped away from the queen. Had the woman brought her here merely to insult her looks? Surely a queen should be above such cruel entertainment. Ellie's hands fell to her sides, and the right one brushed the hard metal sheath housing Belliard's knife. Her fingers clasped around it with sudden need. The feel of the cool metal, the tiny pebbles of the six stones, the sturdy hilt of Bel's Fey'cha dagger, made Ellie's nervousness fade. She, Ellie Baristani, tall, skinny, not very attractive Ellie, was the woman Rain Tairen Soul had declared to be his *shei'tani*.

Her spine went stiff. She straightened to her full—and quite considerable—height. Her shoulders squared, her eyes flashed, and she lifted her chin, staring down her nose at the tiny queen. "Come to think of it, Your Majesty, I believe I must still be growing. Either that, or you are shrinking."

"Ellie!" Lauriana and Sol gasped her name together.

Kieran burst out laughing, and Belliard—too-solemn Belliard—actually smiled.

Queen Annoura's limpid blue eyes sharpened, and she eyed Ellie with new respect. "Very good, my dear," she purred. "I see you are not without claws of your own. You may just survive the coming days after all."

Ellie smiled, showing her teeth. "You may count on it, Your Majesty."

The queen inclined her head, and Ellie returned the gesture warily.

"Enough of my little entertainment." Queen Annoura glanced at Belliard. "The Feyreisa and her parents will remain here until they are called. I will send someone for the children. I'm sure they would much rather play in the palace garden than stay cooped up in this room. I trust you have no objection, Madam Baristani? No? Good. Nurse will be eager to have such pretty little charges in her care, and I'll be sure she knows not to feed them too many more comfits."

In a swish of perfumed skirts, she was gone.

Ellie sank into the nearest chair, covering her face with shaking hands.

"Ellysetta Baristani!" Lauriana flew across the room to stand before her daughter, hands on hips, the light of maternal outrage in her eye. "What were you thinking, speaking like that to the queen? I never raised you to be so rag-mannered!"

"I don't know," Ellie groaned. "I don't know what came over me."

"The tairen, I think," Belliard replied, his cobalt eyes gleaming bright rather than dark.

"I made a fool of myself. I spoke rudely to the queen."

"You spoke like the Feyreisa. You brought pride to this Fey." He glanced at his Fey brethren and cried, "*Miora felah ti'Feyreisa!* Joy to the Feyreisa!"

"*Miora felah ti'Feyreisa!*" the other four shouted back.

Then the very walls seemed to shake with an echoing roar as nearly two hundred Fey voices shouting in unison rose from all parts of the palace.

"Good sweet Lord of Light!" Lauriana exclaimed.

Ellie just stared at her quintet in dismay and prayed her queasy, lurching stomach would settle soon, before she humiliated herself beyond all hope of recovery.

CHAPTER SIX

Fortunately, Ellie's stomach settled and she regained at least the outward appearance of composure by the time another liveried servant came to fetch them. Circled by the Fey, she followed her parents out of the antechamber and down a series of halls until they came to a set of massive, opulent doors manned by two bewigged footmen and a third pinch-nosed man. Four royal guards flanked the doors, spears in hand, swords shining at their hips. They eyed the bristling display of Fey weapons suspiciously, but made no attempt to disarm the warriors.

The massive doors swung inward, and the pinch-nosed man called out in a carrying voice: "Master and Madam Sol Baristani. Mistress Ellysetta Baristani."

Before them, the Celierian throne room loomed large. A wide blue carpet stretched for a very long way down the center of the room, leading to two enormous thrones that ruled over the vaulted space from a raised dais. Hundreds of people stood in crowded masses on either side of the carpet, and balconies up above held another hundred. At least two dozen royal guardsmen stood at attention along the walls of the room.

The Baristanis and their Fey escort walked down the long and daunting aisle. The king and queen were seated on their respective thrones, flanked on the king's right by Dax v'En Solande and his red-shrouded truemate Marissya, the *shei'-dalin*. Two rows of benches, presently empty, sat before the dais. Another small platform surrounded by a semicircular wooden railing stood off to the right between the thrones and the benches, angled so the occupants of the thrones, the benches, and the room at large would be able to see whoever stood behind that railing.

Ellie's mouth went dry and her stomach took another unpleasant lurch as sudden realization struck. This was the annual gathering of the Celierian Supreme Court of Justice, presided over by the king and queen, who served as judge and jurors, and facilitated by Marissya v'En Solande, whose touch could force the truth from even the most hardened criminal. This was the court that rendered final judgment on disputed or undecided cases from all over Celieria. The verdicts of this court were final and irreversible.

And Ellie had just mouthed off to the queen.

Oh, gods. If there's any mercy in you, don't let the queen hold a grudge!

A man in calf-length blue robes met them at the end of the carpet and gestured for them to take seats in the second row of benches to the right. After making their bows and curtseys, Ellie and her parents sat, but the Fey went to stand at the far edge of the benches.

The pinch-nosed man's voice boomed out again: "Master and Madam Gothar Brodson. Goodman Den Brodson." Ellie felt her heart sink into her stomach. Sure enough, there they were. Den was once again stuffed into his too-tight suit, pomaded and curled, and wearing his smug *klat's* smile, as if he knew something no one else did.

The Steward of the Court, wearing blue robes with gold stripes on the lower half of the sleeves, walked to the king and handed him a parchment. King Dorian scanned the parchment, then handed it back and nodded. The steward turned to the benches. "Goodman Brodson," he said, "yesterday you petitioned the court to validate the betrothal contract between yourself and Mistress Ellysetta Baristani. You were granted the validation and have petitioned the courts for a special license to wed her immediately. Is this correct?"

Den stood, his chest swelling, his strong chin jutting forward. "It is, ser."

"You have a contract signed by the girl's father?"

"I do."

The steward referred to the parchment. "The girl bears your mark?"

"She does."

"Is she in this courtroom?"

"She is." Den pointed towards Ellie. "That is my betrothed, Ellie Baristani."

"Thank you, Goodman Brodson. You may sit."

Den shot a gloating look at Ellie and sat.

The steward came to stand before Ellie's father. "Master Baristani, did you sign a betrothal contract promising your daughter in marriage to Den Brodson?"

Sol stood. "I did, ser." He glanced back at Ellie. "But—"

"Thank you, Master Baristani," the steward interrupted. "That will be all." He turned his cold, dispassionate gaze on Ellysetta and called her name. "Ellysetta Baristani."

With a gasp, she jumped to her feet. "Y-yes, ser?" Her heart was racing, her stomach roiling, giving her cause to regret the pastry and keflee she had consumed.

"Do you bear Den Brodson's mark on your person?"

"I had no idea what he was doing!" she blurted. "I tried to stop him!" Guffaws and raucous jeers sounded in the gallery, and her face flamed with embarrassment. The bailiff banged his gavel and called for silence.

"Answer the question, Mistress Baristani. Do you bear Den Brodson's mark on your person?"

Her head drooped. "Yes."

"You may sit."

She sank down on the bench, her shoulders slumped. She

and her father had just confirmed before the king and queen that Den had a valid and binding claim to her. That was the same as clapping a collar round her neck and giving Den the leash. She glanced at Bel, but his face was inscrutable. Not even Kieran was smiling.

"Goodman Brodson." This time it was the king who spoke. Den leapt to his feet again as the king leaned forward. "Celierian laws and customs regarding betrothals and betrothal contracts are clear and immutable, as we are certain you are well aware. So clear and immutable, in fact, that you should not have found it necessary to file your petition. But your case has extenuating circumstances, does it not? Circumstances that we see you excluded from your petition." A little of the smugness faded from Den's face. "It has been brought to our attention that these circumstances alter the very nature of your case from a simple civil dispute to a potentially explosive situation that could adversely affect Celieria's foreign policy, our diplomatic relations, and even our national security. Did you not think those considerations were important enough to include in the statement you filed?"

"I—" Den went pale around the mouth. "But . . . Your Majesty, I—"

"Take your seat, Goodman. There is another who would address this court." The king gestured and the massive doors at the back of the room swung open again.

In deep, ringing tones, the tempo slowed so that each word sounded clear as a bell, the king's man called out, "His Esteemed Majesty, Rainier vel'En Daris Feyreisen, the Tairen Soul, King of the Fading Lands, Defender of the Fey."

Ellie's heart, which had been in her stomach, leapt up into her throat. She jumped to her feet and turned, like every other person in the room, to watch the Fey king make his entrance.

"Dear gods," she heard one woman whisper. "He is magnificent."

Tall, lean, and searingly handsome, Rainier vel'En Daris

exuded the dark, dangerous beauty and mystery of the Fey race as he strode down the blue carpet. His black leather tunic and snug leggings seemed to absorb light, while his bristling collection of Fey blades were so highly polished that they reflected light back with almost blinding intensity. Black boots, tooled with scarlet and purple tairen, crossed the length of the throne room in smooth, ground-eating strides. A scarlet sash embroidered with tairen worked in gold thread draped from his left shoulder to his right hip, just below one of the two crossed bands of Fey'cha daggers, while a chain made of fist-sized squares of gold, each set with large Tairen's Eye crystals, hung from one shoulder to the other. A golden crown circled his head, each of its six points topped with a small globe of priceless Tairen's Eye crystal. Even without the crown, no one who saw him could fail to recognize he was a king. He carried power as effortlessly as his broad shoulders carried the purple-lined black cape that billowed out behind him.

He reached the end of the carpet and condescended to bend his spine in the almost bow made by one king to another. He didn't look at Ellie, but his emotions reached out to her and his voice whispered in her mind, «*Shei'tani.*» She shivered at the liquid caress of the Fey word that meant truemate, wife, and beloved all wrapped up in one. Every nerve in her body was aware of him as he stood only feet away, and when a warm breeze of Air brushed across the back of her neck and swirled around her ear, she almost cried out at the pleasure of it.

The crack of the bailiff's gavel brought silence to the court. "The king of the Fading Lands has approached us with a petition of his own," King Dorian announced. "One that has made us reconsider the validation and license granted to Goodman Brodson yesterday. We have invited the Feyreisen to give testimony." King Dorian gestured to the platform beside him. "If you would step into the testimony box, My Lord Feyreisen."

The Fey king strode to the platform on the right and stepped behind the railing, facing the court. Marissya came to stand close, but she did not touch him.

The steward stepped forward. "Rainier vel'En Daris, you have stated that you have a claim to Ellysetta Baristani that supersedes our laws and you have petitioned this court to dissolve the betrothal contract between Den Brodson and Ellysetta Baristani. Is this correct?"

"It is." His voice was deep and sure, his face proud and uncompromising.

"What is the nature of this claim that supersedes our laws?"

"Ellysetta Baristani is my *shei'tani*." His eyes found hers. "My truemate." A murmur of voices rippled through the crowd.

"Please tell the court what a truemate is."

"A truemate is the person who holds the other half of a Fey's soul." His gaze never left hers, and Ellie felt the magic of his voice wrapping her in imperceptible weaves of longing. "It is the most sacred bond known to any Fey, more sacred than that between a king and his subjects, more sacred even than that between a mother and a child."

"Ellysetta Baristani is a Celierian, not subject to your laws or customs but rather to ours," the king interjected. "Though she may indeed be your *shei'tani*, she is also legally betrothed to Den Brodson according to our laws. He has a prior claim, which he is obviously unwilling to renounce."

Rainier met the king's gaze impassively. "I am the Feyreisen, she is my *shei'tani*. The betrothal to the Celierian must be dissolved. I understand your ways. I will pay Den Brodson and his family restitution for their loss. I do not ask that you break your laws, only that you understand and recognize that there is a higher law at work here. The gods created one woman whose soul could call mine. She sits there. Her betrothal to the Celierian must be dissolved."

"And if it is not dissolved?"

The sudden biting coldness of the Fey's expression chilled the room. "I am the only living Tairen Soul. Any harm to me is harm to the Fey. I have recognized her as my *shei'tani*, and the bond must be fulfilled. If you deny her to me, you do me irreparable harm. The Fey will consider it an act of war."

An audible gasp rose from the gallery.

The Tairen Soul's face smoothed. "But let us hope it does not come to that. As I have said, I will pay the young man's family restitution for their loss."

He gestured and the doors at the back of the throne room opened. Two Fey entered, bearing a huge chest between them. They brought it to the front of the room and at Rain's signal placed it before the Brodsons and opened the lid to reveal a dazzling display of gold and jewels, wealth enough to dower a princess several times over. Gothar Brodson's eyes nearly popped out of his head, while his wife fell back in her seat in a half swoon.

"I know enough of your Celierian laws to know that if the parents accept restitution, the betrothal contract is void." He pinned the Brodsons with a hard, haughty look. "Do you accept?"

"Yes!" Den's parents cried, even as their son shouted, "No!" Gothar cuffed his son on the side of the head. "Quiet, boy. That's a flaming fortune before you. More money than you'll see in a lifetime. No girl's worth losing that." The butcher nodded. "We agree."

"I don't!" shouted Den. When his father would have hit him again, Den deflected the blow and glared ferociously at his sire. "Why do you think he's offering you that money? Because she's worth twenty times that, and he knows it! I won't give up my claim to her. I—"

With a snarl of rage, Rain faced him, and Den's voice suddenly went silent even though his mouth was still shouting words. It didn't take anyone very long to realize what had happened.

"My Lord Feyreisen!" the king snapped. "Release our subject at once. You will not use Fey sorcery to silence a Celierian subject in a Celierian court of law."

Though he had the power to destroy Den Brodson with a

flick of an eyelash—and despite the fact that the tairen in him was eager to take the burden of this *rultshart's* death upon his soul—Rain knew it would be unwise. Ellysetta had not yet entered into the matebond. She and her family were Celierian. They honored Celierian laws, not Fey ones. Besides, a Fey did not call tairen to hunt mice. With a narrow-eyed look at the king that plainly said he released the boy because he wished to, not because Dorian commanded it, Rain dissolved the bonds of Air he had woven over Den's larynx to prevent speech.

"You see!" Den cried, pointing an accusing finger at Rain. "How do you know he hasn't used his sorcery to steal my bride?"

"Goodman Brodson," King Dorian said, "you are beginning to annoy me."

"But, Your Majesty—"

"Be silent. You marked a girl under questionable circumstances, forced a betrothal contract out of her parents based on that mark, and now you object because another man may have laid claim to the same girl using his own superior brand of force? Little boys shouldn't throw torches at tairen, Goodman. The tairen may get a burn, but the boys will be roasted and eaten for dinner." The king turned to Rain. "As for you, My Lord Feyreisen, regardless of whether or not the Brodsons accept your payment, there are still lawful procedures this court must follow—"

"There are no procedures to govern the bond between a Tairen Soul and his mate," Rain interrupted. "I have stated my case before you. She is my *shei'tani*. You have seen the Brodsons accept my payment to them. Dorian vel Serranis Torreval, King of Celieria, son of the line of Marikah vol Serranis of the Fey, do you dissolve the betrothal between Ellysetta Baristani and Den Brodson, holding the Baristani family blameless of any wrongdoing in this matter?"

"My Lord Feyreisen." Queen Annoura leaned forward in her throne before her husband could reply. "You have indeed stated your case." Her blue eyes were narrowed, and there was a snap in her voice. "The Brodsons have accepted your payment, and yet I don't recall hearing Master Baristani grant you the right to break the betrothal on his behalf." She met Sol Baristani's bespectacled brown eyes. "Have you given this right to the Tairen Soul, Master Baristani?"

Sol rose to his feet. He gave Rain a long, hard look. "No, Your Majesty," he said very clearly. "I have not."

"Ah. So it seems, Rainier vel'En Daris, you are incorrect in your assumption that the betrothal is broken merely because the groom's family accepts your very large bribe." The queen smiled sweetly. "Perhaps you are not so familiar with Celierian laws as you thought."

Rain's eyes blazed a furious command at the woodcarver. "You will grant me this right."

"Sol . . ." The woodcarver's wife tugged at her husband's sleeve. Her voice was an urgent whisper that Rain brought easily to his ears on a waft of Air. "Don't do it. Think of Ellie, of what's best for her. You can't mean to cede her over to these . . . these godless sorcerers."

Sol shrugged her off, muttering, "Hush, Laurie. I *am* thinking of what's best for her. She never wanted Den, you know that, but she's dreamed of the Fey—*this* Fey—all her life."

"You've always given her everything she wanted, but not this, Sol. They'll destroy her. They'll corrupt her soul. Everything we've ever done to keep her safe will be lost."

"Maybe, Laurie, the Bright Lord sent these Fey to help her, to protect her from the things we can't."

"And maybe they're the very thing we were meant to protect her against!"

Sol took a deep breath, stiffened his spine, and struck an aggressive, challenging stance that any male of any species would have recognized. He turned to Rain. "I don't know you, my lord, and you don't know me. But lest you think it has escaped my notice, for all this talk of souls and mating, not once have I heard the word marriage fall from your lips. I did not raise my daughter to be any man's concubine, even if he is a king. If you want the right to break Ellysetta's betrothal, Tairen Soul, rest assured you will wed her. And I mean by Celierian custom, in a Celierian church, with her family in attendance and a binding marriage contract in my hand!"

"Sol!" his wife gasped. "No!"

"Papa!" Incredulity and hope warred with fear and pride on Ellysetta's face.

Rain's expression lost its fury. A man protecting his daughter was something any Fey understood all too well. "Agreed." He turned back to the queen. "I believe now your Celierian laws are satisfied. Ellysetta's father has given me the right to offer payment on his behalf. The Brodsons have accepted it. The betrothal is broken."

Seeing Ellysetta about to slip from his grasp, Den jumped to his feet and shouted, "She's mine! She bears my mark! She accepted it willingly! Ask her parents! She never tried to stop me, never called out for help."

A feral growl rumbled ominously from the Feyreisen's throat. He bared his teeth, his eyes flashing hot with power and rage. The guards along the walls snapped to tense alertness. "She called to *me*. I felt her terror, her fear, her outrage across hundreds of miles. Willing? You attacked her in her own home, took advantage of her innocence and her ignorance of your mating rituals to put your filthy mark on her and lay claim to her against her will. You did not know she was my *shei'tani*. It is the only reason you still draw breath."

"My Lord Feyreisen!" The king snapped. "You will not threaten Our subjects in Our presence."

Rain's head whipped around. The torches on the wall flared violently, making the crowd gasp. "Then your subjects had best not lay claim to the Tairen Soul's mate," he hissed. It was not a ruler, not a man of peace, who looked out from Rain's face, but a fierce predator, barely caged. No one in Celieria had seen a Tairen Soul in a thousand years, and no one—not even the king, with his Fey blood—had understood what they were dealing with.

Ellie couldn't help feeling both fear and a thrill of excitement at the display of primitive possessiveness. His savagery, which should have frightened her witless, made her feel protected instead. She had never known what it was to be wanted so badly by anyone, had never dreamed such a thing could happen to her. A tide of longing swept over her, drowning out her fear of magic, her nightmares, even Selianne's warning not to let the Fey control her mind.

She looked at Rain's hands, now clenched into tight fists. She remembered the feel of them sliding into her hair, remembered the closeness of his arms pulling her tight, the way his voice had poured over her like honeyed cream as he spoke the Fey words of *shei'tanitsa* claiming, *Ver reisa ku'chae. Kem surah, shei'tani.* Your soul calls out. Mine answers, beloved. She remembered the warmth and security she had felt with the sound of his heart beating in her ear. Heat bloomed in her breasts and belly, a tingling heat that made her skin feel two sizes too small.

Rain drew a hissing breath, and his eyes, glowing like beacons, fastened on her face. Need, hot and urgent, rolled over her, scorching her, bringing every nerve in her body to quivering life. She could almost feel his desire, like hands, stroking her through the fabric of her gown, touching the aching tightness of her breasts, the liquid heat gathering in her loins. Her breath came very fast, and a fine trembling started in her belly, radiating outward. "Dear gods," she whispered, her eyes starting to lose focus. What was happening to her? "Dear gods."

Then he was there, his strong hands drawing her up against his chest, his arms enfolding her. His cape swirled about her, hiding her from the hundreds of prying eyes surrounding them. She leaned into his strength, pressing her hot face against his throat. Her arms linked around his waist and clung tight, as his head bent to her and his lips rained searing kisses and a storm of passionate Feyan words in her hair.

"You are mine."

The fierce claim sent another bout of shudders rippling

through her. All she could do was cling to him and whisper brokenly, "Yes. Yes."

Rain's head shot up in savage triumph. "She is mine," he growled, his narrowed gaze spearing the onlookers with naked threat, a lethal promise of death to anyone fool enough to try to take Ellysetta Baristani from him.

The scorching heat of the Tairen Soul's desire for his mate was palpable, and his primitive claiming of her raised the temperature of the room several degrees higher. In the gallery, breathless, corseted ladies swooned by the dozens. On the dais, the king swallowed and ran a finger under the suddenly too-tight neck of his tunic, while the queen shifted restlessly on her throne and fanned her face, muttering, "Good sweet Lord of Light."

King Dorian cleared his throat. "It would indeed seem that you and Mistress Baristani are in accord on the subject, My Lord Feyreisen, and this court has heard all it needs to hear." His face settled into a stern expression and he leveled a hard gaze on the butcher's son. "Den Brodson, you claimed the girl by marking her without her consent or knowledge, and when the king of the Fey also claimed her, you filed a petition in the hopes that our court administrators would not yet have heard the name of Ellysetta Baristani and would make your claim binding before anyone was the wiser. You sought to deny the Tairen Soul his truemate through legal maneuvering."

Den opened his mouth to object, but the king's hand slashed up in a curt gesture that silenced the objection before Den gave it voice.

"If Ellysetta Baristani were being claimed by the Feyreisen against her will—if he threatened her in any way—then I might very well refuse the Fey king his mate and face the consequences of that decision, whatever those might be. But you, Den Brodson, not the Tairen Soul, are the one who has molested the girl, claimed her against her will, threatened her family, and tried to manipulate this court in order to force her to your will. I will not—now or ever—plunge Celieria into war in order to support the questionable claim of an unquestionable bully."

"She is mine!" Den shouted. "She bears my mark. Everything she says is being manipulated by these Fey sorcerers, and you are falling prey to their magic!"

"Goodman Brodson, you will be silent!" The king gripped the arms of his throne and glared at the butcher's son. "As my queen correctly noted earlier, the betrothal agreement is between Master Baristani and your father. You have no say in the matter. Your father has accepted payment in lieu of your bride. The betrothal is dissolved. The Baristanis are free of all obligations—material or honorable—entailed by the agreement or the circumstances leading up to it. Ellysetta Baristani may bear your mark, but she is no longer yours to claim. Is that clear?"

"It's clear, Your Majesty!" Gothar replied quickly, grabbing his son up in his arms and clamping one huge hand over the younger man's mouth. "Very clear! Thank you for your time and patience. Den won't be bothering these people."

"See that he does not," the king warned. Then he took a deep breath and leaned back in his throne. "In light of the obviously strong feelings this case has . . . er . . . aroused"—a weak, dazed laughter rippled through the audience—"I call a one-bell recess to allow passions to cool." He nodded and the steward's gavel cracked out the call for dismissal. The king immediately rose to his feet and thrust out an imperious hand to his queen. "Annoura, you will attend me."

The queen eyed the passion-dark eyes of her husband, the flaring nostrils, the ruddy color of his face, and took his hand, allowing him to drag her off her throne and into the privacy of the antechambers beyond.

Only a few paces away, Ellie's Fey protectors watched the throne room empty with astonishing quickness, the majority of observers leaving by twos with flushed faces and dazed eyes. The few dozen who remained were mostly women who stayed behind to ogle the Fey Tairen Soul and his Celierian truemate.

"Any bets on the number of Celierian babies born in nine months' time?" Kiel vel Tomar murmured dryly as he watched the rush of departing couples.

Rowan vel Arquinas ran a hand through his black hair and shook his thighs to ease the tightness of his leathers. "And I thought the keflee thing was stimulating." Beside him his younger brother Adrial gave a bark of laughter that he tried to disguise with a fit of coughing.

Kieran grinned and obligingly thumped him on the back. "What do you think, Bel?"

"She is a fine mate for our king," Belliard replied in a distracted voice. The watchful eyes of Ellysetta's blood-sworn champion were focused on the enraged face of Den Brodson as his father dragged him from the courtroom.

"Bel?" Losing his grin, Kieran followed the older Fey's gaze. "You think the little sausage still hopes to make trouble? Surely even he would not be so stupid."

"Not stupid, no. He was wise enough to see in our Feyreisa what these other Celierian fools did not. What even she does not see in herself." Belliard fingered one of the red-handled Fey'cha sheathed in his crisscrossed chest straps. "A man who has laid claim to such wealth will not let it slip from his hands without a fight."

CHAPTER SEVEN

As the courtroom emptied, Sol cleared his throat to gain the attention of the infamous Fey holding Ellysetta. "My Lord Feyreisen? Er . . . Your Majesty?"

Lavender eyes snapped open, bright and fierce. Sol felt his knees tremble, but he stood his ground. "I am Sol Baristani, sir, the father of that young woman you're holding so closely. It would make me quite a bit happier if you would release her."

"Sol . . ." Lauriana muttered a barely audible warning.

"Ah, the father." Anger skated across the Tairen Soul's face. "The man who would sell my *shei'tani* to the *rultshart* with the filthy, roving mouth and disrespectful hands."

Sol drew in a sharp breath. "Despite what you obviously believe, I love my daughter. I urge you not to cast judgment when you know nothing of me or the reasons for my actions."

"Papa?" Ellie emerged from the folds of the Tairen Soul's cloak. Her hair was mussed. A few of her curls had won freedom from their confinement and now dangled in springy ringlets from their anchor pins. Her green eyes were heavy-lidded and slumberous, though as she glanced from Sol to Rain, her gaze sharpened considerably. "My Lord Feyreisen?"

The Tairen Soul's expression relaxed, and he reached out to wind one loose flame-colored coil around his index finger. He rubbed the curl with his thumb, a tender expression warming his eyes. "I would never bring nor allow harm to my *shei'tani's* family," he announced, and his fingers set to work on the intimate task of putting Ellysetta's escaped curls back in order. "To do so would be to harm her. You may speak your mind, Master Baristani, without fear of reprisal." He tucked the last ringlet in place and secured it with a pin.

The Tairen Soul's knuckle lightly caressed Ellie's cheek while his gaze met and held Sol's. Sol understood. The boundaries had just been established. Though Sol was Ellie's father, the Tairen Soul was her mate and he claimed the right to protect and guide her.

Sol expelled a weary breath. "Den Brodson isn't the husband I would have chosen for Ellie, but once he marked her—with or without her consent—she would have been shunned here in Celieria had I not signed the betrothal. I made what I considered to be the right decision under the circumstances, to protect both Ellie and the rest of my family."

"To protect her, you sell her to a man she despises? A man who takes advantage of her innocence to trap her into a union she does not want?"

"And what of you?" Sol retorted. "Your actions are certainly not beyond reproach. I don't know how things are done in the Fading Lands, but here in Celieria a man of honor does not approach an innocent girl and overwhelm her with intimate attentions the likes of which no decent, unmarried young woman should be subjected to."

"Ah—" Rain's lips curved in a mockery of a smile. "Then I should have come into your house to 'overwhelm her with intimate attentions,' as you allowed the butcher's son to do."

"Don't twist my words."

"They are untwisted. I merely spoke them back to you."

Ellie laid her hand on the Tairen Soul's arm. "Stop," she told him quietly. "He is my father. Do not mock him. In my own ignorance, I have shamed him not once but twice."

The Tairen Soul took her chin between his fingers and compelled her to meet his eyes. "What is between us shames no one, *shei'tani*. And any shame brought by the mark forced upon you lies with your parents and the butcher's offspring, not with you. You are bright and shining."

Despite Sol's distress, he couldn't mistake the astonishing gentleness in the fierce man's face. If Sol had been able to choose a husband for his daughter, he would not have hesitated to choose one who looked at her with such tenderness.

The Tairen Soul raised his other hand to brush a wave of bright hair away from Ellysetta's face. "Where is this mark that has caused such trouble?" When Ellie tugged her chemise aside, he bent his head and frowned at the dark spot on her skin. "Unattractive custom," he murmured. "Why blemish beauty to claim it?"

"I'm not beautiful," she protested.

"You are to me." He raised his head and rapped out a command in Feyan that brought the red-shrouded *shei'dalin* and her mate to his side. When the *shei'dalin* reached out a hand, Ellie shrank away from her touch. "Do not be afraid, *shei'-tani*," Rain said. "Marissya will only remove the mark. Like she healed your hand. There is nothing to be afraid of."

"She won't try to pry into my mind? You promise?"

"*Nei*, she will not. I promise." Black brows arched. "Would you rather keep the mark? I had thought it distressed you and that you would be pleased to be rid of it."

"It does distress me. I would like it removed, if she can do it. But nothing more than that. No . . . probing." Ellie stared at the red-veiled face beside her with trepidation.

"I was wrong to trespass before, Ellysetta Baristani," the *shei'dalin* said. "I will not do so again. You have my oath as

Celieria's Truthspeaker. May I touch you to remove this mark?" Marissya waited for Ellie's nod before proceeding. Even then, Ellie flinched as the *shei'dalin's* fingers touched her throat. "Peace, little sister," Marissya murmured. "You will feel heat and tingling where I touch. I call upon your body to unmake the stain on your flesh, to break it down and expel it." Her thumb brushed over Ellysetta's collarbone, removing the dry dust that was all that remained of Den Brodson's attempt to claim a Tairen Soul's mate. "There. The mark is gone as though it were never there."

Ellie touched her throat, rubbing the spot that still tingled. Her eyes widened in surprise when Rain produced a mirror out of thin air and presented it to her.

"It is made of Spirit," he told her, "but the reflection is true."

"I see," she said, though she didn't really. Understanding the engineering nuances of magic was far beyond her realm of comprehension. "Thank you." She lifted the mirror and ran her fingers over the spot where Den had bitten her. The mark was gone. She released a breath, feeling as if a great weight had been lifted from her. "Thank you, Lady Marissya."

"*Sha vel'mei.* I am glad to be of service to the Feyreisa."

Rain turned back to Sol. "You were chastising me. You may continue."

Sol shook his head. His anger, justified though it had been, was gone. "My point," he said wearily, "is that you are a stranger to me. And you have sent other strangers—lethally armed ones at that—into my home to work gods only know what magical mischief. You appear to care for my daughter, but that doesn't excuse your behavior. You summoned my family to a public forum and put our most private family matters on display for the titillation of the masses, including things better saved for the privacy of a bedchamber. And you've done it all without having the common decency to present yourself to me as any honorable man would have done when seeking to win my daughter's hand."

After a moment of silence, the Tairen Soul bowed his head.

To Sol's surprise, twin flags of color stained the man's cheeks. Who would have thought the king of the Fey could be put to blush? It made Sol like him a bit better.

"The father of my *shei'tani* is right to upbraid me for failing to introduce myself and request his blessing. Even in the Fading Lands, a man must approach his mate's family before he begins the courtship. My only excuse is that the bond caught me unawares and has left me . . . unsettled." The Tairen Soul grimaced, and Sol had the feeling there was a great deal left unsaid on that subject.

"As for the Fey I sent into your home, they are there to protect Ellysetta and your family. I am not without enemies, and they might do you harm to hurt me through her. With your permission, Master Baristani, I would introduce you to the warriors who protect your daughter." At Rain's wave, the five Fey who served in his truemate's quintet came closer.

"This is Kieran vel Solande." He gestured to the brown-haired, blue-eyed Fey who always seemed to be smiling. "He is the son of Marissya and Dax, and as you may have already learned, he enjoys a good joke. There are none among all the Fey who can wield Earth better than he." Four hundred fifty years old, Kieran was the last child born to the Fey people. Though he had only recently completed the final level of the Dance of Knives and earned the right to guard a *shei'tani* outside the Fading Lands, he was so strong in Earth, Air, Spirit, and Fire that Rain had not hesitated to appoint him to Ellysetta's quintet.

"This is Kiel vel Tomar." The lean, blond-haired, blue-eyed Fey bowed low with a supple grace that exceeded even Fey standards. "He is a master of Water magic. He likes small children, and they usually like him, though it appears your Lorelle may have a different opinion." The black eye and scratches Kiel had earned yesterday had healed considerably thanks to the natural Fey recuperative powers, but he still bore the marks of Lorelle's displeasure.

"These two are Rowan and Adrial vel Arquinas." Rain

gestured to the two black-haired, brown-eyed Fey who closely resembled one another. "They are brothers. Rowan is a master of Fire, and Adrial is unbeatable in Air." Both were also strongly gifted in Earth.

"Twins?" Lauriana asked.

"*Nei*. There are seventy-three years between them." Her look of surprise amused him. "That makes them almost cradle-friends by Fey standards."

"And this"—Rain clapped a hand on his friend's leather-clad shoulder—"this is Belliard vel Jelani. The oldest and fiercest of all Fey warriors, and my friend. Bel is a master of Spirit." He was also a master of every elemental magic save Earth, which to his undying shame he could not wield at all. He had walked the earth for more than 1,400 years and was now the oldest unmated Fey warrior in the Fading Lands, a fact that made Rain both proud of and afraid for his friend. It would not be long before the burden of the many deaths on Bel's soul either sent him to eternal rest or eternal wandering as an outcast, a *dahl'reisen*, one of the death-and-sorrow-shadowed lost souls who were forever banished from the Fading Lands.

"Earth, Air, Fire, Water, and Spirit. Each of these 'strangers' I sent to guard your daughter masters one of the four elemental magics and the one mystic that we wield. Alone, they are more powerful in their particular magic than any Fey you are ever likely to meet. Together, they are nearly invincible. I sent the best warriors of the Fading Lands to protect your daughter, Master Baristani. Each of them has pledged his steel and his life to keep her safe. They will remain by her side whenever she is not by mine."

"Well . . ." said Sol, eyeing the Fey warriors with new respect.

"And as for bringing you into this court to air your private affairs, I would never have done so had Den Brodson not tried to use your legal system to rob me of my *shei'tani*. King Dorian and Marissya persuaded me that this was the best way to handle the situation. It was not done to bring shame. The Fey are a very proud people, though I have not done them honor since entering Celieria. With your permission, I would begin anew."

With grave graciousness, Rain Tairen Soul bowed low before the spectacled mortal who, at less than one-tenth his age, would—gods willing—be his bond-father in the not too distant future. "Blessings and peace on the house of my beloved. Life, soul, steel, and magic I do pledge to her protection. May I prove worthy of her trust." In Feyan, then in Celierian, Rain spoke the traditional words of a courting Fey warrior to his mate's family. That much honor, at least, he could do this man, after all the unintentional dishonor Rain had shown him thus far.

Rain bowed again. "These are the words a Fey warrior speaks to the family of the woman he courts." He had spoken those words once before, to Sariel's parents more than eleven hundred years ago. Then, he had failed in his pledge. Sariel had joined him in the matebond and died while under his protection. It would not happen again.

After a moment, Sol held out a hand. "I welcome you as a suitor for my daughter's hand. And I thank you for the honor you do my house." He smiled a little. "Those are the words Celierian fathers speak to young men who come courting their daughters in the proper fashion."

Rain stared at the extended hand in surprise. It took him a moment to realize he was supposed to shake it. Fey senses being what they were, the Fey did not use touch as casually as other races did, especially not the skin-to-skin contact favored by the non-Fey of the earth. Still, to refuse this handshake would be to insult his prospective bond-father.

Rain clasped his hand carefully around the smaller man's and was pleased to sense almost no darkness in the woodcarver. The brightness of his spirit was refreshing, and it proved that he was an honest, humble man who was happy in his life and his family. As Sol shook his hand, his thoughts poured freely into Rain's mind. Out of respect for the man's privacy, Rain tried to block most of them out, but he could not prevent himself from hearing the thoughts concerning Ellie's happiness, her safety, and Sol's related concerns about the security of his family.

Though Rain would have liked to erase the man's fears, he could not promise more than he already had. Danger always courted the Fey people. They had too much power, too much wealth, too much that other races coveted.

"For a Fey, the blessing of a truemate is the greatest gift that can be bestowed. Master Baristani, you have my thanks for guarding her so well and for keeping her safe until now. I add my strength and vigilance to your own until the honor of protecting her becomes mine alone."

"Thank you, my lord." Ellysetta touched the back of his bare hand with her fingertips.

Rain drew in his breath at the sudden rush of feelings that sprang from the simple feel of her skin meeting his. The strength of his connection to this young Celierian went so far beyond what he had felt for Sariel, he could hardly fathom it. She was so young, so incredibly new to the world and to him, and yet regardless of the cost to his soul, Rain would destroy anyone and anything that dared to stand between them. And if any dared to harm her, he would shred them without mercy and dance as he drank their blood.

Ellysetta misunderstood the fierce look on his face, because she snatched her hand back and apologized for touching him.

"*Nei*, do not apologize." Rain could barely restrain himself from reaching for that hand and putting it back on his skin. His fingers itched to do so, and he clenched them into fists. He craved her touch, ached for it as only a Fey warrior could. But admitting to his need was the same as admitting a weakness, something a Fey rarely did willingly. "I was merely surprised. You may touch me if you like." But she didn't lay that sweet hand upon him again. He cursed his own unguarded reaction that had cost him such a small but much-desired pleasure and wondered how he might contrive to get it back. He bent his head to her, his gaze intent as he willed her to touch him again. To his disgruntlement, she did not.

Laughter sounded in his mind. Laughter he recognized but had not heard in any form for centuries.

«Bel?» He turned to his old friend in disbelief. Though to most, the solitary Fey would still appear blank as a wall, Rain knew better. Bel's dark eyes glinted with amusement, and the grim stoicism of his face was less pronounced. There was even the faintest crinkling at the corners of his eyes—humor struggling to find expression.

«If you could see yourself, Rain. Pouting like a tzicaida whose lunch just got away.» The corner of Bel's mouth actually twitched. *«You could always just command her to put her hand back on you.»*

Despite his amazement over Bel's incredible rediscovery of levity, Rain scowled. To issue such a command would be to admit he could not win his desire any other way. It would be the same as admitting defeat, another thing no Fey warrior would ever willingly do. *Nei*, he was tairen enough to be crafty, to lure his *shei'tani* into giving willingly that which he desired, without revealing to her how badly he desired it. *«You babble like a child, Fey.»*

«Aiyah, but then the babblings of a child so often hold truth, My King.»

«What has happened to my fierce friend Bel?»

«Your shei'tani, thank the gods.»

Rain's scowl was immediate, the hand reaching for a Fey'cha instinctive, though before Rain could pull the blade free, Bel's quick denial sounded in his mind.

«Nei, nei. Nothing like that! By the Flame, Rain, no Fey would dare.» In an odd tone, torn between shock and something that almost sounded like hurt, Bel added, *«Red, Rain? You would pull red against me?»*

Rain's gaze darted to the scarlet Fey'cha handle his fingers still clutched. With an oath, he snatched his hand away. *«For-*

give me, Bel.» All Fey steel was tempered in Fire and imbued with magic as a result, but red Fey'cha daggers were doused in tairen venom as they were forged, making them deadly poison, even to Fey. Fey did not pull red against other Fey. To actually attack another Fey with red was a banishing offense. «*These . . . feelings . . . drive me mad. I cannot think.*»

«*Peace, Rain. This is a difficult time for any Fey, you more so than others.*»

Rain nodded curtly and lifted a hand to run his fingers through his hair, only to stop when he realized what he was doing. To continue showing his distraction was yet another sign of discipline unraveling. He forced his hands down and extended an arm to his *shei'tani*. "Come. We are through here. I will escort you and your family home."

When Ellysetta would have linked her arm through his in the Celierian fashion, he stopped her. "*Nei.* In time of need, I would lose time untangling my arm from yours." He took her hand, straightened her fingers, and laid them on his wrist, bathing in the pleasure of her touch and ignoring the sound of Bel's laughter in his mind the whole while. "This is the Fey way. My hands and arm are free should I need to call steel or magic to your defense." In a flash, he had an unsheathed black Fey'cha in his hand. "You see?"

She eyed the naked blade with obvious worry. "You think there will be trouble here? In the palace?"

His lips thinned. "Trouble has begun here before." He regretted the fear that sprang to her eyes, but he could not lie to her. Outside the Fading Lands, danger was never far from the Fey. She must learn that and be wary enough to watch for it. Still, she was his truemate, and it was his duty to keep her from harm and worry. "Will there be trouble today, *shei'tani*? I doubt it. But we must always be on guard." He sheathed the blade and extended his arm to her again. "Come. Let us walk. I will send the Fey to bring your sisters to us."

Before taking his arm, she adjusted a golden chain at her waist and curled the fingers of her left hand around the black hilt of a blade sheathed at her hip. Only then did she place the fingers of her right hand on his wrist in the manner he had taught her. If there were to be danger, she and her Fey'cha would be ready for it. Even as the gesture took him aback—no Fey woman would ever lift a blade against a living creature— gentle amusement and pride mingled inside him. His Celierian *shei'tani* might be foreign and far too young, but her spirit was fierce. She would not cringe from the possibility of trouble; she would meet it with steel.

As Rain, Ellysetta, and her parents made their way through the palace, Rain looked more closely at the dagger in his *shei'tani's* grasp. His brows climbed skyward as he recognized the identifying mark carved into the black pommel. "You have made a conquest, I see."

She blushed faintly. "Belliard gave it to me," she admitted. "In some sort of Fey ceremony. He said I should always look to you to be my first protector, but that he would always be my second. It's all right that I accepted the knife, isn't it?"

"*Aiyah*," Rain agreed, frowning. Bel had blood-sworn himself to her?

«*That's what I was trying to tell you, Rain. She touched me and wished me joy, and now my heart weeps again.*»

«*What?*» What Fey warrior wouldn't blood-swear himself to a woman who could lift the weight of centuries of death from his soul with a single touch? But who was his *shei'tani* that she would have such power? Even Marissya—the strongest of the Fey *shei'dalins*—could not work such a miracle.

Rain turned to Ellie's parents. "Is there a history of magic in your families? Fey blood, perhaps?" Fey had intermarried with Celierians in the past.

Sol shook his head. "No, Laurie and I are both pure mortal. Simple folk from simple stock."

"Not so simple. You have produced a Tairen Soul's *shei'-tani*. That has never been done before in all of Fey memory."

The Baristanis looked at each other, then back at him. "Oh, no," Sol informed him. "Ellie's our daughter, but she's not of our blood." The woodcarver quickly related the tale of how he and his wife had found the infant Ellie in the woods of Norban, a week's journey north of the Celierian capital.

"There was no sign of a parent? Nothing to identify where she came from?"

Sol shook his head. "Nothing except a note asking someone to take her. She was just there, sitting under a tree. I don't think she'd been there very long when Laurie found her. She was awake, but she wasn't crying." He smiled fondly at his adopted daughter. "She was a solemn little waif with big green eyes and the brightest hair you've ever seen. Laurie and I didn't think we could have children, so we took her in. Not that we had much to offer. Poor as mice we were. My hands had been crippled in an accident. I didn't think I'd ever carve again."

"But your hands have healed."

"Yes," Sol agreed, grinning and flexing his fingers. "Better than ever."

"And the little girls with the brown hair? Are they adopted also?"

"No. Lillis and Lorelle are ours. Ellie'd been with us almost fifteen years when we were blessed with the twins. She was almost as happy as we were. She'd been wanting her own little sisters to love."

"You enjoy good health?"

"The best. Hardly ever even get the sniffles."

"And good fortune."

"We do well enough. We've never been rich, but we've never lacked for anything either. And now that we've received a royal commission, we'll not lack for money to dower our girls. We're simple folk with simple needs. And we're happy. That's all that really matters in the end, isn't it?"

"*Aiyah*," Rain murmured. "Happiness is a fortune beyond compare." He glanced at Bel and the other Fey and saw comprehension dawning in their eyes. «*Bel, send two men to Norban. Perhaps someone there knows more.*» Bel nodded, and

Rain turned his attention back to Sol and Lauriana. "So, you took in an abandoned child. After that, your hands, which were crippled, were healed. Your wife's womb, which was barren, bore fruit. You have enjoyed excellent health and happiness, and you've never lacked for anything you truly needed. And when you needed a little more, you received a royal commission. Have there been any other small miracles since you took her in? Any other dreams that have come true?"

"We've always said she was our good luck charm, but surely you're not implying that Ellie . . . No. These are coincidences. Nothing more."

"Any one on its own might be a coincidence. But taken all together, with Ellysetta also being a Tairen Soul's *shei'tani*, it can be no coincidence." The slender hand covering his wrist jerked. Rain caught it in a loose grip before she could pull away.

"What are you saying? That she's Fey?" Sol asked.

"Fey? Possibly. Magic? Most definitely."

With a yank, Ellie pulled her hand free, crossing her arms and stuffing her hands in her armpits where he could not reach them. "I'm not magic. There's not a magic bone in my body. If there are miracles here, it's the work of the gods, not me."

"Do not fear what you are, *shei'tani*. It is a wondrous thing."

"No. I'm Celierian. Just plain mortal like my parents. I'm no different than they are."

"*Las*. Peace, Ellysetta. I do not mean to upset you." The frightened, almost frantic look in her eyes reminded Rain of the desperate fear that radiated from an animal as he swooped upon it in tairen form. "I don't understand why you would fear your magic so."

"What Celierian wouldn't?" That bitter question came from Lauriana. "How many magic-blighted forests do we have, thanks to you and the rest of your kind? How many dark places to trap unwary travelers?" Her mouth turned grim. "Sol and I both knew what it meant when we found Ellie abandoned in the woods. She was born in the dark lands, infected with magic left over from the Mage Wars. But neither of us could bear to leave a child to die, so we took her in and did our best to raise her in the Light and keep her safe from magic and magical creatures." She gave her husband a hard look.

"You were compassionate, indeed, to take her in despite your fears," Rain replied. "But rest assured, she possesses no mere remnant of magic, dark or otherwise. Her power is bright and shining and very strong." It had to be, or she could never have reached Bel's heart.

"Arrogant Fey *rultsharts*. Think they can come in and take whatever they want. Thrice-damned soul-scorched sorcerers." Den Brodson sat at the bar of the Charging Boar pub and glared into his nearly empty pint of dark ale. "Another pint of Red Skull, Briggs," he growled as he downed a swallow of what was already his third pint in half a bell.

"Make that two." The smooth, accented voice behind him brought Den's head around for a quick, assessing glance. The newcomer, a foreigner wearing a blue sea captain's coat, smiled slightly and gestured to the barstool beside Den. "May I?"

Den shrugged. "As you like."

The man straddled the barstool. "I couldn't help overhearing your story. The young woman claimed by the Tairen Soul—she was yours?"

"My betrothed. At least she was until that damned Fey sorcerer stole her from me." Den flicked another appraising glance over the foreigner, noting the man's oiled curls, woven with gold rings, and the dark blue tattoo in the shape of crossed swords high on one sun-bronzed cheek. "What's it to you?"

"A matter of interest. And perhaps a problem I can assist you with."

"What makes you think I need any help?"

The man held Den's gaze steadily, and for a moment, Den glimpsed something hard and dangerous in the man's vivid blue-green eyes. Then the man blinked, and said mildly, "Perhaps I misunderstood you earlier. I thought you wanted the woman back."

"I do."

"Then do not be foolish. A powerful immortal has claimed your woman, and the courts have upheld his claim. You cannot possibly hope to stand against him unaided."

Briggs approached with two pints in hand. The foreigner pulled a money purse from an inside pocket of his coat and extracted a gold coin. "Shall I buy this round?"

Den shrugged again, his eyes watchful. "I never turn down a free pint."

The man smiled, revealing impressively white teeth. He tossed the coin to Briggs, then held out a hand to Den. "The name's Batay. Captain Batay. I sail a merchantman from Sorrelia."

"Den Brodson." Den shook the captain's hand. "And just how, exactly, do you think a Sorrelian merchantman can help me best Rain Tairen Soul?"

"Is there somewhere we can speak privately, Goodman Brodson?"

Without taking his gaze from the Sorrelian, Den called over his shoulder, "Briggs, is the back room open?"

"It is," the bartender replied. "Help yourself, Den."

Den led the Sorrelian to a small, private room at the back of the pub. As the door closed behind them, he turned and crossed his arms over his chest. "Well? How can you help me?"

Captain Batay smiled. "Not I alone, Goodman. I am but the humble servant of a very powerful man. But first, as a gesture of your goodwill—" He pulled a small oval object from his pocket and held it out. The mirrored surface appeared cloudy at first, but then an image began to form in the misty glass. A wizard's glass, Den realized, used for scrying and for recording images. "—tell me everything you know about this woman."

The wizard's glass was clear now, and the image of Selianne Pyerson, Ellie's best friend, stared up at Den from the crystalline surface.

CHAPTER EIGHT

My beloved is the sun
And I am the earth that thrives only in her warmth.
My beloved is the rain
And I am the grass that thirsts for her quenching kiss.
My beloved is the wind
And I am the wings that soar when she fills me with her
  gentle strength.
My beloved is the rock
Upon which rests the happiness of all my days.
                    —*The Elements of Love*, a poem
            by Aileron v'En Kavali of the Fey

That evening, two bells before sunset, Rain presented himself in full ceremonial splendor at the door of Sol Baristani's humble home. Marissya and Dax accompanied him, along with Marissya's quintet and another five Fey warriors carrying several chests.

After introducing Marissya and Dax, Rain bowed to Sol Baristani. "This is how I should have begun, Master Baristani," Rain said. "In the Fading Lands, a man brings gifts to the home of his beloved to ask her family's blessing on the courtship. The gifts"—his hands gestured towards the three chests the Fey had carried into the room—"are intended to show the suitor's depth of feeling for his prospective mate. The stronger the bond to his mate, the more clearly he sees her family through her eyes. If my gifts please you, then I have seen you clearly and the bond is true. Please, open them."

Needing no further prodding, the twins fell upon the chest that bore their name and flung back the lid. Inside, a selection of brightly colored clothes with matching shoes and hairbows and a collection of porcelain dolls in full court dress elicited squeals of delight.

For Lauriana, Rain had selected a dashing burgundy dress adorned with black lace at the cuffs and collar, matching hat and gloves, a pair of gleaming black boots with sturdy heels and buttons up the side, and a black cape with downy soft fur at the collar. The clothes were sensible, but of superior quality and workmanship, obviously expensive but discreet enough that Lauriana could wear them about the neighborhood without feeling as though she were putting on airs. On the collar of the dress, an exquisite sun-and-moonstone cameo set in gold filigree gleamed with subtle and very feminine elegance.

Despite Lauriana's distrust of the Fey, the stern lines of her face softened when she beheld the gifts meant for her. "It's all lovely," she said, running a hand over the fabric before she could catch herself. "Thank you."

Sol's chest contained a collection of raw woods, the finest to be found, including a large block of black, almost grainless ebonwood and a slightly smaller block of pale cinnamon-colored fireoak that would gleam like copper flame once it was properly polished. Also nestled inside was a pouch containing a new burlwood pipe and a selection of fine tobaccos that made Sol smile in pleasure when he sniffed them.

"Well," said Sol, caressing the wood with his master's fingers, already envisioning the beauty waiting to be revealed by judicious application of his chisels and gouges. "The bond must indeed be true. I don't believe you could have chosen better for any of us."

Rain bowed low to show his appreciation of the fine compliment while Ellie's five Fey guardians nodded approvingly and spread the word to the rest of the Fey that their king had successfully made his amends with his prospective bond-family.

"With these, Master Baristani"—Rain touched the ebonwood and fireoak—"I ask that you make a particular piece." He carefully formed the image of what he wanted in his mind and, using a narrow weave of Spirit, placed that image in Sol's mind. "Do you see it?"

Eyes wide with wonder, Sol nodded. "Yes."

"Can you make it?"

"Yes." Rain released his weave, and the picture winked out of Sol's mind. Dazed, Sol touched his temple. "How did you do that?"

Rain explained, at least as well as he could to a mortal with no concept of magic. "It is like drawing a picture, only instead of paper, I use Spirit. All living creatures hold Spirit within them. It is the energy that allows you to think thoughts, to dream, to imagine. Because you possess Spirit, I can communicate with you using it. Fey magic is merely the ability to control the elements and the mystics, to open their natural paths and weave them to our will."

"And the mirror you made earlier?" Ellie asked, beginning to understand.

"Was Spirit. Not real, but a mental projection of a mirror that I created using Spirit. A bit more complex, because I tied to the image the ability to reflect the natural world. The mirror was both a picture of a mirror and a picture of what the mirror would see at any given moment. A master of Spirit can tap all of your senses, building taste, touch, smell, sound, everything into the weave, but an object created of Spirit remains an illusion at heart."

"Bel told me that Kieran commands Earth and that things made of Earth are real."

"*Aiyah*, but to weave Earth into substance, you must first have the substance to weave. You can pull it from the world around you, but that is difficult and takes great care and concentration as well as exceptional command of Earth. If you pull too much from something else, you damage it." Rain's eyes crinkled at the corners. "Fey magic is not without its limitations, despite what mortals believe."

"What of the wizards that come to Celieria? Are all their feats illusion also? Do they control Spirit like the Fey?"

"Some do. Most are charlatans. Others tap the dark magics, Azrahn chief among them. They use spells and charms to trap otherworld spirits and force the elements to their command."

"You're speaking of the Elden Mages," Ellie said.

The Tairen Soul's face hardened instantly into cold, unyielding lines. "*Aiyah.* The black-souled spawn of demons. They use Azrahn and other magics for their own evil purposes. They covet what the Fey possess and kill without remorse—how can death stain a soul already given over to the dark?"

«*Rain.*»

Even without Marissya's silent warning, Rain saw the worry on Ellysetta's face. Frightening her with his hatred of the Eld was no way to court her. "Enough of the Eld," he commanded. "It is never a pleasant subject with me."

He looked at Sol and Lauriana. "I asked Marissya and Dax to accompany me so that we might negotiate the Celierian marriage contract. Is there somewhere we may sit and speak?"

"Of course. Lauriana has prepared the parlor and set out a plate of refreshments in anticipation of your visit. If you will follow me?" Sol led the way into the parlor.

When Ellysetta did not immediately accompany them, Rain paused and held out an arm. "Join me, *shei'tani.* Celierian customs may leave such negotiations to the parents, but in the Fading Lands, the conditions of courtship and matebonding require the consent of both mates."

Surprise and gratitude warmed her eyes. She placed her fingers on his wrist and allowed him to lead her into the parlor.

The small parlor seemed to grow smaller when the two Fey Lords entered. It had been built for Celierian comfort, not Fey, and the ceiling was slightly lower to create a cozy feel. Too cozy, Rain thought, as his head almost brushed the ceiling.

He moved to take the most vulnerable seat in the room, a large green wingback chair with its back to the window, and gestured for Ellysetta to sit beside him on a matching ottoman that placed her securely between the protective strength of himself and Dax. Lauriana bustled about the room serving keflee and frosted hazel-cakes before settling down beside her husband.

"In twelve days' time, immediately after the Prince's betrothal ceremony, the Fey return to the Fading Lands," Rain began. "Ellysetta must accompany me." He felt Ellysetta's quick spurt of surprise and trepidation. «*Peace, shei'tani. I cannot leave you here alone and unguarded, but I cannot stay either.*»

"Twelve days," Lauriana breathed, staring at him in shock.

"I hoped to return sooner, but Marissya has convinced me that Ellysetta needs time to prepare for her new life." Rain chafed at the delay. He wanted Ellysetta safe in the Fading Lands, protected by the magical barrier of the Faering Mists that surrounded the Fey homeland. He could not court his truemate properly here in Celieria, where he must remain vigilant, always on the alert for an attack. Neither could he forget his obligations to the tairen. If the Eye had steered Rain true, Ellysetta was the key to saving the tairen and the Fey, and that meant he must bring her to the Fading Lands as soon as possible. "If you are amenable, we will draw up the Celierian marriage contract tonight and hold the ceremony in two or three days."

"Two or three days?" Lauriana exclaimed. "Impossible!" She clasped her hands to her cheeks, horror etched on her face. "The Church alone requires seven weeks for devotions and the Bride's Blessing. Not to mention all the other necessities. She needs a wedding dress, a trousseau. We must notify our friends and family. And then there are flowers, food, prenuptial dinners, receptions . . ." She shook her head. "No. I'll need three months at least. Unless you wish to shame us and our daughter with some shoddy, rushed little affair?"

Rain's spine stiffened. Shame his truemate? The insult was outrageous. "This I would never do." His voice was cold and clipped. "I do not have three months to give you. In twelve days, I leave Celieria. Ellysetta will accompany me then."

"It is very little time, I know," Marissya broke in. The *shei'dalin* cast a warning glance at her king. «*Their ways are not ours, Rain. You brought me here to negotiate. Allow me to do so.*» Turning her attention to Lauriana, Marissya continued,

"Your daughter's wedding will be as grand as you desire and will bring your family honor, I assure you."

The sudden clearing of Sol's throat made everyone turn to look at him.

"The wedding will not take place until the blessings and ceremonies required by the Church are complete," Sol stated in a mild but firm voice. "In that regard, my wife and I are in perfect agreement. Speak to the Archbishop, if you like—I know the Church will abbreviate their ceremonial timescales under special circumstances—but until the Bride's Blessing is complete, there will be no wedding. And irrespective of the Archbishop's decision, the wedding will not take place sooner than one month from tomorrow. That gives my wife at least some time to prepare, and gives our family and friends a bit of notice so they can have a chance to attend."

"Two weeks," Rain countered.

"Three," Sol returned swiftly. "And that is the absolute minimum."

Rain met his future bond-father's eyes in a brief visual skirmish that ended when Ellysetta placed her hand on the arm of Rain's chair and whispered, "Please."

Though it chafed him to wait a moment more than necessary, Rain put aside his impatience. "Three weeks," he agreed. "But at least three bells of every day will be set aside for our courtship. And the Fey will continue to guard her and your family as they do now. That is not negotiable."

Sol considered the offer for a moment, then nodded.

Rain sat back. "Then we are agreed." His hand covered Ellysetta's, his fingers threading through her smaller ones. Pleasure filled him at the simple touch and made Ellysetta blush.

"This may actually work out better," Marissya said. "Prince Dorian's betrothal ceremony will be over by then, so the wedding won't conflict with those celebrations. Which is good, as I know the king and queen will wish to attend."

"The king and queen? Oh, my." Lauriana sat back in her

chair, fanning a hand before her face. "Three weeks to prepare a wedding the king and queen will attend . . ."

"It will be fine, Mama. Don't worry." Ellysetta gave her mother a reassuring smile. "No one will be expecting a huge celebration, and I would be happy with something simple. A priest, perhaps some flowers." But her words only seemed to distress her mother more.

"*Nei, shei'tani*," Rain interrupted. "Since there is to be a ceremony, it must be grand, else it would not bring honor to your family or the Fey." The Celierians had always adored pomp and ceremony, and that had not changed in over a thousand years. Because Dorian and Annoura were planning to attend, the high-ranking Celierian nobles must also be invited, and Rain would not leave his *shei'tani* vulnerable to their cruel, wagging tongues.

He looked at Lauriana and Sol. "Marissya is correct. I will assign a group of warriors to help you. Those talented in Earth can make what your Celierian merchants cannot provide on such short notice. You may also hire whatever Celierian help you require. Marissya will have Queen Annoura provide the names of tradesmen supplying services for the Prince's ceremonies." Annoura wouldn't like it, of course, which almost made Rain smile. It would be a subtle punishment. Bel had told him of the way she'd dared to test Ellysetta's mettle earlier in the day.

"We will discuss the marriage ceremony again, but for now, let us attend to the matter of the marriage contract." Rain nodded at the *shei'dalin*. "Marissya is more familiar with your customs than I, and I have asked her to speak for me."

Marissya leaned forward slightly. "With your permission, Master Baristani?" She waited for Sol to incline his head before proceeding. "I have taken the liberty of modifying a standard Celierian marriage contract." She nodded at Dax, who produced two copies from thin air and handed them to his truemate. She passed one to Sol. "There is no need to settle a bride price. What Ellysetta brings to this union is beyond price. In that, Den Brodson was correct. The Fey would have paid twenty times, a thousand times, what we did to break her betrothal.

"We will speak to the Archbishop, and if he is amenable, the wedding will take place in three weeks, at which time Rainier will accept full responsibility for Ellysetta's well-being, in accordance with your customs. Though the *shei'tan-itsa* bond will not be fulfilled by this ceremony, in the eyes of Celieria, Rain and Ellie will be man and wife. When the Fey depart Celieria, she will accompany us to her new home in the Fading Lands. Your family, Master Baristani, may travel with us to the Fading Lands and remain there until the Fey matebond ceremony is held. Or we can send escort for you when the time comes."

Sol set his copy of the marriage contract on the small table beside him and pulled a pipe and tobacco pouch from his pocket. He hesitated and glanced at his Fey guests. "Do you mind?" When the Fey shook their heads, he filled the pipe's bowl with dark, moist tobacco, tamped it down, then lit a match against the sole of his shoe and cupped the flame over the pipe bowl. The room was silent except for Sol's quiet puffs as he lit the pipe. Fragrant smoke filled the air, a deep, rich aroma that smelled of flowers and spice. He puffed the pipe for a few moments more, then picked the contract back up. "Why would you not hold the Fey ceremony at the same time as the wedding?"

"Ellie must accept the bond before the ceremony can take place."

"Didn't she already do that this morning in Council?"

Marissya shook her head. "Ellysetta only recognized the bond today. She has not yet accepted it within herself."

"I don't understand." He frowned.

"It is confusing, I know." The *shei'dalin* smiled gently. "Acceptance of a truemate bond is not a conscious act. Ellysetta cannot just say 'I accept' and complete the bond. When she opens her soul to Rain and allows him in without reservation, when she willingly enters into his, then she will have accepted the bond. No one, not even she, can say when that moment will come. The path is different for every truemated couple, and it is never a simple one. Both Rain and Ellysetta will be tested, as will the strength of their bond, and they must prove their worthiness before the bond can be complete. She and Rain will know when it happens, and so will all the Fey. Until then, he must court her, as all Fey warriors court their mates."

Marissya turned her head and captured both Rain and Ellie with her gaze. The *shei'dalin's* voice lowered and grew so gentle it was almost hypnotic. "He must prove himself strong enough to protect her, gentle enough to win her heart, and worthy of the great gift of her love and her unconditional trust. She must find the courage to embrace the darkest shadows of his soul, and the even greater courage to bare the shadows of her own soul to him. When all barriers are sundered, all secrets revealed and accepted, she can complete the bond; and they will no longer be two separate people, but rather one person, one soul, complete for eternity, stronger together than either could ever be apart."

A fierce longing rose up in Rain, closing his throat and clasping a tight, aching fist around his heart. Ellysetta turned her head, and her eyes locked with his. Of its own volition, his hand reached out to touch her cheek, even as her hand reached out to touch his.

«Your soul calls out. Mine answers, beloved.» The sending was a tender caress. Her lashes fluttered down, half veiling her eyes. *«One day, Ellysetta, you will say those words, and this Fey will at last know joy.»*

"What happens if Ellie cannot accept this Fey bond?" Lauriana asked with obvious agitation. "We've raised her in the Church of Light, and she believes as we do that all souls belong to the Bright Lord. Ellie pledged her soul to him at her first Concordia ten years ago."

"Madame Baristani, the Fey worship the same gods as Celierians, including the Lord of Light," Marissya reassured her. "*Shei'tanitsa* does not violate the bond between believers and the gods. Indeed, truemates exist only *because* the gods decreed they should."

But Lauriana wouldn't be soothed. She cast a frightened glance at her husband. "I don't like the sound of this at all. Sol, you know why I insisted she complete her Concordia. And haven't I been right?" Lauriana turned back to Ellysetta, and to Rain's surprise, there were tears in the older woman's eyes. "I know you hated me for pressing Den's suit, Ellie, but at least with him, I knew your soul would be safe from the perils of magic."

"Mama!" Ellysetta pulled away from Rain and crossed the room to kneel at her mother's feet. "I could never hate you." She grasped her mother's hands and pressed them to her face. "You're my mother, and I love you. Even with Den, I knew you had only my best interests at heart. But you heard Lady Marissya: the Fey aren't evil. They walk the Bright Path, just as you've raised me to do." Ellysetta's voice dropped lower. "I promise you, I will not forget the vows of my Concordia. And I do not believe the Bright Lord would abandon a soul in his service. So, please, be happy for me. I want this. It's what I've always dreamed of."

A nearly imperceptible wave of power whispered in the room.

Rain exchanged a look with the *shei'dalin* and her mate. «*Marissya. Dax.*»

«*We feel it too, Rain.*»

All three of them turned their attention to Ellysetta. Surprising, amazing Ellysetta was weaving Spirit. The weaves were delicate, incredibly subtle, invisible even to Fey eyes but faintly perceptible to their heightened senses. Had they not been in such a small, confined room, sitting close to her, with the weaves around the Baristani house buffering them from the random surges of power that came naturally from all living creatures, Rain doubted they would even have sensed her magic at all.

Ellysetta was weaving a *shei'dalin's* calming power with an untutored expertise so natural, and yet so powerfully and flawlessly done that even Marissya could not hide her astonishment. Compared to Ellysetta's weave, the delicate probing touch that Marissya had tried to use on Ellysetta's mind was as subtle as a hammer strike. It was obvious that Lauriana had no idea she was being influenced. It was equally as obvious that Ellysetta had no idea she was doing anything more than offering comfort, and that made her skill all the more incredible.

"Ah, kit, perhaps you're right and I'm being a silly old woman, seeing demons in every shadow." Lauriana wiped her eyes and nose with a handkerchief. "Your faith in the Most High makes shame of my doubts. You've always been a bright soul, even at the worst of times." More tears spurted when she embraced Ellysetta again, and she gave a self-conscious bark of laughter. "Well, now I know I'd best bring several handkerchiefs to the wedding."

Ellysetta laughed, too, as did Sol, and the emotional moment passed. The spidery weave of Spirit dissolved, leaving no trace of its existence.

"Rest assured, Master and Madam Baristani," Marissya continued, "if for any reason Ellysetta does not accept the matebond, she will have the choice of remaining in the Fading Lands or returning to Celieria. Should she elect to return, the Fey will dower her sufficiently so that she may remarry or live independently for the rest of her life."

Sol's brows rose at that unusual generosity. "That is very kind."

The *shei'dalin* inclined her head. "The Feyreisa will be expected to attend at least some of the upcoming court functions. Am I correct in assuming she's had no training in the noble graces?"

"There was no need. We're simple folk."

"I will arrange for her to meet with instructors who will teach her what she will be expected to know, both about the Celierian graces and those of the Fey. Once we return to the

Fading Lands, the Fey will see to any further education she requires to fulfill her duties as our queen. The rest of the marriage contract is standard. If you wish, I can leave it with you so you may have your solicitor review it."

"That's not necessary. I'll look at it now." Sol took the contract and began to read. When he was satisfied there were no nasty surprises, he went to the writing desk in a corner of the room and signed both copies of the contract. Rain signed them also and affixed his seal, a tairen rampant, in a blob of purple wax. Behind them, Lauriana, Ellie, and Marissya began to discuss wedding preparations.

Rain settled back in his chair and let the conversation flow over him. To his credit, he managed to sit through three-quarters of a bell of wedding plans before the first yawn hit him. He managed, admirably he thought, to stifle it, but Sol looked at him and grinned.

"Ellie girl, why don't you take your betrothed for a walk in the park? He looks like he could use some fresh air."

Rain was far too pleased with the idea of escaping the detailed discussion of flowers and color schemes to take offense at Sol's teasing.

The twins, who had been listening at the doorway, jumped into plain view. "Can we come to the park, too?" they asked in eager unison.

"Girls," Lauriana rapped in a stern voice.

"*Nei*. It is all right. They may come." Rain nodded at the young girls and hoped their presence would put Ellysetta at ease. His consideration earned him the silent laughter of the Fey warriors, who were amused their king would stoop to bringing infants along on his courtship. He deserved the teasing, of course. Courtship among the Fey was as much a masculine rite of passage as the Soul Quest and the Dance of Knives. Fey men vied openly with one another to prove their greater strength, bravery, and skill in all such rites. But Rain was the first Tairen Soul ever to claim a *shei'tani*, and he would shamelessly employ whatever methods he could to win her.

★ ★ ★

Ellie's quintet accompanied them, along with thirty other Fey who, fortunately, were little more than dark shadows that she glimpsed now and again as she, Rain, and the twins walked through the streets to the riverfront park a scant mile upstream from the National Museum of Art.

As could only be expected, they garnered a following of curious Celierians, all of whom were suddenly inspired to take in the view of the Velpin River at sunset.

Though the Fey warriors deterred the onlookers from venturing too near, Ellie was painfully aware of the many eyes focused on her party as they made their way to the park. The stares made her realize just whose company she was keeping, and how inadequate and inexperienced she must seem to him.

"What are you thinking?" Rain asked after the silence between them had dragged on for several chimes.

"I was just thinking that I must seem very young to you," she admitted.

"*Aiyah*. Indeed you do."

"I'm sorry." She clasped her work-roughened hands before her and stared hard at her ragged fingernails. "I'm sure you would have preferred someone older, more experienced."

"*Nei*, you misunderstand. If anything, I envy you." When she cast him a startled, disbelieving glance, he nodded. "It is true. To you, everything is still fresh and new. That has its own appeal to someone like me. I had forgotten, you see, what wonder felt like. You have reminded me." He paused. "Those older, more experienced women, they have lost their wonder too, and in their endless searching for something to make them feel it again, they have let darkness into their souls. I would never prefer that."

They had reached the park, and with a natural courtly charm, Rain Tairen Soul opened the gate and ushered her into the park. Thick, green grass rolled out before them like a carpet, while brown graveled paths offered stately, symmetrical walks bordered by blooming flowerbeds and immaculate hedges. Benches sat in select locations alongside the river and beneath the shady canopy of sheltering trees. The clear, Fey-cleansed purity of the Velpin flowed past, singing its soft water music. Rain led her to the walk that bordered the steep granite embankment. There, they stood together and watched the Great Sun set over Celieria, while Lillis and Lorelle played Stones nearby.

"It is beautiful," Ellie murmured as the last golden-red rays of sunlight glimmered on the water.

"*Aiyah*. Celieria has always been beautiful."

As twilight settled over the city, the warm glow of candle-light rose up from thousands of street lamps to replace the brightness of the Great Sun. Once, long ago, the lamps had been lit by small armies of lamplighters carrying lit wicks from lamp to lamp, but now a Fey Fire-spell performed the task in one magical moment each evening. It was one of the gifts from the Fey, like the Velpin Water-cleansing spell, that had been bestowed centuries ago when Marikah vol Serranis became Celieria's queen.

"It's been a thousand years since last you were here," Ellie said. "What was it like then?"

"Not so different from now. Many of the buildings are new, which I would expect, given all the years that have passed, but the city itself remains remarkably unchanged. Except, of course, there are no Elden Mages wandering the streets and working their evil in the palace, thank the gods. And the only Fey here are the ones that came with Maris-sya."

"Do the Fey despise all Eld, or just the Mage families?"

He gave her a sharp look. "Why do you ask?"

She shrank back from the suspicion in his eyes and the sudden frightening fierceness of his expression. "N-no particular reason," she stammered. "I was just curious. A number of Eld families have come to live in Celieria over the last few decades—none from Mage lines, of course—but they've always been quite nice to me."

His hand shot out to capture hers. "Who? Who are these Eld you have befriended?"

Shocked, she tried to pull her hand away. "I haven't befriended any of them," she protested. It wasn't technically a lie. Selianne wasn't Eld, she was Celierian born and bred. "And even if I had, it wouldn't be your business."

"You are my truemate. Any Eld folk who've befriended you are utterly my business. Give me their names, Ellysetta." When she set her jaw and remained stubbornly silent, his eyes narrowed. "Must I summon Marissya?"

Fear shot into Ellie's heart at the thought of the Truthspeaker invading her mind and stripping her soul bare, but even that frightening threat wasn't enough to make Ellie betray her dearest friend. Her spine went stiff. "If you ever order the *shei'dalin* to Truthspeak me, I assure you, I will never accept your bond."

Rain released her hand as if it burned him and spun away.

Bel, who had fallen back to give them a measure of privacy, took one look at their set, angry faces and stepped forward to mend the breach. "Ellysetta, *kem'falla*, you must understand, we have dealt with the Eld for centuries before you were born. The Feyreisen has only your safety at heart. The Eld can do you great harm."

"Because the Mages soul-bind their followers to them," Rain snarled, "enslaving them for their own evil purposes. Once a soul is claimed by the Mages, that person's will is no longer his own. A man would slay his own parents, even his own children, if the Mages ordered him to do so."

A muscle flexed in Rain's jaw. Not even to please his *shei'tani* would he abandon a millennium of suspicion and outright hatred for all things Eld. What the Eld touched, they corrupted. Even an Eld who loved Ellysetta the woodcarver's daughter could be turned into a tool for the Mages to use against Ellysetta the Tairen Soul's mate. Through Ellysetta, the Mages could strike a mortal blow to the entire Fey race.

"Promise me you will not go near anyone with Eld blood, especially not someone born in that cursed land." His voice was a whip cracking with the demand for complete obedience.

"But—"

"*Nei!* You are innocent of the evil in the world, Ellysetta. You have no idea what the Mages are capable of, what they will do to accomplish their goals." Her chin was set stubbornly, and Rain forced himself to take a deep breath. For thousands of years, the daughters of Celieria had been taught obedience from the cradle. How was it that his *shei'tani* was the one Celierian girl in the whole miserable kingdom who had *not*? "Ellysetta . . . *shei'tani* . . . I am sorry I threatened to summon Marissya. I should not have done so. But promise me you will never again go near these Eld. The danger is too great. Even to them. Your presence would bring them to the attention of the Mages."

Her out-thrust chin lowered. Uncertainty crept into her expression. That possibility had obviously not occurred to her. "They would be in danger because of me?"

"The gravest danger."

Tears filled her eyes. She blinked them back quickly, but he saw them. And the sight nearly broke his heart. "You have my word," she vowed, her voice barely audible.

"*Beylah vo.* Thank you." He reached out, wanting to comfort her and mend the breach between them, but she turned away and took a quick step to avoid his touch. He grimaced. Less than one day into his courtship and he'd already all but alienated his *shei'tani* completely. Marissya would scorch his ears if she knew how badly he was bungling.

Gravel crunched beneath his booted heel as he turned, looking for something, anything, to distract Ellysetta. His eyes fell upon the twins, who had ceased playing Stones and were now begging Kieran and Kiel to show them some Fey magic.

"So you would like to see Fey magic, would you?" The forced heartiness in his own voice sounded false to Rain's ears, but the twins didn't seem to notice. Their eyes lit up and their little mouths curved wide in eager grins.

"Oh, yes, My Lord Feyreisen! Please!"

"My name is Rain. You may call me that." He held out his hands to them. "Come, I will show you some magic my father once showed me."

"You have a father?" Lorelle took his hand without hesitation, though Lillis held back.

"I did. He died in the Mage Wars along with so many of my people. His name was Rajahl vel'En Daris. He was a Tairen Soul, like me." He remembered his father as a proud, somber man, devoted to his mate, his son, and the protection of the Fey. What gentleness his father had retained was reserved for his family, and Rain still treasured the memory of his father's rare, beautiful smiles and his even rarer laughter.

"He died with your mother, the Lady Kiaria, at the Battle of Torrin's Pass," Ellie said.

Rain shot her a startled look. "*Aiyah*. He did, though I am surprised you know of it. Torrin's Pass was a terrible battle, but very small. I would not have thought it made the history books."

"It didn't, at least not as more than a footnote. I read about it in an old book of Fey poetry."

"Ellie reads lots of Fey poetry," Lillis offered, now venturing to put her small hand in his.

"She's read lots and lots about you," Lorelle informed him. "And she knows the poem *Rainier's Song* by heart. *All* of it." Which, apparently, was an amazing feat.

"Does she?" Rain's brows arched. Though lamplight made it difficult to be certain, he thought his *shei'tani* was blushing. He opened his Fey senses and became certain. She was blushing, furiously. Curious. "I am not familiar with this poem."

Relief at his ignorance warred with shock on Ellysetta's face. It was as if he'd admitted to some terrible crime not to know the poem. "It's one of the most famous poetic works in Celierian history," she exclaimed. "Required reading in all Celierian schools."

"Ah." There was a poem, about him he assumed, that was required reading in all Celierian schools. Incredible.

«They have put the poem to music, theater, opera, and ballet as well.» Bel's amused voice sounded in his mind.

Rain shot his friend a dark look before turning his attention back to Ellysetta. "Then, of course, I must hear this poem. Would you recite a little?"

Ellie shook her head, avoiding his gaze. "I don't have the voice to do it justice."

"Yes, you do!" Lillis exclaimed.

"She performed it at the All Souls' Eve pageant at our school just last fall," Lorelle added.

"So what is this magic your father showed you, My Lord Feyreisen?" Ellie asked quickly.

"Rainier, please. Or Rain. Or *shei'tan*, if you prefer." In a rare show of tairen-mischief, his lips curved up at the corners. "Else I'll insist you recite this poem."

Ellie's breath caught in her throat. The tiny smile softened the coldness of his face; the sparkle of mischief warmed his eyes. His legendary Fey beauty stunned her senses, but it was the unexpected flash of gentle, laughing humanity that stole a place in her heart.

"Rain," she whispered.

His eyes flared bright. She gasped and pressed a hand to her pounding heart. In an instant, the world ceased to exist except for him. He wasn't touching her, and yet she knew he was clutching her to him with every Fey sense he possessed.

Then, abruptly, she was free, her knees so weak she thought she might collapse.

"*Sieks'ta*. I'm sorry," he muttered, dragging a hand through his hair. "Your father was right to complain about my lack of control." He grimaced, then forced a pleasant expression on his face and took the twins' hands again. "Come.

I will show you this magic. I think you will like it." He escorted them to a riverside bench partially secluded by the long, leafy branches of a burlwood tree, and stood beside the bench as Ellie and the twins sat. Bel and the rest of his quintet formed a protective semicircle behind them.

"Watch the river," Rain instructed. He raised his hands and summoned Water and Fire, easily blending the weaves until spouts of crystalline water fountained up in the center of the river, each fountain lit from within by various colors of Fire.

At his command, Fire and Water danced together in the shimmering patterns of Cha Baruk, the Dance of Knives. A circle of five fountains splashed in perfect symmetry. They sprayed up in a bright flare of light, whirled, and began to move in a perfect circular clockwise motion. A tiny bright blue spurt of water jumped from across the circle, looking exactly like a glowing dagger tossed across a small distance. Another blue blade of water was returned. The number of water blades increased, cartwheeling across the center of the circle until Fire and Water formed a glowing dome of flashing blue lights performing a stunning aerial display.

Water-blades still flying, the five fountains split into five new circles, each with its own dome of flashing Fire-lit Water-knives in a different color, while the blue blades, increasing exponentially in number, continued to dance from circle to circle. The twenty-five fountains became a hundred twenty-five, and now there were thousands of Fire-lit Water-blades flashing an endless rainbow of colors.

Crowds had gathered on both sides of the river and on the bridges to watch the Tairen Soul work his magic. Ellie and the twins gaped at the incredible display in awestruck silence.

Rain shifted the weave from the fierce exuberance of the Cha Baruk to the gently flowing Felah Baruk, the Dance of Joy. The Cha Baruk fountains subsided, and ten new fountains arose to dance in an interweaving loop. Five tall, fierce jets of water circled five gently arcing fountains that twirled slowly within the weave. Watching, Ellie could almost see Fey women bending and swaying seductively as their fierce suitors paid court.

Each twirling fountain, orbited by its fierce protector, danced in an ever tightening ring until they all merged into a single huge plume of water from which rose a blaze of Fire in the shape of a tairen rampant. Burning white, then red, then purple, the Fire tairen roared at the onlookers and lit up the night sky with an exploding blossom of flame before sinking back into the shrinking fountain and disappearing beneath the surface of the river. The light of Fire slowly faded, and the water grew still once more.

After a moment of utter silence, thunderous applause exploded from all sides of the river. Lillis and Lorelle jumped up and down, clapping their hands and clamoring for more. Ellysetta sat in stunned silence, feeling her heart clench into a tight knot.

"You must be very powerful."

Ellie didn't realize she had spoken aloud until Rain replied, "All men of the Fey are powerful, but I am the Tairen Soul, Defender of the Fey. A Tairen Soul is a master of all Fey magics." He looked out over the night-darkened river, glimmering now only with the golden lights of the lamps that lined the streets and bridges. "And I am a very powerful Tairen Soul."

He stood so straight, so tall. So alone. A bulwark of strength standing between his people and the world. Though he had not said as much in words, his skills set him apart, made him different from everyone around him. She knew what it meant to be different. Even when she was among those who loved her most, there was always a part of her that felt lonely, outside the close bond of sameness that everyone else seemed to share.

She reached out and took his hand. She felt him tense as her fingers closed around his; then he gave a little shudder and pulled her to her feet so he could wrap his arms around her. Need and violent passion raged in him, but she felt him battle it back, control it, cage it. That took strength, too, she realized. Immense strength, which he exerted with such fierce will because he did not want to frighten her. She feared both his magic and the savageness that lived in his soul, could not imagine ever having access to such seemingly limitless power, but she also understood what it was to be alone and to long for acceptance and the warmth of a loving embrace.

Her prayer went up, silent but heartfelt, *Dear gods, grant him peace.*

His body went stiff, then trembled faintly. When she would have pulled back in concern, his arms clutched her tight. "*Nei, shei'tani*, do not leave me just yet. Let me hold you a while longer." She felt his lips press against her hair, felt his need for her down to her soul, and for this moment in time she did not feel alone.

They stood there by the Velpin for many long, silent chimes, the woodcarver's daughter and the man who had once almost destroyed the world, the man whose face was now drawn in lines of mingled joy and anguish.

CHAPTER NINE

Ellie wandered, blind and searching, through a dark, black cavern lit only by the faint light of distant flickering fires. The air was hot and heavy, burning her lungs so that her breath rasped harshly in the tomblike silence. Perspiration beaded on her skin.

A rustle sounded down one wide tunnel, a growl, low and dangerous. Fear skated across her nerves, but she followed the sound, drawn to it against her will. Something hissed behind her, making her jump. She turned, squinting into the shadows, but if something was there she could not see it. Heart pounding, she continued forward, one shaky step after another, down a black, twisting tunnel, using the feel of rough rock beneath one hand to guide the way. The glow of red-orange light grew brighter.

Without warning, the dark tunnel opened up to a wide, deep cavern. There, in the flickering shadows beside a river of molten lava, a great black tairen crouched over a torn, bloody carcass, feeding. The carcass moved. A human hand lifted weakly. A ravaged face turned to her. Selianne's blue eyes stared out at her through rivulets of thick, dark blood.

Ellie woke with a sudden jerk and a ringing cry, sitting up and gasping for air.

She was at home, in her bedroom. To her surprise, soft morning sunlight streamed through her bedroom window. Usually her nightmares came in the deepest dark of night, not so close to dawn.

"Ellysetta! *Kem'falla*, are you all right?" Belliard's voice sounded outside her door.

She didn't answer right away. *Blessed gods, what a nightmare.* All Rain Tairen Soul's talk of Eld, death, and dark magic last night must have frightened her more than she'd known.

The door rattled with the force of Bel's staccato knocking. "Answer me, Ellysetta, or I will come in. Are you harmed? Should I call the Feyreisen?"

Before Ellie could answer, she heard her mother's voice. "What it is? What's wrong?"

"I'm fine," Ellie called, hoping to allay their concern. She threw off the covers, dragged a robe over her nightgown and opened her bedroom door to let Belliard and her mother see for themselves. "I'm fine," she repeated. "It was just a nightmare."

Lauriana tugged the belt of her robe. "Another bad one?" she asked cautiously. It hurt Ellie to see the fear, so long absent, back in her mother's eyes.

"I'm sure it's just all the excitement from the last few days." Heightened emotions had always served as a catalyst to nightmares—and other things—in the past.

Lauriana didn't ask what the nightmare had been about, and Ellie had long ago learned not to offer the information. Even when she'd been young, there were things she dreamed that no child should.

Her mother scowled and cast a dark look at Belliard. "I told your father nothing good would come of this. I told him letting these Fey remain beneath our roof was a bad idea, that the last thing you needed was to be around a bunch of magic-wielders, but did he listen?"

"Mama," Ellie interrupted. "You know you can't blame my nightmares on the Fey."

Her mother took a deep breath and clamped her lips

closed. Ellie could all but see her carefully tucking her fears away and forcibly reasserting her normal, steady calm. "You should dress, Ellie. There's much to be done today. And wear something nice. We'll be meeting the queen's personal dressmaker this morning so you can be measured for your wedding gown, as well as half a dozen of the queen's street merchants who'll supply the rest of what you'll need, and then we have an appointment with the Archbishop himself to plan your wedding ceremony." Lauriana gave Ellie a brisk kiss, sniffed at Belliard, and walked back down the short hall to her own bedroom.

The Fey remained where he was, his cobalt eyes intent and searching. "Will you tell me what you dreamed to cause such fear? Perhaps there is something I can do to help."

Considering the subject of her dream, she was even more loath to discuss it with him than with her mother. Telling Belliard about her nightmare could lead to unwelcome questions about Selianne. "I've had nightmares all my life, especially when I've had too much excitement in a day, as I have for the past few days. They mean nothing except that I don't get as much sleep as most Celierians." She forced herself to hold his gaze, but her smile refused to cooperate. It trembled traitorously until she gave up the attempt at false bravado and shrugged. "But thank you for your offer to help, Ser vel Jelani."

After a silent, searching moment, Belliard bowed. "I am Bel to you, *kem'falla*," he reminded her in a gentle voice. "My soul and my steel are pledged to your protection."

"*Beylah vo* is the Fey way of saying 'thank you,' isn't it?"

"It is."

She touched the back of his hand. "Then *beylah vo*, Bel. I appreciate your concern."

His fingers covered the spot she'd touched, and he gave her an odd little half smile. "You do that with so little effort, I can scarce fathom it."

"Do what?"

"Share the warmth of your soul." He tucked away his wonder, and his expression grew serious. "Not all magic is evil, *kem'falla*, despite what your mother believes. To the Fey, magic is a gift from the gods. Only the manner of its using can despoil it." His gaze shifted to a point past her head, and his eyes lightened once more. "Indeed, most magic is a thing of natural wonder and beauty."

She turned to follow his gaze, and her breath caught in her throat.

"What is that?" On the nightstand beside her bed, perched on a tasseled velvet pillow, a bright, spiraling weave of multicolored magic danced within a small, perfect crystal globe.

"A Fey courtship gift," Bel said. "I had thought all poetry had been scorched from Rain's heart by the Wars and Sariel's death, but I see I was wrong."

"What do you mean?"

"The gift is more than what it appears. As with all Fey courtship gifts, it is also a symbol. The deeper and more layered the meanings, the finer the gift. Rain has given you his magic, *kem'falla*, the essence of himself. An eternal fivefold weave of it, embraced forever in a fragile Celierian-made vessel. Strength wedded to vulnerability, magic to mortal craft, him to you. It sings so many different songs. It is a very fine gift, indeed." Bel turned his shining gaze upon Ellysetta. "And you, *kem'falla*, are the greatest gift of all. You breathe life back into the dying ember of our king's soul."

His expression grew somber. "If your nightmares persist, you must promise to tell me or your *shei'tan*. Not all dreams are harmless."

Ellie nodded. That was a truth she'd learned for herself long ago.

A few blocks from the warded and guarded Baristani home, a knock rapped on the front door of a small weaver's shop.

"A moment!" Maestra Tuelis Sebarre, recently ringed mas-

ter weaver, pulled her hair into an untidy knot and clattered
down the stairs from the private apartments above her shop.
What in the Bright Lord's name was someone doing pounding on her door at a quarter before seven bells? It was not as
if normal folk ever woke possessed with a sudden and driving
need to purchase a length of fine cloth.

Maestra Sebarre unlatched but did not unchain her door
and frowned irritably through the three-inch crack at the
man standing on her stoop. Dazzling white teeth flashed in a
dark, well-oiled beard threaded with gold rings. He was a
fine-looking man, with lovely bright blue-green eyes, but
Tuelis was no fool woman to judge a man by a pretty face.
She looked at the cuffs of his blue sea-captain's coat. The
weave was fine, smooth, tight, and unslubbed, the threads of
obvious quality, and the jacket cuffs showed no signs of fray-
ing about the edges. A merchantman, then, and successful
enough to keep himself in good thread.

"What can I do for you, ser?"

"You are Maestra Sebarre, the weaver?"

"I am."

"You have a daughter named Selianne?"

Wariness froze her. "Why do you ask?" Immediately on
the heels of wariness came dread, clenching Tuelis's innards in
an iron fist. "Has something happened to her?"

"What?" The captain evinced utter shock, then humble
contrition. "Oh, no, dear lady. Forgive me for giving you a
start. I simply meant to ascertain that I had the *right* Maestra
Sebarre." The man executed a deep, courtly bow. "I am Captain Batay. I sail a merchantman out of Sorrelia. Forgive such
an early intrusion, but my ship sails at noontide today. At dinner last evening, I heard tales that you could work magic with
a loom. There are nobles in Sorrelia who'll pay a fine price
for quality fabrics, and I still have enough room in my hold
for a dozen bolts or so. I thought I'd seek you out and glance
over your wares, Maestra." The handsome smile widened. "If
you'd care to let me into your shop, that is."

Tuelis didn't unchain the door. "Who was it sent you my way?"

"A gentleman who'd purchased a parlor suite from a local woodcarver, a Master Baristani, who used your fabric for the cushions." When the chain still remained firmly in place, the Sorrelian's smile disappeared. "Forgive me. It's obvious I've intruded with my too early call. The gentleman gave me another master weaver's name as well. A Master Frell. I will try him instead."

Tuelis bit her lip. A dozen bolts would bring a sizable sum of cash. Careful as she was, being a woman alone now that her husband was dead and her daughter Selianne wed and gone, Tuelis was too much a businesswoman to let such an offer slip past. Especially if the business would then go to Frell, the smirking bloat toad. The Sorrelian was well dressed, after all, and he knew that Sol Baristani used Tuelis's cloth for his upholstery. "My pardon, Captain Batay. Of course, you may come in." The chain rattled as she unlatched it and opened the door.

"My thanks." The captain entered the small shop.

Tuelis closed the door behind him. "What would you like to see first? Brocade? Velvet? Or something finer? I've just finished a bolt of spider-silk in a Celierian blue so rich you'd think I'd woven the sky itself."

"To be honest, Tuelis, my pet, what I really want to see is your obedience."

"What?" she gasped in affront. Captain Batay turned to her, his dazzling smile now cold and dreadful. Tuelis fell back a step, pressing a hand against her chest where a long-forgotten ache began to throb. "No! Oh, no!" The sea captain's striking blue-green eyes darkened to deep, shadowy pits that flashed with red lights.

She managed one, two racing steps towards the door, but Captain Batay moved with inhuman swiftness. His bronzed hand, circled with deceptively beautiful blue cuffs, slapped against the door. In her mind, a cold, insistent voice called her name, demanding submission. The pain in her chest grew sharper, and a foreign yet horribly familiar black malevolence consumed her, engulfing her in an icy darkness she hadn't felt since her early childhood in Eld.

Tuelis had one final, desperate thought before her consciousness fell to total subjugation. *Selianne! Dearling, what have I done?*

Several bells later, bright, late-morning sunlight streamed through the curtained windows of Rain's palace suite, casting ribbons of warmth across his skin. Rain lay in his too soft Celierian bed and stared blindly at the velvet canopies overhead. He'd only just awakened from the few snatched bells of restless sleep granted a courting Fey, and his mind whirled with a mix of shock and wonder that had nothing to do with the *shei'tanitsa* need humming through his veins.

For the first time in a thousand years, he had not dreamed.

Not of the Wars. Not of the dead.

Not of Sariel.

How was it possible? Rain sat up and swung his legs over the side of the mattress. He remembered last night, holding Ellysetta beside the riverbank and wondering at the flood of peace that almost made him weep in her arms.

Cautiously he checked the internal barricades that held back the sorrows of all those millions of souls whose weight he carried on his own. The barriers were still in place, and behind them, the torment of a thousand years still throbbed—yet the familiar pain seemed muted now, the burden lighter.

Ellysetta had healed his soul, just as she'd healed Bel's. Not completely—that would have been beyond miraculous—but to a greater degree than Marissya's substantial *shei'dalin* powers or even tairen song had managed over the years. And she'd done it without even trying, in one brief moment of communion.

Who was she? No simple Celierian, that was certain. But if not that, then who? *What?*

He sent a thread of Spirit across the city. *«Bel?»* He didn't even have to ask the question. Bel knew him too well.

«We are on our way to the cathedral to meet with her family's priest and the Archbishop. She is well.»

«I must meet with Dorian this morning. I will join you when I can.» And because he could not help it, Rain sent another thought along a different path. *«Shei'tani.»* He felt her sudden alertness, sensed the moment of fear followed by the hesitant happiness. She didn't like that he could send his thoughts to her, and yet she was glad he did.

«My lord?» It was a tentative mental touch at best, a whisper unbacked by power. It barely reached him. Yet because it was *her* whisper, it sounded in his mind with the force of a gong. His body clenched, his need for her deep and strong and instant.

He felt the jumbled heat of her emotions and knew that half a city away his desire was lapping over, making her nerves sing with awareness, demanding a response. Innocently, doubtlessly unable to prevent it, she did respond. Nectar-sweet, liquor-potent, her own awakening desires reached out with a delicate hand and gripped him with the strength of steel. He staggered from the impact of her untutored, unshielded emotions. He flung out his hand, fingers curling around the bedpost to steady himself, and sucked in a deep, ragged breath. *Gods have mercy.* Within him, the tairen stretched and dug its claws deep. He felt it reach for her, felt her quick flare of fear as she sensed it. He slammed down his mental barriers, groaned as he pitted his will against the tairen's and battled it back into submission.

«I will come to you soon, shei'tani,» he sent when he could, accompanying the thought with the mental projection of a kiss that he placed with warm promise on her lips.

How did he do that? Ellie touched her lips. The Spirit kiss had felt every bit as convincing as the real thing. She could even smell Rain's fresh, distinctive scent and feel the warmth of his arms pulling her close.

"I hope the meeting with Father Celinor and the Archbishop doesn't take too long," she said. She glanced at her mother as they walked down Celieria's busy streets. "I promised the girls I'd meet them in the park for a game of Stones."

"I still don't know why you made that promise, Ellie," Lauriana chided. "You knew how busy we were going to be today."

"I knew," Ellie agreed. "But I suspected I'd need a break after dealing with the queen's craftsmasters. And I was right."

Four unpleasant bells in the company of haughty dressmakers, cobblers, and clothiers had left Ellie aching to leap into the nearest hermit hole. Who knew wealthy people spent so much time in pursuit of the perfect outfit, or that there were so many decisions to be made for so simple a task? Until today, Ellie had never realized that the number of buttons on a lady's boot held some particular social significance. Gods! What utter madness! Not to mention the fact that each and every one of the merchants had sniffed at her common appearance and made it clear they served her only because the queen had commanded them. The worst was Maestra Binchi, the queen's dressmaker, who had sized her up in one cold, calculating glance, sneered, and muttered something about silk purses and sowlet ears.

Lauriana shook her head. "You shouldn't have let them bother you, Ellie. They may be masters of their own crafts, and serving by appointment of the king or queen, but so is your father now. They're no better than you or I, even if they do have a bit more gold in their pockets. In fact—though I still think your father made a dreadful mistake—you're the betrothed of a king now. They should be thanking the gods for the opportunity to serve you."

Ellie didn't answer. Mama was very good at ignoring the opinions of others when it suited her. Ellie wasn't so lucky. She'd felt the dislike of those merchants crawling over her skin until she'd wanted to cry out that she had no more choice about being there than they did.

Ahead, the road curved to the right, and Celieria's Grand Cathedral of Light came into view. Built entirely of gleaming, hand-carved white marble and gold leaf, the Grand Cathedral stood testament to both the glory of the Bright Lord and the mastery of ancient Celierian, Fey, and Elvian artisans. Situated on the small Isle of Grace in the middle of the Velpin River, it rose up from the clear blue depths of the river like a palace of white clouds and sunbeams. Four gilded, sun-bright bridges radiated from the four corners of the island, connecting the holy site to the more mundane streets of the city.

Thirteen spires adorned the cathedral's golden roof, one for each of the major gods. The largest of the spires rose up on six marble columns from the top of the central dome. An enormous statue of Adelis, Lord of Light, stood in the center of those columns, arms upraised, holding aloft a golden crystal globe that blazed an eternal beacon.

Every time Ellie saw the cathedral, it both awed and frightened her. Even now, as she crossed the golden northeast bridge and climbed the thirteen steps leading up to the cathedral's Grand Entrance, her stomach roiled and her palms went clammy. She loved the Bright Lord, but his priests would forever be tied in her memory with the terror of her childhood exorcism.

Father Celinor, the priest from her family's West End church, was waiting in the covered portico just outside the cathedral doors. A young man with bright blue eyes and sandy hair that always seemed mussed, Father Celinor was the first cleric who'd ever managed to get past Ellie's terror of priests after her childhood exorcism.

"Madam Baristani." He held out his hands and exchanged the kiss of peace with Ellie's mother, then turned to her, smiling with genuine affection and welcome. "And Ellysetta." His fingers squeezed hers. "I never dreamed the Most High had such plans in store for you. This is your opportunity to share the Word of Light with those who have not heard its call."

Ellie gave a small laugh. "Let me find peace in my new life first, Father. But you may take comfort that the Fey already do follow the Bright Path."

"Of course." He patted her hand and smiled. "Come meet the Archbishop." He glanced at the Fey warriors. "I'm afraid canon law forbids you from entering the cathedral bearing arms. You must leave your blades at the door. There is a room there to the left where you may check them with Brother Vericel before entering."

"Fey protecting a *shei'tani* do not shed their steel," Bel replied.

"Then you must remain here, outside the sanctuary. Not even the King himself may carry weapons across this threshold. The Cathedral is a holy place, a haven of peace."

Bel exchanged a glance with the rest of Ellie's quintet. Without another word, all five removed their Fey'cha belts, the curved *meicha* at their waists, and the twin *seyani* swords strapped across their backs. They handed the weapons to their Fey brethren. Bel gestured, and all but Ellysetta's quintet and five other Fey fanned out to surround the cathedral.

"We will observe your custom," he conceded, "but no one will be permitted to enter or leave this building or island so long as the Feyreisa remains within."

Father Celinor's jaw went lax. He hurried to the top of the steps and gaped at the sight of Fey weaving magical barriers at the bridges. "You can't block access to the Isle of Grace! This is the Grand Cathedral of Light, a haven to all."

"So long as Celierian custom dictates that Fey steel must remain outside the cathedral while the Feyreisa stands within, *Fey* custom dictates that all haven-seekers will have to wait until she departs." Bel held the priest's shocked gaze without wavering. "As we honor your customs, you shall honor ours."

"I'm sorry, Father," Lauriana apologized in an aggrieved tone. "There is no reasoning with them when it comes to Ellie and what they perceive as ensuring her safety. I've concluded it's best to just humor their requests and ignore them as much as possible." She glowered at Bel.

"The Archbishop will not like this. He will not like this at all."

Ellysetta cleared her throat. "Perhaps, Father, you should introduce us to the Archbishop. The sooner we're done, the sooner the cathedral can return to normal."

The priest ran a hand through his hair, leaving the thick waves of gold-streaked brown in disarray. "Yes, well, I suppose you're right, Ellie. Follow me."

Ringed by her quintet, Ellysetta followed Father Celinor and her mother down the nave towards the large, ornate altar, towering alabaster luminary, and dual pulpits at the center of the cathedral. Behind the altar, a large wedge-shaped portion of the cathedral was reserved for seating clergy and choir, and several doors led to clerical offices and ceremonial chambers.

As they neared the altar, one of the doors opened and a stocky older man emerged. He wore the spotless, ankle-length white tunic and sleeveless, gold-trimmed blue robes of a Church of Light Archbishop. A scowl rode low on his brow.

"Celinor, I distinctly saw Fey warriors weaving magic outside my window."

"Greatfather, Mistress Baristani and her mother have arrived. The Fey escorting her would not remove their weapons without weaving magic around the Isle of Grace."

Bel bowed to the Archbishop. "The weaves are shields of protection, to ensure the safety of the Feyreisa, which you would not permit Fey steel to do," he explained.

If anything, Bel's comment only made the Archbishop's scowl deepen. "I do not approve. Rest assured, as soon as this meeting is over, I will request an audience with the king. I will not have cursed Fey magic stand between this church and the faithful."

Ellie bit her lip. For years now the Church had been growing less and less tolerant of magic in all its forms, a direct result of the sharp increase in the numbers of northern priests moving into positions of power in the Church's hierarchy. But until now, she'd never heard any priest in Celieria City—let alone the city's most senior cleric—openly condemn Fey magic as cursed. As the king himself wielded Fey magic, such a statement bordered on treason.

Bel executed a stiff bow. His eyes had gone flat and cold. "As you will, Excellency. But not even King Dorian can prevent the Fey from protecting our queen."

"Yes, well . . . er . . ." Father Celinor rubbed his hands together briskly. "Let's get on with the introductions, shall we?" He coughed and cleared his throat. "Ellysetta, Madam Baristani, it's my honor to introduce you both to His Excellency, Greatfather Tivrest, Archbishop of Celieria. Greatfather, this is Mistress Ellysetta Baristani, the Tairen Soul's betrothed, and her mother, Madam Lauriana Baristani, wife of master woodcarver, Sol Baristani. As I mentioned to you earlier, their family has been in my West End congregation since I first assumed my appointment there ten years ago."

"Greatfather." Ellysetta and Lauriana sank into deep curtseys.

"Madam Baristani, Mistress Baristani." The Archbishop laid a hand on each of their heads and murmured a blessing, then extended a loosely clenched fist for them to kiss the ring of office on his right thumb. When they straightened, he graced them both with a tight smile. "Well, Mistress Baristani, for the last two days you've caused quite a stir in the city, and I see the commotion is going to continue."

"So it seems, Greatfather," Ellie murmured.

"Hmph." The Archbishop straightened his robes. "First things first. The Bride's Blessing. The king has already informed me of your need for urgency. Though I emphatically do *not* approve of subverting Church protocol for personal whim, precedence does exist for . . . accelerating some of our lengthier ceremonies. It is not the preferred choice—the longer the devotions, the stronger the bond—but it can be done. I have agreed to perform the seven-day version of the

Blessing. Six days of devotion, followed by the Blessing on the seventh day."

"If you need more time, Greatfather, you must say so," Lauriana urged. "I would never forgive myself if any rush on our part weakened the effects of the Blessing."

The Archbishop missed the silent plea shining in Lauriana's eyes. "I wouldn't worry too much, Madam Baristani. Seven is a godly number, full of protection and strength." He turned to Ellysetta. "Who will stand as your Honoria, Mistress Baristani?" Every bride was accompanied at the Blessing by her mother and her Honoria, a married female relative or friend, who served as her attendant and guide in the purification ceremony.

"Oh, no question there, Greatfather," Lauriana answered before Ellysetta could speak. "Selianne Pyerson. Ever since childhood, she and Ellie have been close as two feathers on the same wing."

Ellie's eyes rounded. "Oh, um, Mama, I don't know if she can." She flicked a glance back towards Bel and the others and lowered her voice. "She's a bit . . . intimidated . . . by the Fey."

"Aren't we all," Mama muttered under her breath. Then a bit louder, "I'll send a boy round with a note later today. I'm sure she'll be honored to stand by you."

Ellie opened her mouth to protest again, then saw Bel watching. If she continued to protest, she'd just call undue attention to Selianne. She swallowed the objection quickly and forced a smile. "There's no one else in the world I'd rather have. We always vowed that whoever married first would serve as the other's Honoria."

"Excellent," the Archbishop said. "I'll need all three of you to meet me here at twelve bells on Kingsday for the initial consecration. You will continue to come at the same time every day until the six devotions are complete. On the seventh day, you will be ready for the Bright Bell. Please arrange to arrive no later than eleven bells, so you can begin the Bright Bell precisely at half eleven, when the Great Sun is approaching its zenith and the powers of the Solarus are at their height. If you are even a single chime late, the ceremony will have to be postponed for another day. Do you understand?"

"Yes, Greatfather."

"Good. Now, about the wedding ceremony itself . . ."

Rain strode down the corridor to King Dorian's private office on the second floor of the palace, where Dax and the king were waiting for him to join them. Annoura was in court, as was Marissya, protected for the moment by her own quintet rather than her mate. This meeting with Dorian was one Dax and Marissya had prompted, and Rain had reluctantly agreed to. If *dahl'reisen* had begun murdering Celierians in the north, the Fey must help put an end to it.

A pair of Royal Guardsmen flanked the door to the king's office. They bowed as Rain approached and granted him entrance, closing the door behind him. The office was a spacious, wood-paneled room, designed more for comfort and efficiency than pomp. Tall windows overlooked a view of the south gardens, their partially open, slatted wooden shutters admitting plenty of light while obstructing unwanted observation from below. A matching pair of golden leather armchairs faced the large, heavily carved desk that dominated the room.

King Dorian, standing near one of the windows, smiled pleasantly as Rain entered. "Greetings, my Lord Feyreisen. I hope you have found your palace accommodations acceptable." Rain gave a brief nod. "I regret putting you through that circus in the courts yesterday, but it was necessary. We are a country of laws, and even noble visitors must live by them. I trust the girl, your *shei'tani*, is fine and suffered no ill effects from the excitement?"

Rain's spine stiffened and his eyes narrowed. "She is well. I would not leave her were it otherwise." The implication was a grave insult.

Dorian blinked in bewilderment. "Yes, of course. I meant no offense."

«Celierians consider it polite to ask after the health of one's mate,» Dax murmured silently. *«It was the same, before the Wars.»*

Rain had a vague memory, long forgotten, of a similar incident many centuries past. *«I remember now. I didn't like it then either. They should take better care of their mates, so the question of their mates' health need never be in doubt.»*

With Dax's laughter rippling through his mind, Rain shook off his irritation and got straight to the purpose of the meeting. "I have come to discuss the situation in the north. Dax and Marissya tell me you believe *dahl'reisen* have begun murdering Celierians."

Dorian nodded. "There've been half a dozen attacks in the last two months, and twenty Celierians slain since First Moon this spring. Another ten since harvest last fall. Mostly farmers and village folk along the northern march. The Border Lords had been keeping the situation quiet, but now that the pamphleteers and newspapers have wind of it, all hope of quietly resolving the problem is gone." He explained about the witnesses and showed Rain the recovered Fey'cha. "Dax has already told me it's unlikely the blade was left behind by accident."

"Beyond unlikely," Rain agreed. "All blades forged in a Fey smithy have a weave spun into them so their owners may summon them back to their sheaths after use. The spell works on any blade within half a mile of its owner. It was either left deliberately as a challenge, or stolen and left to cast suspicion on the Fey." He examined the dagger and the name-mark forged on it. "I don't recognize this mark, but it does appear to be a true Fey'cha." *«Dax, send an image of the mark to all the Fey. See if any of them know it.»*

Turning his attention back to Dorian, he added, "As for witnesses to a *dahl'reisen* crime, that, too, is unlikely. *Dahl'reisen* live outside our laws. If it serves them to manipulate mortal minds, they would likely do so. Not even Marissya would be able to tell the false memories from the true ones. Still, you should bring the witnesses in for Truthspeaking, just in case they are using these rumors of *dahl'reisen* murders to hide their own crimes."

King Dorian shook his head. "Sebourne—the lord whose lands were attacked—has already refused. He says the witnesses are terrified of having their minds manipulated by the Fey, and he's angry enough over the number of murders on his land to support them." Dorian cast an apologetic glance Dax's way. To suggest that Marissya would misuse her powers was a grave insult.

"Is there a map that shows where the raids have taken place?" Rain asked.

"Here." Dorian walked around his desk and opened a narrow door in the corner of the far wall. "We started monitoring the incidents after the first half-dozen deaths last year." He pulled out a large map of Celieria mounted vertically on a wheeled spongewood backing. A handful of colored pins set with tiny annotated flags were scattered across the northern border. "Except for the fact that most of the raids have taken place in the villages along the Celierian-Eld border, there is no apparent pattern to the attacks."

Rain examined the collection of pins. The raids had taken place over a thousand miles of border land, ranging from Bolla near the eastern coast all the way to Toulon in the west.

"What would a band of *dahl'reisen* gain from slaughtering Celierian peasants?" Dorian asked. "That's what I cannot understand."

Rain cast a glance back over his shoulder. "Have you considered the possibility that it might not be *dahl'reisen*? Fey enemies are numerous, and as you know, the greatest of them lies just across your northern border."

The king's brows rose. "You think the Eld are behind this?"

"The possibility must at least be considered."

"But the Eld have no more reason to kill Celierian peasants than *dahl'reisen* do."

"Unless they mean to drive a wedge between Celieria and the Fading Lands. Celierians have rarely distinguished between Fey actions and those of the *dahl'reisen*. The Eld know that. They would use it to their advantage." Rain turned back to the map, frowning at the large expanse of border. "How many troops do you have on the border?" he asked.

"Two thousand, give or take a few hundred."

"That's not enough. You should have triple that number at least." Rain straightened and turned around. "I can offer two thousand Fey to ward the borders and track the attackers when they strike again."

Dorian's jaw sagged in surprise. Fey and mortal troops had not stood side-by-side along the Eld border in nine hundred years. Not since Celieria had reconstituted its military after the decimation of the Mage Wars. Fey had periodically quartered themselves in the border keeps to watch for signs of Eld magic and strengthen the wards put in place at the end of the Wars, but never more than that. The Mages had been defeated, and the Fey had withdrawn from the world.

"Your offer is . . . quite generous, My Lord Feyreisen, and an unexpected honor." Dorian cleared his throat. "I don't know what to say."

"I do not offer Fey lives or Fey steel lightly," Rain answered. "I have sensed a growing darkness in Eld. The Mages are at work again. It is one reason why I question whether the *dahl'reisen* are truly behind these raids of yours."

"Do you have proof of this Mage activity? Reports from spies?"

Rain raised a brow. "This I do not need. I sense the darkness, and that is enough."

"I see." Dorian drew a deep breath. "Well, unfortunately, the Council of Lords will require more than just Fey intuition before they authorize tripling the number of troops along our border, or quartering foreign warriors—especially Fey warriors, given the current suspicions about the *dahl'reisen*. Besides, the Eld would view a troop buildup as an act of open aggression.

"You must understand," he added when Rain's expression darkened, "our relations with the Eld have settled considerably in the last decades. In fact, the Elden ambassador was here not a fortnight ago seeking to recommence direct trade between our two countries. He spoke quite eloquently, and the terms he offered were very appealing."

Rain's hands fell to the silk-wrapped handles of the curved *meicha* at his hips. His fingers curled tight around the grips. "You let the Eld ambassador set foot on Celierian land?" he growled. "You're contemplating *trade* with those black-souled vermin?" The windows of Dorian's office rattled in their panes.

The king cast a confused glance in Dax's direction. "We've been trading with them indirectly for more than three centuries . . . ever since the Great Plague threatened the mortal world. They possess the only supply of keio, one of the ingredients required for the cure. We still purchase it yearly through Sorrelian intermediaries, along with a few other goods."

«*Dax . . .* » Rain hissed with silent fury.

«*You had only just regained your sanity. Marissya and I both agreed it was best you did not know. Thousands—hundreds of thousands—had already died. Millions more would have. There weren't enough healers to have stopped it.*»

«*And after . . . when I no longer teetered on the brink of insanity?*»

«*They'd been trading for years by then, with no ill effects . . . and there remained occasional threats of the plague returning. We didn't see any harm in letting it continue.*»

Rain shook his head in disbelief and turned his attention back to Dorian. "You Celierians with your short life spans. The Mage Wars are naught but a distant dream to you, a conflict that happened so many generations in the past it has no bearing on the present. But the Fey fought those wars. We died by the thousands, hideously, in those wars. We remember." He speared Dax with another hot glance. "At least most of us do. We still mourn our dead. The Eld are not to be trusted. Ever!"

"Rain—" Dax held out his hands. "There has been no trouble with the Eld since the Wars. Perhaps Dorian's advisors are right . . . perhaps it is time to heal the wounds."

"Your own mate's sister died at their hands. Her brother became *dahl'reisen*—forever banished from the Fading Lands—because of what he did in vengeance. You dare say this to me? Trade with the black-souled practitioners of Azrahn?"

"It is because of Marikah, because of Gaelen, that I do feel free to speak," Dax returned. "They are gone from the Fey forever. Nothing can bring either of them back to us. But the Mage Wars were a millennium ago. And the Mages were all but destroyed. You saw to that. The other Eld, those not from Mage families, they don't practice Azrahn."

"It only takes one."

«Know your enemy, Tairen Soul. Opening the borders to trade gives us an opportunity to introduce our own eyes and ears into Eld. They can find the proof Dorian needs.»

«Never will I willingly put another Fey life within reach of Eld evil. The darkness is there. It grows. Opening the borders does not help us. It endangers us all the more.»

"Dax is right," Dorian said. "The Mage Wars were a thousand years ago—provoked by a senseless assassination that snowballed into full-scale war thanks to Gaelen vel Serranis's excessive vengeance."

"The assassination," Rain answered with clenched jaw, "was not senseless. It was retaliation by the Eld for a wound your ancestors delivered two thousand years earlier. The Eld don't forget. And they count on the fact that you do!"

"I think perhaps you lack objectivity in this situation. You suffered a great many personal losses in the Wars. You hate the Eld. You'll never see them as anything but enemies."

"Because that is all they will ever be!"

"My advisors," Dorian said, "see this opportunity as a way to provide a needed boost to our economy. As do many of the nobles on the Council of Lords."

"Your advisors," Rain retorted, "and your nobles are greedy fools. When an evil man dangles a heavy purse before you, beware. Have you never learned that?"

"When his children are hungry, a desperate man will do desperate things," the king countered. "The last year has not been easy. Droughts and floods ruined most of last year's crops. Even with the help the Fey provided to manage the weather, our stockpiles of food are nearly depleted. If this year's harvests are not plentiful, there will be starvation come winter."

If Rain could promise Fey help to bring fertility to the Celierian fields, he would. But any such promise would be a lie. Fertility was a woman's gift, and the Fey women had been barren for centuries. "I can send warriors to you, ones strong in Earth, Water, and Air. They can help manage the weather and bring the nutrients in the soil closer to the surface." Fey with Earth magic could create food, but not on a scale large enough to feed Celieria for a winter. Aiding the world in performing its natural functions would produce greater results.

"And in return?"

"Cease your trade with Eld. Do not open the borders. That way is dangerous, the threat far greater than starvation, even if you do not see it."

Dorian turned to Dax. "Lord Dax, I have known you and my aunt all my life. I trust and value your opinion, yet never once have either of you mentioned the possibility of a revived Mage threat in Eld. Why is that?"

Dax didn't answer. Instead, he looked at Rain.

"Marissya and Dax don't sense the darkness," Rain bit out. "Only I do."

Dorian's expression went blank, as if a shutter had been drawn closed. "I see."

"Marissya Truthspoke Rain before we left the Fading Lands," Dax said. "There is no doubt of his honesty."

"Forgive me," Dorian replied, "but as we all know, Truth-speaking only guarantees that the one being Truthspoken believes what he says. It doesn't guarantee that what he believes is true. The distinction may be small, but in this case vital—as I'm sure you agree, or we would not be having the conversation."

Dax's gaze dropped. Fey did not lie. He could not dispute Dorian's conclusion.

Rain swallowed a bitter curse, hating the Celierian for his blind determination to believe the Eld and doubt the Fey. Hating himself for being unable to offer proof or control his temper long enough to make Dorian see reason. Hating the fear that perhaps Dax and Dorian were right, and there was no darkness, only Rain's old companion, insanity, toying with him again.

He couldn't say why he sensed what no one else did. He only knew he did. Perhaps it was all those Mage souls anchored to his own. Perhaps it was because he was a Tairen Soul, and they were not. Perhaps it was because he had spent seven hundred years tormented by madness, his mind a wide-open field upon which all the millions he'd killed trampled without restraint.

Whatever the cause, he knew he was right. Believed it with unswerving certainty. The Mages had regained their power, and the world was in danger once more.

"Believe me delusional if you like, King Dorian, but protect yourself in case I am not. Keep your borders closed. You've survived a thousand years without the Eld. Surely you can survive a few more. At least give me time to gather the proof you require."

"I will consult my advisors. The Eld treaty is scheduled for debate in the Council of Lords next week. We will discuss your concerns, so the lords may take them into consideration before they cast their vote."

"This is not a matter for your advisors and Council to decide, King Dorian," Rain countered. "The monarchy did not give up all of its power when the Council of Lords was established. Invoke *primus*. Make the decision yourself, and keep your borders closed."

Dorian drew back. "*Primus* is a king's tool of last resort," he answered in a low voice. "It is not to be invoked except in cases of utmost urgency. To use it carelessly is to tread the path of tyranny."

"Tyranny?" Rain echoed in disbelief. "It is not tyranny for a king to command the defense of his country and keep his borders closed to his enemies."

Dorian shook his head and heaved a sigh. "You have been too long away, Rainier Feyreisen. The Eld are not the enemies they once were, and I will not invoke *primus* on the basis of groundless speculation and hard feelings. The Lords of Celieria will debate the issue." He held up a hand to forestall Rain's next objection. "And unless you can provide definitive proof to the contrary, *they* will make the decision, not I."

Rain's jaw clenched. Had this fool heard nothing? The Eld were dangerous! They greeted you with friendship, wormed past your defenses, gained your trust, and only revealed the dagger of betrayal as it was plunged into your vitals. Darkness was growing in Eld. The Eld were once again forming ties to Celieria. And Rain had claimed a mate with a Celierian family. It was as if history were repeating itself, only this time the Fey might be too weak to prevail.

"Then think on it and have your debate, Dorian vel Serranis Torreval, but while you do, think also on this." His eyes narrowed, glowing so fiercely Dorian's face was bathed in lavender light. "If you open your borders to the Eld, you terminate your alliance with the Fey." With a final glare for Dorian and Dax, Rain spun on one booted heel and stalked out.

Dorian frowned after the Feyreisen's rapidly departing figure.

"The tairen are creatures of great power and great ferocity," Dax murmured. "So, likewise, are the Tairen Souls, and with them temper is always closer to the surface than with other Fey. It is worse for our king, because of *shei'tanitsa*."

Dorian turned and gave Dax a cool look. "You should never apologize for your king."

"I do not apologize, bond-nephew. I merely explain."

Ellie glanced at her escort of sword-bristling shadows and sighed. She'd hoped to enjoy a quiet outing in the park with her sisters before completing the rest of her day's obligations, but "quiet," it seemed, was a quality she'd lost when she'd inadvertently called Rain Tairen Soul out of the sky.

Despite her objections, all thirty of the warriors who'd accompanied her this morning had insisted on following her to the park as well. They'd posted themselves throughout the park and surrounding streets, drawing all manner of attention and increasing the crowds of curious bystanders. It was just as well Mama had stayed behind at the Grand Cathedral with Father Celinor to discuss the upcoming ceremonies in more detail and make her daily devotions. She'd have curled up in shame over the attention such a conspicuous Fey presence was drawing.

On the bright side, at least the twins were having fun. Earlier, Kieran had made them toys out of Earth magic—a little bear that walked and roared, a tiny kitten that sat in the palm of Lorelle's hand and meowed sweetly, a small yellow bird that tweeted when Lillis stroked its silky feathers. In return, the twins brought their own little gifts to Kieran—a gaily painted wooden top their father had made, a small rag doll with red yarn hair and green button eyes.

He accepted the gifts, to the girls' delight, and let the teasing of his fellow Fey roll off his back. He was courting a pair of infants, the warriors joked, and the infants were courting him back. Lorelle hadn't taken too kindly to being called an infant, and had promptly and fiercely set the record straight. The warriors now bowed and called her "Little Fey'cha" just as the blond warrior Kiel did, which seemed to suit Lorelle just fine.

A delicate, tinkling laugh chimed, and Ellie groaned. The day had just gone from bad to worse. She tracked the familiar laugh back to a crowd of twittering local beauties drawn by all the handsome Fey warriors in the park. In the midst of the crowd stood Ellie's nemesis, the golden-haired, Fey-beautiful Kelissande Minset. Her large, limpid blue eyes, exactly the same pure blue as a summer sky, flirted beneath thick rows of fluttering brown lashes. The delicate heart-shaped face and lush red lips that had brought countless suitors calling over the years now smiled invitingly at the Fey.

Ellie couldn't prevent the stab of envy she felt any more than she could have stopped the pang of wistfulness. She had always longed for a complexion as smooth and creamy as the one Kelissande guarded beneath a wide-brimmed hat and delicate blue parasol, for a figure as petite and curvaceous as the one so exquisitely displayed in a form-fitting powder-blue gown of Capellan silk overlaid with delicate Elvian lace.

Ellie watched from the corner of her eye as Kelissande sauntered towards her. Ellie was instantly and painfully aware of the grass stains on her skirts, the sturdy woolen cloth and simple cotton of her navy dress and white chemise, and the unruly hair that had snuck free of its plait to wave in wild tendrils about her face.

"Hello, Ellie." Kelissande's voice was a honeyed whisper, a perfection of sound cultivated by years of speech tutoring.

"Hello, Kelissande."

"I heard the most amazing story," Kelissande announced, "but I didn't believe it was true until just now." She eyed Bel, Rowan, and Adrial and flashed them a beguiling smile. "People are saying that a Fey warrior has claimed you as his mate."

"The Feyreisen has claimed her," Bel corrected before Ellie could answer. "More than just a warrior." He took a step closer to Ellysetta.

She looked up at him in surprise. His face was expressionless, his eyes flat. That was when she became aware of the tension that tingled in the air. The humor that had danced so subtly between the warriors only moments before was completely erased. Ellie blinked. The Fey were not watching Kelissande with the goggle-eyed admiration Ellie expected. Rather, they had once again affected the stone-faced demeanor that had become as much a hallmark of Fey warriors as the weapons that adorned them. How odd.

Kelissande appeared blithely unaware that she was surrounded by lethal killers. "The Tairen Soul? Isn't he the crazy one who almost destroyed the world?"

Irritation flashed. "He's not crazy." Ellie got to her feet. "Girls, would you like to play Stones?"

"Yes! Yes!" The twins jumped up and raced off to round up a group of local children.

"Will you join us, Kelissande?" Ellie asked politely, though only because she was certain of refusal.

The West End's reigning beauty did not disappoint her. Giving a delicate shudder, Kelissande declared, "And ruin my dress playing a silly child's game? Of course not. Unlike some girls I could name, I'm too mature for such nonsense."

"That's right," Ellie murmured, her hand closing about the hilt of the dagger at her waist. "You're older than I am. Your twenty-fifth birthday is only a few weeks away, isn't it?"

"Four months," Kelissande snapped.

Ellie shook her head. "Who'd ever have thought I would be wed before you?"

"I'm still trying to decide which of my ten suitors to select." Kelissande closed her parasol with a quick jerk. "And who'd ever have thought you, Ellie Spindle-Shanks, would have any suitors at all? Let alone two. Of course, calling a crazy half-man and that loathsome little slug Den Brodson 'suitors' may be a bit of a stretch."

Well. Ellie had definitely managed to ruffle Kelissande's feathers. It had been a long time since the lovely Miss Minset had struck out at her with such a lack of finesse. Surprisingly, the insult didn't cause even the tiniest wound.

Suddenly Kelissande's eyes went wide. "By the gods, who is *that*?"

Ellysetta glanced over her shoulder and saw Rain Tairen Soul striding boldly down the street. Sunlight glinted on the myriad blades bristling from his black leathers, and his long hair blew back off his fiercely handsome face as he walked.

A thrill of pride coupled with the swift bite of desire shivered up Ellie's spine. She straightened to her full height. "That," she replied, "is the crazy half-man who has claimed me."

"He is magnificent." The words were a bare whisper. Ellie doubted Kelissande even realized she had spoken aloud. Her dazzled blue eyes seemed to drink in the sight of Rain as he approached. She turned to Ellie and smiled. "You must introduce him to me."

Ellie's satisfaction shriveled to a heavy rock that sank to the pit of her stomach. Never once in her life had she known Kelissande not to get her way when she had that hungry, determined look in her eye, and now Kelissande wanted to meet Rain? Ellie wanted to scream "No!", rip out Kelissande's silky blond hair, and scratch her perfect skin.

"Of course," she replied politely. And she wondered how she would survive the torment of Kelissande Minset's perfect beauty calling Rain's attention to Ellie's many physical flaws.

Rain sensed his *shei'tani's* unhappiness as he drew near. Her gentle face, with its dusting of golden freckles and large, expressive eyes, was set in a carefully composed mask, and the glowing aura of compassion and fresh innocence that called so sweetly to his ancient soul was dimmed. Something had wounded her tender heart. Or *someone*, he corrected when Ellysetta quietly introduced him to the sun-haired woman beside her. The blond girl was physically beautiful, but darkness hung about her like a shroud.

"Hello," the young woman purred.

"Mistress Minset." He did not bow. Somehow she was to blame for his truemate's distress. Such a woman would receive no honor from him. He turned to Ellysetta. *"Shei'tani."* His voice was a caress. He did not touch her—it was not the Fey way. But he reached out to her with a warm weave of Spirit. «*What has made your heart sad?*» When she did not reply, he sent the same question to Bel.

«*The golden one with the dark soul said unkind things and took the laughter from your shei'tani's eyes,*» Bel replied with disgust. «*We did not know what to do.*» Had Kelissande Minset been a man, she would have found herself facing bared Fey'cha steel. But she was a woman, and no Fey warrior would ever harm even a dark-souled female except to save lives.

"Come on, Ellie!" A chorus of childish voices called out from a short distance away.

"I'm coming!" Ellysetta called back. To Rain, she said, "The children and I were just about to play a game of Stones." She paused in the process of turning away. Hesitant invitation and uncertainty flickered in her gaze. "Would you . . . like to join us?"

A harsh, mocking laugh rang out. "For the gods' sake, Ellie, he's a king," Kelissande sneered. "Kings don't play Stones in the park with a bunch of filthy peasant children."

Rain saw embarrassment redden Ellysetta's cheeks. "I'm sorry," she said. "I wasn't thinking." She turned away quickly.

"Shei'tani." He started to follow her, only to stop in his tracks when Kelissande grabbed his wrist. The instant her skin touched his, the mean, grasping ugliness of her soul poured into him. Her thoughts were hateful and self-indulgent. She was beautiful, Ellie was not. She was the one who deserved a king for a mate. Rain was handsome and powerful, and Kelissande had decided she would have him. Stealing him from Ellie Lack Grace would be child's play.

With a grimace of distaste, he grasped Kelissande's wrist and removed her clinging hand. Deliberately, gritting his teeth against the soul-eating darkness that emanated from her, he gripped her other wrist as well and bent close to her beautiful face.

"You dare too much, foolish Celierian female," he growled. He let power flare in his eyes, and enjoyed the fear that blossomed on her face. How could she think a truemated man would ever have eyes for anyone but his own mate? Stupid woman. Ignorant, primitive, ungifted, dark-hearted creature of no worth. "Even were she not my truemate, I would choose Ellysetta over you every time. Do you think a Fey Lord cannot see past your pretty face to the ugliness inside? All your beauty, all your wealth, could not make any Fey desire you."

He bound her in weaves of Earth and Spirit to keep her still and grasped her heart-shaped face with frightening gentleness. He felt her terror, and it made him smile, made the tairen roar and flex its claws. *«Hurt my shei'tani again in any way, and female or not, you will have made an enemy worth fearing. This I do promise you.»*

«Rain . . . »

Even as Bel's warning voice sounded in his mind, Rain felt the waves of Ellysetta's emotion roll over him, misery bubbling with hurt and anger and disappointment. And something unexpected that Rain recognized as—

Jealousy?

He lifted his head and found Ellysetta staring at him. Her eyes were huge in her fine-boned face, filled with accusation and, yes, jealousy. He gazed at her in bewilderment. Why would she feel such a thing? Had he not claimed her? Had he not set aside even the memory of his love for Sariel to court her? Did she not understand what that meant?

Directly on the heels of that thought, common sense asserted itself. Of course she did not understand what the *shei'-tanitsa* bond meant. She'd been raised Celierian, not Fey.

Thrusting Kelissande from him, he straightened and held out his hands to his truemate. "Ellysetta—"

"The children are waiting. You and Kelissande can join us

or not, as you desire." She spun away and marched off. The elegant line of her spine was stiff as a board, and her thick, flame-red plait twitched behind her as she walked, reminding him of an angry female tairen's very dangerous tail.

CHAPTER TEN

It wasn't jealousy. It wasn't. Ellie wasn't stupid enough to be jealous just because Rain Tairen Soul responded like all men did when the beautiful Kelissande Minset cast a lure their way.

Betrayal. That's what it was. She felt betrayed. He had dazzled her with his masculine beauty, his power, his tairen-fierceness, until she'd actually begun to believe that her plain drabness didn't matter to him, that he saw beauty in her.

"*Shei'tani*." His hand, so strong, so warm, touched her shoulder.

She shuddered from the instant wave of helpless need that flooded her. Dear gods, when he touched her, all she wanted to do was fling herself into his arms. She wanted to forget about the tender way he'd cupped Kelissande's perfect face, absolve him for the quiet words he'd murmured so close to Kelissande's soft lips.

Ellie wrenched herself out of his grasp. Pride. It seemed she actually possessed some. And it would not let her accept a touch from the same hands that had just caressed Kelissande.

"Go back to Kelissande," she snapped. "I'm sure there are many more sweet words you'd like to whisper in her ear."

His eyes opened wide in surprise, then narrowed. "I was not—"

"Not that it matters to me," she interrupted. "I haven't put any claims on you. And despite the claims you've made, you're free to do as you like."

His beautiful lips compressed into a thin line. "And this would not concern you?"

"Of course not," she scoffed.

"You lie."

"I don't lie." But she was lying now. And wretched because of it.

«Shei'tani . . . Ellysetta . . . you don't understand—»

"Get out of my head!" Angry, she wished she had the power to thrust him out of her thoughts, imagined the satisfaction of her anger taking the form of two giant hands that picked him up and flung him out of her mind. A split second later, she felt his surprise followed by a bruising jolt of pain. His pain.

The Tairen Soul staggered.

She couldn't stop the rush of concern that sent her lurching towards him. "Rain?"

He put a hand to his head. "Flames, woman, you pack a punch."

"Are you all right?" She bit her lip to stop its trembling, tried to harden her heart against him. She failed miserably.

"*Aiyah.* Surprised mostly." He shook his head. "Your jealousy is flattering, *shei'tani*, but unnecessary, I assure you."

"Jealousy?" Her spine became a steel poker, her jaw a hard, thrusting rock of feminine outrage. "Jealousy?" She clenched her fists and wished she dared to hit him. Instead, she sniffed and turned away, forcing a tight smile to her face as she met the curious, interested gazes of a dozen or more children. "Come, children, let's play Stones."

As his young *shei'tani* presented Rain with her back, the sound of silent Fey laughter rang in his head. He gave Bel and the others a scorching look, but that only made them laugh all the more. Not that anyone but a Fey would know it. They would not dishonor their King by any outward display of amusement.

He glanced over his shoulder. The Kelissande creature had wisely retreated. She was now ringed by a bevy of panting Celierian fools, dull-witted mortals blind to all but her beautiful exterior. Rain dismissed them. As long as the woman kept clear of his *shei'tani*, he would not concern himself with her.

He turned back to his truemate. She was smiling at the children, laughing as she played their stone-tossing game, doing her best to ignore him.

How different she was from the dark-souled one. And how much more intriguing than he had first thought. She was one surprise after another. Fey-gentle. Tairen-proud. Woman-passionate. And jealous when she thought her mate's attention had strayed. He savored that thought. A woman did not feel jealousy if her emotions were not engaged.

And a wise man did not let it fester.

With sudden purpose, Rain shed his Fey'cha belts and the harnesses holding his sheathed swords. Naked of steel, he stepped towards the ring of playing children.

"It would please me to learn this game," he announced. That earned him all manner of surprised looks, from the children, the Fey, and his *shei'tani*.

"It is a child's game," Ellie told him warily. "Surely nothing that would interest a king." There was an emphasis on the last word, accompanied by a glance in Kelissande's direction.

"Ah, but I am tairen as well," he told her. "And tairen delight in games." It was true, though he had not indulged in tairen games since the Mage Wars. She was his truemate, and he was pledged to win her. If a child's game could help him achieve his aim, then play it he would.

He sent a warm, moist weave of Air, Water, and Fire whispering up her throat and curling around her ear. She shivered and gave him a warning look. The fire in her eyes made the tairen in him growl with appreciation. Tairen females were not timid. They were, in fact, often more dangerous than their mates. "Come," he murmured, his voice low and seductive. "Teach me this game." Satisfaction rumbled in his throat when he saw her nostrils flare in awareness of his pursuit.

She explained the rules with a quick breathlessness that pleased him. Stones was a game of aim, dexterity, and speed. The object was to make a path from one side of a grid to the other by landing your stones on connecting squares, while keeping your opponents from stopping you and simultaneously doing your best to stop them. If two stones landed on the same square in the grid, the two players had to race to it by stepping only on those squares occupied by their stones; whoever reached the disputed square and claimed the opponent's stone first won control of the square, while the other player forfeited his stone. The first player to build an unbroken path across the grid won the game.

"Are there any other rules?" he asked, when she was finished explaining. She shook her head. "Good." Inside his mind, where Ellysetta could not see, Rain smiled. It was a tairen's smile, full of teeth and cunning. "And will you grant me a boon if I win this game?"

"A boon?"

"*Aiyah*. Surely there must be some reward for winning."

"Such as what?"

He ran a finger over her lips. "A kiss, I think."

She swallowed. "A kiss?"

"I hunger for one."

She blinked and visibly struggled to collect her thoughts. "And if you lose?"

"Then I grant *you* a boon."

"Anything?"

"Anything." What would she ask for? A shame he would not find out. He raised a brow. "Well? Do we have a wager?" He enjoyed her wary frown. She knew there was some catch, but she had yet to figure it out.

"Yes," she finally agreed. "It's a wager. If you win, I'll give you a kiss. If anyone else wins, you'll grant me a wish—anything I want."

And with that, the game began. On all levels.

Ellysetta loaned him a spare bag of stones. His were purple with a gold line painted across the diameter of each stone. The players took their spots along the borders of the grid, four on each side, with Rain standing beside Ellysetta. The game began with each player, in turn, dropping a stone on the grid square at his or her feet. It was simple enough, and if truth be told, rather boring, but within three or four plays, things began to get interesting as throwing distances grew greater, paths crossed, and the play converged on the center of the grid.

To his surprise, Rain truly enjoyed himself, and not just because he was looking forward to his reward once he won. In the Fading Lands, even before the Mage Wars, children had been rare and precious, adored and protected by even the most soul-shadowed warrior. Their youthful innocence and wide-eyed delight in the world appealed to the gentle heart that lay at the core of every Fey. The Celierian children, laughing as they leapt like little goats across the Stones grid, were no less appealing for all that they were not Fey.

Even the other warriors were not immune to the lure of childish joy. Fey laughter rang out across the common mental path, accompanied by the picking of favorites and good-natured teasing. No one placed bets. They all knew Rain Tairen Soul played this game to win.

At last, all the players but Ellysetta and Rain had lost their stones. Rain tossed his stone, deliberately landing it on Ellie's square. Like two elf bolts fired from an Elvian fingerbow, the pair of them darted across the grid, leaping nimbly from square to square. She was laughing as she raced across the grid, still laughing as she plowed into his chest when she made the jump to the disputed square he had reached first.

He absorbed her weight easily, and when she raised her face and laughed up at him, he was stunned anew. She was a gift from the gods, this woman with her gold-sprinkled skin, eyes clear and green as lush spring glades, and her soul that shone bright as the Great Sun itself.

Aching to kiss her, he instead stepped back and showed her the red-and-green-striped stone in his hand. "I believe your stone is forfeit, Ellysetta," he told her. He tucked her stone into the pocket on the inside of his tunic, close to his heart. "Do you forfeit the game as well?"

Her eyes had followed the path of his hands and were now fixed on the small vee of pale flesh revealed by the opening of his tunic. At his question, she blinked and dragged her gaze back to his face, the bright smile on her lips not quite masking the hunger in her eyes. "Me? Forfeit a game of Stones?" She forced a laugh and danced away. "Never!" She raced back to her home position on the grid. Pleased with the exchange, he followed at a more leisurely pace.

As he prepared to throw his stone to win the game, she inched closer to him. "Take care with your aim," she advised him, smiling. "If you miss, I have a chance to win."

"I will not miss."

"Care to wager on that?"

Interested, delighted by her daring, he raised a brow. "What did you have in mind?"

"If you don't win on this play, I want to go flying." She paused. "On tairenback."

"And if I win?"

"Your choice."

"Agreed." Rain lowered his lashes over eyes that suddenly glowed with heat and satisfaction. Taking wing with his *shei'-tani* astride him would be no hardship.

Still, no Fey ever lost a challenge on purpose, and he would not be the first, especially not with so many warriors looking on. Taking aim, he drew back his hand and loosed his last stone. At that precise moment, his *shei'tani* stood on her toes and blew directly into his ear.

His entire body clenched. His throw went wild. Rather than landing with Fey precision on the winning square, his stone hurtled through the air over the heads of squealing, ducking children, skipped three times across the surface of the river, and sank like . . . well . . . a stone.

Ellysetta was bent double, laughing. "I win," she gasped between laughs.

"*Aiyah*," he grumbled, eyeing her with new appreciation. That little move was sneaky enough for a tairen. "This wager. But I will win the game."

She regained her composure and tossed her next stone towards an unoccupied square that would bring her one toss away from winning the game. Her aim was true, the arc of her throw perfect. The stone descended . . . then hit an invisible wall of Air and bounced back to land on a disqualified player's square. "What!" Ellysetta exclaimed. "Oh, foul!" She turned to him, laughing all the while she attempted to pretend outrage. "I cry foul!"

"Ha. As if you could." Rain tossed his last stone with negligent ease, this time using Air to direct it to its proper destination. It landed in the farthest row of the grid, completing his line. "I win."

"You cheated," she accused. "More than I did," she added when he raised a brow.

"*Nei*, I did not."

"You used your magic to win."

"You never said I couldn't." His voice simmered with masculine satisfaction. "When you wager with tairen, take care with your words."

Leaving the children to their game, he led her towards a copse of trees beside the river and pulled her close. *Shei'tanitsa* need, never far from him, rose up in swift, insistent waves. "I would collect my prize."

"Now?" she asked nervously. "Here?"

"Now," he confirmed. "Here."

Ellysetta's lips were soft and warm, her eyes solemn, nervous, and wide open. He smiled against her mouth, gently licked at her lips with flickering, teasing touches of his tongue followed by tiny nibbling bites. «*You taste of honeyed cream, shei'tani. Open your mouth to me.*» His hands splayed against her back, clutching her slender body closer as she hesitantly complied with his command. Triumph, pleasure, desire, and protectiveness swirled through him as he laid claim to the secrets of her mouth. Timid at first, she accepted but did not respond to his kiss.

«*Do not fear this,*» he urged. «*Do not fear me. Feel what you do to me, feel how I need you.*» Deliberately he lowered the protective barriers that were as much a part of him as his leathers and steel.

Need and desire poured over her like warm honey, and she gasped against his mouth, closing her eyes against the almost painful pleasure that claimed her senses. He did desire her. Though it made no sense to her, she couldn't deny it. Kelissande, for all her beauty, couldn't make him feel what she, plain Ellysetta Baristani, did. The knowledge was heady, intoxicating. There was such longing in him, such loneliness. It was like a void crying to be filled, and she could feel herself being drawn to it, needing to bring him peace.

Opening his senses to her, aware of every nuance of her emotions, of every beat of her heart, every shivered breath, Rain drank in her sweet response. Hesitant at first, she grew bolder as he greeted each tentative stroke of her tongue with a hungry stroke of his own, building her self-confidence, assuring her that she held the same sensual power over him that he held over her. He took her breath into his lungs and gave her back his own. She shuddered and twined her arms around him, clinging tight. His body grew hard as her feelings flowed to him, through him, saturating every cell of his being, just as his desire, his need, his passion flowed to her. Intensity doubled, quadrupled, as their emotions formed a harmonic frequency and amplified each other.

"Disgusting display," Kelissande's sneering voice declared. "I'd heard he'd all but mated her in public. I see now the stories were true."

Ellysetta gasped and tore her lips from Rain's, a tide of red rushing into her pale face. The banker's daughter stood on the gravel path beside the river, surrounded by her admirers and sneering at Ellysetta and Rain.

He felt Ellysetta's shame for having shared in their passion, and it infuriated him. Power sparked in his eyes. The Minset woman had been warned.

Before he could release his weave, Kelissande shrieked and toppled backwards into the Velpin. Thrashing and sputtering, she screamed for help, and four of her Celierian admirers promptly leapt in to rescue her.

Rain followed the nearly invisible trail of the Air weave back to Kieran. Beside Kieran, Lillis clapped her hands, squealed, and threw herself into the Fey's arms. The young warrior hugged her close and met his king's stern look with a broad grin and a careless shrug, showing not the faintest hint of remorse. Despite himself, Rain almost laughed. How could he upbraid the Fey for doing something he'd been about to do himself?

Unaware of the silent communication going on over her head, Ellie felt a spurt of wicked happiness as she watched Kelissande flounder her way out of the river. The glee was followed immediately by shame at her unkind feelings. She knew what it was to be publicly humiliated, and to take enjoyment in the humiliation of another made her little better than Kelissande. She tried to free herself from Rain's arms, intending to go to Kelissande's aid, but his grip tightened.

He shook his head and cupped her face. "Do not waste your compassion on her, *shei'tani*. Her heart is hard."

Ellie blinked. She was aware of that, but Rain was the first man she'd ever known to see it. "Don't you find her beautiful?" she asked. Surely he did. After all, only a short while ago he'd been whispering sweet nothings into Kelissande's ear. Hadn't he?

"She is like a komarind fruit—beautiful on the outside, but bitter inside. Fey do not prize the komarind. We let it rot on the branches." He touched a finger to her lips. "The Fey find beauty in the soul. That is where true beauty always lies. And believe me, Ellysetta Baristani, your soul is beautiful indeed."

She absorbed his words, scarcely daring to believe that this man could find her more appealing than Kelissande Minset.

She glanced at the other Fey around her. None of them had lifted a finger to help Kelissande out of her predicament. To the contrary, several of them seemed to find the situation amusing. Rain, it seemed, wasn't the only one unaffected by Kelissande's perfect beauty. Somehow, that made the possibility that Rain actually preferred Ellie more believable.

As the dripping, disheveled young woman was delivered from the watery clutches of the Velpin, she shot Ellie a look of such virulent hatred that Ellysetta actually flinched and stepped back. Immediately Rain and the Fey closed ranks around her. Faces hard, their eyes cold and lethal, they glared at the soaked girl. To Ellie's surprise, Kelissande turned pale and stumbled back into the arms of her rescuers. Fear contorted her face. Ellie followed the girl's terrified gaze to Rain, who was watching her coldly, his eyes glowing with faint lavender light.

"What are you doing to her?"

"I am making sure she understands what will happen if she persists in this foolish desire to hurt you."

Ellie frowned. "Well, stop it. You're scaring her."

After one last forceful look, Rain released Kelissande and turned to Ellie. "I am your mate. It is my duty and privilege to protect you, even from your own too-forgiving heart. She hurt you, wounded your feelings, made you doubt the bond between us, and now she thinks dark thoughts that give you fear. Such evil I will not allow. Those gentle words you thought I whispered to her were my first warning of what I would do should she persist in wounding you. Now I have shown her what sort of enemy she has made. Should she think to hurt you a third time, it will be the last." There was no compassion in his eyes, no hint of mercy, just cold, implacable promise. Ellie shivered, and his face immediately softened. "I make you fear me. This is not my intent." He raised a knuckle to her cheek. "Do not fear me, Ellysetta. Never will I harm you. I seek only to ensure your protection and your happiness."

"I know," she whispered, surprised to find it true. Though

the cold power and deadly promise in his eyes frightened her, she knew it was not directed at her, and her fear was more for others than for herself. She would not want to be witness to the unleashing of that power. She did not want to think of it being exercised on her behalf.

He held out his hand, palm down in the Fey fashion. She placed her fingers on his wrist the way he had taught her the day before. Now he did smile, the barest curve of his lips, but the warmth of his approval filled her with joy.

In a shadowed alleyway across from the park, two pairs of eyes had watched the passionate kiss, one gaze blazing with hatred, the other glowing black with hints of smug, satisfied red. "You see how wantonly she displays herself? Would the Ellysetta you know do this? He uses Spirit to force her mind to his will. She is his puppet. He has taken your bride and made her his whore."

"Demon-souled sorcerer," Den hissed. "He's got her so besotted, she'll do anything he asks with her power."

"Her power?" Captain Batay repeated with interest.

"She heals with a touch, finds things that are lost. And I've even seen her . . ." He broke off, flicked a quick glance at his companion, and remembered caution. "Never mind." He frowned and turned his head to study the man beside him. A moment ago, at Den's quick first glance, Batay's eyes had looked like dark pits filled with glowing red coals. It must have been a trick of the light. Now they were their usual blue-green.

White teeth flashed in the shadowy darkness. "Come, my young friend. There is much to be done."

A dark-sleeved arm wrapped around Den's shoulders like a tentacle, making the butcher's son shiver with a premonition of dread. He shook off the feeling. To reclaim Ellysetta Baristani and all the riches that would come when he put her powers to lucrative use, Den would even deal with a Drogan Blood Lord. Compared to those vicious blood-drinking cannibals, what was there to fear from the captain of a Sorrelian merchant ship?

"What would you like to do now, Ellysetta?" Rain asked as they left the park.

She flashed him a surprised look. She had been expecting him to go off to do whatever it was kings did when visiting a foreign city. Surely King Dorian and Queen Annoura had entertainment planned for him. "Don't you have things to do?"

His eyebrows lifted. "You wish me to leave you?"

"Not at all. But I'm sure you came to Celieria for a purpose. Don't let me keep you from it." She bit her lip as his eyebrows rose higher. "That didn't come out right. I don't want you to leave, but I'll understand if you must."

"You think there is business I must attend to, which I put off so I may court you?"

"Yes." She gave him an earnest look. "And you don't have to. I'll understand."

He was silent for a moment, staring so intently into her eyes that she forgot to breathe. His hand came up to cup her cheek, fingers sliding into her hair, the warmth of his palm cradling her jaw. His thumb stroked the high ridge of her cheekbone. "You are the reason I came to Celieria," he told her. "My only purpose for being here."

"How can I be the reason you came?" she whispered. "You didn't even know I was alive until two days ago."

"Three," he corrected. "You called to me three days ago. That was when I first knew of you." His thumb continued to brush across her cheek. "Do you remember what I said when we first spoke? I told you that I had seen the mist of your reflection in the Eye of Truth. It was the Eye that sent me here to find you, though I did not know it until you called me from the sky."

"But why would this 'Eye of Truth' send you to find me?"

He took his hand from her face. Her cheek felt cold and bereft at the sudden absence of his warmth. "You are my *shei'tani*. My truemate."

"Is that what the Eye does? Sends Fey warriors to find their truemates?"

"*Nei*, but you are no ordinary truemate, if there is such a thing."

"What do you mean?"

"I am the Feyreisen, the Tairen Soul, and yet you are my truemate. No Tairen Soul before me has ever had a *shei'tani*."

"What about Lady Sariel?"

He shook his head. "We loved as children. She knew I would never have a *shei'tani* and loved me enough to join her life with mine, giving up her desire for a *shei'tan* of her own."

"I don't understand."

"She was *e'tani*, the mate of my heart. We chose the bond. You are *shei'tani*, the mate of my soul, my truemate. A Fey doesn't choose the truemate bond. It chooses the Fey. For me there will never be another, whether you accept the bond or not."

"And for me?"

His eyes held an odd combination of remorse and satisfaction. "*Nei*. You would not be my truemate were I not also yours. If you do not accept our bond, perhaps one day there might be a man with whom you could find some measure of happiness, but there will be no other mate who can reach your soul."

Why didn't the prospect of never loving any man but him fill her with dread? It should have frightened her, or at the very least made her cry out against the unfairness of it all. And yet she could not help feeling an answering surge of satisfaction as her soul rose up to recognize and thrill in the bond between them.

She knew the instant her feelings reached him. His eyes flared. Magic wrapped around her with sudden electric warmth. But the warmth changed in an instant as a powerful primitive force invaded her mind, calling to her, roaring with triumph and searing hunger, battering at the privacy of her soul. She felt something inside her start to give way, and fear rose hard and fast. With a cry, she flung herself out of Rain's arms.

Rain groaned aloud, a raw hoarse sound. His hands fisted and he closed his eyes. Sparks flashed around him like fireflies.

"*Sieks'ta*," he apologized tightly. "Do not be frightened. It is the tairen in me that frightens you, but I can control it. I will control it, *shei'tani*. I promise you. Please, do not shrink from me." Even as he spoke, the sparks began to fade.

"The tairen?" Her heart was pounding, her breath coming in shallow gasps.

"The tairen lives in all Fey warriors," he replied, opening his eyes. Relief flooded her as she saw that his control was back. His magic no longer sparkled around him, the glow in his eyes was dimming. "In most it is dormant, but when a Fey is born with full strength in all the Fey magics, the tairen awakens. These Fey become Tairen Souls. The tairen is conscious within them, leashed by their will, but always driving the Fey with the same instincts of a true tairen."

"It-it attacked me."

"*Nei*. It did not attack, it tried to claim." His hand reached out, but stopped shy of touching her face. He pulled his hand back, thrust his fingers through his hair, and sighed. "Mating and the claiming of a mate is the fiercest of any tairen instinct. I have recognized you as my *shei'tani*. A moment ago your soul reached out, willingly, to mine. I felt it. The tairen in me responded as any tairen would to its mate. I should have been prepared. I was not." His eyelids lowered. "For this, I apologize. I have dishonored myself."

Even though she was still frightened, her heart could not bear to see him humbled. He was the Tairen Soul, the hero of her life's dreams. And for some strange reason, some joke of the gods she could not hope to fathom, he had claimed her as his mate. She bit her lip in indecision, then dragged a deep breath into her lungs and stepped forward to clasp his hands.

At her touch, his eyes flew open and fixed on hers. "*Shei'tani*?"

"I'm the one who should be sorry," she told him. "You asked me not to fear you, to understand that you would never hurt me, but at the first test, I let myself be terrified. I'm afraid I'm not going to be a very good truemate for a Tairen Soul. I'm a coward at heart."

"You are all that a truemate should be," he told her firmly. "Never think otherwise." The harsh line of his mouth softened. "Come," he said. "The afternoon is ours to enjoy. What would you like to do?"

She bit her lip. "Actually, I have another appointment with the queen's dressmaker to review fabric samples for my wedding dress."

"This does not appear to please you."

"No," she admitted. She wasn't looking forward to yet another half day of sneering dislike from the cold, haughty tradesmen recommended by Queen Annoura. She'd particularly hated standing in the presence of Maestra Binchi, the queen's dressmaker, this morning, being measured—both physically and figuratively—by a woman who obviously found Ellie lacking. "But she's making a special effort to fit me into her schedule. Besides, I have an appointment at the palace with the queen's Master of Graces after that."

Rain glanced at Bel for a moment and his face grew still. A hint of anger entered his eyes, and Ellie realized Belliard had just related the morning's events. Rain's next words confirmed her suspicions. "Bel has told me of this dressmaker. You are the Feyreisa. She will attend your pleasure, not the other way around. As will the queen's Master of Graces."

Ellie blinked at the implacable finality of his statement. "Oh, but—"

"Ellysetta." He gave her a look that made her close her mouth and swallow her objection. "I despise Celieria. I remain here only to fulfill my oath to your father and to give you a little time at least to grow accustomed to me before I take you from all that is familiar to you. I will not cut short my time with you merely to indulge the self-importance of a foolish woman who insults the Tairen Soul's truemate—and I am speaking of both the queen and her servants. The dressmaker will attend you tomorrow morning. Early, before I come to you. The Master of Graces will tutor you after that, while I am there to observe him. And, Ellysetta . . ." He lifted her chin with a gentleness that somehow made the fierce look in his eyes even more terrifying. "If anyone insults you again, you—not Bel—shall tell me of it."

Ellie gulped and nodded. She would promise almost anything to stop him looking at her with those eyes that leapt with flickering lights of cold fire.

"*Beylah vo.* Thank you." The hard lines of Rain's expression softened and his eyes calmed. "Now, what would you like to do?"

"I—" She wet her lips and tried to still her rapidly beating heart. "I don't know." She'd never been courted before, didn't have the first idea of where to go or what to do. Inspiration struck. "You could take me flying. After all, I did win that wager."

"You did, indeed. Very well, then. Flying it is."

CHAPTER ELEVEN

With wings unfurled and joy unbound,
I dance on laughter-spangled winds.
I bathe in freedom's rushing breath
And drink cool nectar from the clouds.
Up, up, through sunlit fields of blue,
I soar through boundless ether.
Look! Starlight shines at height of day.
I hear infinity calling.
                    —*Tairen's Flight*, by Cadrian vel Sorendahl,
                                        Tairen Soul

"Why did I bring my coat?"

Rain cast an amused glance at Ellysetta. His *shei'tani* had been an uncorked bottle of questions since they'd dropped off the twins at her home. Her hesitance with him had been replaced by incessant curiosity and wide-eyed wonder that reminded him very much of a young tairen eagerly examining the world for the first time.

"Because, *shei'tani*," he replied, "it is very cold in the high reaches of the sky. If it gets too cold, I will weave Fire and Air around you to keep you warm, but then you will not feel the wind on your face. Feeling the wind is one of the best parts of tairen flight."

"What if I discover that I'm afraid of heights?"

"You will not be."

"How do you know?"

"Because you know you will always be safe in my care." Ah, blessed arrogance. He wanted to grin. He astonished himself. The Fey and tairen were teetering on the brink of extinction, darkness was rising again in Eld, and Rain Tairen Soul, Defender of the Fey, was happier than he'd been in a thousand years, all because he was taking his mate for a ride in the skies. Even the anger that had simmered in him since leaving Dorian—and roused again upon learning of Ellysetta's treatment at the hands of Annoura's tradesfolk—was gone. If Ellysetta was weaving a *shei'dalin's* peace on him, he could not detect it.

"Lillis and Lorelle are probably still wailing because they couldn't come," Ellie said. The twins had pitched an unholy fit, complete with copious tears, when Lauriana had informed them that, no, they were not going to ride on tairen-back, and, no, they were not going to tag along with their sister and her betrothed this time.

"This I doubt," Rain replied. "Kiel and Kieran would not permit their unhappiness." Kiel and Kieran had both stayed behind to entertain the girls, while the holders of Water and Earth in Ellysetta's secondary quintet took their places for the afternoon.

They walked through the city gates, out into the open fields that ringed the city. "Tell me again, why do we have to come out here?"

"I prefer to have space for the Change. Besides, there are fewer eyes."

She glanced over her shoulder at the crowds gathered on the walls. "Right."

She had a dry sense of humor, very Fey, that made him want to laugh as he had not in centuries. "Just imagine the audience we'd have if we had stayed in the city," he replied.

Rain brought the group to a halt about two hundred yards from the city wall. "Stay here, Ellysetta, and wait until I tell you it is safe to come forward." She nodded.

He turned and began jogging away, slowly at first, then faster and faster until he was sprinting. With a tremendous Air-powered leap, he catapulted himself into the sky and flashed into tairen form, winging high above the earth. Skyward he soared, up towards the mid-afternoon sun and into the bright, endless blue of the warm spring day. Black wings spread wide, he banked left and circled back over Celieria, back over the small knot of black-clad warriors and the single slender figure in navy skirts standing safely in their midst.

He knew he was an impressive tairen, large, sleek, powerful. In flight, his tairen body was even more graceful, forelegs flattened aerodynamically against his belly, powerful hind legs trailing behind, his long, thick tail trailing even further, its blunt, curling tip acting like a rudder in flight. He watched his shadow speed across the Celierian landscape, and basked in the warmth of Ellysetta's dazed admiration.

Slowly, lazily, he glided down to earth and settled with graceful precision on the ground not far from Ellysetta and the Fey warriors. He stretched his wings high, flapped them, then tucked them against his back and padded towards Ellysetta. Stopping a few feet from her, he lay down on his belly beside her and gave a rumbling purr.

« That was a prideful display.» Bel's dry voice sounded in his mind.

Tairen fangs bared in a grin. Bel knew him too well. Rain could have transformed without taking flight, but it wasn't nearly as impressive. And he had wanted to impress his *shei'-tani*. From the dazzled look on her face and the wonderment that he felt through their bond, it was plain he had succeeded.

« Tairen are prideful creatures,» he replied. His glowing lavender eyes turned to Ellysetta. His tail swished slowly. *« You can come closer now.»*

Ellie heard the voice in her mind, but it didn't register. She had never seen anything so incredible or so beautiful as the sight of Rainier vel'En Daris leaping into the sky like a human dart and flashing into a huge, sleek, soaring tairen. He'd ridden the sky on broad, black wings, and she'd stood, earthbound and wingless, aching to fly beside him. Not on him, but with him. Beside him, under the power of her own broad wings.

« Shei'tani.» His voice sounded in her mind again, more insistent this time. His tairen head, larger than her body, bumped her gently, bringing her back to the present.

She laughed as she stumbled back a half step. Lillis's kitten bumped people with her head to demand attention in just the same way, though with considerably less force. An instinctive reflex made Ellie reach out to scratch the bony spot between his eyes. Beneath her hands, his tairen pelt was thick and silky, with a particularly lush nap. She had not expected something so huge to be so soft.

The fur on his majestic head was short, thick, and velvety, growing at a very close crop as it neared his muzzle. His ears, alert and rounded at the tips, were set to either side of his tairen skull. Past his head, his fur grew thick and sleek. He glistened a glossy, intense black, rich and deep, without a hint of brown. His eyes, each larger than her head, were pure lavender with no visible pupil, and they seemed to be lit from within. His proud neck merged gracefully with his powerful chest and the rest of his long, sleek great cat's body. Muscular forelegs ended in toed paws with sharp, retractable, curving ivory claws, while his hind legs bulged with undisguised strength. The end of his long tail curled and uncurled. His wings, tucked tightly against his body, seemed fragile compared to the rest of him, though she could see that the lightly furred membrane stretched across his wing bones was thick and supple.

"You are beautiful," she told him, petting the heavy muscles of his furred jaw, forgetting for a moment that this fiercely gorgeous creature was the same being as the fiercely gorgeous man who had claimed her.

«*I am glad you think so.*» He gave a pleased vibrating purr as she continued to rub his head, and his eyelids half lowered over his large, shining tairen eyes. «*I like that. You have a pleasing touch.*»

Green light flashed, and a small black leather saddle appeared where his neck joined his torso just above the jutting bones of his shoulders and wings. Long leather straps circled his neck and threaded behind his forelegs, holding the saddle firmly in place.

«Come, shei'tani. Let us dance the winds.»

"How will I get up there?" She gave a surprised cry when her body floated up into the air and settled in the U-shaped saddle. The high-backed cantle cradled her body. "Oh my." She felt the unfamiliar sensation of a breeze blowing against her legs, and looked down. Her skirts were hiked up to her thighs, her long legs exposed for all to see. "Rain . . ." Before she could even voice her concern, black leather breeches appeared out of nowhere to cover her. She gaped for a moment, then blinked and closed her mouth. Casual magic was something she was going to have to get used to. "Earth?" she asked, because the breeches felt too real to be even a masterful illusion.

«Aiyah.»

"You made them from nothing. Isn't that supposed to be difficult?"

"It is," Bel said. "He shows off for his mate." There was dry humor, friendly mockery, and a trace of envy in Bel's voice that would no doubt have embarrassed him if he'd heard it.

Rain hissed at his friend and tossed his head. *«Allow me to put your coat away, shei'tani.»* That was all the warning she had before her long leather coat disappeared.

"Where did it go?"

«Behind you.» She twisted in the tall saddle and saw the small, bulging pouch strapped behind her. *«When you need it, I will return it to you. There are grips in the front of the saddle. Use them and hold tight. When I launch us into the air, you will feel a jolt.»* She found the grips and wrapped her fingers tightly around them. *«Are you ready?»*

She swallowed as excitement and nervousness bubbled inside her. "Yes."

«Then hold on.» She could practically feel the power building in him as he rocked back on his hind legs and his muscles bunched tight. His wings unfurled and spread wide. They flapped once, twice, whipping up swirls of dust from the

ground. Then he sprang, a mighty leap, powered by Air that rocketed them into the sky.

Ellie screamed, more from surprise and the queer feeling in her stomach than from fright, though if not for the hand-holds and the tall saddle, she would have tumbled off Rain's back when he took off. As it was, her body rocked hard against the back of the saddle, then snapped forward when the sudden initial surge of power ceased and the more fluid motion of true tairen flight began.

Massive wings beat the air, and Rain's tairen body undulated in a sinuous rhythm like waves rolling in the open sea. His neck stretched out, strong and straight, his head a fixed point that speared through the sky like an arrowhead.

The wind whistled across Ellie's face, fresh and cold and sweet. It blew her braided hair behind her, whipped at her skirts and chemise sleeves, and made her glad for the leather breeches Rain had provided. The ground below swept past, the blocks of fields and tiny villages looking more like a patterned tapestry than the world she knew. Above, infinity waited, beckoning to her with sunlit skies and the delicate puffs of white clouds she could almost reach out and touch.

"I'm flying," she whispered. "I'm really flying." Joy unlike any she'd ever known filled her. She flung out her arms and lifted her face to the wind, laughing with uncontainable happiness. "This is wonderful!"

«You like it, then?»

"Like it? I love it! I adore it!" If not for the waist-high front ridge of the saddle, she would have flung herself against his neck and squeezed him tight. "Oh, Rain. Thank you."

«It pleases me to bring you joy, shei'tani.» Her happiness was contagious. No tairen could ever grow bored of the sky, but sharing it with her, feeling her joy, made Rain recall the thrill of his first flight, the laughing exaltation, the feeling of immense freedom, the knowledge that he was a master of the world and anything was possible. He wanted to give her plea-

sure, open the world to her, and stand by her side as she discovered its wonders. There was so much he could show her—literally an entire world. For the first time in a long, long while, Rain was glad to be alive, glad to be Fey and a Tairen Soul. *«Where would you like to go, Ellysetta?»*

He felt her eagerness, her excitement. "I don't care. I just want to *fly*."

«Then hold tight.»

He folded his wings, and they plummeted fast and hard, diving towards the earth. Ellysetta screamed with laughter and held tight to the saddle, fearless even as the ground rushed up to meet them. Rain's heart swelled at her trust and complete lack of fear. His wings spread wide, and the rapid dive became a swooping ascent that left Ellysetta breathless yet still laughing.

With joy in his heart, Rain Tairen Soul soared across the sky.

Den Brodson smiled as he watched thin, gangly little Tomy Sorris scribble the last of his notes on the pages spread out before him. "You have it all, then?" The pair of them sat in the private back room at the Charging Boar. A nearly empty pint of Red Skull sat on the scarred wooden table before Den, and a half glass of well-watered ale sat before the printer's son.

"I do. Thanks for the story, Den!" Tomy tipped his ink-stained wool cap with one hand while the other busied itself stuffing the pages into his satchel. "It's a beaut. And I'm grateful you took time to write most of it down for me first. The less I have to write, the quicker Da can get it into print."

"No problem at all, Tomy. Give your Da my best. And be sure he uses that one paragraph I showed you, exactly as I've written it." Those words, Batay had promised him, would sway simple minds, in particular the minds of readers who rarely thought for themselves. A spell of persuasion, buried not in the ink or the paper used to write them, but tied to the very words themselves. Already, Den had met and distributed the copied pages to half a dozen pamphleteers and newspaper writers.

"I will," the printer's boy promised. "Exactly as it's written."

"And don't use my name, remember. I don't want to get my Da in trouble with the king." Den pasted a sober expression on his face. "I just want to see justice for Ellie. Sold out, she was. Sold out to a murderous sorcerer for a chest of magic-cursed gold."

"Ooh, that's good." Tomy paused to scratch Den's words down on the last piece of paper before stuffing it away and carefully stowing his ink and pen. He straightened and scratched his head. "But, you know, Ellie's always fancied the Fey. Maybe she's happy with the way things have turned out."

"Women fancy tigers," Den snapped. "Doesn't mean they want to bed down with the beasts." He lifted his now-warm mug of Red Skull and downed the last quarter pint. "No, she's been ensorcelled. Her whole family has. And it's up to us—plain folk like you and me, Tomy—to save her."

The boy squared his shoulders and nodded. "You're right, Den. I'll do my part. People have a right to know what the Fey are up to."

"Indeed they do." Den clapped a hand on the boy's shoulder and escorted him out the Charging Boar's back door. He waited for the boy to disappear down the alleyway before closing the door and making his way back into the main pub. "Thanks, Briggs." He waved to the bartender as he walked past.

"No problem, Den. You off, then?"

Den nodded. "To church."

"Church?" Briggs threw back his head and laughed. "That's a good one, Den!"

Den grinned. "I know. Can't hardly believe it myself. I'll make an offering at one of the altars for you, eh?"

Briggs snickered and shook his head.

Den pushed through the pub's brass-and-leaded-glass

doors and turned left down King's Road. He'd actually
been telling Briggs the truth, though only because he knew
the man would never believe it. His next destination lay
about two miles down, in one of the rougher areas of town,
where the Brethren of Radiance had set up a mission to
minister to the poor and the godless of Celieria City.
Founded more than a century ago by a zealous Church of
Light priest who'd spent too many years in the north, the
Brethren despised magic in all its forms.

Den patted his coat pocket and smiled at the crinkling noise
of several more sheaves of folded paper. Yes, indeed, he could
already feel the Bright Lord's Radiance shining upon him.

As Den completed the tasks set to him, Kolis Manza was busy
with a mission of his own a little further north in the city.
The fourth golden bell of midday had just rung. Time
enough to see to this task before journeying back to Eld for a
meeting with his master.

The Mage smoothed back his bronze-powdered hair and
straightened the fit of his well-tailored but nondescript
brown jacket. He'd discarded his Captain Batay disguise after
leaving Brodson earlier. A Sorrelian captain would garner too
much attention wandering the more affluent residential
neighborhoods of the West End, whereas a well-dressed but
unremarkable merchant would slip by unnoticed. Not even
Fey warriors would connect the bold dress, tattooed face, and
oiled hair of Batay with the sober Goodman Black.

He approached a small, tidy home near the riverfront and
slowed his pace. His watchful gaze scanned the nearby roads
and rooftops, but he detected no Fey warriors, hidden or
otherwise. Even so, he was careful. His brows drew together
in a faint frown of concentration as he formed a weave of
Azrahn and meticulously insulated it in threads of Spirit to
mask its signature from keen Fey senses. Only when the familiar, cold, sweet tang of Azrahn was suitably muffled did he
direct the weave into the house. He felt the woman's quick
start of fear, her pointless struggle to resist, and the satisfying

whimper of obedient subjugation. Pleased, he pushed open the front gate and walked up the gravel path bordered by tidy rows of cultivated flowers. Even before he reached the mullioned front door, he heard the lock click open, and the door swung inward.

The house was as tidy within as without. As Tuelis closed the door behind him, Kolis looked around the modest living room. A smile curved his lips as his glance fell upon the two small children playing quietly on a rug by the hearth. "Aren't you a pretty pair," he murmured.

"Mama? Who's at the door?"

Kolis turned to the young woman who entered the room. She was lovely, with clear, fine skin, deep blue eyes, and an appearance as neat as the home she kept. He smiled. This would be a greater pleasure than most. "My dear, you must be Selianne. Your mother has told me so much about you."

"Are the beaches in the Fading Lands as beautiful as this?" Ellie looked out across the vast expanse of white sand and turquoise waters of Great Bay. She and Rain had flown countless miles with astonishing speed until the tropical beauty of southern Great Bay had drawn their interest. Now they sat on a blanket on the sand beneath the shade of a copse of broad-leafed pella trees. The remains of the picnic lunch they'd purchased earlier in a tiny bayside village lay between them on the blanket they'd been forced to accept from the awed villager who'd sold them lunch. Rain's weapons lay in a pile of steel and leather within easy reach of his hands.

"It depends where along the coast you are," he answered. "On the southern coast, there are pella trees, white sand beaches, and crystal waters like this. In the north, where the Feyls meet the sea, the beaches are black and the waters are a deep, deep blue."

"Tairen like the water, don't they?"

His eyes warmed and the fierceness of his handsome features softened, making him seem more approachable and somehow even more staggeringly handsome. "*Aiyah*, they do indeed."

Ellie's heart turned somersaults inside her chest. "Tell me about the tairen."

"What would you like to know?"

"Everything. What do they look like? Are they the same as you when you are a tairen?"

"*Aiyah*, though they come in many different colors. The oldest female is a deep gray, with white and black in her wings and tail. She is beautiful and very fierce. To the Fey, she is called Sybharukai, the wise one. She is very ancient, very crafty. A powerful friend and an even more powerful enemy." His voice was filled with both pride and respect. "Her mate is Corus. He is a great warrior, with many battle scars and fur the color of twilight. And there is young Fahreeta, all golden fur and green eyes. She likes games and flirting with the other males to annoy her mate, Torasul. He is the largest of the males except for Sybharukai's mate, and he has great patience, which is good, else Fahreeta would drive him mad."

"You make them sound like people."

He smiled. "They are. Just a different kind of people."

"How many tairen are there?"

His smile dimmed. Sadness skated across her senses, then was gone so quickly she thought she must have imagined it. "That, you will have to see for yourself. When you come to the Fading Lands, I will take you to meet the Fey'Bahren pride."

In three weeks, she would wed this man and leave behind everything she knew, everyone she loved. The reminder was an abrupt splash of reality. She drew her knees up close to her chest and wrapped her arms around them. Though half of her longed to go—longed to follow him anywhere, for that matter—the other half was terrified at the prospect. He was so confident, so at ease with himself, his power, the world. He exuded grace and elegance in everything he did, from the way his fingers ran through his hair to the way he sprawled so unself-consciously in the grass yet lost not one shred of dignity or self-possession. Could he possibly be any different from her? And though it only made sense that she would want to follow him to the ends of the earth like the hopelessly besotted romantic she was, what could he possibly see in her?

"Has anyone ever claimed a *shei'tani* by mistake?"

Rain's eyebrows flew up and nearly disappeared in his hairline. Then they came plummeting back down into a fierce, haughty frown. "I am not mistaken, if this is what you imply." His voice was stiff, his eyes hot. Offended pride slapped at her senses.

"I'm sorry," she apologized quickly. "I didn't mean to insult you. I just don't understand how you *know*." She bit her lip. "How can you know? How can you be sure?"

"I am sure." The finality of his tone signaled an end to the discussion.

Ellie subsided into silence for all of five seconds, before the question struggling inside her burst free. "How is it different from what you felt for Lady Sariel?"

Rain gave her an exasperated look. He obviously wasn't used to people who insisted on continuing a discussion once he had indicated he was done with the subject. "Comparing the two is like comparing the Great Sun and the Mother moon. They both shine light on the world, but one is the light itself and the other is a reflection."

"Oh." She frowned. So which was she, the light or the reflection?

"The sun, Ellysetta. You are the sun."

She eyed him suspiciously. "I thought you said you couldn't read my mind."

"And so I cannot. But I would be a foolish man indeed not to know what question would come next once I compared my feelings for you and Sariel to the sun and the moon." His mouth twisted in a wry smile. "Women have not changed *that* much in a thousand years."

Did he really expect her to believe that she, a stranger he'd only met a few days ago, was the sun while Sariel, the woman for whom he'd scorched the world, was the moon?

"Please don't lie to flatter my vanity," she told him in a low voice. "I'd rather have the truth, no matter how harsh the sting that comes with it."

His anger was instant and palpable. "I do not lie, Ellysetta," he snapped. "Especially not to you."

She flinched but refused to back down. "I am young, My Lord Feyreisen, and ignorant—and even foolish at times—but I am not such a silly *pacheeta* as to believe you love me even the tiniest bit as much as you loved Lady Sariel. How could you? You barely know me."

Rain's face cleared and he shook his head. "We are talking at cross-purposes. You speak of love, while I speak of something far greater. You are my *shei'tani*, the other half of my soul. It is a bonding so deep I could never hope to deny it, even if that was my desire. Feelings of the heart are nothing compared to that."

A few days ago, his words would have left her swooning with daydreams of love and romance. Now, however, all she could think of was not what he had said, but rather what he had left unsaid. *When you wager with tairen, take care with your words.* Rain Tairen Soul might not lie, but that didn't stop him from dancing around the truth. Had he said he loved her? No. Had he said he wanted her? No. On the contrary, he said quite clearly he had to claim her even if he didn't want her.

"Somehow, I have upset you," he said, frowning. "This was not my intention."

"No. You haven't upset me." He wasn't the only one who could dance around words. Rain hadn't upset her. She'd done that herself by hoping her silly fantasy of absolute love, spawned by the stirring poetry of his countrymen, might actually come true.

Ellie stared hard at her clenched hands. She'd asked the gods for someone, anyone but Den, and they'd answered by sending her Rain Tairen Soul. She hadn't asked them for true love. She needed to learn how to be thankful for what graces she received, rather than yearning for those unbestowed. She had Rain and his devotion. She could live without his love.

She looked up into Rain's beautiful face and smiled with determined good humor. "I'm fine, really," she assured him. "I'm more fortunate than I ever thought possible."

"Can we do that again?" Ellie asked as she and Rain walked home through the streets of Celieria, ringed once more by her Fey guard. "Soon?" They had flown all afternoon, would have flown longer had they not promised her parents they would return before sunset.

"*Aiyah,*" Rain replied. "If it is your wish."

"I wish," she told him fervently.

His eyes crinkled at the corners. "Then we will do it again." He grimaced ever so slightly. "With your parents' permission, of course."

"Of course." Ellie smiled. The Tairen Soul chafed at the restraint, but she was pleased that he cared enough to honor her parents and her country's customs. "And thank you."

His gaze was tender, as was the faint hint of a curve on his lips. "*Sha vel'mei, shei'tani.*"

The Baristani household, when they returned, was in chaos. Ellie couldn't believe her eyes. Gaily wrapped packages sat on every available surface, while others lay tossed on the floor with their ribbons and paper ripped and tangled. Dress pattern books lay scattered on the settee, several of them open. Shoe boxes, with their contents spilling out, were jumbled beside a lamp table. Swatches of fabric and lace dangled from the back of a chair and made a haphazard path across the floor. The smell of something burning emanated from the kitchen.

Apprehension clutched at Ellie, and she felt Rain stiffen at her side. Drawing blades with a quiet hiss, the quintet of Fey warriors fanned out quickly and silently, like dark shadows whispering through the house. Rain gestured, and light surrounded Ellie.

"Mama?" Ellie called.

"Just a chime!" Lauriana's voice shouted from the kitchen. There was a sound of muffled cursing, then something banged, and Ellie heard the sizzle of water hitting a hot surface.

"I've burned the dinner rolls." Lauriana appeared in the doorway to the kitchen, wiping her hands on her apron and scowling. "What in the name of . . . ?" The scowl darkened and her fists planted themselves on her hips as she surveyed the destruction in the room. "Lillis!" she yelled. "Lillis Angelisa Baristani, come here this instant!"

Ellie heard a door bang at the back of the house, then the sound of small feet racing. Lillis burst breathlessly into the room, followed close on her heels by an equally breathless Lorelle. Their hair was disheveled, but it was obvious they were unharmed.

The glow of magic around Ellie winked out. Rain straightened from the tense, slightly crouching position he had assumed. The Fey warriors who had fanned out in the room returned and sheathed their weapons.

"Yes, Mama?" Lillis gasped.

"I thought I told you to keep that cat out of this room. Look at the mess she's made."

"I know, Mama. I'm sorry. I gave her to Kieran, and she was behaving so well, but then he starting doing magic and—"

"Magic?" Lauriana echoed sharply.

"A thousand pardons, Madam Baristani." Kieran entered the room, followed by Kiel. Lillis's tiny white kitten, an adorable blue-eyed darling named Love, was perched on Kieran's shoulder. Her stubby pennant of a tail flicked continuously at his ear, and she was purring loud enough for all to hear. She looked far too innocent to have caused such wholesale destruction.

"It is my fault," Kieran said. "Kiel and I will clean up the mess."

"Let me assist you," Bel offered, and a white glow of Air lit his fingertips.

"*Nei!*" Kiel and Kieran shouted in unison.

At the same instant, sweet, adorable Love sprang into screeching, insane life and launched herself off Kieran's shoulder, fangs gleaming, claws bared, every little white hair on her body standing straight up. She landed with a thud on top of the pile of pattern books, and the sound of ripping pages filled the air as her claws scrabbled for purchase.

Kieran dove for her, but she eluded him, leaping to the chair draped with fabric. Swatches spat out from beneath her frantically pedaling feet.

"Let go, Bel," Kiel commanded. "She senses when anyone calls magic within a tairen-length of her, and she *hates* it."

Bel released his power and the kitten went skittering across the floor to hide under a tall, carved display cabinet. Blue eyes shone out from the darkness as Love crouched there, hissing and watching them warily.

"She hates Air especially," Kieran added, climbing to his feet and running a hand through his hair. That was when Ellie noticed there were enough bleeding scratches on the backs of his hands to form a Stones grid. "I would have thought it would be Water, wouldn't you?" He shook his head and grinned a little. "Perhaps she's got a bit of tairen in her rather than just plain house cat. Fire, Water, and Earth only get her back up. Air makes her crazy. And if you want to see real feline insanity, try a weave of Spirit."

"*Aiyah,*" Kiel agreed with a shudder. "That's what caused all this." His hands gestured to the destruction throughout the room.

Ellie bit her lip, trying hard not to laugh as Kieran crossed the room to crouch down beside the cabinet and croon, "Here, kit, kit, kit. Come here, little Love. That bad Fey warrior has put his nasty magic away." Kieran turned his head just slightly to flash a laughing blue-eyed look at Belliard as the older Fey's back went stiff.

Within a few chimes, Kieran had successfully coaxed Love out of hiding, and once more she perched on his shoulder, purred, and flicked his ear with her stubby little tail.

"How sweet of you, Lillis, to let Kieran hold your kitten," Ellie remarked.

"I gave her to him," Lillis said proudly. "It was the best reward I could think of."

"Reward?"

"For pushing Kelissande into the river."

Ellie rounded on Kieran. "You were responsible for that?"

Kieran smiled, shrugged, and scratched a finger beneath Love's chin.

Ellie shook her head. Centuries old he might be, but there was still plenty of mischief in him. She turned back to her mother. "Mama, do you need any help in the kitchen?"

Lauriana was still staring daggers at the Fey for weaving magic in her house. At Ellie's question, she gave them one last frowning glare and turned away. "No. Just have the girls clean up this mess. You need to look through those pattern books and make some decisions about what you want. Maestra Binchi said she'll send a lad round tonight to pick up your selection so they can cut the fabric for your wedding gown tonight and do the first fitting tomorrow morning. The other three dressmakers have asked for the same thing." Which explained all the pattern books and fabric swatches Love had scattered everywhere. "And Lady Marissya sent a note saying that you and the Feyreisen are expected at the palace for dinner on Kingsday night. She's already selected a gown for you, and it's being made, along with everything else you'll need to wear." Lauriana disappeared through the kitchen door.

Dinner? At the palace? Three days from now? Ellie stared up at Rain in dismay.

"Peace, *shei'tani*. We do not have to go."

"Oh, and one more thing," Lauriana said, popping back out of the kitchen. "Lady Marissya says you have to go. Something about upholding Fey honor and family ties."

"Where is Marissya's note?" Rain asked. Lauriana gestured to a small table by the front door and disappeared back into the kitchen. Rain crossed to the table in four long strides, read Marissya's note, then crumpled it in his hand, glowering. The note burst into flames.

On Kieran's shoulder, Love hissed and arched her back. Kieran gave his king a reproachful look, then set about soothing his magic-ruffled pet.

"It appears we do have to go," Ellie said. She swallowed her trepidation and smiled bravely. "I'll try not to embarrass you with my poor social graces."

Rain frowned at her. "You bring pride to this Fey," he replied. "Never believe otherwise." He shook his head. "There is an attempt in the Celierian Council to reopen the Eld borders. I have urged Dorian not to do so, but there is opposition in the Council of Lords. He is holding this dinner in our honor in order that he and I might present a united front against those who oppose him. Marissya has sworn a Fey oath guaranteeing that you and I will be there. That makes it impossible for us not to go. But even without Marissya's oath, if Dorian asks for my help to keep the Eld out of Celieria, then I must give it."

"According to the papers, the Elden ambassador just wants to open trade between our countries again," Ellie said. "That doesn't seem like such a bad thing."

"It is never 'just' trade with the Eld."

"How can you be sure?"

"Because I know the Eld. Because I sense the darkness. The serpent is there, waiting in the grass. It has been coiled so quietly for so long, Celierians have forgotten it. Even among the Fey, there are those who have forgotten how quickly the serpent can strike, how insidious and lethal is its venom. They think we can walk the path and not be bitten."

"But you don't think so."

"I am unwilling to take the chance." His face was grim, his eyes shadowed. "I have seen what Elden Mages can do to a Fey. I hope never to see it again."

Ellie remembered the torment Rain had shared with her

in the museum that first night. She never again wanted to witness—even secondhand—anything remotely like the horrors he had experienced in the Wars.

"Then of course we must go," she said, forcing down her own curl of dread. She'd met a number of Celierian nobles when assisting her father, and for every one she'd thought was kind, she'd met ten more who weren't. She had no illusions about the kind of reception she would receive from them. "Perhaps we won't have to stay long?"

"Longer than I would like," he grumbled. "Celieria's noble families are full of dark-souled creatures. I have never been able to abide them."

"Well, let's worry about tomorrow when it comes," she declared, pushing aside her useless fears. "For now, we have a mess to clean up." She bent to gather up the pattern books and all their torn pages.

The sensation came without warning, like deadly ice spiders crawling up her spine. Every hair on Ellie's body stood on end. The pattern books spilled from her hands to the floor. She jerked up and instinctively grabbed hold of Rain's arm, leaning into his strength and shivering.

"*Shei'tani*?" His concern was instant. "What is it?"

"I—" As suddenly as the feeling had come, it was gone. She exhaled. "Nothing."

"Ellysetta." His hands cupped her face, forcing her to meet his eyes. "Do not keep things from me. I am your mate. You must trust me. I can sense your fear, but not what caused it. Tell me what it was you felt." He was frowning, his black brows drawn together, his eyes intent and demanding.

"It's nothing. Just a ghost treading on my grave."

"A ghost? A wandering soul?"

She laughed a little. "I didn't mean that literally. It's just an old Celierian saying for when something makes you frightened for no reason."

"Old sayings are usually grounded in old truths," Rain told her, still frowning. "Have you had such feelings before?"

"On and off, ever since I was a child." She gave him a

lopsided smile. "It's one of the many little oddities about me that make me undesirable as a Celierian bride. The feelings never seem to mean anything in particular. They just scare me a little." But not nearly as much as those waking nightmares that left her sobbing in agony and terror just before a seizure. She forced a reassuring smile to her face. "I'm fine. I'm sure it's nothing."

Opening his Fey senses, Rain stretched the limits of his awareness, his mind filling with thousands of thoughts, mundane, mortal, many dark but none an obvious threat to the young woman by his side. In addition, he probed for the telltale reddish-black glow of Azrahn. He found nothing.

He glanced at Love, but the kitten was still purring on Kieran's shoulder. Whatever the wandering soul was, it did not trigger fear in Love the way magic apparently did.

Because he could sense no danger, he nodded. "Very well, then. It must indeed have been nothing." But his instincts urged caution. He met Bel's eyes. He didn't need to say a word. Bel simply nodded. The Fey would be on their guard.

High Mage Vadim Maur dipped his quill in the inkpot beside him and recorded the details of his latest experiment on a piece of blank parchment. The waterclock on the wall of his office softly chimed the first silver bells of the evening. Even without the clock, he knew the sun had set over Eld. The tingle of magic in his flesh had strengthened, as it did every night when light retreated from the world. Azreisenahn, the dark magic of the Mages more commonly known as Azrahn, thrived in the night. The darker the sky, the greater his magic, and the more powerful the spells he could cast.

Next to the waterclock, a mechanical moonclock ticked slowly. The golden orb representing the Great Sun had disappeared, and the small globes representing the two moons had risen. Painted half white and half black, the globes had rotated on their slender brass rods to show the current moonphase. Unfortunately, both the Mother and Daughter had just waxed full, and his magic was at its lowest ebb of the year. Discovery of the girl—if she was indeed the one he'd been searching for so long—couldn't have come at a worse time.

A knock sounded on his office door. "Enter," Vadim called. He looked up from his desk as his apprentice, the young but very powerful Mage Kolis Manza, entered. The younger man's red robes swirled around him as he walked. About his waist, Kolis wore a scarlet sash embroidered with golden threads and decorated with numerous dark, shining jewels, each a commemoration of a great achievement. Kolis was a Sulimage, the Eld equivalent of a journeyman, and he was famous among the novitiates, apprentices, and his fellow Sulimages for his magical prowess. His current service in Celieria, coveted by even the most experienced, fully ranked Primages, was one of the many important tasks that Vadim had set before him over the years to complete his training.

"Well?" Vadim prompted.

Kolis bowed deep, his vivid blue-green eyes suitably unfathomable, though Vadim thought he detected a hint of excitement. "I'm almost certain it is she, Master," he replied, "the one that was lost. She was found abandoned twenty-three years ago in the forests of Norban. The Celierian who tried to wed her said there are rumors she is demon-cursed, and he claims to have seen her work magic. Healing, finding lost things, perhaps more."

Anger curled in Vadim's belly, and just as quickly was snuffed out. If his pets had deceived him, they would suffer for it . . . but first he must ascertain the depths of their deceit. After a thousand years of captivity and experimentation, they were fragile, close to succumbing to the catatonic death sleep that had claimed all but a few of their fellow captives. He would not risk destroying them without cause.

"If her magic was substantial, I would have detected it before now. She must be powerful to be of use to me." His fingers drummed on the polished wood of his desktop.

"Does it matter, Master? She is the Tairen Soul's truemate. Isn't that enough? Through her you can destroy him."

"No, Kolis. We've seen what this Tairen Soul will do when deprived of a mate. I'm not as big a fool as my predecessor was. We've made too much progress to risk that sort of destruction again without an extraordinary reason. She must have exceptional power, and I must have proof of it." His fingers stilled. His eyes flashed up. "Take your rest for a few bells. Rejuvenate yourself, then return to Celieria," he instructed. "Test her magic. A master's strength in any of the six branches would be enough for me to risk the Tairen Soul's wrath. And bring me back her blood. She hides too well. I need her blood to strengthen the seeking spell."

"But, Master, she is guarded round the clock."

"I trust your judgment, Kolis. You will find a way. Use that Eld girl you told me about and your other *umagi*." He held Kolis's gaze steadily.

"I will not fail you, Master." Kolis bowed again, deeply as befitting an apprentice to his master, as befitting any man before the greatest Mage of Eld.

Ellie was dreaming she was back in the park. Only this time, the girl who was pushed into the river wasn't Kelissande, it was Ellysetta.

Mocking laughter rang out. A crowd had gathered at the river's edge, all the tradesmen she'd met today, the king and the queen, the courtiers, even the Fey. They were laughing and pointing at Ellie as she dragged herself out of the river. Maestra Binchi howled and said, "What did I tell you? Sowlet ears." The Archbishop stood beside Ellie's mother, and both of them pointed at her, shouting, "Demon-cursed!"

"Did you really think he would ever choose you?" Sariel stood with Rain at her side, one hand clutching his arm possessively. "He's mine, and he always will be." Sariel's midnight hair lightened, turning golden blond. Her face changed, too, and then it was Kelissande who stood at Rain's side, sneering, "Ellie Lack Grace."

Ellie stared at the hand on Rain's arm, and a terrible fury bloomed in her heart. She struck out wildly, raking her fingers across Kelissande's face, but her hands had become talons. Kelissande's perfect skin shredded. Blood soaked Ellie's clawed, hideous hands. She screamed and screamed. Fey leapt towards her, blades bared and deadly. Power flamed in Rain's eyes and shot from his fingertips as he cried, "Demon cursed! Servant of the Dark Lord!"

A cold, howling wind swept over her, a maelstrom of darkness that ripped her away and left her alone and shivering in a cold, dead world of shadows. Her own weeping was the only sound in the emptiness. And when that died away, she heard the familiar hissing, malevolent whisper. "Girl . . . you cannot hide forever. Your true nature will reveal itself eventually."

Rain stood on the palace rooftop, breathing in the still-warm night air and absorbing the scents and sounds of the city. Eyes closed, senses flowing out on every path, he searched as he had all evening for traces of the "wandering soul" that had attacked Ellysetta. He found darkness and evil, but nothing more sinister than that which existed in every mortal city.

Horse hooves and steel-rimmed carriage wheels clattered on the cobbles below. He released his weaves and glanced down to watch a noble family alight. Throughout the day, the nobles from the outlying estates had been arriving for Prince Dorian's betrothal celebrations and the biannual convening of the Council of Lords. By this time tomorrow every room in the palace would be full, every grand residence in the city buzzing with activity, and soon the heads of those noble houses would decide the fate of their country.

Too many, he feared, had forgotten the harsh lessons of the past and the sacrifices of their ancestors. Mortals always did. Rain had not. He remembered Dorian I and Marikah vol Serranis Torreval and the abrupt, shocking brutality of their deaths. He remembered Dorian II and his courage as he led his country through bitter, bloody years of war. He remembered the staggering price that Fey, Celierians, Elves, and

Danae alike had paid to live free of Eld corruptions and the domination of the Mages.

Just the thought of Celieria's lords contemplating friendship with their northern neighbor made the tairen scream in fury and Rain's hands itch to bare lethal Fey steel. Free men could never hope to live in peace with the Eld as long as a single Mage held power. Every fool who had ever tried doomed himself and his children to be soul-bound by the Mages and enslaved in the service of Seledorn, God of Shadows. Why was it so impossible for mortals to remember that? Had they become so soft, so certain that peace and freedom were gods-given rights rather than hard-won gifts, that they could no longer recognize evil when it stood on their doorstep?

"Mortal lives are short," Marissya had reminded him earlier. "The ones who remember as we do are dead and gone centuries ago."

"And these newer generations cannot read?" he'd countered bitterly. "The suffering of our friends and our people during the Mage Wars was well documented—specifically so such evil would never be forgotten. And yet it has been."

"You must have patience, Rain," she'd counseled. "Except for my one visit each year, men have lived with little in the way of immortal guidance for centuries. The Elves have kept to their mountains and forests, the Danae to their marshes and groves, and we have sequestered ourselves behind the Faering Mists. You cannot expect the mortals to accept everything we say without question. They never did even when we lived among them."

"And I never liked them then, either."

She'd sighed and shaken her head. "It's best you keep that truth to yourself. If we're to have any hope of keeping the borders closed, we must be patient and diplomatic—and tactful. Even when we would rather do otherwise."

Rain hadn't been fooled. She'd said "we" but she'd meant him. Unfortunately for Celieria, patience, diplomacy, and tact were traits he'd never possessed. He'd always been too quick to

anger, too impatient with the shortcomings of others—
mortals, in particular. And those traits had only grown worse
since the Wars.

Rainier vel'En Daris, the young Tairen Soul, had lost
countless dear friends, his family, his mate, even his own sanity,
to save Celieria once before. Rainier vel'En Daris Feyreisen,
the Defender of the Fey, would not risk another drop of precious Fey blood to protect ungrateful fools who willfully
blinded themselves to the truths and wisdom of the past.

And he would scorch the world ten times over before ex-
posing Ellysetta to the evil of Elden Mages.

Feeling a sudden need to be at his truemate's side, Rain
leapt into the sky and winged west, towards the humbler
homes of Celieria's artisans and craftsmasters. The Fey
guarding the Baristani home saw him coming and opened
their protective weaves to let him pass. He Changed with
fluid ease, streaming through Ellysetta's bedroom window
and regaining Fey form at her bedside, wrapped in Spirit
weaves to hide his presence from mortal eyes.

She was sleeping, but not peacefully. Her head thrashed on
the pillow, and her breath caught on a sob of fear that roused
his every protective instinct. He flung out his senses, testing
all the magical and sorcerous routes he knew, but once again
he found nothing. The source of her distress, whatever it was,
lay beyond the detection of his Fey senses.

He slipped into the narrow bed beside her and wrapped his
arms around her. "*Las, shei'tani*. Do not fear. I am here." She
turned towards him, burying her face in the hollow of his
throat, and her tense muscles started to relax. In sleep, she
trusted him as a *shei'tani* should.

He breathed in the flowery scent of her bright hair and
closed his eyes. For the remaining bells of the night, he lay
there holding her in his arms. The tairen in him lay quietly,
still there, still hungry for its mate, but content to bide its
time, at least for this night.

Ellysetta's nightmares did not return, and Rain filled her
sleeping ears with whispered words, things a man only said to

his mate. Some of the words made her moan a little, others made her smile. And when he finally left her just before the dawn, her fingers clung to him and she gave a little cry of protest in her sleep as he slipped away.

CHAPTER TWELVE

Just after sunrise, the bell on the butcher shop door jingled. Den looked up from his place behind the service counter, and his scowl smoothed in surprise as he recognized the new customer. A faint chill rippled up the back of Den's neck. With a quick glance at his father, Den wiped his hands on his white butcher's apron and said, "Can I help you?"

Batay, the Sorrelian merchant ship captain, smiled. "I hope so, Goodman Brodson. If I may have a moment of your time?"

"Papa, do you mind?" The shop was filled with customers waiting for service. The Brodsons were getting out of the butcher business and had put the last of their stock on sale.

Gothar Brodson eyed the gold braid on the man's coat and nodded. "Go on, then." As Den slipped his apron off, Gothar murmured, "Ask him about the merchant ship business. I've a fancy to buy a ship or two." He grinned and slapped his son on the back.

Den veiled the flash of anger in his eyes and stepped out from behind the counter. "We can talk outside," he told the Sorrelian.

Fifteen chimes later, Den returned to his place behind

the butcher shop counter. Captain Batay's request had been odd, but Den had managed to find what the man asked for. Upstairs in the Brodson home above the butcher shop, on the lint brush Den's mother had used to tidy the blue suit he'd worn the night he had put his claiming mark on Ellysetta Baristani, Den had found three long, curling strands of flame-colored hair.

Why the Sorrelian needed Ellie's hair, Den didn't know. But the man had left with a smile on his face and a glass vial containing the three strands of hair in his pocket.

Outside, on the street corner, a ragged pamphleteer's boy began his morning cry: "Tairen Soul steals local man's bride! King and Queen cower in fear! Read the shocking truth they don't want you to know! Only three coppers!"

Several ragged scraps of paper trembled in Queen Annoura's hand. Before her, Lady Jiarine Montevero, a former Dazzle and current lady-in-waiting, stood waiting while Annoura read the pamphlets Jiarine had just delivered.

"There are many of these, you say?" Annoura asked.

Jiarine nodded. The long, dark curls draped over one shoulder bounced with the motion, and her sapphire-blue eyes shone with earnest concern. "Many times many, Majesty. The presses must have been running all night."

Annoura resisted the urge to crumple the leaflets and instead set them aside on the pearl-inlaid surface of her desk. "Thank you, Lady Jiarine."

Jiarine's gaze followed the discarded pamphlets. Her brows drew together in confusion. "My Queen? You cannot mean to ignore this. The pamphleteers have always been a thorn in the palace's heel, but this time . . . Majesty, those leaflets border on treason. They call your husband a puppet of the Fey, and you—"

"I read what they said, Jiarine," Annoura said, her voice as flat and hard as a marble tile. "You need not repeat it to me."

"I'm sorry, Majesty." The lady bobbed a curtsey but continued earnestly, "It's just that the people are already nervous because of the *dahl'reisen* murdering innocents in the north. And now the Tairen Soul has returned for the first time in a thousand years. Suspicions and fears are rising on many estates. The lords are worried. They can't help wondering if the *dahl'reisen* attacks and the Tairen Soul's arrival aren't in some way connected."

The thought had occurred to Annoura, as well. "I understand your concerns, Lady, but I assure you, the king and I are intimately familiar with the state of our kingdom."

"There's even a growing number of historians who are beginning to question whether the Eld Mages were really behind the assassination that started the Mage Wars," Jiarine persisted. "I know we've all been raised to believe that was true . . . but what if it's not?"

Annoura recalled her Steward of Affairs making some mention of the study in one of his reports a few months back, but at the time she'd dismissed it as nothing more than a handful of elderly men who'd addled their brains inhaling too much moldy parchment dust. She still didn't put much stock in the idea. Give an obsessive scholar a single sentence, and he could extrapolate entire reams of hidden meaning from it—all of it overanalyzed nonsense.

Then again, obsessive scholars and their myopic passions could serve a useful purpose when it came to discrediting political rivals. Rain Tairen Soul had already proven himself willing to use threats and intimidation to force Dorian's compliance. Annoura would not stand idly by while her husband's immortal kinsmen ordered him about like a trained pet. She made a mental note to have her steward find out more about those scholars and their theories.

For now, however, there was the matter of these pamphlets to deal with. Dorian was no puppet, and she—Annoura glanced back down at the illustrated pamphlet and her teeth snapped together—she was no little mouse queen squeaking in fear and fleeing the tairen's paw.

"Thank you, Lady Montevero," she said. "That will be

all." When Jiarine opened her mouth as if to protest, Annoura cut her off. "You are excused, Jiarine."

The lady's mouth closed and her expression faded to controlled blankness. She sank into a formal curtsey. "Your Majesty," she said, then took her leave.

When she was gone, Annoura snatched up the pamphlets, stalked out through a different door, and headed down a series of corridors to Dorian's private office. He was seated at his desk, a pair of spectacles perched on his nose as he pored over a stack of documents. She tossed the pamphlets on top of the papers he was reading. "Have you seen these?"

Dorian's lips thinned as he glanced at the ragged leaflets. "Corrias showed them to me this morning."

Her arms folded across her chest. *And he'd said nothing to me?* "What are you doing about this, Dorian?"

"What can I do, Annoura?" He leaned back in his chair, removed his spectacles, and regarded her with weary exasperation. "You know as well as I do that for every pamphleteer I stop, a dozen more spring up. Short of putting the city under martial law, I can't control what they do. I can only go on as I have been—doing my best to keep Celieria safe and strong."

"You cannot be seen as a puppet of the Fey. If the lords lose faith in you, you lose your ability to rule. You know that. The nobles are unsettled enough as it is. First the *dahl'reisen* begin slaughtering peasants; then *he* comes—Rainier v'el En Daris—for the first time in a thousand years, carrying unfounded tales of Mage power growing in Eld. The timing is suspicious. Can't you see that?"

Dorian rubbed the bridge of his nose. "So I should alienate the Fey—and terminate more than a thousand years of alliance—just because Rain Tairen Soul has come back into the world? What if he's right? What if the Mages really have regained power?"

"There's not a shred of proof to support that."

"Which is why I refused to invoke *primus* when he asked me to. I'm letting the lords decide whom they trust most, just as you advised." He pushed his chair back from the desk and walked over to one of the shuttered windows to look out at the manicured gardens below. His spine was straight, arms folded across his chest, feet slightly apart as if bracing to survive a blow.

Annoura knew that stance. Intractability wasn't far behind. And Dorian, when he dug in his heels, was impossible to budge. Time for a change of tactics.

She crossed the room to his side and laid a hand on his arm, tugged gently but insistently until he turned to face her. His expression was closed, hazel eyes distant. She framed his face in both hands and gazed up with a look of compassion and sympathy, stroking the hair at his temples with gentle fingers.

"Dorian," she said softly, "beloved, heart of my heart, I know this is difficult for you. I know how much you love them—Lady Marissya, Lord Dax, even the warriors who accompany them each year." He'd told her so many times, and she'd seen the reverence in his eyes whenever he spoke of the *shei'dalin*. In the first years of their marriage, before she felt secure in her husband's affections, Annoura had actually been jealous of the effect Marissya had on him. Her hands grew tense for a moment before she forced them to continue their gentle stroking. "But the Tairen Soul is a stranger to us, a dangerous one at that. Celieria is entrusted to your keeping, my love. You must do what's right for us, regardless of what the Fey want."

"That *is* what I'm doing, Annoura."

"I know," she soothed. "I know. But the people—and the Lords of the Council—must be made to see it also. And up until now, all they've seen is you giving in to the Tairen Soul's demands. You broke a lawful betrothal on his behalf. You've allowed him to install a common peasant as his queen and ordered our court to dance attendance on her."

Dorian's expression, which had begun to soften, went suddenly cold and distant. He pulled her hands away from his face and stepped back several paces to fix her with a hard look. "You've just overplayed your hand, my dear. This isn't about me and my perceived strength or weakness. This is about you. He's wounded your pride, and you can't stand it."

"Dorian!" Annoura gasped in unfeigned shock. He'd never spoken to her in such a manner. "You know me better than that!"

"I do know you, my love. You are the reason my heart beats in my chest, but I am just as acquainted with your weaknesses as I am your strengths."

His jaw had tightened. His lips had thinned to an implacable line. Annoura could have screamed in frustration. The familiar expression was the one she'd been trying to avoid: intractability. This was Dorian the King, an immovable rock of authority and command.

"Like it or not, my dear, the Fey are my kin. But even were that not the case, their centuries of service, friendship, and goodwill to Celieria would compel me to consider the concerns of their king with all due respect and grave attention." Each word was fired from his mouth like a bolt from a crossbow. Sharp, clipped, unyielding. "I will afford him the opportunity to make his case to the Council. I will make every effort to smooth his way and encourage the lords to give him a full and fair hearing. And as injurious to your pride as it may be, I will welcome the Tairen Soul's mate as his queen, regardless of her humble birth—and so will you. For in the eyes of the Fey, a queen is exactly what Ellysetta Baristani is. She is a bright and shining light born to bring peace to their king's heart. And I am Fey enough to understand that, even if you cannot."

"Dorian!" Annoura wanted to wail and gnash her teeth.

"Go tend to your business, Annoura. Leave me to tend mine." He stepped around her, avoiding her outstretched hands, and took his seat.

She stood there in impotent frustration as he reached for his spectacles, thrust them into place, and picked up the parchment he'd been reading before her arrival. The pamphlets she'd brought fluttered to the floor. The illustration of the puppet king and squeaking mouse queen stared up at her in silent mockery.

"Close the door when you leave," Dorian instructed without looking up.

Her hands clenched in fists. She would not be made the fool. She would not be mocked and dismissed—not by the pamphleteers, not by the common rabble who gobbled up their insulting leaflets, not by Dorian, and especially not by the Fey or some woodcarver's slut.

She was Annoura, Queen of Celieria.

If Dorian would not stand up to the Fey, she would do it herself. As long as she had breath in her body, the Fey would not usurp the power of Celieria's throne or force their will upon Celieria's people without a fight. And one way or another, she would put that upstart peasant Ellysetta Baristani in her place.

In Celieria City's West End, having replaced the distinctive trappings of Captain Batay with the unremarkable garb of a simple merchant, Kolis Manza stood amidst the throngs of curiosity seekers gathered across the street from the Baristani family home. *Test her magic,* his master had said. *Find a way.*

Determined not to fail, Kolis had not taken his rest last night, but had instead spent several bells poring over book after book of spells and charms from the High Mage's private library. While many spells could force a response from even latent magic, few could do so while penetrating Fey shields and remaining undetected by watchful Fey warriors. Luckily, the Master's long association with the Feraz witchfolk had borne useful fruit, and in an old, handwritten text of Feraz witchspells tested on the High Mage's pets over the years, Kolis had found what he was looking for.

He put his hand in his coat pocket and grasped the small wax *talis* he'd prepared last night in Eld. The spell was so simple, its uses had been long overlooked by serious scholars of magecraft: a simple pressure spell designed to gradually amplify emotion and elicit a magical response, targeted at Ellysetta Baristani by one of the strands of hair Den Brodson had so helpfully produced this morning.

With his eyes on the Baristani house, Kolis began to chant the witchwords under his breath.

If one more person made a sneering remark about the "humble coziness" of her family's home or the "new" Ellysetta Baristani, Ellie wasn't going to be responsible for what happened. Her brows drew together in a thunderous scowl. Despite vague memories of disturbing dreams, she'd woken in an exceptionally happy mood this morning, and Rain's courtship gift of Stones had made her laugh with delight, as no doubt he'd meant her to. That lightheartedness was long gone. Now, it was all she could do to stop from screaming.

The Dark Lord take this whole exhausting, frustrating, sanity-scorching idea of a wedding! She cast a blistering glare at the frenzied mob of seamstresses, florists, caterers, printers, decorators, wine merchants, cobblers, and stuffy wedding advisors surrounding her. They had descended upon her parents' house just after breakfast and turned Ellie's peaceful morning into a war zone of raucous pre-wedding activity. Every half bell, a knock would sound on the door and a new throng of visitors would pour in. Couriers bearing packages, friends wanting to extend their congratulations, neighbors just being nosy, merchants, craftsmen.

The mad, unceasing rush of people and the constant barrage of questions—each merchant had at least a hundred questions, all needing a decision *now!*—had long since taken their toll on her sanity and had wiped every last vestige of good humor from her mood.

Twenty gowns, Lady Marissya had decreed. Twenty! Plus an enormous monstrosity of a wedding gown that required an entire wagonload of fabric and had taken most of the morning to fit. The queen's dressmaker, Maestra Binchi, who had been noticeably more respectful and accommodating this morning, had already departed with her half-dozen seamstresses to begin work on the wedding gown,

but another three court modistes and their respective gag-
gles of assistants were still industriously dedicating themselves to turning Ellie into a human pincushion.

"My lady, please stand still." Kneeling at Ellie's feet, one of
the seamstresses blew a strand of limp brown hair out of her
eyes and attempted—but failed—to sound patiently polite.
The seamstress's lips were pulled taut in a grimace that Ellie
concluded was supposed to be a deferential smile.

"I *am* standing still," Ellie replied through clenched teeth.
An awful, squeezing pressure had begun building in her head
earlier, as if her skull were caught in a tightening vise. The
voices around her formed a merciless, pounding drum, echoing inside her head, beating at the shreds of her control.

«*Las, Ellysetta.*» Bel's cool voice sounded in her mind.

Peace? *Peace,* he said? Over the top of the opaque curtain
of Spirit the Fey had woven to protect her modesty, Ellie sent
Bel a glare so scorching, his leathers nearly caught on fire.
The fierce warrior blinked in surprise and wisely retreated.

"Ellie." Oblivious to the brewing tempest, Lauriana approached with a selection of flowers in her hands. "For your
bridal wreath, which roses do you prefer? Maiden's Blush,
Sweet Kaidra, or Gentle Dawn?" She held up one of each velvety bloom, faint pink, creamy ivory, and pale yellow edged
with the barest hint of orange.

"I don't care, Mama." Ellie tried desperately to hold on to
her temper. "You choose."

«*Ellysetta.*» Rain called to her in a voice of insufferable
calm. But, of course, he would be calm. He'd been *gone* this
whole wretched morning. She ignored him.

"Hmm. I like Maiden's Blush, but the pink might clash
with your hair. Sweet Kaidra is lovely, of course, but it may be
a little too bland. Gentle Dawn . . . well, there's something
about yellow roses that I've always liked and the orange is a
shade that will suit you, I think. Come now, kit, give me your
honest opinion."

"Whichever you choose will be fine, Mama." Ellie could
feel her jaw muscles locking in place. Days from now, she

was sure they would find her, dead from this wedding torture, her lips still frozen and her teeth bared in a grim parody of a polite smile.

"All right, Ellie," Lauriana replied evenly. "I'll make the decision, since you don't care to. Gentle Dawn it is." Her skirts swished with violent little movements as she stalked away.

Ellie scowled, angry at her mother for getting upset, angry at herself for being the one to upset her. The anger was unsettling. Ellie wasn't a volatile person. She worked hard at keeping her emotions in check. Bad things happened when she didn't. Yet the anger was there. And growing. The pain in her head increased.

«Ellysetta.» Rain's voice sounded again, a bit more insistent this time. She continued to ignore him. She'd wanted a simple wedding. Flowers, perhaps, and a priest. But, no. The mighty Rain Tairen Soul mandated a huge court affair. And then conveniently absented himself from the resulting madness. Ellysetta's anger grew some more.

"Mistress Baristani?" A man's nasal voice sounded to her left.

"What?" Ellie barked and turned towards the voice.

The cobbler held up several pairs of shoes. "You've selected your footwear for your wedding, but you still need to select slippers for your ball gowns and a pair of boots for your day dresses. Something—if I may be so bold—a bit more elegant than your current footwear?"

"There is nothing wrong with my current footwear," she snapped. "It is the perfect footwear for a girl like me."

"Of course, Mistress Baristani." The cobbler gave a small, condescending smile and bowed. "But I'm referring to the new you."

Her anger flared higher. "There *is* no new me. I am the same me that I have always been. I will be the same me tomorrow, and the day after that, and the day after that."

"My lady, please, stand still just a few chimes more," the seamstress pleaded.

Ellie scowled down at her. "I am standing still!"

«Ellysetta, you will speak to me.»

He wanted her to speak? «*GET OUT OF MY MIND!*»
She felt his jagged burst of pain as her angry response blasted
between them, and the ache between her eyes became sharp,
gouging daggers thrusting into her brain. Dizziness assailed
her, but she fought it back.

"I apologize if my choice of words has offended you, Mistress Baristani," the cobbler said. "I merely meant that in your
new position, you will require a different form of attire."

"I am very aware of what you meant, ser. But I am now
and always will be a woodcarver's daughter. No amount of
fancy new clothes—or elegant footwear—will ever change
that." Ellie raised a hand to her head and began to rub her
temple.

"Please, Lady Ellysetta, put your arm back down and hold
still," the seamstress begged.

Irritation shrieked through Ellie, but she lowered her arm.

"Ah, Duanniza Baristani," Duan Parlo Vincenze, the elegant
Capellan chef who catered to the cream of Celierian society,
gestured extravagantly with a lace-festooned handkerchief. "I
have sketched the perfect bridal cake for you. Tall. Elegant.
Simple but *boi mezza*, very pretty." He held up the sketch of a
towering wedding cake. "You like, eh?"

Ellie stared at the sketch in horror. Layer after angular
layer of plain square cakes perched on tall, gawky columns.
The cake was stark in its plainness, except for gargantuan
bunches of dramatically sketched flowers that dripped
down the columns. She supposed the chef meant the flowers to complement the minimalist appearance of the cake,
but to her they looked like monstrous weedy growths run
amok. Ill-fitting, ridiculous attempts to make something
pitifully plain look attractive and feminine.

"No. I don't like." Her chest felt tight. The room was too
small, too crowded. Her mind whirled. The pain in her head
was staggering. The anger seemed to be consuming her, stealing the very breath from her lungs.

With a gasp of offended pride, the chef whipped his lacy

handkerchief through the air like a sword. "But, Duanniza, it is perfect for you."

"You must at least select a pair of slippers for the ball. Lady Marissya insisted."

"My lady, please stand still. Pella needs to repin the waist of this gown."

"The cake is hideous! I don't care about the flaming slippers! And for the last time, *I am standing still!*" Gods, she needed air. She was going mad. She couldn't breathe. Her vision began to blur.

"Ellysetta." Rain stood in the doorway, and there was no mistaking the whip of command in his voice.

"*WHAT*?" Anger roared to blazing life. This was all *his* fault! She whirled to face him. Pain stabbed into her waist as she impaled herself on the long, wickedly sharp tailor's pin held in the seamstress Pella's hand.

Ellie screamed.

Every window in the Baristani house exploded in a cloud of shattered fragments.

Rain leapt forward, power bursting around him, his teeth bared in savage fury.

"Get back!" he roared. Most of the people in the room were too stunned to move, but a punishing thrust of Air flung their bodies out of his path. Rain destroyed Bel's opaque weave of Spirit with a single thought. Seamstresses shrieked and fled like mice as the Tairen Soul reached for his mate.

Across the street, as the screams of the milling crowd still echoed in the aftermath of the exploding windows, Kolis Manza cursed and turned away. So close. He'd been so close.

Magic had definitely been released. Elemental Air magic and a masterful burst of it. But just before the burst of Air, the Tairen Soul had arrived, power radiating from him in a huge, shining, barely controlled aura that had distorted Kolis's view. And when the Tairen Soul had released blasting weaves of his own, he'd wiped away all hope of tracing the first weave to its source.

The magic had been hers. Kolis *knew* it had been hers.

But because he hadn't witnessed the source of the magic with his own senses, he couldn't be sure. He *had* to be sure. The High Mage wasn't forgiving of mistakes.

Kolis crushed the now-drained Feraz *talis* in his hand and threw it down a sewer grate. The small piece of beeswax, wrapped tight with a single flame-colored strand of hair, made a tiny, distant splash as it hit the water below and was carried away.

"I'm sorry I acted so badly," Ellie whispered for the thousandth time. "I don't know what came over me. I'm not like that. I don't get angry. I don't treat people rudely."

"Shh," Rain soothed. "*Las, shei'tani.*" He stroked her hair and held her close as they sat together on the narrow bed in her room.

After catching Ellie in his arms, Rain had carried her upstairs to her bedroom and then refused to leave her. Lauriana had strenuously objected to his presence on her daughter's bed, but a hot, dangerous look and a snarling command to hold her tongue or risk having it silenced shut her up. Not the most diplomatic of solutions. She'd turned right around and would have marched out of the house to fetch her husband had not Bel hurried after her to soothe the worst of her maternal outrage. They were still downstairs, Lauriana subjecting Bel to a furious tirade recounting every indignity and offense the Fey had visited upon her family and their good name, but at least she'd left Rain in peace to tend his truemate.

"I didn't mean to yell at you," Ellie said again. "I don't understand why I let them upset me so badly. It was as if there was some terrible, angry force inside me, and it kept growing stronger and stronger, and I kept getting madder and madder."

"It's all right, Ellysetta. Those people are gone." He stroked her cheek. "They won't be back, except by appointment, and I will be with you when they come."

Despite the worry and fear coloring her emotions, she smiled against his hand. "So you can explode all the windows again if they bother me? Maybe we'd better not have them come to the house. Mama might get tired of cleaning up the glass."

Rain stilled.

Ellysetta scooted back so she could look at him. "What?"

He met her gaze. "It was not I who destroyed the windows, Ellysetta."

She blinked. "It wasn't? Then Bel did it?" She gave a small laugh and shook her head. "I wouldn't have thought he was the type for such a display."

"*Nei*. It was not Bel, nor any other of the Fey."

Ellysetta's smooth forehead wrinkled in a confused frown. "Then . . . who?"

Rain gazed at her steadily, saying nothing.

"No," she said. "It wasn't me."

"You used Air. An incredibly fine yet powerful weave that struck only the windows. Every window." He saw her glance at the perfectly intact bedroom window. "The warriors repaired them while you were unconscious. But they were all destroyed. Reduced to dust."

"It wasn't me," she insisted. "You must be mistaken."

"I am not mistaken. There is power in you, Ellysetta. Great power."

"No." She dragged her fingers through her hair, tangling the wild curls.

"Why do you fear what is inside you?"

"Why do you keep insisting that I'm magic?"

"Because you are. I've seen evidence of it several times now. On the day you called me out of the sky, you used Earth. Not much. It was only a small healing weave, but both Marissya and I sensed it. The night of our betrothal, you wove Spirit on your mother with so much power packed in so fine a weave that even most Fey would not have known they were being influenced, or been able to resist. Today, you used Air in a very concentrated and powerful weave. All the Fey sensed it this time."

"Maybe it was someone else who destroyed the windows," she suggested. "You think there are Elden Mages in Celieria. Maybe it was one of them."

His *shei'tani* was grasping at straws, so eager to deny her power. He still did not understand why she would fear it so. Lauriana's explanation of all Celierians' fear of magic-blighted forests didn't ring true. Ellysetta wasn't afraid of all magic like her mother; only her *own* magic truly frightened her. And Rain could not imagine why that would be so.

"This was no Mage, Ellysetta. I saw the weaves with my own Fey eyes, and they came from you."

"Must we talk about this now?"

Rain sighed. "Of course not." He rose, held out a hand, and helped her to her feet. She looked so . . . lost, so worried. He brushed thick spirals of hair away from her face. "It will be all right, Ellysetta." And then, because he couldn't bear not to, he kissed her.

His mouth slanted over hers softly at first. A kiss of reassurance and the gentler side of *shei'tanitsa*. But as her warm breath mingled with his, and the honeyed sweetness of her mouth opened to his, tenderness blossomed into desire. He groaned deep in his throat, a rumbling sound of restraint and longing, and his kiss grew firmer.

Rain's fingers delved into the bright silk of her hair, curving around to the back of her head and holding her fast. All softness fled his body, only a remnant of it remaining in his kiss, but that too burned away the instant Ellysetta's arms wrapped around him and her hands pulled him closer with surprising strength.

The tairen stirred, and Ellie flinched. Rain clamped a ruthless hold on the beast within him. Not this time. The tairen would not rob him of this wonderful moment.

His hands pulled free of her hair, and he trailed them down her back, fretting at the layers of cloth that separated her skin from his. With just a small weave of Earth, he could banish those annoying layers. Rain summoned power to his fingertips.

«*Rain.*» Bel's warning sounded.

Someone cleared a throat loudly from the doorway.

Rain released his power and tore his lips from Ellysetta's. A blistering torrent of curses battled on the tip of his tongue, held back only with great effort.

He dragged in a breath and turned to face Lauriana Baristani.

Color stained the woman's cheeks, but her accompanying narrow-eyed look made it clear the flush did not come from embarrassment at having interrupted an intimate embrace.

"I came to check on Ellysetta," Lauriana said. "As she is most definitely awake, there's no need for either of you to remain in her bedchamber."

Ellysetta blushed. "Yes, Mama."

Lauriana gestured for Rain and Ellie to precede her downstairs—so he couldn't steal another kiss, Rain surmised, cursing Celierians and their restrictive customs. As he entered the small home's main room, Rain met Bel's gaze and wasn't pleased to see amusement lurking in his friend's eyes beside the apologetic sympathy.

«*I'm sorry, Rain.*»

«*So I see.*»

«*Nei, truly.*» But Bel's laughter broke free across their link.

Rain scowled and turned his attention back to his *shei'tani*, who was staring at a wall heaped with packages.

"*More* gifts?" Ellysetta asked her mother. "Who are these from?"

"The gods only know. Simple-gentry trying to ingratiate themselves with the Feyreisen. Wealthy merchants attempting the same. Friends. Neighbors. Complete strangers." Lauriana shrugged. "I gave up inspecting whom they're from and just starting stacking them. The parlor is already full."

Ellysetta shook her head. "Amazing." Then the expression on her face grew somber and she put her arm around her mother's shoulders. "I'm sorry for upsetting you earlier,

Mama. I know everything's in turmoil, and it's my fault. There's so much to do in so little time, and—"

"Shh." Lauriana put a finger on her daughter's lips. "I know, kit. And I'm sorry, too, for snapping at you. It was a madhouse here this morning. There was too much going on all at once. I must admit I'm grateful your betrothed sent them all packing, though I don't much approve of his methods." Lauriana cast a dark look Rain's way. "Exploding windows and flying bodies only added to the madness."

Rain bowed low. "I shall endeavor to show restraint in future." Ellysetta gave him a startled glance. *«Say nothing, shei'-tani. It is best that all believe I am responsible for the windows.»* After a moment, she nodded.

"I have several errands to run," Lauriana said. "Why don't the two of you open the wedding gifts in the parlor, so we can clear some space."

What? Rain opened his mouth to object, but before he could say a word, he heard his *shei'tani* doom them both.

"Yes, Mama."

Rain closed his mouth and carefully blanked his face.

"There's a book in the secretary. Be sure you write down who gave you what, so I have some hope of sending appropriate gratitudes."

"Yes, Mama."

"Well, then, I'd best be going. I've got a hundred things to do. Don't forget that Master Fellows, the queen's Master of Graces, is coming here at fourteen bells to begin your instruction in the noble graces. Be sure to tidy up before he arrives—both the house *and* your own appearance. You don't want to make a bad first impression."

"Yes, Mama." As Lauriana bustled off, Ellysetta glanced at Rain uncertainly. "Do you mind about opening the gifts?"

He did, of course. Opening gifts from Celierians he neither knew nor cared about was not how he would choose to spend his courtship bells. He answered diplomatically. "My time is yours, Ellysetta. If this is how you choose to spend it, then so it shall be spent."

She bit her lip. "It's just that Mama's already done so much, and I've done so little. And it's my wedding. Our wedding."

"I understand, *shei'tani*."

"Do kings even open their own gifts?" she asked as they walked down the short hallway to the parlor.

"Apparently this one does." The grumble in his voice made her smile, as he'd hoped it would. But when they reached the parlor and Rain saw the gifts, crammed into every inch of space and stacked to the ceiling, he called for reinforcements. Ellysetta's quintet came running in response to their king's summons, though when they heard what he wanted of them, their faces went predictably blank.

"It won't be that bad," Ellysetta promised, "especially with all of you helping."

"They live to serve you, *shei'tani*," Rain assured her. After serving as a source of amusement to these Fey over the last few days, it gave Rain great pleasure to turn the tables.

Rain watched as his five best warriors squeezed into the tiny parlor, picked their way through the jungle of wedding gifts as if tiptoeing through a nest of Drogan sand vipers, and settled down with stone-faced stoicism to proceed with the humiliatingly un-warrior-like task of opening presents.

«*You bring pride to this Fey,*» Rain sent on their common path, and his tone rang with amusement.

Five lethal glances speared him. For the first time in a thousand years, Rain Tairen Soul threw back his head and laughed.

CHAPTER THIRTEEN

Ten thousand swords before you, ten thousand daggers
    drawn,
Ten thousand lives defend you, ten thousand warriors strong.
Our blood will spill ten thousand times.
In hope, ten thousand sigh.
For love we face ten thousand deaths,
With joy, ten thousand die.
Ten thousand Fey before you, ten thousand fierce and tall,
Ten thousand souls protect you, beloved of us all.

           —Chorus from *Ten Thousand Swords,*
                a Fey Warrior's Song

Even with seven pairs of hands, unwrapping and recording all the wedding gifts was tedious work. To pass the time, Adrial vel Arquinas began to hum a rhythmic tune. His brother Rowan soon joined him, then Kiel. Then Kieran began to sing. To Ellie's amazement, Rain soon joined in, his voice a deep, rich baritone.

They sang in Feyan, and though Ellie only understood a word or two here and there, the song's beat and the melodious sound of the lyrics made her smile. "That was beautiful," she said when they finished. "What was it?"

"A Fey warrior's song called 'Ten Thousand Swords,'" Rain told her. "It is a song all Fey youths learn when they are training to become warriors."

"Can you translate it for me?" With a nod, he did so, and tears sprang to her eyes as she listened to the words that vowed the death of thousands to protect the life of one woman. She gave a little shiver. "Surely it's just a song. I, for one, wouldn't want any of you dying for me."

"It is the greatest of honors to die in the defense of a *shei'-*

tani," Kiel protested. "Such a warrior will be born to this world again, to find a truemate of his own."

Holding a forgotten package on her lap, she looked at the faces of the men around her. "Do you all believe that?"

They exchanged glances, then nodded. "Of course," Adrial told her, and a chill worked up Ellysetta's spine as she suddenly realized how dear to her the warriors had become in such a short time. The thought of any one of them dying was like a knife to her heart.

"Peace, Ellysetta," Rain murmured. She felt a warm touch on the back of her hand, another on her face, even though he sat several feet away from her and had not moved a muscle. "None of them seek death yet."

"Seek death?" she repeated weakly.

"*Sheisan'dahlein*," Rowan supplied. "The Fey honor death."

"You seek death?" She stared at them all in horror.

"When we must," Belliard said. His cobalt eyes held a calm acceptance she couldn't begin to fathom.

"Why?"

The five warriors glanced at Rain, who hesitated, regarded Ellie with a searching look, then nodded briefly.

Setting aside the small golden dish he'd unwrapped and recorded, Bel began to explain. "Each time a Fey warrior claims a life, he takes the weight of that soul upon his. He absorbs the darkness of that soul and the pain of that soul's unfulfilled promise, its sorrows and regrets, and he carries the weight and the pain of it always, like a burning stone hung round his neck."

Ellie covered her mouth. "I've never heard of such a thing."

"It is the price the gods decreed for the many gifts they have bestowed on the Fey," Bel said. "And it is just. How much more greatly we value peace, knowing the price for taking a life. It is one of the reasons the Fey avoid war. In war, many good men die, and the soul of a good man is far harder to bear than that of one steeped in darkness, even though killing a dark one brings terrible pain." His voice dropped. Shadows dimmed his eyes, turning cobalt to brooding navy. "I would rather slay a thousand dark ones than cut down one good man."

"*Aiyah*," Rowan and Adrial agreed quietly.

"Is there nothing you can do to . . . get free of these souls?"

Bel blinked, and the shadows fled from his eyes. His hard, handsome face softened. His lips curved, not quite a smile, but almost. "If a warrior is lucky enough to find his *shei'-tani*," he said, "she can help ease his burden, for hers is the spirit of compassion and healing and she alone can touch her warrior's soul. He will still feel pain when he takes a life, but she can banish the darkness that comes with the pain and heal his soul."

"But *shei'tanis* are rare and precious," Kiel added. He brushed a lock of golden hair behind his ear, then deftly stripped silver paper from a small package to reveal a delicate china vase. He held it up to the glow of the lamp hanging from the ceiling and smiled as the lamplight illuminated the translucent porcelain. "Most warriors will live and die without ever finding their truemate, yet all of us still hope." With great care, he set the vase aside, and made note of both the gift and its sender on the paper before him.

Hope. Bel's small, not-quite-revealed smile was hope. Ellie felt her throat grow tight. It grew tighter when she realized that even that tiny hint of emotion was already gone from his face, replaced with careful blankness, as if he dared not display his hope for fear of its being stolen from him.

Bel reached for a large package with a huge blue bow. "So, when the weight of the souls he has taken becomes too much for a Fey to bear," he concluded, pulling the ends of the ribbon to unravel the extravagant bow, "when the stain on his soul grows so dark it threatens to consume him, the warrior has only two choices: *sheisan'dahlein*, the honor death, which gives him the hope of being born again to find the one who will complete his soul, or becoming *dahl'reisen*, a lost soul, outcast from the Fading Lands, in danger of turning to Azrahn and other dark magics, doomed for eternity." Bel's face went momentarily grim as he mentioned the last.

"But that's horrible."

"That is the lot of the Fey warrior," he answered. "Of all possible honor deaths, the greatest of them is to die protecting a truemate, for then the warrior is assured of finding his own truemate in his next life. It is one reason we dedicate our lives to the Dance of Knives. We strive for centuries to become the best of all Fey warriors, to earn the right to protect a *shei'tani*, to earn the right to die for her." Pulling a black-handled Fey'cha from the bands across his chest, Bel slit open the seals on the box he had just unwrapped.

"No," Ellysetta protested. "No. I won't allow it. I won't have any of you dying for me, not for any reason."

Silence fell in the room. All rustling of paper ceased. All motion ceased. It seemed to Ellie as if all breathing ceased.

Rain touched Ellie, this time with his hand rather than his magic. His long fingers closed over hers. His lavender eyes shone intently.

"You will allow it, *shei'tani*," he told her in a gentle voice lined with steel. "You will not deny these men their right to the most honorable of all Fey deaths. They live now to protect you, to die for you if they must. Because you represent hope for all Fey, and especially for them."

For a long, shocked moment, Ellie stared into Rain's steady, resolute eyes. It was one thing to believe these warriors were there to protect her. It was another thing entirely to realize that they would die for her. Perhaps she'd been foolish not to realize it before, yet it had never occurred to her that if her life was in danger, their lives were in danger too. Or that they would each die before allowing harm to come to her. Not even Bel's stirring pledge to devote life and soul to her protection had made her realize, truly, what was at stake.

Everything in her screamed against allowing such a thing.

She was plain, awkward Ellysetta Baristani, the woodcarver's daughter, and though for some incredible reason Rain Tairen Soul believed she was his truemate, she knew there was nothing within her important enough for these men, these oddly dear friends, to protect at the cost of their immortal lives. How could she live with herself if even one of them died on her account?

«They will protect you whether you agree or not, because I will command it. You are my shei'tani, and immeasurably valuable to us all,» Rain told her silently. *«But if you rail against their protection, you take away their joy. Do not make this great honor a burden to them.»*

She lowered her eyes and dragged in a breath. "I'm sorry," she said, forcing her voice not to tremble. "Of course, I am honored by your protection."

Breathing resumed. Paper crinkled. Silence lifted.

«Beylah vo, shei'tani.»

Ellie fiddled with the ribbons on the package in her lap and did not respond.

Bel finished unwrapping the large package and held up an object made of shining steel and shaped like a very ugly coiled serpent. "What in the name of tairen fire is this?"

Kieran laughed. "I think it's a keflee pot."

Bel stared at the object in his hand, twisting it this way and that. "And what's the matching cream pot, I wonder? A scorpion?"

They were joking. How could they be joking?

« Would you have them cry every day of their lives?»

She looked at Rain and blinked back the tears that sprang to her eyes. "I thought you couldn't read my mind," she accused. Her anger was weak, but she grabbed it, not wanting to cry in front of these men who had far more reason for tears than she.

Rain only shook his head. "Your thoughts are plain on your face."

★ ★ ★

They managed to open, record, and pack away all of the gifts in the parlor before lunchtime. Lillis and Lorelle returned from their morning's instruction with Madam Nolen, a widow who supported herself by teaching the local guildmasters' children basic reading, penmanship, maths, and household management. Ellie reviewed their morning's work, fed them, then sent them out into the rear garden to play with their kitten so the Fey could do a swift, magical spit-and-polish of the house before Master Fellows arrived.

Lillis and Lorelle weren't pleased when they realized Ellie would be too busy the next three afternoons to take them to the park, and nothing mollified them until Rain offered to spend a portion of tomorrow's courtship bells playing Stones with them in the park. The offer transformed their expressions from utter dejection to soaring delight, and the sudden change of emotion made Ellie's eyes narrow with suspicion.

"I think you've just been manipulated," she told Rain.

He glanced after the girls as they disappeared through the kitchen door, then shrugged. "Ah, well, it pleases me to see them smile. They are young and bright, and their laughter lightens my heart."

She felt her own heart squeeze a little. Behind that simple statement lay centuries of indescribable torment: the pain he'd shared with her that first night in the museum, the loss of the people he'd loved, and now, as she'd just learned, the suffering from every life he'd ever taken in defense of his people. And yet despite all that, he could still find happiness in making a child smile.

She reached for his hand. Her fingers curled around his, measuring through touch the unyielding strength of his grip. She was tall, but beside him she felt slight. He stood a full head above her. His body, while lean, was hard with muscle, his shoulders broad and squared. He was a man built to hold the weight of the world on his shoulders. And she was a woman just learning how much she longed to lighten his burden.

He stood motionless as she reached up to lay her other hand along the side of his face. "You're a good man, Rainier vel'En Daris." She rose up on her toes and pressed her lips to his.

A shudder rippled through him. His free hand slid round her waist, and he started to pull her hard against him, then stopped. Though she could feel the surge of longing in him, the fierce desire to capture and claim, he conquered it. The tairen roared for dominance, but Rain refused to give in. He kissed her with breathtaking passion that left her in no doubt of his desire or need, yet when she broke the embrace and stepped back, he opened his arms and let her go.

He held her stunned gaze with eyes that glowed bright and fierce. "I am not a good man, *shei'tani*," he corrected. "I never have been. But for you I will strive to be better."

She pressed a hand to her lips. He could make her feel so much, so deeply and so quickly it was frightening. Just then, while he'd kissed her, a powerful sensation had moved inside her. She could feel it still, drawing her skin tight, shuddering through her bones as if at any moment they might dissolve.

She took a deep breath and dragged a ragged veil of calm around her, tamping her emotions down until the feeling faded. "I should go freshen up. Master Fellows will be here soon, and I don't want to embarrass you by looking a mess when he arrives."

Rain's brow's drew together. "You bring pride to this Fey just as you are."

She laughed ruefully. "Yes, well, be that as it may, we both know the nobility won't share that view—which is why I spent this morning and last letting the queen's craftsmasters try to change me into something more acceptable. And why I'm going upstairs now to freshen up before Master Fellows gets here." She turned and started for the stairs.

"Ellysetta." The sudden thread of steel in his voice made

her halt and look back. His expression was carved stone. The pupils of his still-glowing eyes had lengthened to slits. "I meant what I said. I have no wish to change you. All this"— he flung out his hand at the mess of fabrics and pattern books still strewn around the main room—"was Marissya and your mother's idea, to help you feel more at ease among Dorian's nobles. For myself, I'd proudly take you as you are. Just say the word, and so it will be."

Her eyes widened. He would do that. He'd take her before the court dressed as a peasant and expect them to treat her like a queen.

And be furious when they didn't.

"I thought the whole purpose of this Kingsday's dinner was to win the favor of the lords so they would vote to keep the Eld border closed," she said.

"And so it is, but any Celierian worthy of Fey regard will appreciate the honor of your presence no matter what your garb."

Her brows almost disappeared into her hairline. "Oh, truly? You know as well as I do that I don't dare appear before the court dressed in anything even remotely resembling this." She waved at her simple skirts and thick-soled boots. "They'd be insulted beyond words, and you'd lose all hope of winning their support."

She wasn't sure she believed the Mages had reconstituted their power. The *dahl'reisen* murdering innocent villagers up and down the borders seemed a greater and more obvious threat than anything in Eld. But she knew Rain believed Eld was the true menace. And he needed the support of Celieria's aristocracy to ensure that his fears did not come to pass. He was already starting off at a disadvantage. No noble—especially Queen Annoura—would easily forgive him for raising a wood-carver's daughter to the rank of queen.

Rain couldn't dispute her reasoning, though the flush of angry color beneath his pale skin said he wanted to. "Be that as it may," he snapped, "we're not talking about the court right now. We're talking about a servant of the court, the queen's Master of Graces. I assure you I don't need *his* vote, Ellysetta, and that means you have no cause to put yourself out on his behalf."

She put her hands on her hips. "No cause except common courtesy and care for my own pride. Master Fellows may look at me and see a peasant, but at least he'll see a tidy one. And thank you so much for making me admit to such conceit."

Rain's brow creased in a bewildered look, as if he could not understand how the conversation had ended here, with her glaring at him for embarrassing her. He shook his head and pinched the ridge between his eyes. "It's been too long since I've been a mate. I had forgotten the two rules."

"The two rules?" she echoed.

"*Aiyah.* Sariel taught me." He held up his index finger. "Rule one: in any dispute between mates, the male is always to blame, even when he is clearly blameless. Rule two"—his middle finger joined the first—"whenever in doubt, refer to rule one."

The laugh popped out before she could halt it.

His eyes crinkled at the corners. He reached out and brushed the back of his fingers across her cheek in a light caress. "Very well, *shei'tani.* Tidy yourself for this Master of Graces if that will put you at ease. Have the seamstresses provided you with a court gown yet?"

"No, I was just going to put on my green gown. The maestras haven't had time to finish anything finer." She gestured to the bolts of cloth stacked against one wall. "I'm still picking patterns and fabric."

He glanced over at the bolts she'd indicated. "I like that silk." He pointed to a bolt of golden yellow watered silk. "The color would become you." His brows drew together in a frown of concentration. A surge of powerful magic burst from his hands. Half the bolt of cloth disappeared. "There," he said when the shining green Earth threads faded. "You have a dress now, in your room upstairs. And don't bother with your hair. Kieran will fix it for you when you come back downstairs."

She shook her head. Now she was the one bewildered. "You just finished arguing with me about how I should not change myself for members of the court."

"That was before you expressed your fear of being shamed. As your mate, it is my duty to protect you in all ways. For the pride of the nobles, I care nothing. For yours, I do." He shrugged. "Go, *shei'tani*, don these garments you think you need. We Fey will tidy your home and wait for this Master of Graces."

She went. Upstairs in her room, laid neatly across her narrow bed, lay an exquisite gown of saffron silk. She tried it on, not surprised to find it a perfect fit. But as she regarded her stylish reflection in the long mirror inside her wardrobe, her pleased smile faded. Despite her angry claims this morning that she was the same person she'd always been and always would be, Ellysetta knew it wasn't true. She'd already begun to change, and she would have to change still more. Fast. Because when he faced the nobles this Kingsday evening, Rain Tairen Soul would need a queen by his side, not some naive, graceless gawk of a girl.

Precisely as the city clock tower rang fourteen bells, Master Gaspare Fellows, the queen's Master of Graces, arrived at the Baristani home. He stepped across the threshold, threw back the edges of his satin-lined demi-cape, and executed a perfect court bow before Ellysetta.

"Ah, My Lady Feyreisa, a pleasure to meet you." He straightened and cast a swift, appraising, hazel gaze around the interior of her family's home. Ellie was glad the Fey had tidied up, because she had a feeling the Master would describe everything he saw in the minutest detail once he returned to court.

Master Fellows concluded his perusal and cleared his throat delicately. "Very quaint."

What was she supposed to say to that? "Thank you for coming, Master Fellows." The slender, elegant little man stood almost a full head shorter than Ellysetta, but despite his small stature, her stomach was still tied in nervous knots. This man was the chief authority on the noble graces to which all members of the royal court adhered.

"Hmm." Master Fellows subjected Ellie to as thorough a gaze as he had the house. Even though she knew she looked her best, her knees were all but knocking as she waited for his approval. "Turn, please," he commanded, wiggling one finger in an impatient spiral. "Hmm," he said again. "Well, I see I have my work cut out for me if I'm to impart some meaningful modicum of the graces to you over the next few days."

"Master Fellows."

"Oh!" The man gave a start as Rain stepped from the shadows behind him.

"I am Rainier vel'En Daris, the Tairen Soul." No hint of welcome softened Rain's expression. Less than half a bell earlier, Ellie had thought him the kindest of men, but now he looked downright frightening. His steel seemed to gleam brighter—and more menacing—than usual against the darkness of his leathers. Apparently, Master Fellows thought so too, because the little man backed up several paces. "What graces, exactly, do you think a Celierian could teach the queen of the Fey that she does not already possess?"

"Uh . . ahem . . ." Master Fellows cleared his throat again and backed up yet another step, only to bump into the equally imposing figure of Bel, who'd come to stand between Master Fellows and Ellie. The Master of Graces swallowed. "No insult was intended, My Lord Feyreisen. The graces are an art. The manner of comportment, of speech, the language of the fans and flowers . . . they take a lifetime to master."

"I see." Rain nodded. Then he smiled, showing teeth. "You have three days."

Master Fellows gasped like a beached fish.

"I suggest you start with the things she'll need to know for the palace dinner we are attending this Kingsday evening. I'm sure you'll find the Feyreisa a quick study."

The palace dinner was to be a formal state affair where the heads of the noble houses would gather together for a reception followed by a banquet. As Master Fellows explained, that meant he had three appointments of four short bells each to teach a completely untrained woman the graces of court greetings, bows and curtseys, polite conversation, deportment, flatware, and dining.

At first, Master Fellows talked so fast he barely took time to breathe. But after he survived the first bell without being skewered on a Fey blade, he calmed down a bit. By the second bell, he had regained his composure, but his patience had begun to go missing.

"If you are to be treated like a queen, My Lady Feyreisa, you must comport yourself as one. If you think of yourself as regal, others will too. You have a lovely neck, my dear. Like a swan's. Hold your head high. No, not that high. Let them see your lovely eyes, not your nostrils. Yes, like that. Now, spine straight. Shoulders back. No, not so far back that your shoulder blades touch one another. You're a queen, not a prize hen." He started to take hold of Ellysetta's shoulders, but the hiss of Fey steel leaving scabbard froze him in place. All five warriors of Ellysetta's quintet had unsheathed their blades. "Sers," he complained. Ellysetta's quintet just stared blankly at him. He turned to Rain. "My Lord Feyreisen, really. I've tried, but I simply cannot do this without touching her."

"I agree," Rain answered. "You cannot do it."

Master Fellows's expression—which had started to brighten with triumph—fell once more. "This no-touching rule of yours is ridiculous! You would not let me guide her through her curtseys. You would not let me show her how to use her hands in polite conversation. And now, you will not allow me to adjust the way she comports herself. How do you expect me to teach her the graces if you hobble me at every turn? This is impossible!"

"Do you shrink so easily from a challenge, then?"

"A challenge, no. But you, My Lord Feyreisen, are setting me up for disaster. Is that what you want? For me to fail and your queen to become the butt of Celierian jokes?"

Every spark of warmth fled from Rain's eyes. "Mind your tongue, Celierian."

"Or what? You'll cut it out? Go on, then! You might as well. My life will be ruined in any event if Lady Ellysetta falls on her face before the entire court. They all know it's I whom the queen tasked with tutoring her in the graces!" With a great flair of drama, Master Fellows yanked open his silk coat, baring the pristine white linen shirt below. "Go ahead, Tairen Soul! Do your worst! Slay me! Drive one of those poison Fey blades through my heart! I'd rather die than live with such shame."

Rain's irritation melted away. It was impossible to stay irritated while trying hard not to laugh. He didn't like Celierians. He'd always found them to be arrogant, false, and weak. But one thing he could respect was a man who took pride in his life's work and had the courage to defend it. Even if he was a dramatic, posing little prat.

"Let him use whatever methods he thinks are best to teach me," Ellysetta said. "I don't want to embarrass you or my family when I'm presented to the court."

"You could never do that, *shei'tani*," Rain replied. "But neither can I allow him to touch you." Silently, he admitted, «*Until our bond is complete, the tairen would never permit it, and I don't want to kill this man, if only because I would regret the loss of entertainment.*»

She looked shocked.

Behind her, Bel smothered a smile. «*You like him.*»

«*I don't,*» Rain denied, then reluctantly recanted. «*All right, maybe a little. A very little.*» Who could completely dislike a banty little mortal brave enough to dare Rain Tairen Soul to do his worst?

Rain turned to Master Fellows. "Will you accept a compromise, Master Fellows? Permit me to read your thoughts with Spirit, and I will give you the use of my hands. You need only think what you would like me to do, and I will do it for you. Will that suffice?"

"I don't know." Master Fellows straightened his clothing and carefully smoothed back his hair. "I'm not sure I like the idea of having you in my head. What would it be like?"

"You would not know I was there. Simply picture in your mind how you wish Ellysetta to stand." He plucked the images easily from the man's mind and wove them in Spirit so Ellysetta could see, then made the smaller adjustments himself, tilting her shoulders and chin gently to achieve exactly the stance Master Fellows imagined. "Like this, Master Fellows?" He heard her breath catch as his hands touched her, felt her helpless rush of desire and the hot echo of it in his flesh. She might fear the tairen, but this much she could not deny. It gave him hope that the rest would come in time.

"Exactly! I mean"—the man coughed—"that will do nicely, My Lord Feyreisen."

"I feel like a posed doll," Ellysetta muttered.

"You look like a queen." Fellows was right; she did have a lovely neck. Rain bent to press a kiss against the soft skin of Ellysetta's throat. "You bring pride to this Fey, *shei'tani*."

"Oh, but none of that," Master Fellows objected, ignoring Rain's frown. "Celierian courtiers may enjoy passion in private, but in public, they must observe all the proprieties."

Ellysetta's lessons in the graces continued throughout the afternoon. It was late when Master Fellows took his leave and hired a gentleman's coach to carry him back across town to the palace, where he was promptly ushered into the queen's private audience chamber to give a report of his session with the Tairen Soul's mate.

Queen Annoura was seated on a carved and gilded armchair, dressed to perfection and shining with a seemingly effortless combination of luminous beauty and regal grace that Master Gaspare Fellows knew had taken years of careful study to perfect. He'd still been an apprentice when the queen had first come to these shores, and he'd helped his old Master train her to take her place at King Dorian's side. The lessons had ended when the old Master died, but by then Annoura had already been transformed from the reserved young princess so in love with her handsome husband into the Moon of Celieria, the Brilliant around whom the entire court revolved.

Lately, Gaspare had begun noticing changes in her: a hardness that had never been there before, a cutting edge to her wit. After the last four bells spent in the fresh, artless kindness of Ellysetta Baristani's company, the difference seemed even more obvious.

Gaspare's gaze flicked to the bevy of Dazzles gathered around the queen, among them many a grasping, brittle beauty like that sapphire-eyed jade, Jiarine Montevero. Youngest daughter of a poor, minor house, she'd ascended beyond anyone's expectations to claim a seat in the queen's inner circle and title to her family's holdings after the untimely passing of her parents and older siblings. Beside her stood one of the queen's Favorites, the handsome Ser Vale, who for no reason at all made the little hairs on the back of Gaspare's neck stand up whenever the man's vivid blue-green gaze was fixed upon him.

As it was now.

Gaspare threw himself into a deep, elegant bow. The bend of his knee was exact, the flourish of his arm a perfection of grace . . . except for the faint tremors which he hoped no one noticed. Ser Vale disturbed him. Almost as much as the Tairen Soul had at first, only with Vale, the unsettledness never went away.

When Gaspare straightened, he focused his gaze on the queen, not allowing so much as a flicker of a glance in Vale's direction. That helped. A little.

"My Queen, you asked me to keep you informed of my progress with the young Feyreisa." Forcing himself to speak in confident, well-modulated tones, Gaspare related the details of his interactions with Ellysetta Baristani and the Tairen Soul.

Annoura kept her grip on the armrests of her chair light as Master Fellows gave his report. She'd hoped he would return full of sneering condescension for the woodcarver's daughter's attempts to master the noble graces, but somehow the girl appeared to have won him over. Oh, he was careful not to sing her praises too loudly—Gaspare Fellows was too experienced a veteran of noble society for that—but Annoura could tell by what he did not say that'd he'd liked her.

"So, in your opinion, Master Fellows," she said when he finished, "Ellysetta Baristani will be able to master sufficient graces so as not to embarrass either the Fey or my husband, at the dinner on Kingsday?"

"I believe so, Your Majesty."

Conscious of the Dazzles observing her smallest reaction, Annoura kept her irritation well hidden. "Let us hope you are right. I realize I've set you a difficult task, Master Fellows. Turning a commoner into a lady fit for presentation to the heads of all Celieria's noble houses is no small accomplishment—and to have only three short days in which to achieve it—well, just consider that a measure of my confidence in you."

Master Fellows bowed with impeccable grace. "Nothing could give me greater pleasure than to be worthy of your confidence and regard, Majesty."

"Excellent. We thank you, Master Fellows." She fixed a coolly polite smile on her face. He recognized her unspoken dismissal and, with a final bow, excused himself.

When he was gone, Vale caught her eye. He'd been gone from her court since that morning in the garden when he'd acted so impudently, and though it galled her to admit it, she'd missed him. Scarcely a year since he'd first joined the court, and already he was indispensable to her. How had that happened?

A mysterious, knowing smile lurked at the corners of his well-shaped mouth, and a tingling shot of energy raced up her spine in response. She'd seen that look before. He was hiding something, some naughty trinket or choice bit of gossip, and he was waiting for a moment alone to share it with her.

She shouldn't let him. He'd grown too bold by half.

But she was still angry at the way Dorian had betrayed her this morning. She'd given him her love, given him years of devotion and loyalty and her tireless efforts to make him the most powerful king in the mortal world. And what had he done when asked to choose between her pride and his Fey kin? He'd chosen them. He'd thrown everything she'd ever given him back in her face.

She looked at Vale. This handsome man had made it clear in so many ways that he longed to serve and please her, that he would do anything for her.

A sharp staccato beat broke the air as Annoura clapped her hands sharply. "Out. All of you. Give me a moment." She held Vale's gaze for a steady, expressionless moment. His faint smile deepened—then was wiped away as he turned towards the door and exited with the rest of the courtiers. The door closed behind them.

Silence fell over the room. She drew a deep breath, her breasts straining against the tight confinement of her corset. Her heart was beating quickly. This was not wise. Dorian was not a jealous or suspicious man—she'd never given him cause to be—but many a courtier with whom she'd battled in the past would leap at the chance to disgrace her.

Nerves shrilling, Annoura rose from her chair. Across the room, the door through which the courtiers had exited beckoned. Already she was having second thoughts. She should leave. Now. Before she encouraged Vale's improprieties any further and gave herself cause for regret. Before she gave her enemies a weapon to use against her.

She started for the door to her bedchamber.

From behind, the sound of tinkling dishes and a low murmur

of voices drifted in through the half-closed door leading to the adjoining antechamber. She stopped. Drew another deep breath. Turned.

Vale stood in the doorway, elegant and sensual, thick, smooth waves of dark hair gathered in a queue at his nape, blue-green eyes vivid in his bronzed face. Expertly tailored clothes hugged his body, outlining his muscular limbs, broad shoulders, trim hips.

She yanked her gaze back from where it had wandered and gathered her composure, drawing on every lesson engraved upon her being by the stern taskmaster who'd been Gaspare Fellows's old master. One silvery brow arched. "You wished to see me privately?"

Vale smiled. It was not the smile of a supplicant or a courtier. It was, instead, a man's smile, brimming with dangerous promise, whispering of silken sheets and forbidden desires. "I've brought you a gift, My Queen." He gestured behind him, to a small silver serving cart.

Annoura's tension changed to irritation. "Keflee? Vale, really, my nerves are strung tight. They need no further stimulation." Keflee, the powdered nut of the kefloa tree, was a sensory enhancer. When brewed with cinnabar water, it acted as a mild stimulant to the senses, creating a feeling of invigoration and higher mental acuity.

Vale lifted a purple silk bag from the tray, and handed it to her. "Ah, but My Queen, this is no ordinary keflee. I know you to be a connoisseur, and this is a very rare and potent blend. One I think you will enjoy. Open the bag and just smell the aroma. It's enthralling."

Intrigued, she loosened the braided ties holding the top closed, parted the opening of the bag, and took an experimental sniff. A rich, dark fragrance filled her nostrils, heady, dizzying. A potent blend indeed. And now she knew the reason for the wicked light in Vale's eyes.

For a rare few, the more potent forms of keflee could cause mild aphrodisiacal effects—and occasionally even more than mild, depending on the concentration of the brew, and the imbiber's level of susceptibility and state of mind. Annoura had never experienced those side effects herself, but Dorian had a particularly interesting response to keflee in its most concentrated form. Ever since discovering that, she'd made a point of stocking new blends, and encouraging him to try them whenever she was feeling romantic.

"I made a special trip to my estate just so I could bring it to you," Vale said, pouring the steaming liquid into two porcelain cups. He added a stream of thick, chilled honeyed cream, stirred, then held one cup out to her. "I thought if my gift pleased you, you might forgive me for my earlier transgression. I cannot bear to be out of your favor, My Queen."

She gave a brief, disbelieving laugh. "So to apologize for one boldness, you offer an even greater one?"

"Is it boldness to offer my queen a treasure I know she enjoys?"

A quick, sharp yank on the silk cords closed the purple bag tight. She tossed it on her desk and turned away, regretting the irritation and spurt of wickedness that had led her to encourage him. "You presume too much, Vale, and for your information, keflee does not have the effect on me you may think. My . . . ardent pursuit of the rarest blends is an interest I indulge for reasons of my own."

"Then my gift is not bold in the least," he returned smoothly, "and there is no reason why you should not share a cup with me." He smiled invitingly. "Come, will you not at least taste a little? The blend is sinfully delicious."

She started to refuse and dismiss him, but he lifted his own cup of keflee and blew to cool it. The rich, moist aroma swirled around her. Sweet Lord of Light, the fragrance alone was intoxicating . . . as was the spellbinding intensity of Vale's vivid eyes. Between his look and the seductive aroma of the keflee, she had trouble remembering what was so objectionable about an innocent drink between friends.

"Oh, very well. Where's the harm?" She took the cup

from him, started to raise it to her lips, then stopped with a faint smile. "You first, though, Vale. Old habits die hard." Growing up in Capellas, where poisons and potions were standard fare among courtiers, she'd long ago learned to be wary of gifts. Except for Dorian, she trusted no one.

"Of course." Vale didn't hesitate to raise his cup. "To your beauty and grace, Majesty." He took a small sip, then gave a short laugh when she did not respond in kind. "Your suspicion cuts me to the quick, My Queen." With a shrug and a wry smile, he tilted his head back and emptied the remaining keflee in one quick gulp.

She sipped hers, then made a pleased sound and sipped again. He was right about the blend. She did like it. The brew was strong, like nothing she'd ever experienced before. Pure enchantment in liquid form. She sipped again, taking more of the keflee into her mouth and letting the flavors caress her senses.

"Well? Is it everything I promised?"

She swallowed and stifled a moan as the languid warmth slid down into her belly. "Hmm?" She struggled to pull her thoughts together. "Oh, yes, it's quite good."

"I'm so glad. Here, let me warm your cup." He poured another small stream of steaming liquid into her half-full cup, and the gentle splash of liquid became a soft melody ringing in her ears. The room grew warmer, the scent of the keflee stronger and more intoxicating. Her eyes closed against the riot of colors and sensations bombarding her. Her hands—or were they someone else's?—guided the cup to her lips. A voice crooned, urging her to drink more, and, helpless to resist, she did.

A fresh wave of warmth suffused her body. The cacophony of sound faded, grew muffled, and then there was only a voice, low and hypnotic, murmuring to her, saying something about Dorian, something troubling.

Feeling dizzy, Annoura lifted a hand to her head. Just that faint tightening of her bodice as her arm moved sent bursts of heat exploding all over her body. Fire raced through her veins, licking at her skin with hot little tongues. Her knees went weak. Gods have mercy. The sensations flooding her body were more potent than the sexual energy that had rushed through the courtroom the day the Tairen Soul had claimed his mate. Her eyes fluttered, trying to open, but her lids were so heavy.

"Shh. Hush, my sweet." A hard hand slid round her waist, a man's hand, firm and strong, fingers splayed on her spine, pressing her forward. She leaned into a hard, muscular chest, and moaned as lips tracked burning kisses up her throat and swirled around her ear. Tremors shot through her like lightning bolts. Ah, gods, Dorian had always delighted in tormenting her ear, knowing what it did to her. He would laugh deep in his throat and do it again and again until she melted against him, pleading for mercy.

"Dorian," she protested.

"You don't want him, darling. He doesn't appreciate you the way he should. I've seen how he puts the Fey before you, how he allows the rabble to hold you up to ridicule."

She frowned. No, no, that was wrong. Dorian was the only man for her. She'd never known what love was until she'd met him. Her parents led cold, political lives, using each other, their children, any and everyone to their personal advantage. Dorian had shown her a different way. He'd been the first man to make her believe there could be—should be—something more to marriage than power, politics, and procreation. He'd come to Capellas as an envoy from his father. And when he'd been brought before the royal family for presentation, he'd taken one look at her and forgotten every word he'd been supposed to say. His steward had had to read the message for him from the parchment that had slipped out of Dorian's hands.

For the next two months, he'd pursued her with such single-minded dedication and romance, she'd been utterly overwhelmed. He'd made it clear he wanted her for his queen, and made it equally clear that his desire had nothing to do with politics or power. When he left the shores of Capellas, she went with him, his ring on her finger. She'd never once looked back, never once missed the cold beauty of her homeland.

"You should be more than a queen." The voice pulled her back from her memories. "You should be an Empress. The Fey should bow to your rule, not you to theirs."

Yes, that was what she'd always wanted. Glory for herself and Dorian, the power to rule with wisdom and benevolence. He'd always been content with Celieria alone, but she was Capellan enough to want more.

"You can have all the power you desire. All you have to do is give yourself to me."

A hand slid up her waist. A rich, male scent, cool and darkly sweet, filled her nostrils. She frowned in confusion. That wasn't Dorian's scent; it was another's. Fingers cupped her breast and squeezed through the stiffened layers of her bodice. Not Dorian's hand.

"Give yourself to me, sweetness," the voice crooned again. Her flesh swelled at the sound, aching, eager to obey. But the speaker wasn't Dorian.

Her eyes flashed open and she looked up into Vale's face, beautiful, sexual, ruddy with passion. He was holding her in his arms, his hips tilted in and up, pressing his sex against hers through the thick layers of her skirt, touching her with an intimacy no man but Dorian ever had. Shock shattered her strange hypnosis. She wrenched herself out of his hands and shoved him away.

"Oh, gods." She cupped her hands over her mouth. Her blood was still pounding, her breasts and womb aching, all but weeping. Her whole body was on fire, screaming for release, but she couldn't—wouldn't—do this. "Oh, gods, what am I doing? What was I thinking?"

"Annoura?" Vale reached for her.

She lurched back, evading his hands. "Don't call me that!" Only Dorian called her that. Only he had the right. "You must go! Now! *Now!*" she shrieked when he reached for her again. No matter how hurt and angry Dorian had made her this morning, she still loved him. Even if that weren't the case, she was his queen, and this was *treason*.

Vale drew back instantly. "I'm sorry. Forgive me." His face had lost its color. "The brew went to my head. I'll go, of course." He bowed low, and for the first time his movements were stiff and graceless rather than the dance of sensual masculine beauty that had always so enticed her. "Forgive me, My Queen. I never meant to cause you such distress."

"Just go," she cried. "Get out of my sight!"

Straightening, he pivoted on one heel and strode out.

Oh, gods, oh, gods. The keflee pot was still steaming its treacherous seductive fragrance. She snatched it up in a burst of fury and threw it against the wall. Dark liquid splattered, spreading out in a huge, ruinous stain, a blot as dark as the one on her honor. The smell became an overwhelming stench. She ran for the garderobe, leaned over the privy shaft, and vomited in violent, racking heaves until nothing remained in her stomach but emptiness and bile. Frantic to rid herself of every last vestige of the hideous potion, she rinsed and scrubbed her mouth and teeth again and again until she could no longer taste the slightest hint of keflee.

When she was done, she dragged in a long, shuddering breath and tried to calm herself. The task was an impossibility. Vale's brew was still inside her, still working its vile magic upon her. Every move was a torment, every swish of silk an acute torture.

She needed Dorian. Now.

Pausing only to straighten her hair and appearance—there was nothing she could do about the wild glitter in her eyes—she exited the chamber through the main door. She sailed past the crowd of courtiers lingering in the sunlit atrium nearby and walked as swiftly as she dared to Dorian's office. He was still there, his steward with him.

"Leave us," she commanded.

The steward cast her a startled look, then glanced uncertainly at her husband. Dorian eyed the flush of color on her cheeks and signaled the steward to obey.

"We aren't to be disturbed," she ordered, then closed the door in the steward's face.

"What is it, my d—" Dorian's voice broke off. His hazel eyes widened as she strode towards him, ripping at the laces of her bodice as she went. "Annoura?"

The bodice string snapped in her hands. The stiffened fabric parted. "Dorian . . ." She ripped at the sleeves of her gown, almost sobbing as she struggled to pull the loose fabric free and shove it down in a puddle at her feet. She stepped out of the pile of silk, clad only in a sheer chemise, corset, silk hose, and heels. He started to rise from his chair, but she pushed him back down and straddled him. "Dorian, tell me you love me. Tell me now."

Bewildered, he said, "Of course, I love you. You know I do." He frowned. "What's wrong, my dearest?"

"Nothing. Everything." She clutched his face in desperate hands and kissed him, rocking her hips against his until she felt his body begin to harden in response. When his arms came up around her, she closed her eyes to hold back the tears of relief. "Love me, Dorian. Right here, right now. Love me and make everything all right."

Yanking off Ser Vale's silk doublet to cool his overheated body, Kolis stalked down the palace hallway. Fury vibrated in his bones and his blood thundered in his veins. Dark Lord steal his soul! He'd almost ruined everything. The keflee had been potent indeed, laced with a Feraz additive intended to drive her into his arms. He'd had to drink it too, thanks to her suspicious nature, and the effects were far stronger than even the most concentrated keflee could have been. He'd thought that drink would be enough to cloud her senses and get her to accept the first Mark. Instead he'd come close to destroying months of work in one rash, unthinking act. If he lost the queen—if she banished him from her court—the High Mage would be enraged.

He opened the door to the small suite Annoura had given him when Ser Vale had become one of her Favorites. A flash of bright color caught the edge of his vision and he turned to see the trailing edge of a woman's skirts disappear around his bedchamber door. Temper bit hard. Lust bit harder. "Come here," he commanded.

Fabric rustled. Jiarine Montevero stepped out of his bedchamber into the small parlor of his suite. "It didn't go well, I presume." Her lips twisted. "I told you it wouldn't. It's too soon. She still loves him. You must break that before you can break her."

"I said come." The temperature in the room dropped sharply.

Jiarine turned pale. The sardonic triumph fell from her like an untied veil. She hurried towards him. When she drew close enough, he grabbed her arm and pinned her against the wall, grinding his hips against hers. His hands plunged into her bodice and tugged her generous breasts free of their confinement, finding the nipples and squeezing them until she cried out.

"You find my failure amusing, *umagi*?"

"No!" she gasped, groaning as he twisted her flesh. "Never."

"Whom do you serve, Jiarine?"

She gasped again and offered up her mouth, her throat, those lush, lovely breasts. "You, master. Only you."

His head ducked. He took a nipple in his mouth and bit down. She moaned, her hand clenching tight in his hair, a shudder rippling through her. The hot, sweet smell of surrender burst from her in a heady rush, sweeping across his heightened senses. He traced his fingers over the creamy skin of her left breast. Trails of carefully masked magic followed behind. Six shadowy Marks grew visible on her flesh, six small points of darkness forming a circle over her heart. Six Mage Marks that ensured his absolute power over her.

"I own you, my sweet *umagi*. Let me hear you say it."

"You own me, my lord, body and soul. I live only to serve you."

Savage triumph roared through him at the completeness of her willing, even eager, surrender. He spun her around roughly and flipped up her skirts. Beneath them, she wore the pleasure girl's undergarments he'd given her months ago, slippery red satin, slit from crotch to anus for his convenience. Plump, shaved flesh pouted through the edges of the fabric, and the scent of musk wafted up in rich waves. His cock jumped in response.

"Then find a way to break her for me, pet. You've had a year, and still she resists. You must do better." He grabbed her hair and pulled her head back, forcing her back to arch. The motion shoved her bare breasts against the chamber's fabric-covered walls. Her nipples, already tight, became diamond-hard points as the textured fabric rubbed against them.

She was sobbing, hips squirming. "I will, master. I promise."

"Good. You won't like the consequences if you fail me."

He kneed her thighs apart, and drove into her in one brutal thrust. There was no time for niceties—not that he'd ever been a tender lover, and not that Jiarine had ever minded. Her body slammed against the wall from the force of his penetration. She gave a soft, choked cry, then a raspy, muttered plea for more as her hot, wet flesh clasped tightly around him. Sweet, succulent Jiarine. Such a pleasure in so many ways. So willing to take whatever he had to offer, no matter how brutally he offered it. Obligingly, his hips drew back, then rammed forward again.

CHAPTER FOURTEEN

The Great Sun had just risen when Sian vel Sendaris and Torel vel Carlian, the two Fey warriors dispatched by Belliard vel Jelani to seek information about the Feyreisa's origins, arrived in the small northern city of Norban. They'd made good time, traveling light and moving fast, resting one bell for every three they ran and shaving seventy miles off the journey by running cross-country from Vrest to Hartslea before picking up the North Road for the remaining distance. They had actually arrived the night before and waited just outside the village, watching until the shadows of night retreated and the residents began to stir.

Sian and Torel entered by the main road, meeting scores of surprised and suspicious stares with stone-faced calm, and began to systematically work their way through the city. From home to home, shop to shop, they searched for answers to the mystery of the Feyreisa's past. They did not ask about a red-haired infant abandoned in the forests two dozen years before. Instead, they inquired after Pars Grolin, a journeyman smith with bright red hair to whom the Fey owed a debt of gratitude. He might, Sian told the people he questioned, have been traveling with his small daughter.

It was the truth, though it had been stretched a bit. Fey honor prevented warriors from telling outright lies, but tairen craftiness allowed them to dance on the blade's edge of truth when necessary. There really had been a red-haired journeyman smith named Pars Grolin, and he really had traveled through Norban. About seven hundred years earlier. Sian and Torel simply avoided mentioning specific timeframes. And—who knew?—maybe Pars really had brought his daughter with him on one of his travels.

Though it pained them to do so, Sian and Torel attempted to shake hands with each individual they met, using skin-to-skin contact to probe the minds of Norban's citizens and follow any memories aroused by the mention of bright red hair and small girls. Many of the Celierians refused to touch the Fey, either from fear or distrust, and Sian and Torel resorted to probing the minds of those doubters with careful weaves of Spirit.

The warriors' progress through the town was slow, and they did not go unnoticed.

Ellie spent a much quieter morning than the one she'd suffered through the previous day. She woke to find the top of her nightstand draped with a diamond necklace fit for a queen, the stones large and of obvious quality, the chains so delicate she could break them without effort. The message of the gift, she surmised, ran something along the lines of "wear the trappings of a queen if you must, but know you can shed them any time you choose."

To the consternation of Lauriana and all the tradesfolk, Rain arrived very early and made himself both visible and threatening as he stood at her side, arms crossed over his chest, fingers touching the scarlet hilt of his deadly Fey'cha. When any of the tradesfolk became the least bit pushy or rude, he would fix glowing eyes upon the offender and growl deep in his throat. Three seamstresses had to be carried out after they fainted in fright. And even though Ellysetta chided them for their wickedness, the Fey warriors laughed silently among themselves and cast bets on how long it would be before the next young lady keeled over and how many would swoon before lunchtime.

The morning passed quickly, and soon Lillis and Lorelle returned from their studies and clamored for their promised afternoon in the park. At least five dozen children were waiting when the four of them arrived. Ellie recognized barely half of the waiting youngsters; the rest were children she had never met, a mix ranging from the well-dressed off-spring of merchants and simple-gentry to ragged street urchins and every social stratum in between. Each child clutched a Stones pouch and sported a wide-eyed, hopeful look as the Fey king entered the park.

Ellie bit her lip to stop from laughing. Word of the earlier Stones match with the Feyreisen had obviously spread through the West End and beyond. "I hope you're feeling up to another match, Rain," she murmured. "Because I don't think they're here to play with me."

Rain looked utterly taken aback. "Do you think they just decided to gather here on the off chance I would show up?"

"Oh, no. I think they had forewarning." She tilted her head towards Lillis and Lorelle.

"Ah." He seemed to gird himself. "Well, I suppose *we* shouldn't disappoint them." Holding out his wrist for Ellie's fingers, he escorted her to the Stones grid.

There were too many children to include all of them in a single round of Stones, so Rain divided them into groups by producing a handful of small coins that, once divided among the children, changed color to separate them into teams. Rain shed his weapons, and the games began—though only after Ellie made certain the rules prohibited all use of magic.

On their third game, Ellie and a boy she didn't know—a street child, by the unkempt look of him—raced to claim a contested square. Laughing, she reached the square first. A split second later, he plowed into her at full speed, knocking them both off their feet.

"Ow!" She landed hard. Her elbows cracked on the unforgiving surface of the Stones grid. The boy's knee caught her in the belly and drove the air from her lungs. As she lay there, gasping for breath, she caught a brief glimpse of the boy's eyes beneath his grimy mop of hair.

For one strange, surreal moment, she could have sworn the child's eyes were black, glowing with tiny red sparks.

She blinked, and the image was gone. The boy's eyes were brown and filled with fear. He didn't even bother to look over his shoulder at Rain, who was bearing down on him. He just scrambled to his feet and ran as if pursued by the Hounds of the Seventh Hell.

"*Shei'tani?*" Rain dropped to one knee and reached to help her up. "Are you hurt?"

"Just winded," she wheezed. She held out her hands and stared in shock. Red blood—quite a bit of it—covered one hand. She looked down at her waist, and light-headedness assailed her. Her side had been laid open by the slash of a knife, the wound deep enough that her skirts were already dark with blood.

The boy had stabbed her.

Rain swept her into his arm and barked out a rapid spate of orders. "Fey! *Ti'Feyreisa!* Bel! *Kaiven chakor!* Catch that boy. Quickly, before he gets away. The rest of you, to me!"

Ellie's quintet raced after the street boy. Moving in a blur of speed, another dozen Fey snatched up Lillis and Lorelle and carried them off to safety. The rest formed a tight protective ring around Rain and Ellysetta.

Ellie stared up at Rain's pale, drawn face and blinked as his image wavered. Had the boy poisoned as well as stabbed her?

"I've got to stop the bleeding before I take you to Marissya," Rain told her. He clasped a hand over her wounded side, and a bright glow of green Earth flowed from his fingertips. Her skin tingled, then began to sting. She hissed as the sting became sharp needles of pain lancing through her side. It felt as if he were tugging the torn edges of her flesh together.

Rain swore with quiet bitterness when she flinched. "Forgive me, Ellysetta. I was not thinking to stop the pain, only the blood." Cool lavender Spirit joined Earth, overriding her protesting nerves with an illusion of normalcy. Then it was only the tumult of his emotions that beat at her. With inexplicable surety, she not only sensed each emotion distinctly, she *knew* exactly what motivated each of them: fury over her wounding, shame that he'd let it happen and that he'd caused her further pain.

Fear that the wound might be worse than mere rent flesh.

Ellysetta cupped a hand to his face. "I'm all right," she assured him.

He grasped her hand and pressed a kiss into her palm. "Of course you are," he agreed. Against her palm, she felt his lips tremble, and in her mind she heard his quiet, shocked thought: *so dear, in so short a time.* The thought wasn't sent on a thread of Spirit, it was simply *there*, in her mind. He kissed her again on the lips, quick and fierce, then clutched her close to his chest and stood. *"Fey!"* he cried. *"Bote lute'cha!"*

The remaining Fey circled tight around Rain, red Fey'cha gripped menacingly in their hands. Moving as one unit, they raced towards Celieria's palace and Marissya's healing hands.

The boy ran like a rabbit.

Bel swore as he skidded around a corner and smashed into a fruit seller's cart. Fruit went everywhere, apples and oranges rolling across the narrow cobbled lane. Bel stumbled on a raft of apples and went sprawling. He tucked in his head and shoulder and turned the sprawl into a diving roll, coming up on one knee in time to see the boy duck down a small alleyway.

The rest of the quintet vaulted past Bel and cleared the river of rolling fruit in great, Air-powered leaps. «*Down the alley on the right!*» he commanded.

What advantage the Fey had in speed, the boy negated with his intimate knowledge of the city's many side streets and alleyways and what appeared to be an innate ability to avoid capture—learned, no doubt, from years of evading the authorities after picking pockets and thieving. The boy led them on a wild chase, twisting through a labyrinth of uneven roads and narrow alleys, ducking through shops and darting through merchant stalls, always managing to spin away just before the Fey's weaves could reach him. Rowan and Adrial took to the rooftops to try to cut the boy off while Bel and the others remained in pursuit on the ground.

The child burst out of the alley, darted under the wheels of a moving wagon, and hotfooted it down yet another narrow side street. He skidded to a halt when the cobbles in front of him bulged upward and a wall of Earth erupted out of the ground to barricade the road. Rowan and Adrial leapt down from a rooftop, breaking their descent with a cushion of Air. Bel and the others blocked the other end of the street.

The boy feinted right towards the back door of a baker's shop, then dodged to the left, pelting down a dank, narrow alley—little more than a moss-and-slime-covered footpath—between buildings. Bel charged after him, closing the distance between them. The boy was tiring, but the Fey were scarcely winded. The end of this chase would not be long in coming.

The boy knew it, too. He cast a wild-eyed glance over his shoulder and put on a burst of desperate speed, heading down yet another side street. He spun around a lamppost and launched himself down a short, narrow alley.

"Got you, boy!" Bel growled. The youth had made a mistake. This alley offered no outlet. Three solid brick walls hemmed the boy in, and Kieran wove Earth to weld shut the back doors that opened to the alley. There would be no more dodging through back rooms and kitchens, and no more escaping Fey weaves. "Now throw down that blade of yours and come with us. The Feyreisen has some questions for you."

Bel moved in, arms spread wide, his palms open. He didn't want to kill the boy, only catch him and bring him in for questioning. After that, the King's justice could decide what to do with him. If the child decided to get difficult, Bel would simply weave the Air out of his lungs to render him unconscious.

The child spat out a filthy oath. Suddenly his thin body went poker stiff. He clutched at his throat and chest and gave a gurgling cry.

"Boy?" Bel abandoned caution and ran towards him. Only then did he sense the weave. Air and Earth, and something else Bel couldn't quite make out, something masked by the other weaves, but it set his teeth on edge.

Blood vessels burst in the boy's wild eyes, turning them into pools of scarlet framing terrified brown irises. His lips went purplish blue. His eyes rolled back, and he crumpled to the damp filth of the alley ground.

Bel didn't need to check the boy's pulse to know he was dead.

His eyes scanned the alleyway, seeking the path of the weave that had killed the boy. The murderer had already erased his tracks, leaving nothing, no fragment of a weave to trace back to its source.

"The knife, Bel," Kiel reminded him. "Rain will want the blade that cut his mate."

Bel knelt to rifle the urchin's ragged clothes. He found a sheathed blade tucked in the boy's waistband. "Spit and scorch me," he whispered as he recognized the distinctive, black-silk-wrapped hilt of a Fey'cha. What was a street urchin who'd attacked the Feyreisa doing with a Fey'cha? The name-mark etched into the blade's pommel chilled Bel's blood.

Without warning, the knife grew hot to the touch. Swearing, Bel released the weapon and leapt back just as it burst into intense, blue-white flame. The boy's body began to burn, too.

"Murder!" The scream came from the mouth of the alley where a crowd of Celierians had gathered. A woman pointed at Bel and cried again, "Murder!"

Kolis Manza turned away from the crowd across the street, a satisfied smile lurking at the corner of his mouth. That should keep the Fey busy for a while. Let them deal with the accusations of murder now, on top of all the suspicions of *dahl'reisen* raids and the new, dark distrust quietly spreading among the lower classes and the religious zealots.

He walked three blocks down to the Inn of the Blue Pony and entered unobtrusively by way of the back door and servants' stair. Young Birk, friend of the dead urchin, was waiting obediently for him. Wordlessly, the boy handed him the long, wavy-edged dagger the now-dead Beran has tossed to him before leading the Fey on that wild chase through the city streets. The black metal blade was dry, but the dark jewel in the hilt throbbed a rich, satisfied red, testifying to its recent taste of Ellysetta Baristani's blood.

"Excellent, boy," Kolis said. "You did well." Even Beran had served his purpose—though he'd nearly killed the girl rather than merely nicking her as he'd been ordered.

Kolis sheathed the dagger and tucked it inside his vest. Vadim Maur would be pleased.

"So much for my second lesson with Master Fellows." Ellie forced a weak laugh. She lay on a chaise in Rain's palace suite, her body tense despite the soothing warmth of Marissya's expert healing weave and gentle touch. Even the shock of her stabbing had faded in the face of her fear of the *shei'dalin*.

She imagined herself surrounded by a solid, impenetrable wall of stone and steel, her thoughts and emotions safely barricaded within, but shivers still racked her body and her teeth chattered uncontrollably as the warmth of the *shei'dalin's* magic penetrated her flesh.

At last the glow surrounding Marissya's hands dissipated and she stepped back.

"Will I live?"

A tired smile curved the *shei'dalin's* lips. "*Aiyah*, I am glad to report that you will."

Ellysetta's eyes narrowed as magic tingled across her skin and she saw a faintly unfocused look enter both Rain's and Marissya's eyes. "Speak so I can hear," she told them. "As I was the one stabbed, I have a right to hear what you are saying."

"*Sieks'ta*," Marissya murmured. "I was telling Rain the blade wasn't poisoned but there were remnants of a pain suppressant in your blood. The blade was treated with a numbing agent, which explains why you didn't feel anything even though the boy stabbed so deep he pierced a kidney." She glanced up at Rain. "It was good you stopped the bleeding as quickly as you did."

"That boy meant to kill me." Even though Rain had warned her of such a possibility, it hadn't seemed real until now.

Rain's lips thinned. "It appears so, *shei'tani*."

A warrior approached. He gave a short, brisk bow and whispered something into Rain's ears. Rain's brows drew together in a sudden scowl. Whatever the news, it wasn't good.

"What is it?" Ellie asked.

"Something has happened, *shei'tani*, and I must go. Ravel and his *cha'kor* will see you safely home. Do not leave your home again today no matter what the reason."

Irritation flashed. He was shunting her aside as if she were a child to be sent to her room while the grown-ups tended to important matters. "Tell me what's going on, Rain."

For a moment, she thought he might not answer. And when he did, she almost wished he hadn't. "Bel has been taken into custody by the King's men. The boy who attacked you is dead. A dozen witnesses claim to have seen Bel murder him."

Ellysetta swung her legs over the edge of the chaise and stood. "I'm coming with you."

"*Nei, shei'tani*. Your family is worried, and they need to see for themselves that you are unhurt. Ravel will take you to them while Marissya, Dax, and I deal with this." He raised her face to his and held her gaze steadily. "Go to your family, *ajiana*."

"But Bel—"

"Trust me. I will not allow him to come to harm."

Ellysetta searched his gaze and found resolve and reassurance. "I do trust you," she said.

His eyes glowed with sudden emotion. The hand beneath her chin slid round to cup her head and draw her closer. He bent his head and took her lips in a kiss that left her breathless.

"*Beylah vo, shei'tani*. Your words bring joy to this Fey's heart." He straightened and met Ravel's gaze, then the gaze of each member of her secondary quintet. "Guard her well, my brothers."

"With our lives, Rain," Ravel replied.

Rain tracked Dorian down to his council chamber, where he was meeting in private session with the twenty Great Lords who between them governed more than half of Celieria.

News of the would-be assassin's death had traveled through the city faster than magic-fed flames, rousing an astonishing furor. Outside the palace, the Fey reported seeing flurries of inflammatory pamphlets and small mobs of citizens gathering to march on the palace and demand justice for the dead boy, and when one of Dorian's advisors broke the privacy seal on the council chamber as he stepped briefly outside to request a book of legal precedents, Rain overheard at least half a dozen voices within calling for an inquiry and trial—of Bel.

"My Lord Feyreisen!" the council attendant yelped as Rain brushed past. "You cannot go in there! The Council is in session!"

Rain didn't spare the man a glance. He threw open the doors to the council chamber and swept inside. Dax and Marissya followed close behind him.

The great round marble chamber, its raised tiers filled with enough velvet-upholstered chairs to seat the two hundred lords of Celieria's noble houses, was mostly empty. Only the gold and silver thrones of the king and queen and the semi-circle of twenty lesser thrones belonging to the heads of the Great Houses were currently occupied.

Dorian and his Great Lords regarded Rain with a mix of shock and affront as he strode towards them across the chamber's gleaming marble floor. Annoura narrowed her eyes.

"My Lord Feyreisen"—the king's chief advisor jumped to his feet from his chair behind the king's throne and rushed forward to block Rain's advance—"this is highly irregular. I'm afraid I must ask you to leave. This Council is in private session."

Rain waved an arm, silencing the man and nudging him aside with a single, swift weave. "King Dorian, you are holding the *chatokkai*—the First General—of the Fading Lands. I have come to demand his release."

"How dare you burst into this chamber and issue demands!" One of the lords in the blue-velvet-upholstered lesser thrones surged to his feet.

Rain did not recognize the man, but the coldness in his brown eyes and the arrogance etched into every line of his face were not strangers to him. The man's heavy, well-defined musculature, emphasized rather than hidden by the tailored cut of his expensive garments, bespoke a long familiarity with the arts of mortal warfare.

«Lord Sebourne,» Dax informed Rain. *«A lord of the northern march. His family took over Wellsley's land three centuries ago after the Great Plague.»*

"You do not rule here, Tairen Soul!" Lord Sebourne continued. "And this is not one of the remote villages in the northern provinces where Fey crimes go unwitnessed and unpunished!" He jabbed a finger in Rain's direction. "Your general murdered an unarmed Celierian citizen—a child, no less! He will be held accountable for his actions!"

Several of the Twenty nodded in agreement.

"*Fey* crimes?" Rain drew himself up to his full height. "My truemate—*my queen*—" he emphasized, casting a hard glance Annoura's way, "was stabbed by that Celierian citizen you call an 'unarmed child.' Be grateful I haven't burned this city to ash around your ears!"

Annoura sat up straight in her throne. "Are you *threatening* us, Feyreisen?"

"Annoura!" Dorian snapped. His queen glared but fell silent, and he turned back to Rain and Sebourne to say in a more conciliatory tone, "Gentlemen, please, hot tempers and threats are no way to solve anything." He rose from his throne and gestured for the Fey to approach. "My Lord Feyreisen, Lord Dax, Lady Marissya, a private word please?"

Grudgingly, with a hard look for Sebourne and Celieria's too-proud queen, Rain followed Dorian into a small adjoining antechamber.

"There are witnesses," Dorian informed them as soon as the door closed; "dozens of them, all who claim the child was an innocent bystander."

"That boy was no innocent," Rain replied. "He joined Ellysetta and me in a game of Stones for the express purpose of stabbing her."

"He could have killed her, Dorian," Marissya added, "and would have if Rain had not been there to stop the blood loss."

Dorian eyed both of them. "I have to ask . . . is there any possibility Ser vel Jelani made a mistake? Could he have slain the wrong child by accident?"

"*Nei*," Rain said without hesitation. "Bel is the most experienced warrior in the Fading Lands. He would not have been so careless. But even so, he didn't kill the boy. Kieran tells me someone else wove death on the child the moment he was trapped—to keep him from revealing who hired him, no doubt."

The Celierian king rubbed a hand over his face and sighed wearily. "I have no wish to prosecute Ser vel Jelani, but Sebourne and several others who are already concerned about the recent *dahl'reisen* murders see this as yet more proof of Fey magic run amok. Sebourne is demanding a full-blown inquiry and trial, and he's got four of the Twenty agreeing with him."

Rain's eyes narrowed. "If someone means harm to Ellysetta, stripping Bel from her *cha'kor* could be part of a plan to make her more vulnerable to attack. I cannot allow you to endanger her that way."

"And I've just explained why I cannot simply pardon Ser vel Jelani out of hand."

"Then don't." Rain swept an arm towards Marissya. "We have a Truthspeaker. Have Bel swear a Fey oath, under *shei'-dalin* touch, that he did not kill this boy."

"You want us to trust *her*?" Lord Sebourne cried when Dorian announced his intentions. "Your Majesty, this is an outrage. How could we possibly trust the Fey Truthspeaker to tell us the truth if the man is guilty? She's one of them!"

Rain grabbed Dax before the man pulled steel in the council chamber to defend his truemate's honor. What had the world come to that a Great Lord of Celieria would cast doubt on the integrity of Marissya v'En Solande?

"Do not push us too far, mortal," Rain warned. "Were Queen Annoura attacked on foreign soil, this Council would howl for war. The Fey have not done so. But be warned, we will not meekly accept insult atop an already grievous injury."

King Dorian cleared his throat, the sound drawing all eyes to him. "Lord Sebourne's holdings have suffered considerable loss of life in the recent *dahl'reisen* raids. Those losses have obviously affected his normally sound judgment."

"Your Majesty!" Sebourne protested.

Dorian didn't spare a glance for the angry border lord but kept his gaze firmly fixed on Rain. "Of course, the Lady Marissya's honesty stands above reproach. She has served with honor and integrity on every Supreme Council we have convened for the past thousand years. No clear-thinking lord of Celieria would cast her centuries of service in doubt."

Now he did level a steady, steely-eyed look on Sebourne and held it until the nobleman subsided and sat down.

"We are grateful for her gracious counsel and her service, and we hold her in the highest regard," Dorian continued, allowing his gaze to sweep the council chamber, making eye contact with each lord of the Twenty. "The witnesses are being brought to the palace. As soon as they arrive, we will hear their testimony and that of Ser vel Jelani, and we will accept the Lady Marissya's Truthspeaking to determine Ser vel Jelani's guilt or innocence."

Ravel vel Arras, leader of Ellie's secondary quintet, and the rest of her Fey guard hustled Ellie through the city streets towards her family home. More than once they encountered small mobs of people who watched them with accusatory glares. Ellie couldn't understand it. She could practically feel the fear and loathing emanating from them in waves.

Scraps of paper littered the roads like fallen leaves, and on several street corners, shabby pamphleteers' boys shouted, "Fey murders unarmed Celierian child!" and handed out their leaflets as fast as their little fists could collect coin. Pamphleteers were always quick to print and disseminate their "news," but this was fast even for them. They must have run straight from the scene of Bel's confrontation with her young attacker to their presses.

Ellie bent to pick up one of the abandoned sheets and gasped at the awful, hate-filled accusations printed in lurid detail and presented as fact. *Innocent Child Burned Alive by Savage Fey,* the headline screamed. The text below was worse. Reading the vile words actually made her stomach clench and her chest feel tight, as if a cold, heavy weight were pressing against her heart. The headache that had savaged her yesterday began to throb anew.

"Ravel," she murmured in concern, handing him the sheet.

He scanned the paper with grim eyes, then crumpled it and threw it in the gutter. "Do not worry, Feyreisa. These accusations are groundless. Rain will not let Bel come to harm."

For a full bell, Rain sat grimly silent in Dorian's council chamber as witness after witness testified they'd seen Bel burn a helpless, unarmed Celierian boy to death. Afterwards, only years of hard-won discipline kept Rain's face expressionless as he listened to Lord Sebourne and several of his fellow pompous noble windbags howl about the Fey's blatant disregard for Celierian lives. As if a single one of them would not have seen the boy hanged for pinching a dinner roll from their supper tables.

The Tairen Soul's mate—his queen—had been stabbed, in public, on Celierian soil by a Celierian citizen, and these honorless *rultsharts* squealed as if *they* were the injured party.

"I have listened to the charges and accusations of your countrymen as you insisted," Rain interjected when the current speaker paused to take a breath. "I do not dispute that they believe what they saw, but that does not mean what they think they saw is what truly happened. Now bring Belliard forth. Ask him to swear an oath of honor that he did not murder this boy."

Dorian nodded. Near the back of the room, a door swung inward and Bel entered, bound in chains and surrounded by the King's Guards.

Marissya stifled a gasp, and Rain stiffened with outrage. Bel had been stripped of his blades, his tunic, and his boots, leaving him barefoot, bare-chested, and weaponless. Black metal manacles had been clamped around his wrists and ankles, and a matching black collar circled his neck. Short chains tied the bindings all together and restricted Bel's walk to a shuffle. Though the warrior held himself proudly erect, his face was drawn and pale, and his hands trembled, a testament to the terrible pain he was suffering.

"You dare bind a Queen's Blade in *sel'dor*?" Rain hissed in a low voice. A wave of heat swept over the council chamber, and the flames in the sconces flared.

Shocked silence was the only answer to his challenge until Annoura sat up in her throne. "The man stands accused of murder," she pointed out. "Should his guards have left his magic unrestrained? I, for one, will not condemn them for taking precautions."

"Precautions don't include torturing him until he scarce can stand! *Sel'dor* burns like acid on Fey flesh." He shot a furious, commanding glare at Dorian. "Remove that vile Eld filth this instant, or by Adelis's holy light, I swear I will visit Bel's torment upon you all so you may know what harm you do him." His hands clenched in fists at his sides. Hatred of all things Eld swirled around him like a black cloud, and he struggled to keep his violent emotions in check. Tiny sparks of escaping power flashed around him. "*Now!*" he barked.

"Do it," Dorian commanded, and the guards surrounding Bel hurried to unlock and remove the restraints. "My Lord Feyreisen, I assure you I did not order this."

When Bel was free of the cursed Eld metal, Rain spun a rapid weave of Earth to replace Bel's boots and tunic and re-store at least a modicum of his dignity. Marissya reached out to Bel with healing weaves to soothe the worst of his burns.

Rain waited for her to finish before turning back to Dorian. Fire still sparked in his eyes and anger clipped every word. "Question him and be done. I'll not abandon this honored hero of the Fey to your country's unkind custody a moment longer."

Bel stood in the center of the council chamber and sub-mitted willingly to Marissya's touch as he swore a Fey oath that the dead boy was the same one who had stabbed Elly-setta, and that he had neither murdered the boy, nor ordered his murder, nor harmed him in any way.

"Truth," she announced when he finished.

"If you did not kill the boy, who did?" Lord Sebourne demanded.

"I don't know," Bel said. "We saw no one."

"Truth," Marissya said.

"So, you're asking us to believe that a young Celierian boy—a boy you were pursuing for the attempted murder of the Tairen Soul's mate—just happened to spontaneously combust when you cornered him?"

"I am not asking you to believe anything, my lord. I am merely telling you in all honesty that neither I nor my men killed that boy, and we did not see who did."

"Truth," Marissya confirmed.

"But he died by magic, did he not?"

"Someone spun the weave that slew him," Bel admitted.

Lord Sebourne pounced. "Someone Fey?"

"Fey are not the only race to weave magic, my lord. The Eld do as well. And others."

"Ah, yes, the Eld." Sebourne cast a speaking glance around the chamber. "That's who you really want us to believe is to blame, do you not?"

Bel ignored the lure dangled before him. "My lord, as I told you, I did not see who spun the weave. I cannot tell you who wove it, but I can assure you who did not. If you are truly interested in finding the killer, I recommend you start by asking who would benefit most from making Celierians doubt the Fey. And while you're at it, also consider this: I am a Master of Spirit. I weave illusion as easily as you draw breath. If I really had killed that boy, why in all the gods' names would I have been stupid enough to let anyone see me do it? And why would I leave them with memories of the crime intact so they could accuse me?"

Sebourne's mouth opened, then closed again without saying a word. Nonplussed, he glanced round the council chamber and saw similar confusion on the faces of his supporters.

"Enough of this farce." On the opposite side of the chamber, a lord who had thus far remained silent now stood up. He had pale, faintly luminous skin, long black hair, and catlike eyes that proved more than a hint of Fey blood ran through his veins.

«*Who?*» Rain asked Dax

«*You don't recognize him? You once called his ancestor friend, and I've always thought the family resemblance striking.*» When Rain didn't answer, Dax surrendered the name. «*Teleos. Devron Teleos. He guards the Veil now, as well as the Garreval.*»

Rain eyed the young border lord with greater interest. Teleos was indeed a name familiar to him, and neither the Veil nor the Garreval were insignificant stretches of land.

"Ser vel Jelani has sworn a Fey oath, under *shei'dalin* touch, that he did not kill the boy," Lord Teleos continued. "That proves his innocence. And frankly, even if he had slain the little *rultshart*, you lords should applaud rather than condemn him. Which man among you would have let the boy live had he attempted to kill *your* queen?"

"Well said, Teleos." A second, previously silent lord stood up, this one as dark and bronzed as Teleos was pale. There was a no-nonsense sturdiness to him that Rain liked instantly.

«*Cannevar Barrial,*» Dax supplied. «*Another lord of the northern march. His daughter recently wed Sebourne's heir.*»

"Sebourne, you're being an ass." Lord Barrial made the accusation with casual familiarity rather than ire. "The Fey obviously didn't kill the boy, no matter what the other witnesses think they saw, and the young would-be assassin has paid for his crime with his life. Justice has been done. My lords, let us bring this unfortunate incident to a close and move on to the other very serious matters awaiting the review of this Council." Several lords murmured their agreement.

"Agreed," King Dorian said, cutting off Lord Sebourne as he opened his mouth to protest and silencing the grumbling of several of Sebourne's supporters. "My Lord Feyreisen, accept our apologies for the injury done your lady, and for the accusations made against Ser vel Jelani. I promise you Celieria will make every effort to find the culprit responsible for this unforgivable attack." He turned to address Bel directly.

"Belliard vel Jelani, you are free to go. Please accept my personal apologies for the manner in which you've been treated."

Bel bowed to the king and rejoined his countrymen. All the Fey bowed again and filed from the room. They didn't speak until they reached Rain's suite and the privacy wards were once more in place around the room.

"There is more," Bel said as soon as the privacy weaves were complete. "The knife that set off the Fire weave was a Fey'cha, and I recognized the name-mark on it." He cast a brief, unspoken apology Marissya's way. "It was the mark of Gaelen vel Serranis."

"Impossible," she exclaimed. "He is *dahl'reisen*. I would have sensed him."

"There was some other magic hidden in the weave that killed the boy," Bel said. "I don't know what it was. Perhaps your brother has found a way to mask his presence from you the same way he masked his magic from me."

Was it possible? Rain wondered. Fey used red to fight their enemies and those unworthy of the honor of a duel with clean blades. They used black against each other—always. The numbed black blade used to stab Ellysetta could have been a taunt, an insult to Rain's ability to protect her, and arranging for the injury to be dealt by a child could have been just a way to further underscore that contempt. Was vel Serranis calling him out?

Worse, if Gaelen was responsible, the possibility that he was also behind the murders in the north—possibly even in league with the Eld—suddenly became much more likely. Rain prayed it was not so. Sending warriors to kill the *dahl'reisen* would take a terrible toll on the rapidly dwindling strength of the Fading Lands and push the Fey even closer towards extinction.

Marissya didn't want to believe Gaelen had engineered the attack, but Rain could take no chances. He spent the rest of the afternoon with Bel, retracing the boy's wild chase and visiting the site of his death. Nothing remained but a scorch mark on the cobbles. There was no remnant thread of magic, no sign of any other's presence, and no hint of *dahl'reisen*. Whoever had engineered the attack had covered his tracks well.

CHAPTER FIFTEEN

Ellysetta spent the afternoon pacing the floor of her family home and waiting for news of Bel. She kept her mind occupied by practicing her spoken command of Feyan with Ravel and the other members of her secondary quintet. They shared anecdotes of life in the Fading Lands, all spoken in Feyan, and periodically checked in with Kieran via Spirit to find out what was happening at the inquiry and reported those updates in Feyan as well.

News of the attack on her left her father more worried than she'd ever seen him. He'd even abandoned the mountain of work that had been keeping him busy morning till night and came home to assure himself she was safe. When he'd hugged her tight and told her gruffly, "I love you, Ellie-girl," she'd seen tears in his eyes.

Mama, too, was clearly shaken, but the fear only reaffirmed every concern she'd already voiced about having the Fey become part of her daughter's life. She spent the day holding Lillis and Lorelle so tightly they squealed, and no amount of calming discussion would placate her. Even after word came that Bel was free, Mama's dire predictions and recriminations continued until Ellie fled to her bedroom and paced the tiny space like a caged tiger.

She wanted to climb out the window and run until her emotions settled, but she wasn't fool enough to consider it. Rain's warnings had proved true. Enemies of the Fey would hurt her to harm him. She'd almost died today . . . would have died had Rain not acted as quickly as he did. As Bel had warned that first night, the world was no longer a safe place for her.

Several bells after sunset, the sound of wind whooshing past the rooftops and a powerful tingling rush of magic sent her racing to the window in time to see Rain slip from the night sky and land on the flagstones of her family's small courtyard. She raced downstairs to meet him at the kitchen door, but her parents had heard his arrival too and were already there, standing on the back stoop. Mama was wearing one of her looks and roundly berating Rain for not protecting Ellie better, while Papa stood beside her, puffing rapidly on his pipe.

"—our daughter stabbed while under your protection?" Mama was saying. "A boy with a knife nearly killed her right beneath your nose?"

A small muscle flexed in Rain's jaw, but he stood silent as Ellie's mother continued her tirade. When she ran out of steam—even Mama couldn't rail for long against a man who simply stood there and accepted it in silence—Rain bowed. "The mother of my *shei'tani* is right to berate me. I was careless with your greatest treasure. My enemies knew I would not expect the attack to come from a child, and they used that to their advantage. I will not be so blind again."

"Your enemies?" Sol asked. "So you know who attacked Ellysetta? Did you find them?"

Rain shook his head. "*Nei*, Master Baristani, which means that henceforth, we must all be more vigilant. There will be no more games in the park. Ellysetta will leave your home only when she absolutely must, and only with a full complement of warriors in attendance. When I come for our courtship bells, we shall either remain here in your courtyard, or I will take her away from the city, someplace where my enemies cannot surprise me again."

Lauriana started to object, but Sol gave her hand a warning squeeze. "You did warn us of the dangers that first night of the betrothal," he said, "but I must admit, I didn't take your warning as seriously as I do now. We will all be more cautious." He glanced at Ellie. "I suppose you'd like a little time alone with our daughter."

Rain bowed again. "*Beylah vo*, Master Baristani. I would indeed. But elsewhere, if I may. Somewhere quiet, where the thoughts of so many do not beat at me as they do here."

"It's late," Sol said. "Please, don't keep her out more than a bell or two."

"Agreed." Rain held out a hand to Ellysetta.

"Sol!" Lauriana protested. "But—"

"Shh, come inside, Laurie. If it were you who'd been stabbed, I'd want to have you to myself for a bit, to make sure you were safe and unharmed. Let them have their privacy." He put an arm around his wife's waist and led her into the kitchen. "We'll just sit here, sweetheart, and share a quiet cup of tea together until they come back."

They flew east past the lights of the city towards the rolling hills surrounding the moonlight-silvered waters of Great Bay and landed in a small hilltop glade overlooking the bay. There, Celieria City was little more than a distant glow of lights at their backs, and even that was hidden by the treetops. The silence was broken only by the rustle of the ocean breeze in the trees and the faint sound of waves rolling onto the sandy beaches below. Undimmed by the lights of the city, the stars overhead gleamed like diamonds strewn across a black velvet sky.

Magic tingled in the air as Rain wove protective shields around the glade. When he was done he turned to Ellysetta, his face solemn and beautiful, the glow of his Fey skin a shimmering aura. He regarded her in deep, searching silence, then pulled her into his arms and simply held her.

"You frightened me, today, *shei'tani*. A bit of poison on that blade, and I would have lost you." His arms tightened.

"But you didn't."

"*Nei*, thank the gods, but I was careless with you. I won't be again—and I know that will be hard on you." He drew back to look into her eyes. "You need freedom to thrive, just as I do."

"I'll manage." Somehow, she would. She'd sensed Rain's fear and guilt when she'd been stabbed, his terror at the prospect of losing her. She would not intentionally cause him such distress again. "How is Bel? Ravel told me he'd been chained in *sel'dor*."

"He's fine. The effects of *sel'dor* are painful but not permanent. I told him to stay at the palace and rest tonight. He wasn't happy with me, but he'll be back tomorrow."

"I can't believe King Dorian allowed them to bind Bel in *sel'dor*." She'd read horrible accounts of what the evil Eld metal could do to Fey, how painful and debilitating it was. How could Dorian, who was part Fey himself, have authorized its use on Bel?

"Dorian said he didn't know about it. Marissya believes him." He released her and stepped back. "The Celierians who did it claim they were acting out of self-preservation. Bel stood accused of murdering a Celierian with magic, and they wanted to be sure he couldn't murder them as well. Though they wouldn't admit it, I think Annoura authorized their actions."

Ellie's eyes closed briefly in shame. "Rain, I'm sorry."

"For what? You are not to blame for the actions of your countrymen."

"Maybe not, but if it weren't for me, Bel wouldn't have been accused of murder." She still wanted to weep for what he'd suffered. "Do you have any idea who was behind the attack?"

"We were meant to think *dahl'reisen* sponsored it."

"But you're not so sure?"

"Marissya didn't sense them, and *dahl'reisen* don't hire children to make their kills." His lips thinned. "The Eld aren't so discriminating. Using a child to attack you is just the sort of thing they'd do."

"Did you find any proof it might have been the Eld?"

"Proof? The hard, irrefutable kind needed to convince your countrymen? *Nei*, for that we'd have to catch a Mage red-handed in the act of subverting a Celierian's mind or weaving Azrahn before a hundred witnesses." His mouth twisted in a grimly sardonic smile. "Unfortunately for us, they usually aren't so blatant. The Eld work in subtleties until they consolidate a base of power. They sow doubts, disagreements, suspicions, fears—the kinds of things that can be explained away. They play on mortal weakness and self-indulgence. And through those small, steady corruptions, they begin to claim souls."

Ellie could feel his anger building with every word. "Rain . . ."

He caught himself and drew a deep breath. As he exhaled, she could almost sense him forcibly expelling his rage. "*Sieks'ta*," he apologized. "Let's not talk of the Eld. I can never speak of them without hatred welling up within me." He turned away and walked closer to the edge of the steep hill. The ocean breeze blew his hair back from his face as he stood there, looking out over the dark, shining waters of the bay. "No matter who sponsored the attack, it will be a long time before I forgive myself for underestimating my enemies. I was too arrogant, too confident in my own abilities to protect you. I failed you."

Her heart contracted. She went to him, reaching out to grasp his arm. "You didn't fail me, Rain. You saved my life."

He glanced down at the pale hand gripping his arm and gently removed it. "*Nei, shei'tani*. Your heart is kind, but do not try to weave peace on me. I deserve my guilt. I may have saved your life this time, but only because I got lucky."

Her fingers curled around his, holding him when he would have pulled away. "Luck springs from the hands of the gods," she reminded him. "Even if that *was* what saved me, it only proves the gods don't want you to fail. You should be thanking them for their blessing, not railing against it."

Silence fell between them. A wolf pack howled in the distance, and down below, a flock of seabirds squawked and took to startled flight at the sound.

"I do thank them, Ellysetta," Rain said quietly. "More than I thought would ever be possible for me again. But I cannot rely on their grace. I know better than most how unkind the gods can be to those who do not prove worthy of their gifts."

"Oh, Rain." Through the clasp of her hand around his, she could feel the echo of raw grief, the memory of a loss so devastating it had driven him to scorch the world. "Do you think Sariel would want you to carry the blame for her death? Everyone in the world knows how much you both loved each other, and you yourself told me how kind and gentle she was. Surely she wouldn't want you to torment yourself over things you cannot change."

"*Nei*," he agreed, "but she was always too quick to forgive." He drew in a short breath and squared his shoulders, already tucking the old, painful emotions back under careful guard, hiding them from her. "And I did not bring you here to discuss my ancient grief or guilt." He turned to her and took both of her hands in his, lifting her fingers to his lips. "I meant to give us a few quiet bells together away from the pressures of the city. Somewhere quiet and peaceful where we could simply . . . be . . . together. Somewhere I could hold you without an audience." The corner of his mouth curved up. "Perhaps share another kiss or two, if you were willing."

She wanted to protest the change of subject. His grief, his guilt, was a festering wound inside him, and it needed to be purged. Respect for his pride kept her silent. Battered and bruised, but still fighting for dominance, his was not the selfish, petty pride that made bullies of lesser men, but rather the quiet, determined dignity that turned men into heroes and made heroes crawl back to their feet from the bitter dust of defeat and stand tall once more. She dare not take that from him. She remembered what lay beneath his carefully constructed discipline: the screaming torment, the endless barrage of accusing voices.

She stepped closer and lifted her hands to frame his face. "Then hold me, Rain, and kiss me, for I want the same things."

Emotions chased across her senses: humility, sorrow, gratitude, devotion. His fingers brushed back spiraling tendrils of hair from her face. "You are more than I deserve, *shei'tani*."

He bent his head and took her lips in a tender kiss. Sweet, gentle, barely more than a brush of his lips against hers, tiny nibbles along her lower lip, a caress of fingertips across her skin, light as mist. His lips started to move away, but she turned her head, following, wanting. Her hands caught his face more firmly, holding him still. She rose up on her toes, her mouth seeking his, asking for the passion he'd shown her before.

He rewarded her boldness. His fingers delved deep into the heavy mass of her hair. His head dove down and his lips claimed hers with fierce and sudden hunger. Need rolled over her senses in hot, heavy waves. His arms slid round her waist and tightened, pulling her hard against him. She felt the crush of his knives, the hard, lean strength of his body.

Then he pulled back, leaving her hands grasping empty air and her brows tightening in a bereft frown. She opened her eyes and saw the long fall of his dark hair streaming down the equally dark expanse of black leather covering his back. He was walking away. "Rain?"

He cast a glance over his shoulder. His eyes were glowing, his skin luminous, and his expression potently male. "Patience, Ellysetta. There's no need to rush."

Tiny explosions of heat fired all across her body, leaving her knees weak and her breathing shallow.

He waved a hand. Magic flowed from his fingers in a sparkling stream. A thick blanket unfurled in the center of the clearing and a myriad of tiny lights floated out to flicker in the grass and surrounding trees, lending the meadow a verdant, magical quality, as if Ellysetta and Rain were standing not on a hilltop in the mortal land of Celieria but in an enchanted glade, deep in the misty wonders of Elvia or the Fading Lands. She stared around them, mouth open, passion momentarily forgotten as the power and beauty of his magic enthralled her senses. She could not tell what was real and what was illusion.

"Come, *shei'tani*, sit here beside me." He drew her down onto the blanket and joined her, his long legs folding gracefully beneath him as he sat.

"This is beautiful." She couldn't stop looking at the lights twinkling in the grass and trees. One of the lights flew closer, and she saw it was a tiny, glowing creature with gossamer wings. Its phosphorescent form shifted and glimmered, leaving an impression of slender limbs and great beauty, and then it darted off, a trill of delicate, crystalline notes trailing in its wake.

"There is a glade like this in the Fading Lands," Rain said. "Near Blade's Point, overlooking the Bay of Flame. When the sun sets, the waters of the bay turn to liquid fire, and the fairyflies awake and light up the hills just like this. Legend says a great tairen called Lissallukai, the first ever to cast a wingshadow over the Fading Lands, once breathed her fire across the waves of the bay at sunset and sang the magic of this world to life."

"That's a beautiful story."

He smiled faintly. "Oh, *aiyah*, we Fey are known for the beauty of our tales."

The warm night air swirled over them, fragrant with the verdant lushness of the glade, an intoxicating mix of wildflowers and the fresh scent of the night sea. He turned his head towards her, his long, dark hair draping down around his face like onyx silk. His skin shone with Fey luminescence, a light in the darkness.

"Wilt share with me the joy of your kiss, *shei'tani*?" A finger brushed across her lip. "*Ku'shalah aiyah to nei.*" Bid me yes or no.

"*Aiyah*," she whispered. His head bent towards her, his mouth touched hers with exquisite lightness, letting her confirm her choice. With a sigh of breath that he drank as if it were the water of life, she parted her lips and melted into his arms.

Up until now, modesty had made her reticent to offer him passion without his first coaxing it from her, but this time she met his desire with hunger of her own. Kiss for kiss, breath for breath, she matched him, and his soul rejoiced. The tairen roared, but Rain held it fast and bound it with flows of steel-clad will.

Ellysetta threaded her fingers through Rain's silky hair and ran them over the smooth, warm leather covering his back. A whisper of frustration snaked through her at the small barrier that stood between her touch and his skin. She brought her hands around to his chest, fretting at the maze of fastenings that kept his tunic closed and kept her hands from touching him. She wasn't bold enough to release the numerous catches, nor to ask him to remove his tunic. Irritation over her own cowardice and thwarted desires made her nip at his ear.

A low, purring growl rumbled in his chest. "Wouldst share more than a kiss, *shei'tani*?"

"I . . ." The temptation was great. Heat pooled deep in her belly at the mere thought of it. Her flesh felt hot and swollen, and she could feel the hot, rapid throb of her heart pounding through her veins. "We shouldn't. We're not yet wed."

He pulled back just far enough to meet her eyes. "Since the moment you called me from the sky, I have been more wed to you than any Celierian who stands before a priest to take a wife." He stroked her lips with his finger. His eyes flared with a slight glow, and invisible lips traced his finger's path, pressing fevered kisses across her skin. He smiled a little as she gasped and her eyelids fluttered down. "But I will not take more than you are willing to give. Besides, your father made me swear a Fey oath that there would be no mating before the marriage."

Her eyes flew open. "He did *what*? When did he do that?"

"That first night, after we returned from the river. . . . Why else do you think your parents allow us to spend our courtship bells without a chaperon?" He gave a rueful smile. "He is canny, your father. And protective. Good traits for a father to have."

"You and my father talked about mating . . . about you and me and . . ." She sat up and covered her hot cheeks with her hands.

His eyebrows lifted. "Why does this embarrass you? There is nothing more natural than mating. When tairen mate, it is a spectacle of great drama and beauty in the sky. All the Fey within a hundred miles come out to watch. When people mate, it is a bit less spectacular, and certainly more private, but no less beautiful in its own way."

"Rain . . ."

"I can show you."

She pulled back, shocked. "But you just said Papa made you promise not to. You swore a Fey oath." He couldn't seriously be suggesting he would break his oath?

He shook his head. "I vowed not to mate you. I never said anything about showing you with Spirit what your father has forbidden me in flesh." His eyes were slumberous and filled with masculine satisfaction. "When you wager with tairen . . ."

". . . take care with your words." They finished the Fey maxim in concert.

"Well?" he prompted in the brief ensuing silence. "Would you like to know what it is like to mate with this Fey? In all modesty, there are few who can equal my mastery of Spirit. You would not know it was a weave."

Her cheeks felt as if they were on fire. "I don't think that's the best idea . . ." She didn't even want to contemplate facing her parents after such a thing.

Rain laughed softly, not offended by her refusal. "Little coward. No mating, then, in any form, just a deeper taste of pleasure." He bent his head again, and his tongue did things to her ear that made all thoughts of her parents fly out of her head.

She moaned helplessly, and her eyes squeezed shut as sensation grew to stronger pleasure. "Is that Spirit?"

"*Nei*, that's just me . . . do you like it?"

Gods help her. "Too much, I think."

His lips brushed her cheek. "*Parei* is the Fey word for stop. Say it, and I will cease. No matter when, no matter why. *Ku'shalah aiyah to nei.*"

There was no possible answer but one. Despite a lifetime of modesty reinforced by her parents' strict but loving guidance, ever since the moment Rain had given Ellysetta her first, searing taste of passion, she'd wanted more.

"*Aiyah*," she said, and her breath caught in her throat as the pleasures of Rain's touch multiplied exponentially. Real and Spirit hands held her, stroked her. Real and Spirit lips rained kisses on her mouth, her throat, the soft skin exposed by her gown's modestly scooped neckline.

He tracked nibbling kisses around her ear and the sensitive nape of her neck. His hand stroked a searing path down her side, then back up to cup her breast. Her back arched, filling his palm more fully with her flesh. He ran a finger down the center of her bodice, and the fabric parted without protest, forming a long, deep vee that exposed the inner curves of her breasts. The warm summer air felt cool against her heated flesh. Rain stroked the soft, exposed skin.

Invisible Spirit limbs guided her hands to his chest, as swirling Earth magic effortlessly peeled away his black leather tunic and Fey'cha belts, baring the pale, leanly muscled perfection of his Fey flesh. At last she could touch him as she'd wanted to do just moments ago.

Fevered heat and naked skin filled Ellysetta's palms. Her fingers clutched at the rock-hard swell of pectoral muscles, felt the pounding drum of his heart. He brushed aside the remaining scraps of fabric covering her breasts and lowered his head.

Incredible, searing, glorious heat consumed her. Coherent thought eluded her. She could not think. She could not speak. With a helpless gasp of pleasure, she surrendered. Her arms twined around his neck, clutching him to her.

Kolis Manza locked his door at the Inn of the Blue Pony, closed the shutters, and activated the privacy wards he'd set into every surface of the room. On the desk near the bed lay the paraphernalia he hated but was forced to use to avoid Fey detection: the silver salver, the sacrifice, and the Mage blade whose *selkahr* crystal pulsated with sated fullness.

It was time to return to Eld and make his report to the High Mage. He prepared the physical ingredients of the spell, then began to murmur the Feraz witchwords he had long ago committed to memory. Energy gathered, then pulsed in a bright flash. If not for the blackout spell laid on the window shutters, passersby in the street would have seen a curious blast of light emanating from one of the windows on the third floor of the inn.

When the light dimmed, the inn's bedchamber was empty.

The sensation of ice spiders came without warning, crawling up Ellysetta's spine and dousing passion with brutal force. She tore herself out of Rain's arms and jerked into a sitting position, gasping for breath and crossing her arms as violent shivers shook her body.

"*Shei'tani?*" Rain drew her back into his arms. He chafed his hands across her shivering skin. "What happened?"

"I—" Already the feeling was gone. She pressed a hand over her heart where a cold chill still throbbed with every beat. "I'm sorry. It's nothing." Suddenly conscious of her nakedness, she fumbled to draw the scraps of her gown over her breasts.

He spun swift Earth to repair her clothing. His eyes held hers, full of concern and worry. "Ellysetta, that was not 'nothing.'"

"It was just another ghost treading on my grave." She rose on unsteady legs. "I told you, it happens all the time."

He rose to his full height, looking very intimidating as he towered over her, frowning. "This I do not like."

She laughed without humor. "Believe me, neither do I." She glanced up at the position of the dual moons in the sky. "We should go. It's getting late."

"Very well," he conceded with obvious reluctance. "But we'll talk of this again." He dispersed the magic woven over the glade, then moved to the center of the clearing and summoned the Change.

Throughout the return flight, occasional, involuntary shivers that had nothing to do with the chill of the high-altitude air shook Ellysetta. The ice spider sensations were happening too frequently. In the past, they had often preceded the other, more frightening episodes. The seizures that left her howling and shrieking like a wild thing, that made her family fear for her sanity and their own safety. That made her terrified of her own existence.

Because when those seizures came, she knew there was something inside her, something dangerous and evil that must never be released.

The twin moons had reached their zenith when a knock on Vadim Maur's door heralded the arrival of his apprentice. Kolis Manza entered and made a deep bow.

"Do you have it?" the High Mage demanded brusquely.

"I do, master." The Sulimage straightened and held out a sheathed Mage blade. "Her blood, my lord—more than enough to strengthen your seeking spell."

Vadim snatched the knife, half pulled it from the sheath, and inspected the ruby lights flickering in the pommel's dark jewel. He pressed his thumb to the razor-sharp edge to test the blade's hunger and glanced up sharply. "You did not get this much blood without calling attention to yourself. How badly did you wound her?"

Kolis's skin lost some of its color. Vadim made a mental note to himself. Such a betrayal of emotion was a tell that Kolis would need to overcome if he was ever to become more than just a skillful tool. The younger Mage was a mere two hundred years old. Barely beginning his first incarnation. Gifted, but still too inexperienced to control his weaker emotions.

"How badly?" Vadim asked again. If the Sulimage had slain her . . . The temperature in the room grew notably colder. A tell of his own, but one he allowed himself to reveal. Showing fear was a weakness. *Inducing* it was something quite different.

The sudden chill had the desired effect. Kolis's reply spilled from him in a rush. "My *umagi* struck her more deeply than he should have, but the Tairen Soul was with her. She was healed and had been returned to her home before I left. There was no lasting damage to her, and my *umagi* paid for his mistake with his life."

"But now you have raised suspicions."

"The suspicions were already there, master. The Tairen Soul has sensed our growing strength."

Vadim's brows drew together. "Impossible. We are warded by *sel'dor*, witchery and magecraft. No hint of our existence should be felt by any Fey." He'd tested the wards on many subjects over the centuries. There was no doubt as to their effectiveness.

Kolis did not back down. "Possible or not, master, the Tairen Soul has Dorian half convinced the Mages have regained power in Eld."

The Sulimage had regained his color. He was telling the truth—at least insofar as he knew. It made no sense. Vadim had tested the shields of Boura Fell and the other Mage holds often enough throughout the years to be certain of their efficacy. Had the Tairen Soul truly sensed the growing Mage power in Eld, or was he merely passing off suspicion as fact in an effort to revitalize his faltering alliance with Celieria? The former was a troubling concern, the latter an encouraging sign of weakness but still an unwelcome development. They had been making such excellent progress these last few years.

"Do not let the Tairen Soul trick you into acting rashly," Vadim warned. "Overt hostilities now will undermine decades of careful planning." The girl might yet prove prize enough to capture even at the cost of revealing their existence, but failing that, he still had many months of preparation to complete before he was ready to move openly against Celieria. He pinned his apprentice with a cold stare. "I would not kindly view the ruination of those plans."

"My every effort has been designed to turn suspicion away from us, master." Kolis related how he'd arranged for the Fey to find vel Serranis's blade on the dead boy, and how he'd used the boy's death to accuse the Fey of murder. "The warrior was released, but the seed of doubt has been sown. Already it is taking root. Our efforts to make the mortals fear Fey power are working."

"But not well enough yet to countenance haste," Vadim cautioned. "Patience must be our watchword." Much as he longed to conquer Celieria, such things took time. The world was full of useful fools; the trick was cultivating the right ones . . . and carefully encouraging them to usher in their own destruction. "How go your efforts to turn Celieria's queen?"

Kolis's eyes flickered. He drew a breath. "Not as well as I'd hoped, master. She's proving much more resistant than I'd expected. As proud and power-hungry as she is, I thought she would be an easier mark."

The failure didn't please Vadim, but Kolis's honest admission of it did. "Kin of the Fey don't wed easy marks, young Mage. There may not be a *shei'tanitsa* bond between them, but it's as close as a mortal bond can come. She loves her husband. Make her doubt that love, and you will break its hold on her."

The Sulimage bowed. "You are wise in all things, master."

"As will you be, in time, Kolis." Of all the apprentice Mages who had served him over the years, Kolis was the one most like him. Powerful, inventive, hungry for advancement and conquest. One day, Vadim might have to kill him. For now, however, he had proved more useful than most veteran

Primages with a host of jewels on their sashes. "Continue your efforts to discredit the Fey, make it difficult for the nobles to support them. I want those borders open. When we control Celieria from the inside and have isolated the Fading Lands from her allies, then we will strike. As powerful as the Fey are, they cannot stand alone against us."

"And the girl, master?"

Vadim held the Mage blade up to his nose and breathed in as if he could detect her scent still clinging to the metal. "You have not seen proof of strong magic?"

"Not enough to be certain."

"Then continue testing her. If she is what I suspect, her existence changes everything." He wrapped the blade carefully in a silk scarf and set it on his desk. "Dorian and his queen are hosting a dinner for their Fey guests tomorrow, are they not?"

"Yes, master, they are."

"Good. Come, and let's discuss what I would like you to do."

CHAPTER SIXTEEN

Ellie's pillow smelled like Rain. She turned and pressed it to her face, remembering the scent and feel of his skin pressed close to hers. He'd brought her home last night, then scandalized her by sneaking in through her bedroom window after her parents went to bed. Despite her halfhearted efforts to shoo him out, he'd stayed long past a decent bell, lying with her on her narrow bed, holding her close. They'd talked in quiet whispers about everything and nothing: their childhoods, their parents, Rain's life before the Wars. She'd even come close to telling him about her childhood exorcism and the terrors that still haunted her, but fear of replacing that shining, affectionate light in his eyes with suspicion and horror had kept her silent.

Finally, regretfully, he'd left her a few bells before dawn. Not long after he'd left, weariness had tugged her eyes closed, but for the first time in over a week, no nightmare plagued her, as if Rain's presence had kept her troubling dreams away.

Smiling at the fancy, she set the pillow aside and sat up. It was early yet. Outside, the first soft rays of the Great Sun had barely begun to lighten the horizon, and judging by the silence from the room next door, her parents were not yet stirring. She rose, grabbed the robe from the wall hook opposite her bed, and slipped out of her bedroom. Downstairs, her quintet was waiting, Belliard vel Jelani among them.

"Bel!" she cried softly. She rushed across the room, ignoring his shocked look to throw her arms around him in a fierce, happy embrace. "I'm so glad you're safe." She pulled back. "Ravel told me they'd chained you in *sel'dor*. Are you all right?" She grabbed his hand and pushed back the leather cuff to inspect his wrist. Please, gods, let him not have suffered the slightest lasting hurt on her behalf.

His fingers curled around hers, warm and steady. "I'm fine, *kem'falla*."

"And getting better by the moment," Kieran quipped, smiling.

"*Aiyah*," Bel agreed. He cocked his head to one side, cobalt eyes shining with affection and pride. "*Ve stral miora la sa'dol stral liss, kem'feyreisa.*"

"I weave joy like the Great Sun weaves light?" she repeated.

His brows rose. "A perfect translation. You've been practicing."

"Ravel and his men worked with me all yesterday afternoon while we were waiting for word about you." The afternoon of immersion had helped tremendously. Once she'd figured out how the words were pronounced—and which vowels and consonants tended to be dropped or stressed when spoken—she'd been able to associate the sounds of spoken Feyan with her thorough understanding of the written language. A few more weeks and she'd be speaking like a native of the Fading Lands. "Are you truly all right? And what do you mean, I weave joy?"

"You were sharing your soul's warmth again, *kem'falla*." The rare beauty of Bel's smile brought tears to her eyes. "And, *aiyah*, I am truly all right. I deserved much worse than a few short bells in *sel'dor* chains for allowing you to come to harm while under my protection."

"Don't say that!" she protested. "What happened to me wasn't your fault. No one could have known what that boy was going to do. Even I didn't realize he'd stabbed me until I saw my own blood." She squeezed his hands. "You aren't to blame in any way."

"You are too kind, *kem'falla*, but yesterday I did not prove worthy of your trust. I promise to fulfill my bloodsworn oath better in the future." Bel dropped to one knee and bowed low, touching his forehead to the backs of her hands. "May every blade aimed at you find my flesh instead, and may I deal death to your enemies without hesitation and never fail you again." He lifted shining eyes. *"Miora felah ti'feyreisa."*

Garbed once more as the unmemorable Merchant Black, Kolis Manza stood in the shadows of the garden beside Selianne Pyerson's small house. Through the curtained windows of the side door, he could see Tuelis and her daughter sitting at a table in the home's tiny kitchen, two steaming cups of keflee and a plate of small frosted cakes before them. As he watched, Selianne took a sip of the keflee her mother had prepared. A few chimes later, she slumped in the chair. The kitchen door opened, and Kolis walked past Tuelis to her daughter's side.

The vacant expression on Selianne's face didn't change as he slit the soft flesh of her inner wrist with his Mage blade and lifted her wrist to his mouth, drinking the salty sweetness of her blood directly from her vein. He drank until he could feel the buzzing connection of his previous bindings and the shadows of his first two Mage Marks darkened the swell of her left breast. He gave the small incision a final lick and closed it with a whisper of Earth.

As carefully as before, he summoned the sweet darkness of Azrahn, wrapped it in insulating Spirit, then plunged the binding magic deep into Selianne's heart. Her eyes went wide, and despite the powerful sedative she'd ingested, she gave a soft cry and struggled against his hold.

"Don't fight it, pet," he crooned. "Remember your sweet Cerlissa." The threat worked, as it had at their previous two meetings, and the barriers she'd thrown up against him wavered. "Yes, pet. That's it." He held the penetrating cold of the Mark until it extinguished the last defiant threads of her current resistance.

Unlike her mother, Selianne had been born in Celieria, not Eld. She'd not received the bonds of blood that were made at birth for all Eld's children, nor been subjected to the ritual binding of souls that started on the first anniversary of the child's birth and were completed on the day the child turned six. Because of that, he'd been forced to bind her himself, using a less effective six-day method. A knife at the throat of her infant had convinced her to accept the first blooding and Mage Mark. Sedating herbs and threats had coerced her acceptance of the second—and now the third. But Selianne was no willing follower. She would continue to fight his control until she bore the full six Marks, and even then his hold over her would require effort to enforce.

He trailed a finger down the side of her face. Spirit and tiny, imperceptible threads of Azrahn sank into her skin. Though he could not yet force her compliance or inhabit her body without either her consent or a forceful use of Azrahn, he could plant directives in her mind and guide her thoughts and actions without her knowledge.

"Your mother told me you are having second thoughts about serving as Ellysetta Baristani's Honoria." His thumb brushed across her lips. "You must not let fear stop you from doing what is right. Go to the Cathedral this morning, but be sure you tell Ellysetta and her mother how concerned you are. The Fey aren't to be trusted. Look how they murdered that unfortunate boy and got away with it."

He wove the whispered instructions into her mind on compulsion threads of Spirit and Azrahn. When he was done, he wiped the memory of his visit from her mind, leaving only a subconscious certainty that the people she loved were in terrible danger if Ellysetta's marriage to Rain Tairen Soul could not be stopped.

"Selianne!" Standing on the steps of the Grand Cathedral, Ellysetta held out her hands to her approaching best friend and masked trepidation behind a bright smile. After yesterday's attack, she'd realized that Rain had been right about Fey enemies targeting her, and she worried that Selianne, with her Eld blood, might be in danger because of their friendship.

But what was she to do? Mama had gone on and on to Greatfather Tivrest about how Selianne and Ellie were inseparable friends and what a beacon of light Selianne was, what a dedicated daughter and wife and mother. Ellie's quintet had listened to every word. Rescinding the invitation now would not only hurt Selianne deeply, it would make her the object of Fey suspicion. Considering Rain's deep-seated hatred of the Eld and Bel's lethal oath this morning, Ellysetta feared what the Fey would do if they discovered Selianne's heritage.

"Look at you. You look like a princess." Selianne stood back to admire Ellie's exquisite new gown of lavender silk and Elvian lace. "Kelissande would kill for that gown. And your hair is stunning." Thanks to Kiel and Kieran's artistic efforts this morning, Ellie's thick tangle of curls had been pulled back and tamed into a sleek cascade decorated with delicate amethyst flowers that trembled like fairy wings with every turn of her head. "Are those wisp-roses?"

Ellie started to touch the fragile flowers tucked into her hair, then stopped. "They are."

"They die at the first harsh touch. How on earth can you wear them in your hair without destroying them?" Selianne's confused look cleared. "Magic," she said flatly.

Ellie nodded, determined not to feel guilty despite Selianne's disapproving expression. "Rain put a protective weave around them." That had been the second part of his gift, and the second layer of its meaning: fragile life protected by unyielding Fey strength. These flowers, so rare and precious the blooms rarely lasted more than a day, would bloom forever so long as Rain's weave stood strong.

Selianne tucked an arm through Ellie's and lowered her voice as they walked into the cooler shadows of the cathedral. Ellysetta's mother was up at the altar, speaking with Greatfather Tivrest. "How are you, really? I read about what happened yesterday." Selianne asked.

Ellie grimaced. Everyone, it seemed, had read about what happened. The flood of pamphlets yesterday was nothing compared to the storm that all but papered the streets this morning, decrying the release of the child murderer Belliard vel Jelani. The crowds outside the Baristani home had doubled since yesterday thanks to all the protestors, rabble-rousers, and Brethren of Radiance fanatics joining their ranks.

Mama couldn't quite decide whether she was more worried about the damage to her family's reputation and Sol's business or enraged at the gall of the fanatical busybodies who had decided they had some right to camp outside the Baristanis' home and destroy the peace of the neighborhood. She'd even appealed to Rain, saying, "What in the Haven's name good is your magic if you can't make that rabble clear off?" When Ellie had stared at her in shock, Mama had shrugged defensively and said, "Well? It's clear the Fey aren't going anywhere. Since they're determined to stay, they might as well make themselves useful."

The gods weave as the gods will, Ellie thought with a smile. She would have volunteered for getting stabbed earlier if she'd known how it would alter Mama's opinion of the Fey.

Dragging her thoughts back to the present, she smiled at Selianne. "I'm fine, Sel. Lady Marissya healed me and no matter what those pamphleteers are saying, Bel didn't kill that boy—and don't believe for one second that child was an innocent bystander, either." Quickly Ellie recounted what had happened. "Rain thinks the Eld may be behind it. He's been trying to keep the northern borders closed, and the accusations leveled against Bel seem specifically designed to rouse more suspicion and ill will between the nobles and the Fey."

Selianne glanced at the surrounding Fey. "Can you have them do that privacy thing?"

"Of course." Ellie made the request, and Bel spun his weave in a matter of seconds. "It's done. What is it, Sel?"

Selianne turned her back to the Fey and reached out to clasp Ellie's hands. "The nobles aren't the only ones feeling suspicious. Ellie, I'm serving as your Honoria because you're my dearest friend in the whole world, but I wouldn't be any kind of friend if I didn't tell you how worried I am. I don't think you should wed the Tairen Soul. I'm terrified of what will happen to you if you do."

Ellysetta stared at her in surprise. "What? Selianne—"

"Hear me out, Ellie. What do you know—what does anyone really know—about the Fey? They're magic. And no matter how beautiful they are or what the legends say about them, not one of us really knows what goes on behind the Faering Mists. Once you go to the Fading Lands, you'll be locked away from all your family and friends, caged by magic just like those flowers in your hair. Who's to say what will happen to you then?"

Ellysetta pulled her hands free. "Selianne, don't be silly. Rain's not plotting to imprison me. He's been nothing but kind and attentive and caring."

"Of course he has. You're still in Celieria. But don't you realize, the only woman to leave the Fading Lands since the Mage Wars is the *shei'dalin* Marissya? Once you're through the Faering Mists, the Fey can make up any story they like about why you don't wish to return, and no one in Celieria will be able to gainsay them. Not even your family."

Ellie gave a troubled frown as a bobble of doubt rose inside her. Guilt followed fast behind. Simply contemplating such an idea seemed so disloyal to Rain.

As if sensing that brief doubt, Selianne leaned forward. "Ellie, my mother has a friend. A sea captain. He has no love for the Fey, and he's offered to take you someplace where you'll be safe should you choose not to wed the Tairen Soul."

Ellysetta reared back in surprise. "No."

"Ellie—"

"No! I could never do that. Even if I wanted to leave Rain—which I don't!—Papa would never condone breaking another betrothal. He wouldn't have allowed it the first time if the king hadn't interceded. And if I ran off by myself, my family would be shunned, beggared. You know that, Selianne. I would rather sacrifice myself a thousand times than bring such hurt to them. How could you even think I could be so selfish?"

Tears pooled in Selianne's wide, guileless blue eyes. "I'm just so worried for you. I would do anything to keep you safe."

"But not at the expense of my family, Selianne. You'd buy me only misery at that price."

"I'm sorry." She wiped at her eyes and sniffled.

"As am I. Please, let's speak of it no more. You obviously weren't thinking clearly to make such an offer. Agreed?"

Selianne nodded with obvious reluctance. "If that's what you want, Ellie."

"It is." With a forced smile, Ellysetta hugged her friend and tried not to flinch. Selianne's embrace felt oddly oppressive. *Just my imagination*, Ellie thought. As was the trick of light that made Selianne's eyes seem to flicker with black shadows, reminding Ellie unpleasantly of her young attacker. Still . . .

"Sel," she whispered hesitantly, "is everything all right with you? You're not in any sort of trouble, are you?"

Selianne pulled back. "Me? I'm not the one marrying the man who scorched the world."

"It's just that Rain warned me that Mages could control anyone born in Eld." She bit her lip. When Selianne didn't respond, she added, "Your mother was born there. She didn't leave until she married your father. According to Rain, she could be used to hurt you . . . and me."

Any hint of shadow in Selianne's eyes was gone now—as

was her earlier guilt—replaced by horror. With a quick twist, she broke free. "Did you tell him about her?"

Ellie's jaw dropped. "Of course not! I would never do that!"

"Then how would he know it?"

"He doesn't. I didn't mean that." How had this gotten twisted around? "He wasn't talking about your mother specifically. He was talking about the Eld in general, and how the Mages can control them from childhood."

"Ellie, my mother loves me. And you too, for that matter. She'd die before doing anything to hurt either of us."

"I know she loves you, Sel. That's not what I meant. I—"

"I think you'd better not say anything more. It would break my mother's heart to know you could even think something so vile. She's not some . . . some slave of the Mages."

"Sel . . . please . . . I'm sorry. I didn't mean to imply anything bad about your mother."

Selianne sniffed. "We'd better go. Your mother and the Archbishop are waiting."

Ellie's brows climbed halfway up her forehead. "Selianne, you little prig. I just forgave you for suggesting I should abandon my honor and my family and run off with some sea captain. And now you're all in a twist because I'm worried the Eld might try to hurt you and your mother to get to me?" She laughed in disbelief. "I was *stabbed* yesterday. Can you not understand why I might be a little more suspicious than usual?"

Selianne's irritation fled. "What an idiot I'm being. I swear I don't know what's come over me." She shook her head. "I'm supposed to be your friend and beacon, and here I am being an obnoxious ninnywit. I'm sorry. Friends?"

"Of course. The very best." They hugged again, a tight squeeze, and this time Ellie sensed nothing but genuine concern and love in the embrace. When they broke apart, she saw her mother gesturing with escalating ill temper. "I guess we'd better go," she said. "Greatfather Tivrest is getting impatient."

Ellie signaled to Bel, and the privacy weave dissolved. She and Selianne hurried to join Lauriana and the Archbishop.

The initial devotions of the Bride's Blessing were a lengthy, sonorous affair, full of prayers and hymns and meditation. Fortunately, everything proceeded smoothly. When they were done, Ellie gave Selianne and her mother quick hugs and hurried home to meet Rain and Master Fellows.

Lauriana stayed after Ellie's departure in order to discuss the upcoming services and the wedding schedule with the Archbishop. To her surprise, Selianne was waiting for her when she left the cathedral a full bell later. "Selianne? What are you still doing here?"

The young woman Lauriana had known since childhood twisted her hands together in the same way she and Ellie always had when confessing a misdeed. "I needed to talk to you, Madame Baristani, and I couldn't do it in front of Ellysetta and the Fey."

"Talk to me about what, Selianne?"

"About Ellie, Madam Baristani, and about the Fey." Selianne clasped her hands. "I'm very worried for her. Very worried."

Rain wasn't alone when Ellie returned home. Marissya and Dax were with him, and a vehement argument—one that clearly had begun quite a while ago—was in progress. The three of them fell silent when Ellie walked in, but the tension in the room remained so thick it set her teeth on edge.

"What is it?" she asked. "What's happened?"

"Nothing," Rain said. He stalked off to one corner and stood there, arms crossed, glaring out the window.

"Not nothing," Marissya corrected. "Tell her, Rain. Tell the Feyreisa what her *shei'tan* has been doing. She has a right to know."

Ellie stared at Marissya as if she'd grown a second head. The *shei'dalin* actually sounded . . . *angry*. Furious even. And with her veils thrown back, her cheeks hot with color, her appearance confirmed it. If she weren't seeing the proof with her own eyes, Ellie would never have believed it possible. She glanced at Dax. His head was down, shoulders slumped, and he was pinching the bridge of his nose as if he were painfully resigned to suffer through an argument he'd already heard many times over.

"Tell her, Rain," Marissya barked again. When he didn't, the *shei'dalin* turned to Ellie, hands on hips, and said, "He's been using the Lords of Council for *target practice*!"

Ellie's jaw dropped and she stared at Rain with wide, disbelieving eyes. "You didn't."

Flags of red darkened his cheeks.

She put her hands to her face. "Oh, gods, you did."

His jaw clenched. "It wasn't like that. I didn't start firing off Fey'cha by the dozen. It was only one Fey'cha, and I was making a point."

"The point had to be made with a *weapon*?"

"I was trying to explain about the return weave that is spun into Fey weapons when they're forged, to prove that finding a Fey'cha where a crime has been committed doesn't necessarily mean *dahl'reisen* are involved. I thought a demonstration would be more effective."

"He nearly pinned Lord Bevel's ears to his chair," Marissya interjected.

"I used *black*," Rain exclaimed when Ellysetta continued to gape at him in horrified disbelief. "That insolent little *bogrot* was never in any danger."

"That insolent little *bogrot* is a lord whose vote we needed in Council," Marissya retorted. "I asked you to meet with those nobles to befriend them, not alienate them still more. They're never going to support us, Rain, if you can't show them more than anger and threats."

"I tried reason—and that got me nowhere. If they're all too blind and too arrogant to secure their own safety, then let them choose death! After these continued affronts to Fey honor, this pervasive contempt for our many sacrifices, I no longer care what happens to these fools!"

"Well, I care," Ellysetta said.

Rain turned towards her in surprise. Dax started to say something, but Marissya caught his arm and shook her head, then turned to watch Ellysetta with an encouraging look. «*Speak, little sister. You can make him hear.*»

"This is my homeland," Ellysetta said. "These are my people. My family. My friends. Hate the nobles, if you must, but they aren't the only ones in danger."

"Ellysetta—" Rain stepped towards her. Her raised hand halted him.

"No, listen to me. If the Mages are rising again, as you believe, then Celieria is in danger. We have no defense against magic. Without you—without the Fey—we will fall to them. You know that."

"You speak of Celieria as if you still belong with them and not with us," Rain said.

"You have all accepted me as if I were one of you, and for that I'm more grateful than I can say, but I *am* Celierian, Rain. This *is* my homeland. What happiness can we ever find together if I abandon my country and my people to destruction?"

He went very still. "Are you saying you will refuse our bond if I cannot stop the Eld agreement from passing?"

"No, of course not—"

"Because Celierians are free to make their own choices, but that freedom has a price. They must live with the consequences of their choices, just as the Fey do. I have warned Dorian. I have told him that opening the borders will end the alliance between our two countries. I have begged him to invoke *primus*. He could put an end to this right now, but he will not. Without stone-hard proof, he will not act against the wishes of his Council. They have usurped his power, and he allows them to do it."

"And if the Council passes the agreement because you made no effort to prevent it, what then?" she returned, refusing to back down. "If you're right about the Mages reconstituting their power, then abandoning Celieria to them will only give them millions more souls to claim, millions more soldiers to swell the ranks of their armies. Can the Fey afford *that*?"

The corner of Rain's mouth lifted in a snarl.

"What I'm saying," Ellysetta concluded quietly, "is that you must at least *try*. It doesn't matter how you feel about the nobles, because this isn't just about them." She gave a short laugh. "I'm terrified about tonight's dinner. I'm terrified that my presence will do more harm than good. I know the nobles will be watching every move I make, and many are likely hoping to find something to mock, something with which to discredit you. But King Dorian asked us to attend, and so I will go, because, no matter what I think, I know *you* believe the Mages are a very real threat, one that must be stopped. I've done my best to adapt, to change how I dress, how I speak, how I act, because I know you'll need every advantage you can muster to win over the Council of Lords, and I couldn't bear it if I were the cause of your failure."

"I've already told you, you don't have to change. You are perfect just as you are."

"That is Rain, my mate, speaking, not Rain, the Fey king. I'm a woodcarver's daughter, a commoner without a drop of noble blood in my veins. There are lords who will consider it an insult even to have me in the same room with them. And that makes me a liability."

He made a sound—half guttural snarl, half bitter curse—and came to her. His hands reached for her, slid over her cheeks into the thick spirals of her hair. Gentle, unyielding pressure tilted her head back, forcing her to look up into his face.

"You are our queen, our Feyreisa. You are the beacon that shines for us all. And if a single one among them offers insult, they will all feel the edge of my wrath."

Her hands covered his. He would not hear the truth. Not on this. But he could not afford to let anger blind him. Not if he was right about the Mages. "Promise me, Rain. Promise that regardless of what insults the nobles may hurl—at you, at the sacrifices of the Fey, even at me—you will not abandon my people to the Mages."

"You cannot ask a Fey to ignore insults to his mate."

"But I'm asking all the same."

"*Shei'tani*—"

"Promise me, Rain." She held his gaze, refusing to back down. "Promise me, *shei'tan*."

His eyes closed in defeat. It was the first time she'd called him *shei'tan*, and the sound of that single, much-longed-for word on her lips shattered his resistance. Husband, beloved, mate of her soul: when she called him that, he could deny her nothing. He bowed his head and brought her hands to his lips for a kiss, then pressed his forehead against them in a gesture of surrender. "I cannot promise to hold my temper, but I will try. And for your sake alone, *shei'tani*, I will not allow insult to prevent me from fighting for Celieria's safety."

A muffled sound came from the direction of the front door. Master Fellows stood on the threshold, his eyes suspiciously shiny. "Now, that," he declared, "was the grace of a queen."

Accompanied by Jiarine Montevero and two more of her ladies-in-waiting, Annoura walked through the palace kitchens, personally inspecting the preparations for tonight's state dinner as she did for every such occasion. As much as it annoyed her to throw a lavish reception for the Tairen Soul and his peasant bride, she would never let it be said that Annoura of Celieria had not entertained her guests to the fullest extent of her considerable palace resources. Opulence and perfection were the hallmarks of her reign. To offer less than that tonight would reflect badly on her.

Duan Parlo Vincenze stood beside her, clad in a pristine white chef's robe, detailing the final changes to the menu while she and her ladies sampled the tidbits he'd prepared for them.

"Thank you, Duan Vincenze," Annoura said when he

concluded his presentation and she had finished tasting his sample dishes. "You have outdone yourself once again."

The chef bowed and thanked her effusively and returned to his kitchens as the queen and her entourage moved on to the palace wine cellars. Master Gillam, the man who personally inspected and approved every beverage that found its way to the royal table, was waiting for them by the large, heavy doors that led into the cool cellars. He greeted them with a bow and led Annoura and her three ladies-in-waiting to a small table where he'd set out the suggested wines for this evening's dinner, six in all, each carefully selected to complement Duan Vincenze's menu.

Annoura and her ladies tasted each of the wines, and as always happened at these tastings, by the end of the fourth small glass, the women had lost some of their carefully cultivated starch and begun to laugh and share pointed jokes about other members of the court. By the sixth glass, the jokes turned toward the Fey and the Tairen Soul's peasant-born truemate.

"I don't know about the rest of you, but the Tairen Soul makes me nervous." Lady Thea Trubol, senior lady-in-waiting to the queen gave a dramatic shiver. "I was there in the court the day the girl's betrothal was broken, and honestly, ladies, there's something positively . . . animal about him. Did you hear he nearly pinned back Bevel's ears with one of those Fey'cha of his?"

Jiarine snorted. "With a head as big as Bevel's, how could he have missed?"

The three ladies burst into tittering laughter, and even Annoura smiled. Bevel was an infamous lecher with a lustful appetite for very young, very innocent newcomers to the court. From serving girls to noble Seras not attached to an important family, the more helpless they were, the better he liked them.

"Well, let's just hope Bevel isn't idiot enough to chase after the Fey King's girl tonight," Lady Thea said. "You know how randy he gets after the first few glasses of pinalle."

Jiarine burst into a fresh bout of giggles, then clapped a hand over her mouth. "No, no, here's an even better idea. Wouldn't it be amusing if the *girl* got drunk and made a fool of herself tonight? The Fey would never live it down!"

The women all laughed their agreement and finished the last sample of Master Gillam's selected wines. When they were done, he led them to a smaller table in front of the open keflee pantry door and invited the women to sample the keflee blend he'd chosen to clear heads after dinner. Annoura declined the proffered cup and moved a few steps away from the rich aroma steaming from the keflee pot.

The move brought her closer to the open pantry door, and she froze at the sight of a distinctive purple silk bag sitting on one of the keflee casks. "Master Gillam, where did that come from? That purple bag."

Master Gillam looked at it blankly. "Why . . . I . . . I . . . Your Majesty, I'm appalled to admit I don't know."

Cup and saucer in hand, Jiarine tripped over and peered past Gillam's shoulder into the keflee pantry. "Oh, that? One of the maids brought it to me yesterday, when you were with the king, Your Majesty. She said she'd found it in your office. It had the look of one of your expensive rare blends, so I had Bili, Master Gillam's assistant, run it down here last night." When Annoura didn't respond, Jiarine frowned. "Your Majesty? Did I do something wrong?"

"What?" Annoura shook her head, shoving back memories of dangerous intoxication and near betrayal. "Oh, no. Thank you, Lady Jiarine. And thank you, Master Gillam. You have everything well in hand, as always."

She turned and walked quickly away from the cellars and the keflee pantry and that damnable purple bag of powdered ruin.

In Norban, Sian vel Sendaris forced a genial smile as he waited for the stocky pubkeeper of the Hound and Boar to ruminate over twenty years of memories. A full day of searching and inquiries yesterday had turned up nothing, and today wasn't shaping up any better.

"No," the pubkeeper said. "No, I can't say as I recall a man named Pars Grolin."

"He was about this tall, with bright red hair and green eyes." Beside Sian, Torel vel Carlian waved his hand at chin level. "And may have been traveling with his baby daughter."

"Mmm, no, doesn't ring a bell. Sorry." He finished drying the pint mug in his hand and set it on the shelf with several dozen others.

"Well, thank you for your time." Sian reached a hand across the bartop.

The pubkeeper hesitated a moment, then said, "I served in the King's Army as a lad. About forty-five years ago, when Fey swordmasters still taught the king's men how to use a blade. Best damned swordsmen I ever saw." He shook Sian's hand. "One of them even took the time to teach me a thing or two when he caught me watching the practices."

A deluge of memories rushed through Sian as he gripped the man's hand. Images of the pubkeeper's days in the army, of a dark-haired Fey warrior conducting training exercises, frightening images of war. Sian tried to filter out those images and concentrate on the thread he'd planted about strangers, red hair, and baby girls, but the pubkeeper's memories of war and the Fey were very strong.

"I was just a kid and a cannon's mate," the man continued. "No reason for him to teach me, but he did. Enough, anyways, so I could throw a dagger accurate at twenty paces and parry a sword thrust. And that saved my life in '43. I've had a fond spot for the Fey ever since. More so than most of the folks 'round these parts."

The handshake ended, and a final flood of images poured from the pubkeeper's consciousness into Sian's. Disturbing images of a priest standing in the pulpit, denouncing the Fey as soulless servants of the Dark Lord. Calling for Celieria's people to turn from the lure of evil that wore a pretty face and cleanse Celieria of the Shadow's servants. The town square was ablaze with some sort of bonfire, and villagers approached to throw what looked like personal belongings into the blaze. A priest with white-blond hair stood nearby, watching, his voluminous hooded cape swirling in the fire-generated winds.

"If you don't find news of this Grolin fellow here in town, you might try Brind Palwyn. He lives in the woods near Bracken, about thirty miles west of here, but he used to live just north, near the old quarry. His pa was a woodcutter. Your journeyman friend might have done some smithy work for Brind's parents before they were murdered."

Sian's ears perked up. "Murdered?" Murder was an unusual event in a sleepy little hamlet like Norban.

"*Ta.* Both of them slain by brigands about twenty-three years past, their home burned to its foundations. Brind was just a lad at the time. Come to think of it, they died around the time you said your journeyman friend was in town." Caution clouded the pubkeeper's previously open gaze. "No one ever did find the men who killed them."

"Pars was an honorable man, one who'd give his life defending a stranger," Torel assured the man. Not even seven hundred years after Pars Grolin's death would Torel let another impugn his friend's honor. "The Fey do not grant their regard lightly, nor to the unworthy."

The pubkeeper flushed. "My apologies. Suspicion is second nature in the north. If you want to speak with Brind, take the King's Road north about two miles to Carthage Road, then head west for another thirty or so. His place is just off the river, by the falls. He's suspicious of strangers, so tell him Wilmus sent you. And have a care if you're out past sunset. These woods aren't the safest after nightfall."

"Our thanks," Torel said. "The gods' blessings on you."

"What do you think, Torel?" Sian murmured as they left the inn. "Should we head west to visit this fellow?"

"Let's finish here first. Another few bells won't hurt."

Torel's lips lifted. "Unless you're afraid of the woods after nightfall."

Sian gave Torel a shove. "Get scorched." Then his expression grew serious. "I don't like those memories we've been getting from folk about that pale-haired priest and the bonfire. Since when did the Church of Light start preaching that Fey serve the Dark Lord?"

"Good question. That's certainly something we should include in our report to General vel Jelani tonight."

Ellysetta's lesson with Master Fellows passed far more quickly than she would have liked. All too soon, the clocktower rang, and Master Fellows prepared to take his leave. "Thank you for everything, Master Fellows," Ellie said as she walked him to the door. "I hope I will do credit to your instruction tonight."

"A sentiment we both share, believe me." Master Fellows's expression softened. "Just remember, don't let anyone call you Mistress Baristani tonight. It's Lady Ellysetta or My Lady Feyreisa. Anything less is a deliberate insult. And don't smile; they'll think you're currying favor. Just be grave and gracious. Don't fidget, don't laugh, and for the Haven's sake, don't speak unless you're directly engaged in conversation by another. The Fey have named you their queen. It is far better to remain silent and be thought aloof, than to speak and be proven a fool."

He stepped across the threshold, then paused and turned back for one final word of advice. "And remember this, My Lady Feyreisa: being regal is a state of mind. Act like a queen, believe it in your heart, and a queen is what everyone will see."

As twilight settled over the city, Den entered the Inn of the Blue Pony and headed for the stairs leading to Captain Batay's room. He'd done all the Sorrelian had asked, and he was still no closer to getting Ellie Baristani. It was time to lay down the law to the good captain. Den Brodson was no man's lackey. He wanted results for his efforts.

"He's not there," the innkeeper said as Den passed him.

Den paused and growled, "What did you say?"

"The Sorrelian. He said he was going out tonight and wouldn't be back until late. He left this for you, though." The innkeeper drew a sealed note from his pocket.

Den snatched the note and broke the seal, irritated that Batay had skipped out before he could catch him. Then grew more irritated by the command scrawled on the scrap of paper. A music box with paste jewels on the lid? What in the name of the Seven Hells did Batay need with something like that?

Den crumpled the note and stuffed it in his pocket. "When he gets in, tell him I was here. I'll be back tomorrow."

In the private carriage he'd hired after leaving the Inn of the Blue Pony, Kolis shed the hooded cloak he'd worn to cover the nondescript clothing of Goodman Black and whispered the unmaking spell to erase Batay's blue crossed swords tattoo from his cheek. He folded the cloak and tied his hair back in the neat queue Goodman Black wore, then sat back as the carriage rolled through the cobbled streets towards a boarding house not far from the brothel district by the wharf.

The common room there was empty, save for the house mistress, who bobbed a respectful curtsey as Goodman Black walked past her up the stairs, then bobbed again a few chimes later when a mysterious beauty in a concealing hooded cloak entered, went up the same stairs, and knocked on the door the merchant had entered.

Kolis Manza turned as the door opened and smiled at Jiarine Montevero. "You look ravishing, my pet. Come in, and close the door behind you."

Half a bell later, Jiarine departed. On the bed in the room she'd just quit, Kolis's body lay vacant and chilling while his consciousness marveled at the feel of existing inside Jiarine's young, lithe female form.

Ellie stared at her reflection in her bedroom mirror. In less than a bell, she would be presented to the highest-ranking nobles of Celieria, and with only two brief afternoons of Master Fellows's instruction to teach her how to comport herself in their company, she was terrified she would make a mess of it.

"You look lovely, Ellysetta," her mother said from the doorway.

Ellie turned and gave her mother a searching look. Mama had been unusually quiet since returning this afternoon. "Do you really think so?"

"Yes, kit, I do."

Ellie turned back to her reflection. She did look better than she ever had before. Her first new ball gown had arrived, and it was gorgeous. Fashioned of a rich purple brocade that made her skin seem to glow, the dress hugged her torso, enhancing curves Ellie never knew she had, and the low, square neckline flattered her corseted bosom. Tight sleeves fit snugly over her upper arms, ending at her elbows in a fall of red silk-lined drapery that brushed the floor when her arms were lowered. The skirts fell in straight, flowing lines to her feet. The gown's elegant simplicity and becoming cut made Ellie look regal rather than tall and gawky. Her hair, which had been dressed by a seasoned apprentice to the queen's own coiffeuse, was piled high, woven in an elaborate display of plaits and curls. Against one hip, Belliard's dagger hung in Kieran's golden sheath.

She put a hand to her throat to touch the diamond necklace Rain had given her. "I'm so afraid they will laugh at me, the woodcarver's daughter pretending to be a queen."

"In the Lord of Light's eyes, we're all equally worthy." Lauriana put her hands on Ellie's shoulders and met her daughter's eyes in the mirror. "Promise me you'll keep to the Bright Path, Ellie. Promise me that even in the Fading Lands you'll observe your devotions and guard your soul against evil."

"Mama?" Ellie turned in surprise and took her mother's hands. "What's wrong?"

"Just promise me."

"You know I will, Mama." But Ellie bit her lip. Apart from today at the cathedral, she hadn't said her devotions since the day Rain Tairen Soul entered her life. Was that what her dreams were telling her? That without constant vigilance, her soul would fall into darkness? "I'll say my devotions right now, with you, if you like."

"Would you?"

The surprise in her mother's eyes hurt. Ellie blinked back tears. Had the last few days torn such a rift between them? "Of course I will." She took her mother's hand and knelt beside the bed. Devotions were the one thing Ellie had always been able to share with her mother no matter what, the times when she'd always felt her mother's love the strongest. She bent her head and closed her eyes and murmured the familiar words. "Holy Adelis, Lord of Light, shine your brightness upon me. Glorious Father, Sun of my Soul, grant me strength to stand against darkness. Adelis, Bright One, Lord of my Heart, bless me and keep me always in the Light." She gave the fanning wave of the Lord of Light.

"Blessed be," Lauriana murmured. When they rose to their feet, Lauriana had tears in her eyes, and she clasped her daughter to her in a tight hug. "I love you, kitling."

"I love you, too, Mama. You're my beacon."

Mama stepped back, wiping her eyes with the heels of her palms. "Go on, then," she said gruffly. "I won't follow you down. I wouldn't want to embarrass myself by turning watering pot in front of the Fey."

Rain was waiting when Ellysetta descended the stairs. He was once again dressed in magnificent black, red, and purple, with the chain of large gold disks and Tairen's Eye crystals around his neck. The six-pointed crown rested on his brow, and he looked imposing and kingly.

He was scowling.

The knot in Ellie's stomach tightened.

His gaze raked over her in one critical sweep. "You won't need that necklace tonight. Bel, bring her jewels."

Ellie lowered her eyes to hide a sudden flare of hurt and reached behind her head to undo the clasp of her necklace. What had she expected? That he would be dazzled just because she was wearing a gorgeous dress and had done her hair?

Bel approached, carrying a silk-covered box. *«You are lovely, Ellysetta Baristani.»*

She gave him a tremulous smile.

Beside her, Rain gave a quiet grunt, as if someone had just hit him. His scowl deepened, and he flashed a dark look at Bel. Then he returned his attention to Ellie, and warm approval touched her senses, mingled with faint apology. "You bring pride to this Fey, Ellysetta."

She nodded, not looking at him.

She heard him draw a breath as if he were about to speak, heard him let it back out again on a sigh. "Open the box, Bel," he said.

Bel drew back the lid of the silk-covered box, and Ellysetta caught her breath in awe. Against the rich velvet lining gleamed a stunning golden tiara set with pearls and precious jewels and three large, shimmering Tairen's Eye crystals. Two equally stunning crystals adorned a pair of magnificent matching golden bracelets.

"These jewels are a gift for tonight only," Rain said. "The Tairen's Eye crystals are the *sorreisu kiyr*, the Soul Quest crystals, of your quintet. They requested the honor of having you wear them as we present you to Celieria as our queen."

Ellysetta glanced around the room, meeting the shining eyes of each warrior in her quintet. "The honor is mine. Thank you all."

She stood still as Rain settled the tiara in place and clasped the bracelets on her wrists. Her skin tingled where the jewels touched her flesh, as if the *sorreisu kiyr* hummed with warm, living energy. And Rain's emotions seemed clearer, sharper. She could feel his coiled tension and the sparks of anger flashing through his veins.

"Rain?" She touched his hand.

"We should go."

"Just a moment." Sol stepped forward. "I need to kiss this pretty young woman before she leaves." Warm, loving arms wrapped around her. The familiar scent of fresh wood shavings and pipe smoke filled her nostrils. "I love you, Ellie-girl," Sol whispered.

Fresh tears sprang to Ellie's eyes. She blinked them back before anyone saw them and returned her father's hug. "I love you, too, Papa."

"Enjoy yourself tonight."

"I will," she lied.

A royal carriage was waiting outside. The bewigged footman standing attendance beside the carriage door helped Ellie into the vehicle. She took her seat on the blue velvet cushions, folded her hands in her lap, and stared out the far window at the throng of people surrounding her family's home. A strange, disturbing sense of darkness brushed her mind, and the hair at the back of her neck rose. Troubled, she scanned the crowd. Den Brodson's face stared back at her from a distance, his eyes filled with malevolence and thwarted desire.

Black leather moved at the corner of her eye, and Ellie turned her head to watch Rain take his seat opposite her. When she glanced back out the window, Den was gone.

"Ellysetta?" She felt Rain's concern even before she heard it in his voice. "Something frightens you?" The carriage lurched forward and began to roll through the parting crowds.

"No, I'm fine." Den was no threat to her or her family. The Fey had seen to that.

Rain's lips tightened in a faint grimace. "I did not mean to hurt your feelings a moment ago. Bel tells me I am an insensitive *rultshart* for not telling how lovely you look."

"It's all right."

"*Nei*. It is not." His hands fisted, then opened with obvious effort and pressed flat against his thighs. "I do not wish to attend this dinner. I do not wish to take you there. Not"—he added quickly, holding up a hand to forestall any misunderstanding—"because I am unhappy to take you, but because I do not want to expose you to their darkness. Or my anger."

"Because of what happened yesterday?"

"In part, I suppose. But even without the current unpleasantness, I would feel the same. The last Celierian dinner I attended ended badly, and I cannot forget the memory of it."

Ellie suddenly understood Rain's scowl, his inattentiveness, and the tense anger coiled inside him. The last Celierian dinner Rain Tairen Soul had attended had taken place a thousand years ago and ended in the assassination of Marikah vol Serranis and her husband King Dorian I of Celieria. That dinner provided the spark that Gaelen vel Serranis, Marikah's twin brother, fanned into the flames that became the Mage Wars.

"I'd forgotten you were there," she admitted.

"I expect many have forgotten."

"I imagine it was horrible." Ellie heard the words leave her mouth and could have groaned. Of course, it had been horrible. It was a bloody, evil night that had led to an even bloodier and more evil war. "I'm sorry," she apologized. "You don't have to talk about it."

"*Nei*, it's all right. It was a very long time ago. The wound is no longer fresh."

"But it still has the power to hurt."

He smiled a little. "Your heart is kind, *shei'tani*, to worry over such an ancient wound." Then his smile faded. "Marikah died. Gaelen, her twin brother, gave himself to the

Wilding Rage to avenge her and plunged us into war. Millions died. These things I cannot change, and I no longer weep for might-have-beens. It's simply that my memories remind me of what can happen at such seemingly innocuous events."

She leaned across the carriage and reached out to take his hands in hers. She meant the gesture to be comforting, friendly. Loving, too, but in a gentle way. Perhaps it was his unsettled emotions. Perhaps it was her own unsettled emotions. Perhaps it was just the *shei'tanitsa* hunger rising in both of them. Whatever the reason, the moment she touched him, sudden desire roared up inside her, a gout of invisible flame leaping from her body to his.

Ellie's field of vision narrowed until she saw nothing but his eyes, searing amethyst, piercing her senses, her consciousness, then deeper. She felt her soul stir in response. A restless disquiet, a yearning . . . for something more than physical, something more than emotional. Her breath rasped down her dry throat on a ragged inward moan.

He gave a low, deep-chested growl, the warning purr of a stalking tairen, and invisible hands, hot and hard, cupped her through her dress. Invisible lips, firm and silky, tracked a burning path down her neck.

Her pulse thundered in her ears. Her eyes closed on a swell of unbearable pleasure. Her head tipped back, and real hands reached out to grasp her waist and bring her hard against his chest. Real lips devoured the too sensitive skin of her neck, dragging up, teeth grazing the curve of her jaw. His mouth claimed hers in a hot, demanding, erotic kiss.

In her mind's eye, she saw the tairen. Magnificent, sleek, as black as death itself. Its eyes were burning lavender fire, its fangs white, sharp, deadly, bared in a snarl of feral wildness that had slipped its leash. It leapt towards her, massive wings unfurled, gigantic paws outstretched. So beautiful. So wild. So terrifying. White, sharp, curving claws dug into her flesh, holding her fast. The tairen screamed with hunger and dragged her close.

With a small choked cry, she tore her lips from Rain's and pushed against his shoulders.

Rain's empty hands curled slowly into fists that shook with visible effort as he once more caged the wildness within him. He groaned, closed his eyes, and banged the back of his head against the coach wall.

"*Sieks'ta*," he apologized, his eyes still closed. There was a fine sheen of perspiration on his face, the first she'd ever seen, a testament to the force he was extending to keep himself in check. "When you reach out to me, I lose all reason. The tairen is hungry for its mate. As, gods help me, am I."

"It was my fault," she told him, shivering as she tried to recover her composure and still her racing heartbeat. "I started it."

"*Aiyah*, you did. Which gives me hope at least." He scrubbed his hands over his face. "But I should know by now that I must go slowly with you. Your ways are not ours, and you are still so young. I will do better the next time, Ellysetta. I do not wish to frighten you."

"It's all right." She didn't deny that he had frightened her. She knew he had felt it.

"*Nei.*" He gave a slight, hoarse laugh. "When you accept the bond, it will be all right." His eyes opened, pinned her with glowing intensity. "Until then, it is quite the opposite."

She bit her lip, feeling miserable. She could feel his pain and the sharp edge of temper he was struggling not to release. "I'm sorry."

"Do not be. I assure you, I will endure. Just be patient with my lapses, and know that I would never harm you." He closed his eyes again and leaned his head back. "And Ellysetta?"

"Yes?"

"Do not touch me that way again tonight. Please."

CHAPTER SEVENTEEN

The palace was lit like a garden lantern, blazing against the Celierian night sky. The carriage slowly made its way up the crowded carriage path towards the massive palace steps and the waiting footmen, dazzling in their blue-and-gold livery and silvery-white powdered hair.

Ellie stared out the window, up the wide expanse of stairs to the brightly lit interior of the palace beckoning from the opened doors at the top of the stairs. How many young Celierian girls had dreamed of a moment like this? She had dreamed it countless times, and yet now that the dream had become reality, she couldn't stop wishing she were safe back at home, spending another dull night wrapped in the security of the familiar. Even while another part of her was eager to climb those stairs and taste the wonders of the dream.

"What are you thinking?" Rain was watching her with an intent expression.

"That I'm an awful lot like Ashleanne the hearth-minder," she replied with a self-deprecating smile. "And you're the Fey giftfather and the handsome prince all rolled into one."

"Then perhaps that is to your advantage. The weave doesn't have to unravel at midnight if you don't wish it."

"I'm not so sure I don't want it to unravel right now. I'm feeling cowardly."

The corners of his eyes crinkled. "You are not the first to dread a royal dinner. Even without my dislike of the nobles and the memories of what happened here before, I admit I have never enjoyed these affairs. Especially in Celieria. Your people use far too many forks."

She laughed, grateful to him for trying to put her at ease even when he himself was not.

The carriage pulled to a stop before the blue-carpeted stairs. Protective shields sprang up around them as they descended from the carriage and remained in place as they climbed the palace steps, not disappearing until they passed through the palace doors.

A servant appeared before them. His livery, the same rich Celierian blue as all the other servants wore, was much more elaborately decorated with gold braid. His hair was gold-powdered and tied at his nape with a Celierian blue bow. He bowed deeply to Rain. "Your Majesty." He hesitated briefly, then bowed again just as deeply to Ellie. "My Lady. If you will both follow me, please? I will escort you to the ballroom, where the guests are gathering before dinner."

The corridors were brilliant with light and peopled with servants and courtiers dressed in dazzling displays of gilded cloth, sparkling jewels, and piles of glittering powdered hair. The extreme radiance of wealth was stunning to a girl so used to sensible moderation, and Ellie found herself holding her breath and trying desperately not to look like a goggle-eyed fool while still attempting to drink in every sight, every sound.

When they entered the upper level of the already crowded ballroom and stood at the top of the curving staircase awaiting their introduction, Ellie became instantly and self-consciously aware of how her deep purple and Rain's black leathers stood out like dark beacons in a sea of gilded pastels. As they stepped onto the landing, every eye in the room below focused on them.

She shrank back against Rain.

«*Peace, Ellysetta. There is nothing to fear.*»

She tried to stiffen her spine, tried even harder not to let her fear show on her face. Her free hand fell to the Fey'cha at her waist, fingers closing around the black handle with desperate need, but Bel's dagger did not offer her the comfort it usually did. Perhaps because she knew that if she made a fool of herself tonight, it would reflect badly on Rain and the Fey.

The servant who had led them to the ballroom whispered their names to another servant, this one dressed in pure silver. The silver-clad man announced in ringing tones, "His esteemed majesty, Rainier vel'En Daris Feyreisen, the Tairen Soul, King of the Fading Lands, Defender of the Fey, and Lady Ellysetta Baristani Feyreisa, truemate of the Tairen Soul, Queen of the Fading Lands."

Ellie had an hysterical urge to laugh at the titles attached to her name. Oh, gods, this *was* all a mistake. Who did Rain think he was fooling? She was plain Ellie Baristani, woodcarver's daughter, not a queen. And judging by the haughty, sneering looks on the faces of the nobles below, every one of them was thinking the same thing. How could Rain hope to win their respect and convince them to stand firm against the Eld when he confronted them with a peasant on his arm? Even the servants of the aristocracy looked down their noses at her when they visited her father's shop at their masters' bidding.

Bel and Kieran preceded them down the stairs. Kiel, Adrial, and Rowan followed them. Ellie's knees trembled as she and Rain descended the stairs into the ballroom. She was aware of King Dorian and Queen Annoura sitting in gold and silver radiance on their thrones at the far end of the room, watching her with unblinking eyes. She looked out over the sea of faces and sensed the courtiers' swelling out-rage and stiffening pride. They resented having a peasant's daughter shoved down their noble, aristocratic throats. She was beneath them. She didn't belong here. She sensed anger, rapidly escalating, and thought it came from the nobles.

When they reached the bottom stair, Bel turned his head to give her a warning look. «*Peace, Ellysetta. Your emotions wake the tairen.*»

Her gaze flew to Rain's unsmiling, stone-carved face. His eyes were on fire with power. His mouth was grim. The anger she felt was his, and he was struggling hard to contain it.

"Rain," she whispered. "I'm sorry."

«*Apologize for nothing. Not to me, and especially not to these dark-souled mortals. You are the Feyreisa.*»

She winced at the harsh bite in his Spirit voice.

"My Lord Feyreisen." A glittering man in a blue-and-silver coat dripping lace and jewels stepped forth from the throng. His hair was silver-powdered, his blue eyes cool above a pleasant smile. Though Ellie had never met the man, his face was famous throughout Celieria. Lord Corrias, Celieria's prime minister, bowed very deeply to Rain.

"Mistress Baristani." Lord Corrias bowed to her as well, more deeply than a woodcarver's daughter had a right to ex-pect, but less than a quarter the depth of the bow he had given the Tairen Soul. Not that it mattered to Ellie. She was too busy struggling with the nervous fear that clogged her throat to care about the implications of a bow.

It mattered to Rain.

"She is the Feyreisa." Rain's voice was an iced shard of sound, the barest whisper, and yet it sliced across the rising murmurs of the onlooking crowd with chilling ease. "You insult her at your gravest peril."

The prime minister blanched and immediately fell into a bow even deeper than the one he had offered Rain. "My Lady Feyreisa, please accept my apologies. No insult was intended."

"Peace, Lord Corrias. No insult is taken." Marissya v'En Solande's calm voice broke the tense silence. Deeply veiled and exquisitely gowned in unrelieved scarlet, the *shei'dalin* descended the stairs on the arm of her truemate. Tairen's Eye crystals flashed at her throat and wrists, and dozens more hung about her hips on golden chains. "Lady Ellysetta is the first Feyreisa in over two thousand years, and the only one ever to be truemated to our King. One small lapse in protocol can be forgiven."

As Lord Corrias rose, Marissya's voice sounded in Ellie's head. *«Las, little sister. Rain will not be able to keep his promise if you cannot control your fears.»* Then, hesitantly, *«I can help calm you, if you will permit me.»*

Ellie shook her head. She wanted no *shei'dalin* mind control worked on her, even if it was to make her feel better. The very thought of it made her stomach clench.

«Don't be frightened. I will do nothing without your permission. You must calm yourself so Rain can control his temper.»

Ellie took a deep breath and tried to do as Marissya asked, but she was too conscious of the many eyes on her. Whenever Ellie drew too much attention, she could almost *feel* people looking at her, as if their sharp gazes were fingers pinching and poking at her. It was an unpleasant, unsettling sensation, and trying to combat it always gave her a sick headache. Tonight, the sensation was stronger than ever before.

«Peace, shei'tani.»

"I'm trying," she muttered. "Can we just get this over with?"

«Of course.» Even though Rain's eyes still glowed fiercely, his mental voice was warm and gentle and almost as soothing as the *shei'dalin's*.

"Lord Corrias." None of the warmth Ellie felt from Rain was apparent in his voice as he turned his attention back to the prime minister. "Please escort us to the king and queen so that we may pay our respects. Then you may introduce us to your other guests."

The prime minister gave another deep bow. "Of course, My Lord Feyreisen," he replied, with only the faintest hint of stiffness in his voice. "It will be my honor."

When they reached the dais at the end of the room, Rain bowed his head in greeting to King Dorian and Queen Annoura. He saw Ellie begin to sink into a deep curtsey and formed a rapid weave of Air to keep her upright.

«Nei, Ellysetta,» he advised. *«You are our queen. Do not humble yourself before the throne of another. It is acceptable merely to bow your head to them to acknowledge their sovereignty in their own land.»*

Blushing, she did as he instructed.

Garbed completely in gold, with huge yellow diamonds draped around his throat, sparkling on his fingers, and winking from every fold of his gold-cloth doublet, King Dorian was the sun. His dark hair had been pomaded, curled, and powdered with gold dust. A bright Celierian blue sash was angled across his chest and fastened at his hip by a large gold disk stamped with Celieria's royal seal. His feet, clad in gold shoes with stacked heels and yellow-diamond-encrusted buckles, were crossed comfortably before him, and his strong, sun-bronzed hands curled with familiar casualness on the arms of his massive throne.

Beside him, shining in cool silver and diamond-white radiance, Queen Annoura was the moon, though in truth she outsparkled her husband. Her hair was powdered silver, her eyebrows gilded to match. Brilliant blue-white diamonds set in shining platinum cascaded like a waterfall down her slender throat and across the deep expanse of skin exposed by the low heart-shaped décolletage of her gown. One large egg-shaped diamond trembled between her breasts. More diamonds winked at her ears, on her fingers, around her wrists, from the silver fabric and lace of her gown. Even the tips of her silver-polished nails gleamed with small diamonds.

The overdone brilliance of the king and queen offended Rain's Fey senses. In the Fading Lands, elegance and beauty were found in simplicity rather than ostentation. Ellysetta's unadorned gown and the restrained dazzle of her Tairen's Eye jewelry were far more appealing to him.

The queen's sharp gaze roved over Ellysetta. Her lips tightened as she examined the bracelets and tiara, and Rain knew Bel and the others had been right in offering their *sorreisu kiyr*. Annoura had no doubt hoped the Fey would forget the Celierians' custom of declaring social rank by the quantity and value of the jewels they wore. Instead, each one of Ellysetta's crystals surpassed the combined worth of all Annoura and Dorian's diamonds.

Finished with her perusal, Annoura arched a mocking silvered brow that set Rain's teeth on edge. His expression, however, remained stone blank. He would rather dance naked before the entire court than give Celieria's queen the satisfaction of knowing she could annoy him.

"My dear," the queen purred to Ellysetta, "you must meet the ladies of our Great Houses. Jiarine, Lady Montevero, will introduce you."

Annoura waved and a sapphire-bedecked young woman came eagerly to the queen's side. Her large, silver-lidded eyes swept over Ellysetta, and a too-sweet smile curved her pretty lips. Rain didn't like the look in her eyes or the hint of darkness that clung to her neatly packaged form. She reminded him too much of the Kelissande creature who took such pleasure in wounding his *shei'tani's* heart.

"That is unnecessary," Rain interrupted, flashing a cold look at Lady Jiarine. "Lord Corrias has graciously offered to introduce us."

The silver lace fan in Annoura's hand snapped open and pumped drafts of air onto the queen's flushed cheeks. "How kind of him."

Now Rain permitted the barest hint of a smile to reach his eyes. "Indeed."

«Must you go out of your way to annoy her?» Marissya asked in an aggrieved tone.

«Only when she begs to be annoyed.» The queen might enjoy playing her game of Trumps, but her attempt to use Ellysetta as a pawn would stop tonight. If Annoura persisted, she

would soon discover that a Celierian queen was no match for a Fey Tairen Soul.

"Corrias is going to introduce you?" Dorian gave a hearty smile, either ignoring or oblivious to his wife's stifled pout. "You couldn't ask for a better man to steer you through this court's shark-infested waters."

"Then we shall be well served." Rain gave a shallow bow.

As Rain turned to leave, the king's voice stopped him. "Be sure he introduces you to Lords Morvel and Barrial. Both have indicated their interest in pursuing closer ties to the Fey. I understand the Feyreisa's sisters will soon be of marriageable age." Ellie gasped in surprise, as did the courtiers close enough to hear the king's comment. A rapid murmuring rose up around them. "A happy way to strengthen the bond between our two countries, wouldn't you say?"

«*Border lords,*» Dax supplied before Rain even asked the question. «*Barrial was the one who stood up with Teleos yesterday. He holds the land along the Elden border from Carthage to Kreppes. Morvel controls everything from the Estemere seaport to Norwal.*»

Dorian was offering nearly a sixth of the Elden border.

Rain eyed Dorian with new appreciation. The king had been very busy—and much more effective in dealing with his nobles than Rain had been. "Indeed. Such consideration is a great honor to the Baristani family and the Fey."

"Excellent. My queen and I hope you and your Feyreisa will honor us with your presence at Prince Dorian and Lady Nadela's betrothal ball." The ball would initiate a week of city-wide celebrations leading up to the betrothal ceremony itself.

"We will be there, and we thank you for the honor of the invitation." Rain bowed.

"Your attendance will bring us joy." Dorian smiled and laid his hand over his wife's. Her face was a frozen mask.

«*Lillis and little Fey'cha are but children.*» Stalking at Rain's right hand side as he and Ellysetta walked away from the throne, Kieran did not even attempt to disguise his displeasure. »*Fey do not sell children, not even to protect Eld border land.*»

"I don't like the idea of betrothing Lillis and Lorelle to anyone," Ellie whispered at the same time. "They should have a chance to grow up and find someone they can love."

Rain wove a quick net of Air and Spirit about their small group to ensure privacy before he responded. "It is the offer of alliance that is important, not the manner of bonding."

"Then why would the king mention marriage?" Ellie asked, frowning at Rain.

"He was telling us Lords Morvel and Barrial are willing to garrison Fey warriors in their holdings," Dax said. "Ellysetta, they know the Fey would not leave your family members anywhere in Celieria without a substantial number of warriors to protect them."

Rain wondered how the king had achieved such a coup. As he'd spent the past few days discovering, reason alone didn't seem much of an inducement to the nobles.

"And," Marissya added, "by publicly inviting you to the Prince's ball and mentioning the possibility of a betrothal between your sisters and two of the Great Houses, the king has also made it clear that you and your family are to be accepted by the other nobles."

"That's all well and good, but I don't want Mama or Papa thinking high-ranking political marriages are in the girls' best interest. Lillis and Lorelle aren't chattel to be bartered and sold."

"Las, shei'tani." Rain said. "I will speak to Morvel and Barrial and make it clear that no formal offers of marriage are to be extended to your parents." He dispelled the privacy weaves and turned to the prime minister. "You may begin the introductions, Lord Corrias."

★ ★ ★

During the next two bells of introductions and polite mingling, Lord Corrias introduced Ellie and Rain to what seemed like hundreds of Celierian nobles and whispered a steady stream of information into Rain's ear as they went, identifying each individual's estate holdings, and what each one stood to gain or lose if the Eld borders were opened for trade. Ellie's head was swimming with the bombardment of information, but Rain seemed to take it in and process it with enviable efficiency.

She stood at Rain's side, trying her best to be "grave and gracious." It was a good thing Master Fellows had told her not to smile, as that would have proven difficult. The Tairen's Eye crown and bracelets, while physically light, discomfitted her. A low, constant hum of power radiated from the crystals, resonating in her skin and setting her nerves on edge.

Despite the king's announcement, many of the approaching nobles made a point of eyeing the sparkling crystals before forcing themselves to bow before the woodcarver's daughter. Some pretended to be more welcoming. They smiled with too-bright smiles, complimented her hair and dress, and murmured concern about yesterday's attack, but she knew their hard, glittering eyes were sizing her up and searching for any little fault in her appearance or behavior that would put Rain to shame. She refused to give it to them. Holding her head high, she greeted each with solemn reserve. Rain, to his credit, kept his temper in check—and was even on occasion rather charming. The nobles who'd come hoping to gawk at a wild tairen and his peasant bride found themselves meeting a Fey king and his reserved queen instead.

After the first dozen or so introductions, Rain began sending little private communications to her on weaves of Spirit, things like *«You didn't like Lord Braegis at all, did you, shei'tani? Can you tell me why?»* or *«You seemed to like Lady Clovis. Perhaps we should arrange for you and Marissya to meet her for tea.»* His Spirit voice was calm, reassuring, and even occasionally wicked: *«Lady Zillina had best not lean over tonight or those breasts might just leap for freedom.»* The intimacy of the conversation—private words shared only between the two of them—made the ballroom seem less crowded and the nobles a bit less terrifying. Occasionally Rain would reach over to stroke the hand she kept on his wrist, lift the corner of his mouth in the faintest of smiles, and whisper in her mind, *« You're doing fine, shei'tani. You bring pride to this Fey.»*

One of the few genuinely friendly faces in the crowd was a Fey-eyed border lord named Teleos from the west, whom Rain greeted with a warmth he'd not shown any other Celierian. Even without Lord Corrias's whispered summation, Ellie knew who Lord Devron Teleos was. His family's ancestral estates lay at the foot of the southernmost Feyl mountains, guarding the Garreval, gateway to the Fading Lands. On that land, fifty miles north of the Garreval, the battle of Eadmond's Field had been waged, and Sariel had died.

"Lady Ellysetta." Teleos bowed to her. "The gods have shone their grace on the Tairen Soul indeed. You make me envy him his good fortune."

Ellysetta blushed at the generous compliment. Just as she'd sensed the false welcome in the other lords, she sensed the truth in Teleos. Like the Fey, he looked at her and saw beauty. How amazing. "You are too kind, Lord Teleos," she replied, "but in truth, I received the greater grace. What girl has not dreamed of Rain Tairen Soul and Fey devotion?"

"And all this time, I believed the thought of me would send them fleeing in fear," Rain quipped with a faint smile. In a more serious tone, he told Teleos, "My thanks for your courage in Council yesterday. It is good to know that common sense still prevails in some parts of Celieria."

"I should have spoken sooner." Teleos's green eyes held genuine regret. "Had I known what was done to Ser vel Jelani, I would have, but I never suspected such animus."

"Dax tells me you are the descendant of an old friend of mine, Shanis Teleos," Rain said.

"My great-grandfather's great-grandfather," the border lord confirmed.

"He was there that day at Eadmond's Field. I am glad to know he survived it. He was a great warrior, and a true friend."

"According to the family history I learned as a boy, he saw an opportunity to flank the Merellians and took a force of his best men to circle round from the north. He wasn't on the field when you . . . when the Rage took you."

Rain nodded somberly; then a ghost of a smile lightened his eyes. "He always could read a battlefield . . . and had the gods' own luck. We were *chadins* together in our youth at the Warrior's Academy in Dharsa. Then I found my wings, and he went south to Tehlas, to continue his training under the tutelage of his uncle and namesake, Shannisorran v'En Celay."

That was a name Ellie had read in numerous tomes of Fey history and poetry. Shannisorran v'En Celay, Lord Death, one of the greatest, deadliest Fey warriors ever to have walked the earth, as infamous in battle as Rain was for the scorching of the world and Gaelen vel Serranis for sparking the Mage Wars.

"I did not see your folk there by the Garreval when we passed through the Mists," Rain said. "Shanis always kept the custom, but I suppose things have changed."

Lord Teleos smiled at the probe. "The land remains in our family, but we no longer live there. After the Wars, the king granted Shanis a northern estate bordering Eld and the Feyls. We now guard Orest and Kiyera's Veil."

Rain nodded. "So Dax told me. It is a handsome land . . . and a dangerous one. The Eld I knew always coveted that stretch of the river." Orest, the City of Mist, lay at the foot of the Feyls, wreathed in the mists and rainbows of numerous waterfalls that fed the mighty Heras River. About a mile northwest of the city in the river gorge, Kiyera's Veil was a legendary gauntlet of towering waterfalls pouring into the Heras from opposite mountains, filling the gorge with water and mist and blocking a pass rumored to lead into the Fading Lands.

"And still do." The border lord's expression became grim. "I lose a dozen villagers every year to Eld raids—not murdered, just gone—but the attacks seem to be lessening of late."

"You're the first I've heard to blame the Eld and not *dahl'reisen*."

Teleos grimaced. "Yes, well, Sebourne and his pack don't think a fly dies on the borders these days except by *dahl'reisen* hand, but the raids on my land just don't have the feel of *dahl'reisen*. I can't really explain why."

"Do not discount your intuition, Lord Teleos. You're Fey enough to perceive things beyond mortal senses. The Eld I knew always longed to drive a wedge between Celierians and Fey. Murdering Celierians and blaming the Fey—or the *dahl'reisen*—is just the sort of deception they would employ." From the corner of his eye, Rain saw Lord Corrias signal. "It has been a pleasure meeting you, Lord Teleos. I hope we have the chance to speak again."

Teleos bowed graciously. "The pleasure is mine, My Lord Feyreisen. It would be my honor to host a dinner for you before you return to the Fading Lands. Though I'm unlikely to instill trust in those who doubt the Fey"—his Fey eyes gleamed with wry humor—"I know many lords who remain more open-minded about certain things than Sebourne."

Rain inclined his head. "A most generous offer, my lord. It would be our honor to attend." He offered an arm clasp and a traditional Fey warrior's greeting which roughly translated to "Sharp blade, sure aim, swift strike."

Teleos returned the greeting in perfectly accented Feyan and added on the common Spirit path, «*You can count on my support, My Lord Feyreisen. Both my voice in Council and my sword, if you need it. These are unsettling times, but I fear much worse is yet to come.*»

«*Beylah vo, young blade brother,*» Rain answered. «*And for a son of Shanis's line who guards the Veil, the doors of the Warrior's*

Academy in Dharsa are always open. When you wish it, I will send a warrior to guide you through the Mists.»

Lord Teleos's eyes widened. *«You honor me.»*

«That was very kind of you,» Ellysetta sent as they walked away.

«Not entirely unselfish,» Rain admitted. *«Any man who guards the Veil should be Fey-trained in weapons and war. You liked him?»*

«Very much. More than anyone we've met so far.»

«Good. I liked him, too.»

In sharp contrast to Lord Teleos, Lord Morvel was a towering iceberg of a man with thick, unpowdered white hair, a hawklike nose, large nostrils, and piercing blue eyes. After a brief, chilly greeting, those eyes speared Ellie, delved ruthlessly into her very soul, then withdrew with an indecipherable look that left her wondering if he despised her or simply found her unworthy of even that much of his great regard. She was in good company. Lord Morvel's dissecting gaze fell upon Rain and withdrew with the same results.

"Let me be frank," Lord Morvel said bluntly. "I'm not offering marriage to any of my noble sons or grandsons. But I do have a son, duAlbuth, whose mother was my armorer's daughter. I've had him trained in warfare, and he currently serves in my infantry. Marriage to a woodcarver's daughter would not insult his lineage, given his already-common stock. I would, of course, expect a dowry at least as generous as what you gave the butcher, so he could purchase a lower-gentry title and a bit of land and still have enough to ensure advantageous marriages for his own children."

"I see." To his credit, Rain did not pull steel. "And what might the Fey receive in return—besides the gracious offer of blood-ties to the House of Morvel and an opportunity for the Feyreisa's sisters to ascend beyond their lowly roots?"

If Morvel noted his sarcasm, he showed no sign of it. "The king shared your concerns about the Eld with the Twenty. I have eight castles on the Elden March between Eastmere and Norwal, each capable of garrisoning between one and two thousand men. If it's men on the Marches you want, I can help . . . depending on the outcome of our negotiations, of course."

"Of course." Rain smiled without a hint of warmth reaching his eyes and bowed his head. "I look forward to further discussions. Dax and I will call on you tomorrow."

«*Never,*» Ellysetta bit out as she and Rain shook off that wintry encounter and moved on to greet the next group of nobles. «*Never will either of my sisters wed into that man's family. And I don't care if the entire world depends on it.*»

«*Las, shei'tani. An offer is not a betrothal. Besides, you heard him say everything was negotiable. Woodcarver's blood may insult him, but he seems rather fond of Fey gold—and you did notice, I hope, that I let his insults pass without challenge.*»

«*I expected them to insult me, not Lillis and Lorelle,*» she admitted, then looked up sheepishly. «*I was ready to go for his throat myself.*»

Rain's teeth bared in a predator's smile. «*Release me from my oath, and I will make him scream for forgiveness.*» When she didn't, he sighed with mock disappointment. «*More's the pity. So, aside from his insulting arrogance, what did you think of him? Does he strike you as a man of honor? Is he someone a Fey can trust, once he gives his word?*»

She stopped in her tracks and gaped at him. "How should I know?" Surprise made her blurt it aloud. "I'm no *shei'dalin* to read the truth in a man's soul."

Rain wove a quick web of magic to catch her words and keep them from traveling. «*Silently, Ellysetta. Corrias is recording every word for his report to Dorian and the queen. And as for reading a man's soul, aiyah, you can. You've been doing a shei'dalin's service all evening.*»

«*What?*» Her eyes went wide with shock, then narrowed as her brows drew together. «*Is that why you've been asking for my opinions all night? Not to put me at ease, but to use me? Or rather, to get me to use the magic you claim I possess?*»

«*You do possess magic, Ellysetta. Denying it won't change that.*

And nei, I was not using you. If anything, I was testing you. Maris-sya has already read most of the nobles at this gathering. You read every one of them exactly as she did. Exactly, Ellysetta. Do you honestly believe it's pure coincidence that your intuition aligns per-fectly with the reading of our most powerful shei'dalin?»

Her anger faltered, shaken by the possibility he was telling the truth. She'd always had a sense about people. Her father often asked for her opinion before making a purchase from a vendor he didn't know. "You have an eye for an honest man, Ellie-girl," he'd always praised, and she'd never thought more of it than that. Now Rain claimed her "eye for an honest man" was magic. *Shei'dalin* magic.

"My Lord Feyreisen?" Lord Corrias turned back to them. "Is there a problem?"

Rain looked down at Ellie, his eyes steady, his face an im-passive mask.

She took a breath and gathered her composure. "No, my lord. No problem." She put her hand back on Rain's wrist, and his emotions surged up her arm at the first touch: deter-mination, pride, a hint of remorse, but not much. She had a gift, one he was determined she would accept and learn to use. As frightening as that seemed, she'd already been using some measure of that gift all her life. Did it really matter whether she called it magic or an eye for an honest man? Her shoulders squared. Her chin lifted. *«Lord Morvel will honor his contracts to the word, but not one letter more.»*

A quick, surprised glance brushed her cheek, then warm approval flowed across her senses. The arm beneath her fin-gers lost a bit of its tension. *«Beylah vo, Ellysetta.»*

She gave a small nod, but kept her eyes fixed forward and forced a pleasant expression as Lord Corrias introduced yet another noble couple. "Lord Durbin, Lady Durbin. It is a pleasure to meet you both."

When they met Lord Cannevar Barrial, Rain could tell that Ellysetta liked him more than anyone else save Teleos. So did he. The border lord had a sturdy, no-nonsense look about him. His clothes were impeccably fine, but tailored for practicality with no long swags or bulk of fabric to hinder him should a ballroom unexpectedly turn into a battlefield. He wore two long, jeweled daggers at his waist—one on each side—and Rain would be surprised if both weren't razor sharp and made to fit in Lord Barrial's hand with comfortable ease.

The most intriguing thing about Lord Barrial, however, was the heavy gold chain draped around his throat—or rather, the large, cabochon Tairen's Eye crystal hanging from it, surrounded by a sunburst of diamonds in a graduated rainbow of shades. How had Cannevar Barrial, a Celierian border lord, come to possess a Fey warrior's *sorreisu'kiyr*?

"Have you or a member of your family performed some special service to the Fey, Lord Barrial?" Rain asked when the introductions were complete. He gestured to the jewel around Barrial's throat. "A Tairen's Eye that size doesn't usually find its way out of Fey hands."

"It's been in my family for centuries." The border lord's brow lifted. "Who knows? Perhaps there is a Fey ancestor somewhere far back in the Barrial family tree."

"Perhaps there is," Rain acknowledged seriously. "Guard it well, Lord Barrial. There are those who would kill for such a prize."

Lord Barrial gave a smile that changed him instantly from wealthy courtier to dangerous predator. "The warning is appreciated, My Lord Feyreisen, but unnecessary. I am well able to defend what belongs to me. It's something of a requirement for surviving on the borders."

Rain liked the man all the more. "Dax tells me you have several children."

"I do. Four sons and one lovely daughter who recently wed the heir of my neighbor Lord Sebourne, whom you met yesterday."

"Then I am doubly in your debt for your words in Council yesterday and your willingness to entertain a close connection with the Fey. I hope your support did not cause a breach between you and your daughter's bond-family."

Lord Barrial smiled. "Sebourne and I share long years between us. It would take more than a simple disagreement in Council to set us at each other's throats." The smile faded, and seriousness took its place. "He's not a bad sort. Pompous, yes, but the zealous dislike of *dahl'reisen* is a recent development. Too many of the attacks have been focused on his lands, and he's begun seeing enemies in every shadow. That's one reason I agreed to the king's request. My daughter lives on Sebourne land now—or will once she and Colum return from their bridal voyage. For her sake, I'll do whatever I can to help put an end to those attacks."

"Was your daughter betrothed at a young age, Lord Barrial?" Ellysetta interrupted.

"Why do you ask?"

Rain pressed his fingers against her waist. «*Shei'tani, leave it. I have said I will speak with him.*»

Ellie firmed her jaw and blurted, "I don't approve of betrothing young children. They should have a choice of whom they wed. A chance to find love."

The border lord drew back in surprise and Rain cast her a reproving glance. Blood rushed to her cheeks, but she set her face in a mulish expression and held Lord Barrial's gaze.

Rain sighed. «*You must learn to trust me, Ellysetta.*»

Looking from Rain to Ellie, Lord Barrial said quietly, "I would never willingly do anything to cause my children unhappiness. Nor would I propose a union that was unwelcome."

"The Feyreisa is very protective of her sisters' happiness," Rain told him. "And she was recently betrothed to a man not of her choosing. She has asked that no betrothal offers be made to her parents at this time."

"Ah." Understanding dawned. Lord Barrial nodded to Ellysetta. "I heard of your betrothal, and your day in court. On the borders, happiness is too fleeting to waste a moment of it trapped in a cold marriage. Talisa wed the day of her twenty-fifth birthday, by her own choosing, because she had never found another who suited her better than Colum diSe-bourne. It is not the love match I wanted for her, but they are friends." The border lord bowed to Rain. "My offer was merely that—an offer. Any bond between us is negotiable."

Rain returned the bow with a nod, and Lord Barrial moved away. When he was gone, Rain turned to Ellie and shook his head. *You may think you are a coward, shei'tani, but you are mistaken. No other woman in this room, with the possible exception of Annoura or Marissya, would have challenged a man of Lord Barrial's standing as you just did.* He lifted her hand to his lips and pressed a kiss upon it. *When it comes to those you love, Ellysetta, you are fierce as any tairen.*

Across the room, Annoura watched the Tairen Soul kiss his peasant-bride's hand and escort her around the palace ball-room as if she were the Queen of Queens.

Already, many of Celieria's best had begun softening towards her, thanks to Dorian's infuriating surprise an-nouncement. Lords who might have remained hostile to a foreign king and his unacceptable bride would not risk in-sulting one of the Great Houses. Who would have guessed Dorian could ever arrange such a coup, let alone arrange it so swiftly? And he'd not once said a word to her about it!

Furious, Annoura snatched a glass of pinalle from a passing waiter and took a long, satisfying sip of the chilled alcohol. Heady warmth followed the sweet, cool flavors of the wine, and she regarded Dorian's two prize bulls over the rim of her wineglass.

Barrial's participation in this farce didn't surprise her much. He fancied himself an everyman's lord: the sort who would happily roll back his sleeves and toil in the dirt along-side his men. He'd toss out the offer just to prove his willing-ness to accept a person on merit rather than position. As if that were somehow an asset. She hadn't forgotten how quickly he'd jumped to the Fey's defense in Council yester-day. Only Teleos and Dorian were bigger Fey-lovers.

But Morvel . . . the way he bragged on the purity of his noble House, you'd think each thimbleful of seed that spewed from his loins was worth a fifty-weight in gold. How in the name of all the gods had Dorian convinced Albuthnas Morvel even to consider merging his highly pedigreed bloodlines with a woodcarver's whelp?

Somehow, some way, Dorian had managed it. If it had been for any other purpose, she'd be luminous with pride, ebullient with the proof of her royal husband's irrefutable power. But not for this. As always, he stirred himself most not on behalf of his own family, his own wife, but for those gods-cursed, soul-scorching Fey.

Annoura downed the rest of her wine in one angry gulp, then shuddered a little as the warmth washed over her in waves. She'd have to be careful. She hadn't eaten much to-day, and the deceptively sweet blue wine would quickly go to her head.

Wouldn't it be amusing if the girl got drunk and made a fool of herself? From nowhere, the memory of Jiarine's wicked laughter popped into Annoura's head.

She stared at the empty glass in her hand. A small blue drop of liquid still clung to the rim. She scooped it up with a diamond-dusted fingertip and licked it slowly from her skin as she watched Rain Tairen Soul squiring his woodcarver's daughter from one group of nobles to another, watched the obsequious smiles and the fawning that had already begun.

The dinner gong rang. Annoura handed her glass to a pass-ing servant, forced a serene smile to her face, and offered her hand to Dorian. Together, shining like stars beneath the palace chandeliers, they led their guests to dinner in the ban-quet hall adjoining the ballroom and took up their seats at the head table.

As they waited for their guests to be seated, she called the wine steward responsible for serving the head table to her side. He was a discreet man, one she'd brought with her years ago from Capellas. "Do be sure to keep the Feyreisa's wine-glass full," she murmured to him. "And when keflee is served, brew her a special cup from my private stock. Use the new blend in the purple silk bag." She smiled sweetly. "I wouldn't want to offer anything but the best to the Fey's new queen."

CHAPTER EIGHTEEN

Sing and dance the razor's edge, men.
Weave your magic fierce and strong.
Let your steel drink deep of blood, Fey.
Loose the tairen in your souls.
　　　　　　　—*Call to Battle*, a Fey Warrior's Song

As the night deepened over Norban, Wilmus Able, pubkeeper of the Hound and Boar, stood behind his bar, deftly drying the last of the day's freshly washed shot glasses and humming the tune of an old Fey warrior's song he'd learned as a boy.

"Hmm hmm hm hmmm hmm. . . . loose the tairen in your souls. Yah!" With a grin, he tossed several of the shot glasses in the air and began juggling them just like the Fey warriors he'd worshipped in boyhood used to juggle their razor-sharp blades. The glasses went up smoothly and stayed up as his hands remembered the long-ago rhythm.

Ah, Light! The visit by those two Fey today had stirred up a host of memories he'd all but lost. Hard times, but good ones. Some of the best days of his life. How could he have forgotten those years, his youthful love of the Fey? He added a fifth and sixth glass to the four already flying in great loops above his rapidly moving hands, and grinned proudly. "Eh, now, Wilmus, old man. You haven't lost your touch.'Deed you haven't."

Behind him, the hinges of the front door squeaked as

someone entered the pub. *Drat that Mary Betts,* Wilmus thought with a spurt of irritation, embarrassed to be caught juggling. *Useless girl never remembered to lock up after leaving.* "Sorry," he called. He kept his eyes on the airborne glasses, catching the first four as they descended and setting them on the counter. "We're closed."

Silence answered. A draught of chill air swirled around him. He frowned in confusion as his breath fogged before him. Oddest damn thing. He caught the fifth shot glass out of the air and flicked a glance at the mirror hung over the bar. His face went white.

"Light save me." The sixth glass dropped past his nerveless fingers and shattered on the floor at his feet.

Mother and Daughter moons rose over the treetops of Greatwood Forest. Their dual brightness illuminated Carthage Road so clearly, Sian and Torel didn't need to rely on Fey vision as they loped down the rutted dirt track.

Somewhere in the miles of forest behind them, an unearthly scream ripped the night, then abruptly fell silent.

Sian's smooth stride faltered. "Did you hear that?"

"Lyrant," Torel said. "They scream like a dying man."

"You sure?" Sian cast a cautious look around, pupils widening as he tried to pierce the darkness of the surrounding forest. "Sounded human to me."

Torel rolled his eyes. "They scream like a dying *human* man. I thought you said you weren't afraid of the woods after dark."

"The woods didn't flaming well scream, now, did they?"

"You going to quiver at every twig snap?"

"Get scorched."

Torel's teeth flashed. "We've thirty miles to go, my blade brother. Race you?"

Sian grinned. "Beat you!" He took off, long Fey legs sprinting rapidly, dust rising up in his tracks.

Torel swore and leapt after him. One day. One day he would stop falling for that.

Celierians *did* use too many forks.

Sitting in the place of honor beside King Dorian at the head table, Ellysetta stared at the intimidating collection of flatware surrounding her plate. There were at least ten forks of varying sizes and shapes to the left of her plate, plus six knives and four spoons on the right, and another selection of spoons, forks, and small knives spread in a decorative fan at the top of her plate. Six crystal goblets shimmered in the Fire-lit glow of the chandeliers. Three decoratively folded napkins in gold, silver, and Celierian blue stood sentry over a stack of four plates of graduating sizes, topped with a small cobalt and gold bowl.

Were the chefs actually intending to serve enough food to use each of the utensils, goblets, and dinnerware set out before her? Her stomach hurt at the mere thought of it.

She glanced to her right and watched Rain's long, elegant fingers pluck his gold napkin from its place, unfold it, and lay it in his lap. Throughout the banquet hall, others were doing the same. She reached for her gold napkin, intending to follow suit.

"And how are your wedding preparations going, Mistress Baristani?"

Ellie jumped and sent one of her goblets toppling. The crystal made a loud pinging noise as it rolled against the selection of small knives at the top of her place setting. Several heads lifted, dozens of eyes looked her way. She made a hurried grab for the fallen goblet, but Rain beat her to it, righting the glass and feathering a cool, reassuring touch across the back of her hand as he smoothly handed her the gold napkin.

"You will address her as My Lady Feyreisa," the Tairen Soul corrected softly. "Or Lady Ellysetta."

Bright flags of color spotted the pale cheeks of Lady Thea Trubol, senior lady-in-waiting to the queen, who sat directly across the table from Ellie. "My apologies, Lady Ellysetta."

Ellysetta forced her nerves to calm before unfolding her napkin and draping it across her lap. "There is no need to apologize, my lady," she said. "And as far as the wedding plans, they are going as well as can be expected. My mother and Lady Marissya have done most of the real work, and the queen has been very generous in sending her craftsmasters to aid us."

"Weddings are exhausting events, are they not?" Lord Barrial remarked. As an eligible widower, he'd been partnered with the equally eligible Lady Thea for dinner. "Having recently survived my daughter's wedding, I can honestly say it required more strategic planning and careful execution than most sieges I've led."

"That explains my battle fatigue," Ellie answered without thinking, then bit her lip. Had that sounded ungracious? Luckily, both Lord Barrial and the king thought she'd been joking and laughed with good humor. A servant appeared at her elbow and poured pale blue chilled wine in one of her six goblets.

"Celierian pinalle," King Dorian informed her. "Have you ever tasted it?"

"No, Your Majesty." She'd never had anything stronger than the much-watered red demi-wine served at weddings and funerals in the West End.

The king smiled. "It has quite a heady kick, so sip it slowly."

Nodding, hoping to calm her nerves, Ellie reached for the goblet and took an experimental sip. The pinalle was lovely: refreshingly cool, sweet and tangy. Following the iced chill and the fruity sweetness came surprising warmth, the heady kick King Dorian had mentioned. Her roiling stomach relaxed. She took another sip. "It is very good, Your Majesty," she murmured, because the king was still looking at her as if he expected her to say something. "Thank you." After a third sip, she put the goblet down.

"The queen tells me your father is quite a brilliant craftsman. Woodworking, I believe?"

"Yes, sire," she managed to reply. "He's a Master woodcarver." She couldn't believe the king of Celieria was sitting beside her, shining like the sun, asking after her father's abilities. It was with a surreal sense of disbelief that Ellie noted King Dorian had warm, thickly lashed hazel eyes, and a pleasant smile that showed a slightly crowded set of white teeth.

After a moment of silence, the king prompted, "My queen has commissioned a piece from your father, I believe."

"Yes, Your Majesty." *Manners, Ellie. Remember your manners.* "We were very honored to receive her request." She reached for the pinalle and took a quick gulp.

"Will you be remaining in Celieria long after your wedding, Lady Ellysetta?" That question came from Lady Thea. Ellie turned her head quickly, eager to escape conversation with the king before she made a fool of herself.

"The Fey depart after the prince's betrothal," Rain answered before Ellie had the chance.

Lady Thea smiled at Ellysetta. "I envy you. Legend has it the Fading Lands are a paradise beyond compare."

"I *am* looking forward to it," Ellie admitted. "I can't wait to see Dharsa and Fey'Bahren and the ivory towers of Cresse and Tairen's Bay on the southern coast where Fellana the Bright first met Sevander vel Jiolan."

Rain gave her a look of surprise. "The legend of Fellana and Sevander is older than time. I would not have thought anyone in Celieria still remembered it."

"A small collection of Fey poetry survived the burning of the western libraries," Ellie replied. "The books are kept in the museum now, but the curator allowed me to make copies of them. 'Fellana's Tale' was one of the poems in the books."

"Who is Fellana?" Lady Thea aked

"According to the poem," Ellie answered, "Fellana was a female tairen who fell in love with a Fey king named Sevander. She wanted to live her life with him, so she asked a powerful Elden Mage to transform her into a Fey woman. He agreed, but only on the condition that Fellana would seal her tairen soul into a dark crystal and give it to him. She loved Sevander so much that she did as the Mage asked, and for several years, she and Sevander lived happily. They had a child together, a boy named Tevan."

"I take it their happiness didn't last?" Lady Thea prompted.

Ellie smiled. She wasn't the only one who loved Fey tales, apparently. "No, it didn't. What Fellana didn't know was that the Mage intended to use her tairen power to destroy Sevander and the Fey. With the crystal's power to aid him, he gathered a vast army and invaded the Fading Lands.

"When she discovered how she'd been tricked, Fellana and Sevander gathered their own army of Fey and tairen and confronted the Mage. They killed him in a terrible battle, but not before Fellana and Sevander were mortally wounded. On her deathbed, Fellana gave her son Tevan the dark crystal containing her soul so that the tairen part of her would be with him always. And when he put the crystal around his neck, he found he could transform into his mother's true form. And Tevan, son of a Fey and a tairen, became the first Tairen Soul."

"So Tairen Souls only exist because of the Mages," Lord Morvel noted from Rain's right.

"The tale is a myth," Rain replied. "Spoken of only in very ancient Fey poetry written before the dawn of the First Age. But it is interesting to note that even then, in the time before memory, Elden Mages were an evil, corrupt lot seeking conquest over the Fey."

"Then it's a good thing you destroyed all the Mages a thousand years ago," Queen Annoura replied coolly, "and that we've seen no sign of their revival since."

Ellysetta saw Rain's fingers tighten around the stem of his wineglass. She caught his other hand in hers. He sent her a disgruntled look, but held his silence.

"Now we have only to worry about murderous *dahl'reisen* like the Dark Lord, Gaelen vel Serranis," Lady Thea agreed. "Though, of course, some say he's a myth too."

"No." Beside her, Lord Barrial took a long gulp of pinalle. "The Dark Lord is no myth. He definitely still exists. And while I remain skeptical about his involvement in the recent troubles on the borders, I don't doubt that many of the legends about him are true. A more deathly, frightening being I've yet to meet." He glanced at Marissya, who sat out of earshot at the far end of the head table, then looked at Rain. "No offense to the Fey, or to Lady Marissya."

"I am well aware of what Celierians say about Gaelen vel Serranis," Rain said.

Ellie shivered. Although most believed that Marissya's brother, Gaelen vel Serranis, had died in the Mage Wars, Celierian legend proclaimed that he—or his ghost—still roamed the borders, hunting for Eld and stealing the souls of the unwary.

"You say you've met him?" King Dorian inquired. "He's still alive?"

"*Ta.*" Lord Barrial slipped into his native border dialect before remembering himself. "I mean, yes. He is alive, and I have met him. Twice, actually. Once when I was a lad of five, during the Elden raid that caused my parents' deaths. Then again this year, just before my daughter wed diSebourne."

"What is he like?" Lady Thea whispered.

Lord Barrial stared into the pale blue depths of his goblet for a few silent moments. "Cold," he replied at last. "When he's near, the world grows cold and your breath mists before your face, as if his presence sucks all the warmth from the living. That's the only sign that tells you he's nearby. Other than that, you don't see, sense, or hear him, unless he wants you to."

"Bah," Lord Morvel scoffed. "Nothing but nonsense and ghost stories, Barrial. Quit trying to scare the ladies."

Lord Barrial gave his fellow border lord a hard look. "You don't believe, Morvel, because you don't want to believe there's a presence on the border greater than yours. But Gaelen vel Serranis is real."

Morvel huffed. "Never once in all my years have I seen anything to make me believe that some soul-damned ghost warrior roams the borders in search of Eld prey. It's a silly story made up by parents to keep their children from wandering too far from the safety of their own keeps."

"Morvel, I saw him gut the ten Elden raiders who had killed my parents and were about to kill me. I saw his face, his eyes a blue as pale and cold as glacier ice, and his *dahl'reisen* scar. Running from the center of his forehead, bisecting his right eyebrow, and ending here just below his right ear." Barrial's hand traced the path of the scar on his own face. "It was the Dark Lord."

"You were in shock from seeing your parents killed. You saw what you wanted to see."

"And how do you explain the second appearance, three months ago when he appeared in my own gardens, the night of Talisa and Colum's prenuptial dinner?" Lord Barrial retorted. "It was definitely vel Serranis. He walked through the wards around my keep as if they weren't there, and he was real enough to make even my *dahl'reisen* nervous." Lord Barrial leaned forward, his brown eyes narrowing. "Do you have any idea, Morvel, what it takes to make a *dahl'reisen* nervous?"

"Bah," Lord Morvel snorted. "They're probably in on it too—same as they're probably behind all this killing that's been going on. They can charge a much higher fee for their services by keeping Celierian fears alive."

Ellie glanced at Rain. Did Lord Morvel not care who was sitting beside him? But Rain raised his goblet and drank a deep draught of pinalle as if the border lord's insulting remark rolled right off him.

«*The dahl'reisen are beyond the honor of the Fey, shei'tani.*» he told her silently. «*They are capable of much that the warriors of the Fading Lands would find abhorrent.*»

Despite his mild words, she could sense the curl of anger tightening within him. The men Morvel discussed so contemptuously were people Rain would have known, perhaps even loved. *Dahl'reisen* or not, she knew he did not like to hear them disparaged.

Lord Morvel continued in the same oblivious, insulting vein. "Your visitor was probably just another *dahl'reisen* cloaked in Spirit to make him look like vel Serranis, and the cold was probably caused by someone weaving Fire and Air."

"It was the Dark Lord, not some other *dahl'reisen* masquerading as him in order to bilk me of my gold. Flaming souls, Morvel, they're Fey!" Lord Barrial met Rain's gaze briefly in an unspoken apology. "They can make their own damned gold if that's what they're after. And for your information, there are twenty-five *dahl'reisen* living on my lands, and I only pay the two who've been with my family for the last three centuries."

Beside Ellie, Rain went still. She glanced at him in surprised inquiry.

«*Twenty-five is no arbitrary number, Ellysetta. It is five sets of five, a combination capable of weaving vast power.*»

She swallowed, sensing enough concern in him to know what he had left unsaid. If twenty-five *dahl'reisen* had come to Lord Barrial's land, there was a reason for it. And if Gaelen vel Serranis was behind it, there was reason to fear.

"It was the Dark Lord," Lord Barrial continued. "He told me darkness was rising and said I should guard my children and wear my crystal." He looked at Rain. "Those were his exact words: 'Darkness is rising.' He was warning me the Mages have returned to power."

"Ha. Sounds more like a warning to quit drinking so damn much pinalle. That's what it was."

Lord Barrial glared. "You're a blind, hardheaded fool, Morvel."

"And you're a superstitious idiot, Barrial."

"Peace, my lords," the king interrupted as servants approached with a cart bearing a huge soup tureen. "Our first course is served. Let's not spoil the meal with harsh words."

Ellie shifted in her seat as the servant leaned over her left shoulder to fill her soup bowl with a clear brown broth swimming with thin slices of mushrooms and onions.

"Thank you," she murmured, earning a startled look from the servant, who then glanced at the king, flushed, and whispered back, "You are most welcome, my lady."

Beside her, Rain allowed the servant to fill his soup bowl, then selected the gold-handled soup spoon from the far left of his selection of cutlery. Ellie picked up the same spoon from her own place setting but waited for the king to begin eating before she did.

"You employ *dahl'reisen*, my lord?" Lady Thea asked Lord Barrial after everyone at their part of the table was served. She made a show of fluttering her long thick lashes, causing Ellie to blink in surprise. Weren't noblewomen supposed to be adept at flirtation? Even Kelissande could teach Lady Thea a thing or two about subtlety. "With all that's going on, do you think that's wise?"

Lord Barrial frowned at his dinner mate. "Unlike some, I'm not convinced *dahl'reisen* are behind the murders in the north. As I said, they've served my family for generations, and there's no record of their ever giving cause for concern. In fact, it used to be common for all border lords to employ *dahl'reisen*. They're much better than wizards when it comes to countering the magic of the Eld."

"Useful or not, I think I'd be terrified to have so many *dahl'reisen* in such close proximity." The lady gave a delicate shiver.

"Yes, well, that seems to be the common female sentiment. My daughter has never cared for them much, either." There was a cool finality to his tone that discouraged Lady Thea from continuing her flirtations.

"Lord Barrial," Rain said quietly in the ensuing, slightly awkward silence, "after dinner I would like to hear more about your visit with Gaelen vel Serranis."

"It would be my pleasure, My Lord Feyreisen," Lord Barrial replied with a nod.

"So, Lady Morvel"—Lady Thea cast a determined smile at Lord Morvel's wife—"I understand you're to be a grandmother again."

"*Ta*. Our oldest daughter is expecting her fifth," Lady Morvel answered, and a light exchange of pleasantries followed as they attended their meal.

Across the room, Kolis watched through Jiarine's blue eyes as servants tended the royals, Fey, and Great Lords at the head table. He had tested the Fey numerous times tonight—sending Jiarine close to several of the warriors standing guard throughout the banquet hall—but despite the Tairen Soul's apparent ability to sense the growing Mage presence in the north, neither he nor any of his Fey entourage seemed able to detect Kolis's presence within his *umagi's* delectable young body.

Now the wine was being served, and Annoura's careful attention to the level of pinalle in the Feyreisa's glass told him she'd taken Jiarine's suggestion to heart. That would make things easier. The alcohol would lower Ellysetta Baristani's defenses and leave her more susceptible to the influence of his pressure spell.

He reached Jiarine's hand into the hidden pocket in her skirts, and closed her fingers around the small wax *talis* secreted there. The pads of her fingers stroked the wax, warming it slightly and brushing across the single strand of hair curled tight around the tiny magical charm. He wove the Feraz activation spell into her mind, directing her to whisper it beneath her breath and keep her focus on Ellysetta Baristani.

Sian and Torel left the Carthage Road and followed Wilmus Able's directions down a narrow wagon road and into a small clearing where they found Brind Palwyn's house just as Wilmus had described it. The house, a small but sturdy structure built of well-hewn logs and weathered shingles, sat in the middle of the clearing. Light shone golden from the windows and through the faintest of cracks at the bottom of the carefully fitted door. Smoke curled up from the stone chimney, carrying the scent of roasted meat. Someone was home.

As the two warriors approached the house, an arrow

whooshed past, nearly spearing Sian's ear. The Fey dove and rolled for cover, shields springing into place around them.

"Peace, Goodman!" Torel called as Sian scanned the forest for their attacker. "Put your weapons down! We mean no harm!"

«There, Torel,» Sian sent. «In those trees to the left.»

Torel nodded as Sian shimmered and vanished. "We're Fey warriors, not *dahl'reisen*. We're looking for Brind Palwyn. Wilmus from the Boar and Hound in Norban sent us." He heard the twang of a bowstring and threw himself left just as another arrow sank quivering into the ground where he'd been. "Wilmus warned us you didn't like strangers, Goodman, but he didn't mention you were so fond of bloodshed. We only want to ask you a few questions."

"What could the Fey possibly want with a woodcutter?" a disembodied voice called out from the shadows of the trees.

"We were looking for news of a redheaded journeyman smith who might have passed through Norban many years ago, possibly traveling with his young daughter. Wilmus thought he might have done work for your parents."

Half a dozen arrows came spewing out in rapid succession. Torel grunted in pain as one made it through his shields and caught him in the leg. He heard sounds of a skirmish in the woods, filled with curses and struggling. Moments later, a thin man clad in homespun and leather stumbled out of the darkness. Sian walked behind him, holding the man's bow and quiver and prodding him with the pointy end of a curved *meicha*.

Torel yanked the arrow out of his leg and threw it on the ground, spinning quick Earth over the wound to stop the bleeding. He stood up to greet the mortal, a man with an unremarkable face, a shock of brown hair, and eyes filled with an all-too-familiar sorrow.

"Brind Paldwyn? I am Torel vel Carlian. I take it you do indeed know something about a redheaded child in the forests north of Norban—say about twenty-four years ago?"

Ellysetta rubbed her aching temples. The headache from the other day was back, a slight but persistent pressure that grew stronger as the evening progressed. The footmen served course after course of rich food: shellfish on golden skewers, twelve fish, poultry, and meat dishes accompanied by a vast selection of grilled, sautéed, creamed, and casseroled vegetables, frozen sorbets to cleanse the palate between courses. Thankfully, Ellysetta worked her way through the staggering array of silverware without any noticeable gaffes.

Throughout the meal, her goblet of pinalle never seemed to fall below half full. The wine helped keep the headache at bay, and though she couldn't tell how many glasses of the stuff she'd actually consumed, she had a good idea it was several more than she should have. When a servant offered her a cup of keflee, she accepted eagerly.

She poured in enough honeyed cream to chill it, then drank it down in several quick swallows, hoping to clear her head. Instead, the warm, sensuous blend of flavors—more potent than any she'd ever tasted—hit her system with the force of a blow. Heat rolled down her body in undulating waves. Rather than clearing her head, the keflee only clouded it all the more. Feeling boneless and dazed, she melted against the back of her chair.

Her eyelids drooped, and she regarded Rain through her lashes. He was, she thought hazily, the most beautiful man ever created, saved from prettiness by the strong masculine thrust of the bones beneath the luminous paleness of his unlined flesh. Saved also by the palpable aura of danger, power, and scarcely leashed wildness that surrounded him.

Inky black hair fell back from his smooth brow, spilling over broad, well-muscled shoulders in straight flows that seemed to merge with the coal-black shadows of his leathers. In the bright glow of Fire-lit chandeliers, his hair reflected a rich dark sheen, like the glimmer of nearly grainless ebonwood. She wanted to touch it, sink her hands into its silky softness. Her fingers flexed and tingled at the prospect.

Annoura hid a pleased smile as the woodcarver's girl downed her keflee in a few quick gulps. *This should be interesting. Let*

Dorian just try to win favors for the Fey after this. She sat back in her chair and laughed at a comment murmured in her ear by Lord Nin, the Great Lord sitting to her left.

A few moments later, satisfaction turned to worry as a heightening tension spread through Annoura's body. Her skin grew warm. She reached for her fan, snapped it open, and began fanning her flushed face. What was happening? She'd avoided the keflee—and even if she hadn't, she'd watched her steward serve the girl a special cup, one already poured and ready for her. All the other guests had been served a normal blend poured from silver kefleepots.

She glanced over at Dorian and saw him running a finger under his collar. Ruddy color had darkened his cheeks. Her womb clenched. She wanted to touch him. Right now. She wanted to crawl into his lap, run her hands through his hair, and rub her body against his.

Dorian turned his head. His hazel eyes were dark and glowed faintly as they did sometimes when his Fey blood rose. Moisture drenched her silk undergarments. Good gods, she was ready to climax just from a single hot look. What was happening?

Rain was speaking with Lord Barrial. Sighing to herself, Ellysetta watched the masculine beauty of his mouth form each word, each syllable. Like a kiss, she thought. His lips framed each word like a kiss. The steward had brought her another cup of keflee. She sipped this one, savoring the potent flavors and imagining she was instead sipping heady kisses from Rain's lips.

Her gaze slid down his throat to the lean power of his dagger-bedecked chest, clothed in snug black leather. The leather, she knew, would be warm to the touch. And it would hold the aroma of magic and Rain. She remembered the feel of his leathers against her cheek, the hard press of his knives against her jaw and temple, the sound of his heartbeat in her ear, low and pounding, a thrumming, sensual beat that sang a magical weave of compelling desire. She watched in appreciative wonder as his spine stiffened and his chest expanded on a deep breath.

She stared hungrily at Rain's arms, remembered them closing about her, wrapping her in alternating layers of protection, unyielding strength, and hot, carnal need. Beneath her gaze, his biceps bunched tight, straining against the seams of his leather tunic. His hands clenched and shook. She stared at them, willing the fingers to unbend and reach out for her, but they did not. With vague regret and growing hunger, her gaze trailed back up his chest, caressing the heavy beating pulse in his throat, whispering invisible dreams of kisses against his squared jaw and sumptuous mouth. At last, her eyes met his, and she found herself staring into the blazing heat of the Great Sun.

Kolis kept Jiarine chanting the Feraz spell in a voice so quiet not even the lord sitting next to her could hear it over the buzz of conversation that filled the banquet hall. Across the room, the Baristani girl had taken on a glow. The hint of light was so faint it would be undetectable to any non-magic-wielders in the room, but Jiarine Montevero had been born in the north. In addition to her many other useful talents, she possessed a fair command of Spirit. Enough, in any case, to recognize the unmistakable signature of the faint lavender flows spinning out from Ellysetta Baristani. He felt Jiarine's body grow tense.

Spirit. The girl was weaving Spirit.

But what strength? The weaves seemed too fine and fragile. A minor command was not what the High Mage was looking for. Only a master's strength would do.

He made Jiarine focus more energy into the *talis* spell, pushing the girl harder to see how strong that faint weave would become. A few chimes later, the glow around her grew brighter, the threads of her weave intensified, light shot out across heretofore invisible streams that had already blanketed the room from one corner to another without anyone being the wiser.

Only then did Kolis realize the weaves were already work-

ing on Jiarine, had been for longer than he knew. The clenching tightness that he'd mistaken for tension was her female
body growing hot and aching with need.

A hand squeezed Jiarine's thigh. Kolis looked down and
followed the plump hand to the portly body of Lord Bevel.
Perspiration gleamed on the man's bald pate, and his thick lips
glistened with saliva. He was leaning forward, breathing
heavy hot breaths against the bare, plump tops of Jiarine's
breasts.

Kolis's consciousness reeled back in disgust. Surely she
wouldn't. Jiarine appreciated her own value too well to hump
a foul *rultshart* like Bevel.

But the Baristani girl's weave was no slight suggestion, and
Jiarine could not resist its dictates despite Kolis's attempts to
stop her. When Bevel's fat tongue slid across her skin and
dove down to curl around one diamond-hard nipple, she
came in an ecstatic gush and reached hungrily for the thick
bulge tenting the man's trousers.

Sickened, Kolis fled Jiarine's body and left her to her rut-
ting. He had what he'd come for. Ellysetta Baristani was a
master of Spirit, powerful enough to exceed even the High
Mage's lofty standards.

Ellysetta couldn't look away from Rain's burning eyes. She
was distantly aware of the shrieking madness of the tairen.
She was even more distantly aware that the room had fallen
silent, the quiet broken only by the shallow gasps of hundreds
of lungs desperately seeking air. She wanted to speak, but her
tongue felt too thick, her throat too dry. Her mind was a
whirl of feelings and incoherent thoughts, simple sentences
stripped to their barest essence.

I want. I need. I ache. I burn.

«Burn with me.»

And then Rain's arms were around her, sweeping her out
of her chair and against his chest, and air blew in a cooling
rush against her hot skin as he sped up the stairs and out of
the palace into the cool Celierian night. Her head fell back

against his arm, her eyes drank in the star-jeweled sky. The sky whooshed past in a dizzying rush. Rain was running, with her in his arms. Then they were home in the night-darkened front room of her house. She was reaching for Rain, trying to hold him, needing him, wanting . . . something. The ache was a terrible pain inside her. "Rain, please."

His face was drawn tight, his eyes burning. "I can't, *shei'tani*. If I thought I could give you what you need and still keep my oath, I would. But this is too much. Don't ask it of me. I would break my honor. Forgive me." His mouth turned grim, his eyes went bleak. "And forgive me for this as well." He raised his hand. She watched without comprehension as magic gathered at his fingertips, then spun out to surround her. She fell, unconscious, in his arms.

He passed her gently into Ravel's keeping. "Guard her," he bit out. "Keep her safe." He didn't wait for Ravel's answer. He simply stepped outside and leapt into the sky. The tairen's roar rattled windows in panes across the city, and a fierce jet of flame lit up the darkness. He shot up into the icy ether and arrowed east through the night, away from the city.

Sian and Torel ran south through the forest, dazed and shaken by what they'd learned from the woodcutter Brind Paldwyn. They didn't speak, didn't look at each other. For a full bell at least, they just ran.

«We should call General vel Jelani,» Sian finally said, breaking their long silence. *«He'll want to know.»*

Torel stopped so abruptly, Sian went pelting ten yards past. "All right," he said. "We'll call him now. You're stronger in Spirit than I. Do it. I'll stand guard."

Torel's nerves were singing as Sian closed his eyes and summoned his power. If the information they now carried was true, it was beyond deadly.

Twenty miles back, in the hut Sian and Torel had left in such a hurry, long, pale fingers passed over the sightless eyes of Brind Palwyn, pulling the lids shut. A pale hand turned over, palm upward. Fingers curled as if cupping a ball. A shadowy spiral, glowing with red lights, rose up from the fingers. Black eyes flickering with red lights stared deep into the whirling spiral of Azrahn. Light and shadow flickered on the ridges of the scar running from the center of his forehead and through his eyebrow to just below his right ear. A moment later, the Azrahn weave dissolved, and the weaver's eyes faded back to their normal piercing pale blue, colder than the glaciers beyond the Mandolay mountains to the far north, the elongated pupils narrowed to thin slits.

The crouching black figure rose to an imposing height and pointed one long finger, calling Fire. Brind Palwyn's body burst into flames, searing, unnaturally hot flames that turned his body to ash in moments, yet never spread to the rest of the cabin.

Swift and agile as a deer, black-booted feet raced through the night-darkened forest, the footsteps soundless, as if they never touched ground.

CHAPTER NINETEEN

Flaming gods, Rain was never going to survive this courtship.

Lying on his back on the still-warm sands of Celieria's Great Bay, he stared blindly at the sky as the salty, rolling surf of the Pereline Ocean washed over him. Every muscle in his body was still drawn tight in throbbing knots, desperate for the release he was beginning to doubt would ever come. Or if it did come, it would be too late to save him from insanity.

His need for Ellysetta was an intense, living, driving thing, a relentless torture that kept him near to screaming on the razor-sharp edge of his control.

Gods rot the soulless bastards who invented pinalle. Plague take the servant who kept pouring the bottled blue frustration into her glass. And Rain hoped to all the seven bitter hells that Dorian mated the very life's essence out of Annoura tonight for her thrice-cursed, sowlet-stupid idea of plying Ellysetta with pinalle in the first place.

Because Ellysetta had not only roused Rain's passion with her sensual, heavy-lidded glances and unguarded emotions. Oh, no, it went far, far beyond that. In her uninhibited, pinalle-induced and keflee-enhanced daze, she had woven a

Spirit web of carnal hunger so subtle and yet so scorchingly strong that she had sent every breathing person in the banquet hall—mortal and Fey alike—spiraling into an abyss of driving sexual need before anyone knew what was happening. When last he'd seen his fellow dinner attendees, they were falling upon one another like ravening wolves, some couples staggering off to find privacy while others shed every last ounce of reserve they ever possessed on the very spot where they stood.

Bel and the rest of Ellie's quintet had barely managed to make it to the Baristani home before pleading for Rain to release them from their duties. He did, of course. They would have been useless in the state they were in. They'd all five taken off walking towards Celieria's brothel district, but by the time they reached the end of the block, they were running.

After leaving Ellysetta in Ravel's care, he'd thrown himself into the sky and flown here, to the silver beaches of the southern coast, hoping to find some respite—or at the very least a lessening of the weave. He'd found none.

The gods alone knew how long the effect of her weave would last, but it was still going agonizingly strong three bells after its inception. Even with hundreds of miles separating himself and Ellysetta. Lying in the surf, Rain shrieked his fury to the open skies above and pounded his fists in the wet sand around him.

Torel paced restlessly as Sian attempted for the sixth time in the last two bells to contact Belliard vel Jelani and relate what they'd discovered.

"You still can't reach him?" Torel asked in concern. He ran his hands through his dark hair and blew on his fingers. The woods seemed colder than they had just chimes ago.

Sian shook his head and dissolved his weaves.

"Try someone else."

"I already have. I can't reach Bel or any of the Feyreisa's quintet, nor Dax, Lady Marissya, or any of her quintet. I even tried to contact the Feyreisen. None of them are answering me. They must still be at that palace dinner Bel mentioned earlier today. We dare not pass the information on to anyone else."

Although Brind Palwyn had steadfastly insisted he knew nothing about a redheaded child, Sian had woven Spirit between them and retrieved the man's memories. Those memories had contained exactly the information Sian and Torel had been sent to find, but not at all what they'd expected.

As a child of ten, Brind had seen his parents tortured and killed by an Elden Mage looking for an escaped slave and a flame-haired child. A child the Elden Mage had claimed was the stolen daughter of his master, the High Mage Vadim Maur.

Even now, Torel wanted to cry out that it wasn't true, that it couldn't be true. He'd seen the Feyreisa with his own eyes, seen her brightness. But Brind's memories were so vivid, he couldn't doubt they were real.

The Paldwyns had only offered a night's shelter to the slave and the child, but afterwards, unbeknownst to his parents, Brind had agreed to hide the baby in the woods while the slave drew off her pursuers. That task had kept Brind from dying with his parents. The slave girl, he later discovered, had set her own body aflame and thrown herself off the cliffs of Norban's quarry to avoid being tortured and questioned by the Mage. Brind had retrieved what little remained of her burned and broken body, and had buried it alongside his parents. As for the baby, Brind had followed a Celierian couple traveling through the woods and put the baby beneath a tree where they would find her. He'd stayed hidden until he was sure they would take the child, and then he'd spent the rest of his life trying to forget everything that had happened.

He'd been relatively successful, too, until recently. While searching Brind's memories, Sian discovered another disturbing image of local villagers bringing treasured Fey-gifts passed down through generations into the town square to be destroyed in a huge bonfire, while a white-haired priest in a voluminous, hooded blue cloak stood by and collected shards of Tairen's Eye crystal from the villagers. Brind had inquired about the bonfire later, but none of the villagers remembered anything about the Fey-gifts they'd thrown into the fire, or the Tairen's Eye shards they'd given to the blue-cloaked priest. It was as if those memories had been wiped clean. But Brind, who'd watched from the woods rather than participating in the bonfire, remembered—and he'd suffered nightmares about his parents' deaths ever since.

Sian had erased all memory of Mages, death and Ellysetta from Brind's mind, then gave the poor man what he'd wanted his whole life: memories of a happy childhood, unmarred by tragedy, memories of parents who died happily in their sleep after a satisfying life. It wasn't legal. It broke the Fey-Celierian treaty and several Fey laws, but Sian did it anyway and dared Torel to say a word.

Torel wouldn't, of course. He'd still been young when the Mage Wars started. He hadn't even completed his first level of the Dance of Knives. But he, too, had seen his parents slaughtered by the Eld, just as Sian and Brind had, and there were days Torel wished someone would weave Spirit to remove *his* memories of that horror.

"Come on, then," Torel said, clapping his friend on the back. "With a little effort, we might just make Celieria City by moonset tomorrow."

"Do you think it's true?" Sian didn't elaborate, but he didn't have to.

Torel didn't want to believe it, but Fey didn't lie, so instead, he forced a chiding look on his face and said, "She made Bel's heart weep again. Do you think she could have done that if even the smallest part of her were tainted by Elden evil?"

"Of course. You're right." Sian nodded and stared at his booted toes.

"Silly *pacheeta*." Torel grabbed his friend around the throat and scrubbed his knuckles against Sian's skull through his wavy brown hair. "Come on, then. All doubts are forgotten. Let's get back to our brothers."

They were still smiling when the *sel'dor* shrapnel ripped through them.

Sian and Torel staggered, fell, then leapt back to their feet with red Fey'cha steel bared, automatically assuming the slightly crouched battle stance of a Fey warrior. Only then did they detect the reek of Azrahn and see the red-black glow of it around them. Only then did they see the shadowed mob of attackers lying in wait for them.

There were fifty or more, Torel estimated. Too many to beat. He and Sian were already surrounded, so there was nowhere to run. It was a fight to the death, then, his and Sian's.

"Where did they come from, Torel?" Hands moving at incredible speed, Sian fired red Fey'cha into the surrounding mob with deadly accuracy.

"Scorched if I know. Guard my back." Torel cursed as a barbed *sel'dor* arrow pierced his thigh, then gritted his teeth and sent four of his own red Fey'cha whirling into the shadows that surrounded him. Muffled shrieks, quickly silenced as tairen venom did its job, made him grin with savage victory. He would take as many with him as he could before he died.

Though he had yet to see the face of a single attacker, Torel was certain they were Eld. The sickly sweet reek of Azrahn was too strong for them to be anything else. He and Sian should have sensed them miles away—if only through their Fey instinct for danger—yet neither of them had detected the Eld even when standing virtually on top of them.

The *sel'dor* piercing their flesh prevented Torel and Sian from summoning magic to their defense. The black metal of Eld burned Fey flesh like acid and twisted even the weakest weave into agony. They could not weave Spirit to cry out a warning to the Fey warriors in Celieria.

But they could fight. With naked steel, deadly skill, and grim determination, Torel and Sian fought like the Fey warriors they were.

Within mere chimes, dozens of their attackers lay dead about them, and more fell dead each moment. It wasn't enough. Torel and Sian were bleeding heavily, both from the hundreds of tiny shrapnel wounds and the numerous arrows bristling from their bodies like quills.

Torel heard his cradle-friend grunt in pain as another of their attackers' arrows pierced his body. Sian fell heavily to one knee.

«I hear the tairen calling, Torel.» Sian's breath wheezed out of lungs rapidly filling with blood. His hands, though, still fired Fey'cha daggers with the fierce precision perfected over a thousand years as a warrior.

«I know, my brother,» Torel replied. Even the small thread of Spirit required to mindspeak over the short distance between them caused agony to rip through him as each tiny piece of *sel'dor* shrapnel in his body twisted his Spirit weave into pain.

It would all be over soon. When Sian fell, Torel's back would be open to attack.

And they had not even had a chance to let Belliard vel Jelani know what they had found.

«It's beautiful, Torel. So beautiful.» The sending was a whisper of sound.

«Save a piece of the sky for me, Sian. I'll fly with you soon.» Torel heard the rattle of his cradle-friend's last breath followed by the low, heavy thud of his lifeless body falling to the ground. A tear slid from Torel's eye. Over a thousand years they had known each other. *Soar, Sian. Soar high and laugh on the wind.*

Dark, shadowy figures moved closer, circling.

Torel pulled his two *seyani* longswords free of their scabbards. "Come, then!" he shouted. "Come dance with the tairen, if you dare! *Miora felah ti'Feyreisa!* Joy to the Feyreisa! And death to you all!"

And he became a whirling blur of motion—black leather, shining steel, red blood—spinning in the moonlight, delivering death to all he touched until he moved no more.

It was time. Dawn was only a few bells away and the Daughter moon had nearly set. The sky was as dark as it would become tonight.

Vadim Maur entered his spell room. Rings gleamed on three fingers of each hand: five colored cabochon stones and one gleaming black *selkahr*, each surrounded by a rainbow of smaller cabochon stones in repeating six-color patterns. Rings of power, worn in the most powerful configuration possible: Earth, Water, and Spirit on his left hand, mated by Air, Fire, and Azrahn on his right. On each wrist, he wore thick gold bands that held dark, gleaming *selkahr* crystals—Tairen's Eye altered by Azrahn to unleash its vast, dark power. He carried Kolis's Mage blade, placed it on the stone table, and began the cleansing ritual.

When he was finished, he plunged the Mage blade into the clear water in the offering bowl and murmured the spell to release the rich blood stored in the dark Eld metal. Streamers of red billowed out from the blade, tinting the water. He added a fresh vial of blood from his prisoner in the levels below and submerged the Tairen's Eye crystal to complete the spell. When the water cleared after his last incantation, he dipped his cup and drank.

Magic flowed over him in a rush of near-sexual pleasure, making his eyes flutter half closed. She *was* powerful. With just that little bit of her blood to strengthen the spell, he could feel the promise of her power coursing through his veins.

He summoned his own magic, wove the camouflaged rope of Azrahn, and sent it spiraling upwards through the pipe and into the world.

"Girl," he whispered in the darkness. He sensed her frightened flinch, felt the brief twinge of his own muscles as her blood reacted in his veins. Oh, yes, she was there, and still trying to hide from him. She would not be able to hide any longer.

A smile widened on his rapidly chilling lips.

Rain swam down to the deepest depths of Great Bay's main channel, where the water was only a few degrees above freezing. Even that did not cool the need that had driven him for

nearly seven full bells now. Giving up, he swam back to the
surface and made his way to shore.

He was close to the city, less than twenty miles away, and
desperate to keep that distance. Already he'd let the tairen
draw him back towards Ellysetta. Control was but a ragged illusion, a bare thread he clung to with desperate hope.

If the weave didn't end soon, gods help him. He had no
more strength to resist.

*Ellysetta dreamed of heat. Rain was with her, eyes glowing like
lavender suns, arms holding her close. His hands and Spirit weaves
played over her skin in endless, breathtaking torment. Dear gods, she
wanted . . . so badly. What she wanted, she didn't know, but the
need for it burned inside her, hungry and yearning, desperate for ful-
fillment.*

*They were in the glade overlooking Great Bay. Soft, cushioning
grass lay beneath her back. The warmth of Rain's body pressed
against her. His lips tracked down her throat, leaving a path of fire in
their wake. "Ku'shalah aiyah to nei."*

*"Aiyah," she breathed. Her fingers threaded through the silky
thickness of his hair as his head lowered. Cool air rushed across her
breasts. She gasped, then arched her back as his mouth closed around
her. "Rain," she cried.*

*He laughed softly against her skin. "You are so sweet," he mur-
mured, "so very, very sweet." His teeth nipped at her with just
enough force to make her gasp in surprise and shiver from the resulting tumult of sensation. His hand slid down her side, found the hem
of her skirt, and ducked beneath. His fingers swept up her leg,
towards the tight ache burning inside her.*

*Alarmed and shocked, she caught his hand. For the first time ever
in his company, a feeling of wrongness came over her. "Rain?" She
shivered again, but this time from cold, not pleasure. The night air
had grown chill and biting. Rain's body no longer offered the warmth
it had only moments ago.*

*He acted as though he had not heard her. His fingers dug into the
soft skin of her thigh. "Give yourself to me. Open up and let me in,
my sweet."*

"No," she said, pushing at him. The arms that had held her close now seemed like shackles, imprisoning rather than embracing her. "No, this is wrong. You promised my father . . ."

He laughed again, but the sound was ugly this time, mocking. "You think any oath to a mortal could ever keep a Fey from taking what he wants?" He lifted his head, and ice rushed through her veins. His eyes! Instead of the glowing lavender eyes she'd come to love, there were only pits of blackness, flickering with malevolent red lights.

She screamed and shoved him away.

Mocking laughter rang in her ears, and Rain disappeared in a swirl of black smoke. The twinkling glow of the fairy flies was extinguished, plunging her into darkness.

"Bright Lord protect me," she whispered. She knew where she was, knew what was happening. This was a place she'd been many times before. This was the malignant womb from which all her nightmares sprang, the dark home of monstrous horrors and unspeakable evil.

This was the pit where the Shadow Man dwelled. Haunting her. Hunting her.

Hide deep and well. Never let him find you. If you reveal yourself to him, all will be lost. The urgent directive that had guided her from her earliest memories now shrieked from the depths of her soul. Hide, child! Hide now!

It was already too late.

She tried to flee, as she'd fled so many times in the past, but something held her fast, trapping her in the dark nexus. Panic rose, swift and sharp. Unable to escape, she tried to make herself small and invisible and tried to direct her consciousness, her thoughts, her entire being inward—hoping silence could conceal her. But she could feel him coming closer.

Cold enveloped her. Terror choked her. Each beat of her heart became a painful blow, as if someone were hammering spikes of ice into her chest.

Whispers snaked around her, the sibilant voice ancient and sinister and harrowingly familiar. "Girl . . . I know you're here . . . I can taste your nearness . . . Show yourself."

Something brushed against her, something small and furry with *sharp little claws. A rat running across her hand. She bit back a scream, knowing the Shadow Man would hear. Knowing, somehow, it was what he wanted. If she made a sound—even the tiniest whimper—she would seal her doom.*

The rat brushed against her again. Its sharp claws scratched her skin. The long, naked tail slithered across her hand, twitching back and forth like some hideous pendulum as its pointed snout poked and sniffed at her. She squeezed her eyes shut, shrieking in silent horror and revulsion as the verminous creature crawled over her. She didn't dare move, didn't dare fling the filthy thing away.

Something else brushed her hip. Another rat had joined the first. A third climbed over her leg, then a fourth brushed her foot. Soon there were dozens, circling around her, crawling over her skirts and up her arms, growing bolder as she offered no resistance.

"I sense your fear. Have my little friends found you?" When she didn't respond, his voice hardened, "Come, now. Show yourself. I can use much more unpleasant methods to get what I want."

Sharp teeth sank into her finger as the first rat closed its jaws and bit. Agony lanced up her arm. Another rat bit, then another. Oh, gods! The silent scream ripped through her soul. She was being eaten alive!

Her flesh was on fire. Though her eyes were blind in the utter darkness, she could feel each tiny scrape and bite, the pierce of long sharp teeth, the agony of skin peeling back from bone in bloody shreds.

With frantic urgency, she began to whisper the Bright Lord's de-votion in her mind, reciting the words again and again. Holy Adelis, Lord of Light, shine your brightness upon me. Glori-ous Father, Sun of my Soul, grant me strength to stand against darkness. Adelis, Bright One, Lord of my Heart, bless me and keep me always in the Light. *The devotion offered only a fraction of the peace it usually did, but even that little bit she grasped with desperate gratitude.*

Again and again, she repeated the devotion, and with each repeti-tion, the pain in her flesh grew slightly more distant. Still there, still agonizing, but muted. As if she'd managed to push it into a small corner of her mind and lock it there.

Time crawled by. Moments stretched out for what seemed like bells. She clung to her silence with ragged determination. No matter what he did to her, she mustn't reveal herself.

"You are stronger than I believed." The Shadow Man sounded triumphant, almost . . . proud. "But your efforts are in vain. You will reveal yourself to me." His voice became a cold whip of compulsion, battering at her mind, eating away at her defenses as relentlessly as his vermin gnawed at her flesh. "You want to reveal yourself to me. You can feel the darkness within you, demanding release."

She closed her eyes and swallowed a silent cry, trying to block out the sound of his voice, the insidious words worming past her defenses. She wanted to scream out that he was wrong, that she wasn't dark, that she didn't feel the evil inside her. But she couldn't. Such a claim would be a lie. Deep, deep inside, in a place she had long ago refused to look—in a place so terrifying she'd never spoken of it to anyone, not even her father—something monstrous lived. An evil thing she'd always feared, a terror that dreamed of rending flesh with fangs and drinking blood rain from the sky.

It shifted inside her now, restless and hungry, its rage growing by the moment. Her skin felt stretched. Her hands clenched in fists. She mustn't let that thing out. Not now. Not ever. The world would fall to darkness if she ever set it free.

"You think the Fey can protect you. But who will protect them from you? Shall I show you what you will do to them?"

Around her, the pure, blind blackness began to lighten. Shadow became gray fog, swirling in eddies. Smells rose up, thick and overpowering: smoke, scorched flesh, blood, death. Gradually the mists began to clear, enough to see the aftermath of a terrible battle stretched out before her.

She was standing in a field of corpses. Shattered swords lay useless in dead, decaying hands. Torn pennants of a once proud army fluttered on broken shafts. Blood soaked the ground and congealed in dark pools. The stench of death filled the air, so thick each breath made her gag.

Horror mounted as she realized all the bodies strewn around her were either Fey or Celierian. King Dorian, Queen Annoura, Lady Marissya, Lord Dax, Bel, Kieran, Kiel: faces she knew, and thou-

sands more that she didn't. Flies filled the air in swarms so thick they darkened the sky. Rats and crows flowed over the bodies like hideous rivers, feasting on the dead.

"Do you think it's only the Fey who will suffer on your behalf?"

A loud caw drew her attention. Atop a piled mound of bodies, a pair of crows were fighting over something long and pink, tugging it between their beaks and flapping their wings angrily. Their clawed feet hopped back and forth over a tangle of bloodless limbs.

Ellysetta's heart clenched with dread as she saw a child's hand. The fingers were still plump with youth, the lifeless grip clutching a small Stone painted in a pattern she recognized. Oh, gods, please, please no. Her gaze climbed up, following the slender child's arm to the tangle of mink-brown curls. Lillis lay dead upon the pile of bodies, Lorelle beside her. Mama and Papa lay close by, faces etched with expressions of horror, dead arms still reaching protectively towards their children.

Ellysetta wept with voiceless grief and denial. Although some part of her knew this was just another of the Shadow Man's tricks to force her to reveal herself, the sight of her parents dead before her, of Lillis and Lorelle's small bodies being ripped apart and fought over by carrion birds, was more than she could bear. She tried to close her eyes against the hideous vision, but even that escape was denied her. The scene played relentlessly against the backs of her eyelids, refusing to be shut out.

A shrouded figure stood on the hillside. Behind the figure, black-armored soldiers stretched out towards the horizon like a stain upon the earth. The Shadow Man's army. The dark promise of what was yet to come.

"You'll kill them, girl. You'll kill them all. It's what you were born for."

Something brushed against her ankle. She looked down and found Rain lying on the ground at her feet, his throat and chest slashed open, his eyes milky and dead. A crow perched on his head. The dark wings flapped and covered his face like some hideous shroud, brushing against her ankle again as the bird bent to peck at one dead eye.

It was too much.

The scream ripped from her, the sound a shriek of anguish and despair.

"Get away from him! Don't touch him!" She flung herself at Rain's body, tearing in hysterical revulsion at the birds and vermin feasting on him. Fury gathered inside her and pulsed in a fierce, hot blast of rage. The rats and crows burst into flame. *"Liar! Foul, evil liar! I'd die before hurting the people I love!"*

A hand clamped hard around her throat. The Shadow Man who had been on the hillside just a moment ago now stood before her, shrouded in black, his face hidden by the deep hood of his cloak. Ice froze her blood in her veins.

"Bright Lord save me," she whispered, more from instinct than hope, knowing it was already much too late. She'd given herself away, revealed herself to him.

Worse, she'd revealed her magic.

The Shadow Man laughed, the sound triumphant. *"The Bright Lord doesn't live here, girl. And he wouldn't save you even if he did."* Her tormentor threw back his hood, and Ellysetta cried out in denial. Instead of the monstrous visage she'd always expected, her own face stared back at her, pale and ravaged, with twin black pits—bottomless and flickering with red lights—where her eyes should have been.

"I see you . . . Ellysetta." The voice came out of her own mouth, but the sound was a familiar, malevolent hiss. *"You can't hide from me any longer."* The cloaked Ellysetta lifted a wavy black blade and sent it plunging towards her heart.

"No!" She shrieked and threw her hands up. The savage thing inside her howled with wrath. Fire boiled from her hands in voracious incendiary clouds. The cloaked Ellysetta shrieked in agony as the flames enveloped her.

Hot wind blew across Rain's face. He stared with dazed incomprehension at the flames leaping all around him as pella trees crackled and burned. The sand at his feet smoked and shattered as a wave tumbled over molten glass. Some small part of his mind registered the memory of furious heat rolling through him, but all that remained now was fear.

"Ellysetta." Oh, gods. *«Ellysetta!»*

No answer.

«Ravel! Fey! Ti'Feyreisa! Ti'Feyreisa!» Rain sprang into the sky, shooting high over the trees in a stream of sparkling gray mist that solidified instantly in tairen form. Air-powered wind filled his wings. He wheeled west towards the glow of Celieria City in the distance. A command barked on a dagger of Spirit sent the Fey rushing to reinforce the protective weaves around Ellysetta's home, and check on his truemate. Something had attacked her, but none of them had sensed it.

«She is here. She is unharmed,» Ravel called back, *«but hurry.»*

Rain streaked across the sky, covering the miles in a hand-ful of chimes. He reached the Baristani house and arrowed out of the sky, Changing as he descended. The Fey hurried to pull down their weaves to grant him access, but those threads they didn't have time to unmake shredded before him, curl-ing back from the buffeting force of his power as he streamed through Ellysetta's bedroom window and reclaimed Fey form at her side.

She sat huddled on her bed, pressed into the corner, eyes squeezed shut, her body racked with violent shudders. Her fists were clenched, her arms crossed protectively over her head and chest as if to ward off an attack. Ravel and her par-ents stood beside her, distraught and helpless. Her room was a shambles, her mirror shattered and smoking, the walls shred-ded as if great razor-sharp claws had sliced through the wood and plaster in a rage and scorched as if by sudden searing flame.

"She was like this when I came in," Ravel said. "She won't let any of us near her."

"What have you done to her?" Lauriana burst out. "What have you done that sleep would bring such torments?"

"Laurie, shh." Sol tried to calm his wife, but she batted him away.

"No, Sol! I won't hush. I've held my silence too long al-ready! I told you this was a mistake. We were meant to pro-tect her from magic, and instead we've flung her back into its teeth! Her nightmares have returned, Sol. Because of *them*."

She jabbed an accusing finger in Rain and Ravel's direction. "You can't deny it any longer! And you know where it's going to lead!"

Ignoring her, Rain knelt on the floor beside Ellysetta and laid his hand on her shoulder. She cried out and tried to fling herself away, but he caught her and held tight as she struggled against him. Her skin was cold as ice. "*Shei'tani.* Ellysetta. *Las, las, kem'san. Ke sha taris. Ke sha avel vo.* I am here. I am with you." He held her close, rocking her, whispering a soothing litany of words into her ears while in silence his heart swore bitter vengeance against the monster who had visited this torment upon her.

The convulsive shudders racking her slender form gradually diminished. "Rain?" Her eyes opened, then flooded with tears when she saw him. She flung her arms round his body to clutch him tight and buried her face against the bare skin of his throat. "Oh, Rain. You're alive. Oh, thank the gods." Wrenching sobs shook her.

Though her grief tore at his heart, his eyes closed with relief. She was safe and unharmed. She was whole and in his arms, where she belonged. "I'm here, *shei 'tani.*"

"Hold me," she whispered. "Hold me and don't let me go. I'm cold, so cold."

His arms tightened, pulling her closer, wrapping around her as if with his body alone he could shield her from whatever evil hunted her.

"Ellie!" Lauriana rushed forward, hands outstretched, but as she neared, Ellysetta flinched away, burrowing deeper into Rain's arms. Desperation flooded his senses.

«Rain, tell her to go. Tell them all to go. I can't bear for anyone to touch me right now. No one but you.»

"Leave us, all of you," Rain barked. *«Ravel, get everyone out.»*

The Fey nodded and tried to usher the Baristanis out the bedroom door. Lauriana resisted the eviction. "Don't you dare touch me! I'm not leaving my child here with you, not after this! I won't do it anymore!"

Sol flung out an arm towards Rain and Ellysetta. "Can't

you see Ellie doesn't want either of us here right now? He's the only one who's even been able to get near her. Clearly, he's what she needs now, not us. For the gods' sake, Laurie, if he can bring her peace, let him do it."

"He can't bring her peace, Sol. He's only brought all her old torments back, worse than they ever were before. How can you not see that?"

"Mama." Lauriana and Sol both turned. Ellysetta was still in Rain's arms, but she had lifted her head. Her face was pale and drawn, her eyes as bleak as Lauriana had ever seen them. "Please go. You can't help me. I'm not sure anyone can help me anymore."

"Ellie . . ." Lauriana started forward, arms outstretched, tears in her eyes. "Kitling."

Ellysetta flinched away. "Don't touch me. Just go. I need you to go."

Weeping, broken by her daughter's plea in a way no angry words could have done, Lauriana left. Sol and the Fey followed her out, closing the door behind them.

"What happened, Ellysetta?" Rain asked when they were finally alone.

"It was a dream," she whispered. "A very, very bad dream."

"Will you tell me?"

In a slow, halting voice, she did. She stumbled over the part where he'd tried to coax her into mating with him and the horrible way he'd laughed, and her voice cracked when she told him about the bodies shredded into bloody meat, rats and crows flowing like a river of disease all around her. She broke into helpless tears once more when she told him about finding him dead at her feet, carrion for the crows. "Oh, Rain, gods save me, I was the one who'd led the army to destroy you. I saw myself there, leading them. I looked into my own face—and knew what I had done. And my eyes—oh, gods, my eyes—it was like looking into the fire pits of the Seventh Hell. It was . . . pure evil." A fresh bout of shuddering shook her. Nothing could block the memory of those dark, burning eyes.

"Is this what you saw?" He spun Spirit in the air between them, weaving an image of a pale face dominated by dead black wells where the eyes should have been.

She shrank back in sudden fear.

Rain's mouth tightened. The nightmarish image dissolved. "Powerful magic always reveals itself. When someone weaves Azrahn, their eyes turn black and flicker with red lights, like the dying embers of a fire. Ellysetta, I doubt the dream was your own—or anything even remotely resembling truth. The purpose could be many things: an attempt to sow doubt between us where none can exist, an attempt to use my face to spring some sort of trap. Bel told me you've had other nightmares. Were they like this?"

She closed her eyes. The time for hiding the truth was past. "I've had nightmares all my life, some worse than others. Even when I was small, I saw horrible things no child should ever see. Wars, murder, people dying. I don't know why I dream what I dream, but I've always known he was searching for me. And that if he found me, something terrible would happen."

"He who?"

"The Shadow Man. He's there in the darkness when I sleep. He was gone for years, but he came back again about a week before you arrived in Celieria. He's been searching for me, calling to me in my sleep, urging me to show myself." She wrapped her arms around herself, chafing her hands on her cold skin. "It's one of the reasons I've always feared and denied my own magic, Rain. I was afraid if I used it, he would find me. And now, I think he has." Her throat closed up. Tears welled in her eyes. "I tried to stay hidden, but he knew I was there. He wouldn't stop tormenting me until I showed myself. Everyone was dead: Bel, Kieran, all the Fey, Mama, Papa, the twins. And you—at my feet and the crows were . . . were . . . oh, Rain, I couldn't bear any more! I screamed at him to stop. I revealed myself to him, and now he knows how to find me. And I think he intends to use me to kill the people I love."

His arms tightened around her. One hand cupped her chin and urged her to look up at him. "I will permit no one to harm you or the people you love, Ellysetta. And if this Shadow Man thinks to try, I promise you he will regret it." The look in his eyes was lethal. This was the man who'd once scorched the world, and for the first time she realized he was fully capable of scorching it again on her behalf. Would scorch it again, if the evil that stalked her laid claim to her soul. "I make you fear me," he said. The fire faded from his eyes. He pulled her tight against his chest and held her close. "Do not fear me."

"It's not you I'm afraid of, Rain." She had to tell him about the exorcism, about the demons the priests said haunted her soul. Now that the Shadow Man had found her, she couldn't afford secrets. Whatever evil lived inside her, he might find a way to use it against Rain and the Fey. "It's not even the Shadow Man. Not really." She blurted out the truth before fear could silence her. "It's me."

He drew back and stared into her face. "What do you mean?"

She tried to speak, but the words caught in her throat. Would he revile her? She pulled herself out of his arms and huddled closer to the wall, needing to put some distance between them.

"Ellysetta . . ."

"No. Listen to me. I've been afraid to tell you, but you need to know." She took a deep, shuddering breath. She could do this. She could. She *must*. "He told me I was evil. He said he knew I felt darkness calling me. And he was right." The admission came hard, each word forced out of her through sheer will, but once the first secret found freedom, the rest followed in a rush. "From the time I was very small, I've had . . . seizures. There's nothing particular that makes them happen. They just do. An unbearable pain engulfs me, and all I can do is fall to the floor, screaming. Sometimes it can go on for days."

Memories, long buried, swirled in her mind, as vivid and terrifying as they had been the day she lived them. The echoes of her own wild screams rang in her ears. Her vision turned red as if veiled in blood. She pressed the palms of her hands to her eyes and whimpered.

Rain's hand covered hers, offering strength and comfort. She clutched it tight and held on until the worst of the memories faded and she could speak again.

"When I was little, the seizures came every few months, sometimes more often. They frightened Mama and Papa. They didn't know what to do. The doctors didn't know what to make of it. They said it was demon possession, something wrong in my soul. Mama brought in the exorcists from the Church of Light. I was very young . . . but I remember . . ." She bent her head, and her hair fell forward to veil her face. She remembered the candles and the chanting and the fierce eyes of the exorcists as she screamed and her small body convulsed.

"At first they just prayed and rubbed me with sago flowers. But the seizures began to grow worse, and they decided they must do something more . . . aggressive . . . to draw the demons out. They had a little box filled with needles . . ." Long, shining needles lying on a bed of red satin. Needles to pierce her so the demon could escape her body, each topped with a tiny, dark crystal bead the exorcists claimed would draw the demon out.

"They thought that if they drove those needles into me, they could trap the demon." Ellie rubbed her arms as the memories washed over her. She was screaming . . . screaming as the needle sank into her flesh.

"Ellysetta . . ." Rain pulled her closer, his body so warm against her chilled skin.

"They put one needle through my shoulder and another through my leg before Papa made them stop."

Papa, so fierce, snatching her up and shouting, "Are you mad? You torture her more? She's only a child! Get out of my house!" How she'd loved him in that moment. He'd pulled the needles out of her body and flung them away as if they were polluted things. He'd held her close, rocking her and weeping. "Papa's sorry, precious kitling. They'll never come back, sweetheart. Papa won't ever let them hurt you again."

Never again did he allow them to enter his house, never again did he allow Mama to speak of the exorcists, not even when seizures flung Ellysetta howling to the floor. Thereafter only Papa could get near her when the seizures came, and he would hold her and rock her as every muscle in her body clenched in agonizing pain. He would sing to her, softly, his tears spilling on her skin, his love wrapping around her. And she would cling to him, finding refuge in his unwavering love, anchoring herself to him until the torturous seizures passed.

"He is a good man, your father," Rain murmured.

"Yes. The best I've ever known." But she knew . . . she'd always known . . . that as much as Papa loved her, he also feared the thing that lived inside her.

And she knew he was right to fear it.

"Rain, if he hadn't stopped the exorcists, I don't know what would have happened, but it would have been bad. Very bad."

"What do you mean?"

"I wanted to kill them, the men who drove those needles into me. I was only a child, but I'd already seen death through my nightmares. I saw it again then, in my mind, but this was different. It wasn't a nightmare. It was what I *wanted* to happen, what I wanted to do to them. I saw those men torn apart, screaming as their limbs were ripped from their bodies. I saw myself laughing, dancing in a shower of their blood, drinking it like a child drinks rain as it falls from the sky." She pressed her hands to her cheeks. "Oh, Rain, what kind of monster am I?"

She waited for his horror or revulsion, but it never came. Instead his arms enfolded her and pulled her close against his chest. "Ellysetta . . . *Shei'tani* . . . You are not evil to have wished those exorcists dead for torturing you as they did. And do not believe you could have killed them, even though you dreamed of it. Fey women cannot kill, not even to defend their own lives. Their natural empathy prevents it."

"But Rain—"

"Shh. Hear me out. Even though your physical appearance seems mortal, there is little doubt in my mind that your blood is Fey. Who your parents are and why they did not return to the Fading Lands before your birth, I cannot say, but your soul shines too brightly and your magic is too strong for me to believe you are anything else.

"When those men hurt you, adding more pain on top of that you were already suffering, your Fey heritage must have stirred in anger against the crimes done against you. The tairen lives in us all, and it is not a tame creature." He smoothed her hair back from her face and stared earnestly into her eyes. "Do you think Marissya has never wished death upon another? *Nei*, Fey women are not so timid as that. They are gentle, *aiyah*, and compassionate, but even they feel the tairen rouse when pushed hard enough."

Hope flickered in Ellysetta's heart. "Do you really think that's what it was?"

"I have no doubt." The unwavering certainty in his eyes made her consider, for the first time in her life, that perhaps the dark, dangerous thing inside her wasn't evil after all.

"But . . . even if that's true, it doesn't explain why all my life I've suffered those horrible seizures and nightmares."

"That is a separate matter." Cold anger flickered in his eyes, making them glow. "If I am right, this Shadow Man of yours is a Mage, and he's been hunting you all your life. Definitely in your dreams. Night is the time when Azrahn grows strongest, and dreams are one realm where Azrahn lives in us all. I suspect your nightmares, your seizures, and probably those wandering souls, those ghosts you feel walking across your grave, are all connected, and all in some way spawned by the Mages." He stroked her hair.

"But why would they do that to me?"

"You are a Tairen Soul's mate. Your magic, though you keep it locked away, is powerful beyond measure. Even as a child, they must have known something about you—or known enough to hunt for you. Soon we will be wed, and I will take you back to the Fading Lands. We will search for answers there. When I discover who has been tormenting you, I will make certain they can never do so again."

This time, the cold, implacable promise of death and retribution did not frighten her. It made her feel safe instead. She'd told him the worst nightmare of her soul, and he had not reviled her. She turned to him, burrowing into his arms, pressing her face to the warmth of his throat. "Hold me, Rain. Keep me safe."

"I will give my life before allowing harm to come to you, *shei'tani*." He rested his cheek against the soft spirals of her hair and closed his eyes, breathing in the delicate scent that was already imprinted on his soul. The tairen in him stirred to life, but this time with fierce protectiveness rather than hunger, solicitous of its mate and her fragile state.

With more instinct than thought, Rain began to croon a soft, wordless, purring song, a song of thought and magic and emotion all woven together in silken, resonant waves.

In his arms, Ellysetta went still. He felt her breath catch in her lungs, then release in shallow, delicate gasps filled with wonder. Within her soul, a tiny, unseen door cracked open. Communion, like a shimmering beam, fell upon him and in that shining sliver of warmth the first, fragile bond between them was formed. A tender, tremulous thing. A warm light where moments ago there had been only cold, dark solitude.

His ancient soul trembled, its fierce arrogance humbled. Tears—his first in a thousand years—glimmered in his eyes. He blinked. The tears spilled down his cheeks, and he marveled at the feel of them, warm and wet, cooling rapidly. One tear tracked to the corner of his mouth, and the long-forgotten flavor of salty wetness touched the tip of his tongue.

"What was that?" Ellysetta whispered when his song died away into silence.

He tightened his arms around her and buried his face in

her hair, breathing her in, rubbing his skin against her, like a tairen exchanging scents with its mate. "Tairen song."

She tilted her head back to stare up at him, her eyes filled with as much wonder as his own. "I could feel it. Inside me, in my heart and in my head." She raised a hand and touched the cooling tracks of his tears.

"My song sang to you, as a tairen's song sings to its mate." His voice sounded low and husky to his own ears, rough with longing and long-buried emotion. Hope was a fragile flicker that he wanted to cup with both hands to protect against the harsh winds of reality.

Ah, gods, I know I am not worthy, but I will devote my life to becoming so.

He bent his head to kiss her, mating his lips to hers, his breath to hers, mating even the beat of his heart to hers. His lips tracked fevered lines across her face, her throat, her hands, then found her mouth again to give her back the passion and essence of his own self. He kissed her as if life itself lived in the wonder of her mouth, to be drunk from her lips lest he die.

Her hands fluttered against him, then clutched at him. Her fingers threaded through his hair, holding him tight. Her arms wound around his neck, slender, silken chains he knew he would never want to be free of. She kissed him back with an intensity to match his own, fearless and fierce, and the beast in his soul roared with triumph and desire.

"*Shei'tani*. Ellysetta." He gasped her name and tore his lips from hers while he still could. It was no easy task, when his instinct, driving and powerful, was to lay his body over hers and claim her. His body shuddered in protest, muscles trembling with enforced restraint.

"Rain?" Ellysetta laid her hand upon his face. Her concern lapped at the ragged edges of his control, as did the innate, calming power that soothed him from her first touch. She was so gentle, so endlessly giving, and yet so strong in ways he was only coming to recognize. For all her outward timidity, she possessed an underlying will of purest steel, tensile and enduring. Her courage was so quiet, most would never see it. Even she did not see it. She would bend, but never break. She would not fight unless she had no choice, but when she did, there would be no defeating her.

He kissed her once, fiercely, then regretfully started to pull back. *«I should go. You have already been through too much tonight, and my control is not what it should be.»*

She clutched his hand. "Please. Don't go. Stay with me tonight."

He shook his head. "*Sieks'ta, shei'tani*, but I cannot." He bent his head to hers and admitted softly, "This Fey aches to mate with his beloved, even if only in Spirit, and the need is more than I could bear if I stayed."

Ellysetta tilted her head back and stared up into his eyes. "I don't want to be afraid anymore, Rain," she said. "I don't want to give him that much control over me. *Teska.*" She guided his hand to her breast. "Take away the nightmare. Give me something else in its stead. Show me the wonders between a *shei'tan* and his mate. *Ku'shalah aiyah to nei.*"

"Ellysetta." Pride and devotion set his eyes aglow. "Your warrior's heart humbles me, *shei'tani.*" Because he couldn't bear not to, he ducked his head and took her lips in a passionate kiss. "*Aiyah, shei'tani.* A thousand times, *aiyah.*" Green Earth swirled around him, depositing his swords and weapons belts on the table nearby.

More magic gathered inside him, and she felt the throbbing heartbeat of living energy and harnessed power. Spirit exploded from his hands in a complex weave of stunning mastery. The shinning mass surrounded them both, alive with form, texture, tastes, and scents, so real that even knowing it was a weave, she could not tell the difference. No longer were they lying on the narrow bed in her room. Instead, they were stretched out on cushioned divans, in a silken tent where perfumed breezes flapped long swaths of fabric in a sensual, hypnotic dance. The air was warm and dry, smelling of cinnabar oil and magic. Outside the tent, the low, feline roar of tairen sounded in the distance.

"Where are we?" she whispered.

"This is my *shellaba*, a private retreat on my family estates, near the Feyls in the Fading Lands. When you accept my soul into yours and our matebond ceremony is complete, I will bring you here for the first night of our oneness, to mate with you on the lands of my ancestors, in the shadow of Fey'Bahren, and ask the souls of those who came before me to bless our union." Rain leaned over her, robes of purple satin sliding across her skin as he moved.

He trailed kisses down her throat, parting the satin of her own robes and laving devoted attention to each breast until her nipples were tight, aching buds and her legs fell open in restless invitation. Obligingly, the warm press of his palm cupped her. The dance of his fingers, so much broader and stronger than her own, caressed her most sensitive flesh. She kept her eyes open, fixed on his face, watching the play of emotion as he felt her body begin to respond. He took his time, patient and thorough despite his own needs, smiling into her eyes as he drove her body wild.

Her hips arched, bucking up against his hand. Weave or no weave, her response was utterly real. Heat raced through her veins, and her breath grew shallow. She reached behind her head to grasp the sides of the divan. Her fingers gripped the softness of cushioned velvet, and the smooth, polished hardness of wood. She squeezed, hanging on tight as waves of sensation washed over her.

"I will touch you like this," he whispered. He kissed his way down her body, following the earlier path of his hands. The long, silken swaths of his hair trailed across her skin, adding yet another subtle friction to tease nerves left throbbing with heightened sensitivity in the burning wake of his mouth. "I will set your body afire, until you think you can take no more. Until you beg me to come inside you and unite our flesh as the matebond unites our souls."

"I'm begging already."

He purred deep in his throat, the sound low and stirring. "Not enough. Not yet."

He lowered his head, replacing the tormenting dance of his hand with the seductive heat of his mouth. His tongue stroked, hot and wet, deep, long laving strokes that made her groan, tiny, flickering strokes that made her shudder and gasp.

"Rain . . . oh, gods save me . . . Rain! Please!"

«Not yet . . . » It was a thrill like no other to make her fly apart in his arms, even if only through Spirit. She was so open, so responsive, an alluring mix of innocence and sensuality. Again and again he brought her to shattering release, wiping out every remnant of fear from her nightmares, replacing each doubt and dread with passion and glorious sensation until there was no room in her mind for anything but him and the feelings he wove upon her.

Only then, only when no hint of fear remained in her eyes, did he draw upon every erotic thought and dream he'd had since her soul first called to him, spin them into each thread of the weave and slide his Spirit body deep into her waiting warmth. He poured his thoughts, his strength, his emotion, his very soul into the weave, fashioning touch, taste, smell, until she could feel his body moving on hers, in hers, until he could feel the tight, wet clasp of her muscles closing around him, pulling him deep. The tendons in his neck drew tight, the muscles in his arms clenched and shook. Part of him was aware of her wide, stunned eyes, her shallow, gasping breaths, the other part was only aware of the naked, sweat-glistening bodies of Spirit that mated in his mind and hers.

"I want to be inside you like this. I would crawl inside your soul and live there if I could. *Ver reisa ku'chae. Kem surah, shei'tani.*"

"Rain," she gasped. "*Shei'tan!*"

He pulled her to his chest and plundered her mouth, as the bodies in his weave arched against each other in screaming, shuddering release. He felt her quake in his arms, felt his own body give itself over to a powerful orgasm that ripped through him with stunning force.

The weave dissolved. The images of his *shellaba* faded into mist, leaving only Rain and his mate, still fully clothed and lying boneless as sated cats on the bed in her tiny room in the woodcarver's house.

Much later, when he rose to leave, Ellysetta's hand curled around his wrist. "Don't go," she whispered. "Stay with me. At least until I go back to sleep."

The glow in his eyes warmed to tenderness. Green Earth swirled in a fresh mist, smelling of springtime and blossoming life. His leather tunic dropped neatly beside the blades and weapons belts on her nightstand. Warm, pale flesh lay beneath her palms, strong arms wrapped tight around her, and the aching beauty of tairen song purred across the newly-forged first thread of their bond, singing a stirring vow.

Rain kissed her with exquisite care and smiled into her eyes. "I will stay with you for eternity, if you allow it, *shei'tani*."

Key Celierian Terms

Bell: hour

Chime: minute

Dorn: Furry, round, somnolent rodent. Eaten in stews. "Soggy dorn" is an idiom for someone who is spoiling someone else's fun. A party pooper.

Keflee: A warm beverage that can act as a stimulant or aphrodisiac.

Lord Adelis: God of light. While Celierians worship a pantheon of gods and goddesses (thirteen in all), the Church of Light worships Adelis, Lord of Light, above all others. He is considered the supreme god, with dominion over the other twelve.

Rultshart: A vile, smelly, boar like animal.

Key Elden Terms

Azrahn: The soul magic forbidden by the Fey for its corrupting influence but used and mastered by the mages.

Primage: master mage

Sulimage: journeyman mage

Umagi: a mage-claimed individual, subordinate to the will of his/her master

Key Fey Terms

Beylah vo: thank you (literally, thanks to you)

Cha Baruk: Dance of Knives

Cha'kor: Literal translation is "five knives." Fey word for "quintet."

Chatokkai: First General. Leader of all Fey armies, second in command to the Tairen Soul. Belliard vel Jelani is the chatokkai of the Fading Lands.

Chervil: Fey expletive similar to bastard, as in "you smug chervil."

Dahl'reisen: Literally, "lost soul". Dahl'reisen are unmated Fey warriors who have been banished from the Fading Lands either for breaking Fey taboos or for choosing to walk the Shadowed Path rather than committing sheisan'dahlein, the honor death, when the weight of all the lives they have taken in defense of the Fey becomes too great for thier own souls to bear. Dahl'reisen recieve a physical scar when they make the kill that tips thier souls into darkness.

E'tan: beloved/husband/mate (of the heart, not the truemate of the soul)

E'tani: beloved/wife/mate (of the heart, not the truemate of the soul)

E'tanitsa: a chosen bond of the heart, not a truemate bond

Felah Baruk: Dance of Joy

Fey'cha: Fey throwing dagger. Fey'cha have either black handles or red handles. Red Fey'cha are deadly poison. Fey warriors carry dozens of each kind of Fey'cha in leather straps crisscrossed across their chest.

Feyreisa: Tairen Soul's mate; Queen

Feyreisen: Tairen Soul; King

Ke vo'san: I love you.

Kem'falla: my lady

Kem'san: My love/My heart

Krekk: Fey expletive

Ku'shalah aiyah to nei: Bid me yes or no.

Las: peace, hush, calm

Maresk, mareska, mareskia: friend (masculine, feminine, plural)

Mei felani. Bei santi. Nehtah, bas desrali: Live well, love deep.

Tomorrow, we (will) die.

Meicha: A curving, scimitar-like blade. Each fey warrior carries two meicha, one at each hip.

Miora felah ti'Feyreisa: Joy to the Feyreisa

Pacheeta: A silly bird; not very smart.

Sel'dor: Literally "black pain." A rare black metal found only in Eld that disrupts Fey magic.

Selkahr: Black crystals used by Mages. Made from Azrahn-corrupted Tairen's Eye crystal.

Sheisan'dahlein: Fey honor death. Ceremonial suicide for the good of the Fey. All Fey warriors who do not truemate will either commit sheisan'dahlein or become dahl'reisen.

Shei'tan: beloved/husband/truemate

Shei'tani: beloved/wife/truemate

Shei'tanitsa: the truemate bond, a mating of souls

Sieks'ta: I have shame. (I'm sorry; I beg your pardon)

Tairen: Flying catlike creatures that live in the Fading Lands. The Fey are the Tairenfolk, magical because of their close kinship with the Tairen.

Tairen Soul: Rare Fey who can transform into tairen. Masters of all five Fey magics, they are feared and revered for their power. The oldest Tairen Soul becomes the Feyreisen, the Fey King.

Teska: Please

Ver reisa ku'chae. Kem surah, shei'tani: Your soul calls out. Mine answers, beloved.

For My Readers

Thank you so much for picking up this book. I hope you've enjoyed meeting Rain and Ellie as much as I've enjoyed writing about them. Their story continues in *Tairen Soul: Lady of Light and Shadows,* coming November 2007 from Leisure Books, and I hope you'll give it a try. It's full of exciting surprises you won't want to miss!

Please be sure to visit my Web site www.clwilson.com, to sign up for my private book announcement list, enter my online contests, and scour the site for hidden treasures and magical surprises. I hope you linger a while to learn more about the Fey and the Fading Lands—as well as other Fey tales and C. L. Wilson novels coming soon.

I'd love to hear from you. Please, send me a Spirit weave, or you can take the non-magical route and just e-mail me at cheryl@clwilson.com.